THE
BEST SHORT STORIES
1938
AND THE
YEARBOOK OF THE AMERICAN
SHORT STORY

EDITED BY
EDWARD J. O'BRIEN

BOSTON AND NEW YORK
HOUGHTON MIFFLIN COMPANY
The Riverside Press Cambridge
1938

The Riverside Press
CAMBRIDGE · MASSACHUSETTS
PRINTED IN THE U.S.A.

TO
PIETRO DI DONATO

BY WAY OF ACKNOWLEDGMENT AND REQUEST

GRATEFUL acknowledgment for permission to include the stories in this volume is made to the following authors and editors:

To the Editors of *Story, The Atlantic Monthly, Scribner's Magazine, Esquire, The Yale Review, Short Story Manuscripts of 1937, The American Mercury, New Masses, Harper's Bazaar* (New York), *The Virginia Quarterly Review, Harper's Magazine,* and *The Prairie Schooner*; and to Mr. Robert Ayre, Miss Libby Benedict, Mr. Stephen Vincent Benét, Mr. Nelson S. Bond, Mr. Morley Callaghan, Mr. John Cheever, the heirs of the late Mr. Vladimir Cherkasski, Mr. Whitfield Cook, Mr. Richard Paulett Creyke, Mr. Pietro di Donato, Mr. Michael Fessier, Mrs. Alberta Pierson Hannum, Mr. Manuel Komroff, Miss Meridel Le Sueur, Mr. Don Ludlow, Miss Dorothy McCleary, Mr. William March, Mr. Elick Moll, Mr. Prudencio de Pereda, Mr. Frederic Prokosch, Mr. George Thorp Rayner, Miss Elizabeth Madox Roberts, Mr. Mark Schorer, Mr. Allan Seager, Mr. John Steinbeck, Mr. Jesse Stuart, Mr. Harvey B. Swados, Mr. Robert Penn Warren, Miss Eudora Welty, and Mr. Ira Wolfert.

I shall be grateful to my readers for corrections, and particularly for suggestions leading to the wider usefulness of these annual volumes. In particular, I shall welcome the receipt from authors, editors, and publishers of stories printed during 1938, which have qualities of distinction and yet are not printed in periodicals which are brought regularly to my attention. Editors of new periodicals are invited to assist me by calling attention to their undertakings.

Communications may be addressed to me at 93, Canfield Gardens, London, N.W. 6, England.

E. J. O.

CONTENTS

CONTENTS

CONTENTS

INTRODUCTION

I

HOW STARS FALL ON STORIES

By Manuel Komroff

OPEN the heavens wide with that celestial cleaver that you reserve for Herculean tasks and what happens? Nothing. Will the stars fall into your pocket? Not one. Slice off a bit of sky with Omar's slick scimitar and still no stars come loose. Fold up the great cloth of blue and shake it out of Juliet's balcony of romance and still not a crumb of star will fall loose. How then do stars fall on stories?

On a certain day, it may be any day, the door bell rings and soon the maid announces in her soft Irish voice: 'Mister O'Brien. Your correspondence has arrived.'

Eighteen mail bags, each filled fat with the pig of advertising prosperity, are dragged into the living-room.

'Ruth,' he calls, 'the bags! They are here!'

A cry of joy fills the air. What excitement! The children burst out of the nursery and tumble, skipping and running, down the stair. You must know that no stars can fall without the children.

The eighteen great American sacks are opened and their contents scattered over the floor. Ruth has returned with the garden rake and hoe that once belonged to Hardy, and soon a heavy paper magazine soil is evenly distributed over the room. The children slush around; their little feet kick the rude advertising and turn up the story pages.

At last, with the paper soil prepared and a million words shining in the light, Ruth runs into the kitchen to prepare the stuff that stars are made of.

Into a battered old coffee-pot that once belonged to Synge and Riders to the Sea, Ruth pours a whole pound of lead birdshot. These little pellets made for the death of birds are in Edward's home converted into messengers of peace. A whole pound of birdshot Ruth empties into the coffee-pot. Over this half a bottle of

the best grade of jet-black ink is poured. A pinch of salt and a dash
of pepper, quite necessary to make the ink stick to the metal shot,
are added. Then the whole is warmed on the stove for a brief moment and stirred about vigorously with that large pewter spoon
that once belonged to Anne Hathaway and is engraved with those
odd initials W. S.

At last the stuff that makes stars is finished and the coffee-pot
is brought into the living-room. During the whole time Edward
has been levelling off the high spots with the hoe and the children
have been walking behind him stamping down the up-cropping
pages. But now at last....

He takes the coffee-pot in hand and beginning in one corner of the
room pours the lead shot through the spout. The little spheres
strike the pages and with the sound of hail the warm ink leaves its
mark.

The children cry out for joy. 'One,' 'Two,' 'One,' 'One,' 'Oh,
Daddy, three!' they cry. 'Another three!'

Soon the whole room has been covered and all the stars that may
fall in a single month have been evenly scattered. The hoe and rake
are now put away and the great work is done.

The children pick up the pages that are marked with the star-
stuff and as they do so they sing that beautiful carol:

> *Open, ye Heavens, wide*
> *And let the stars fall, fall*
> *On Edward's Stories.*

II

THE AUTHORIZED VERSION

By The Editor

To repeat what I have said in these pages in previous years, for
the benefit of the reader as yet unacquainted with my standards and
principles of selection, I shall point out that I have set myself the
task of disengaging the essential human qualities in our contemporary fiction, which, when chronicled conscientiously by our literary
artists, may fairly be called a criticism of life. I am not all interested in formulae, and organized criticism at its best would be
nothing more than dead criticism, as all dogmatic interpretation

of life is always dead. What has interested me, to the exclusion of other things, is the fresh, living current which flows through the best American work, and the psychological and imaginative quality which American writers have conferred upon it.

No substance is of importance in fiction unless it is organic substance, that is to say, substance in which the pulse of life is beating. Inorganic fiction has been our curse in the past, and bids fair to remain so, unless we exercise much greater artistic discrimination than we display at present.

The present record covers the period from January 1 to December 31, 1937, inclusive. During this period I have sought to select from the magazine stories published by American authors those which have rendered life imaginatively in organic substance and artistic form. Substance is something achieved by the artist in every act of creation, rather than something already present, and accordingly a fact or group of facts in a story only attains substantial embodiment when the artist's power of compelling imaginative persuasion transforms them into a living truth. The first test of a short story, therefore, in any qualitative analysis, is to decide how vitally compelling the writer makes his selected facts or incidents. This may conveniently be called the test of substance.

But a second test is necessary if the story is to take rank above other stories. The true artist will seek to shape this living substance into the most beautiful and satisfying form by skillful selection and arrangement of his materials, and by the most direct and appealing presentation of it in portrayal and characterization.

The short stories which I have examined in this study, as in previous years, have fallen naturally into four groups. The first consists of those stories which fail, in my opinion, to survive either the test of substance or the test of form. These stories are not listed in the yearbook.

The second group consists of those stories which may fairly claim that they survive either the test of substance or the test of form. Each of these stories may claim to possess either distinction of technique alone, or more frequently, I am glad to say, a persuasive sense of life in them to which the reader responds with some part of his own experience. Stories included in this group are indicated in the yearbook index by a single asterisk prefixed to the title.

The third group, which is composed of stories of still greater distinction, includes such narratives as may lay convincing claim to a second reading, because each of them has survived both tests, the test of substance and the test of form. Stories included in this group are indicated in the yearbook index by two asterisks prefixed to the title.

Finally, I have recorded the names of a small group of stories which possess, I believe, the even finer distinction of uniting genuine substance and artistic form in a closely woven pattern with such sincerity that these stories may fairly claim a position in American literature. If all these stories by American authors were republished, they would not occupy more space than a few novels of average length. My selection of them does not imply the critical belief that they are great stories. A year which produced one great story would be an exceptional one. It is simply to be taken as meaning that I have found the equivalent of a few volumes worthy of republication among all the stories published during the period under consideration. These stories are indicated in the yearbook by three asterisks prefixed to the title and are listed in the special 'Roll of Honor.' The general and particular results of my study will be found explained and carefully detailed in the supplementary part of this volume.

THE BEST SHORT STORIES
1938

MR. SYCAMORE [1]

By ROBERT AYRE

(From *Story*)

FOR a long time now John Gwilt had been meditating a change in his way of life. John Gwilt was forty-five, and he had been a postman in the town of Smeed, plodding the streets of Smeed mechanically, punctually, up and down, back and forth, day in and day out, rain and shine and snow and slush, for twenty years, never hoisting his bag on his back without a sigh of weariness and never casting it off at the end of the route without a groan of relief.

While his wife, Jane, knew of his discontent, she was nevertheless somewhat surprised when he announced, one evening at supper, his intention of becoming a tree.

'I'm tired of locomotion,' he explained. 'I've had my fill of tramp-tramp-tramping all day long and trudging up and down stairs. I've made up my mind to stand still for the rest of my life.'

Mrs. Gwilt looked at him and sighed. She looked at him and bowed her head and said, 'What's to be, will be.' She was a religious woman. She sighed and asked her husband if he would have more coffee.

'The house is paid for,' said John Gwilt, passing his cup, 'there is a little money in the bank, and I have kept up the insurance. You will be well provided for, Jane.'

'I could take a few piano pupils.' There was just a touch of reproach in Mrs. Gwilt's gesture as she turned the wedding ring on her finger.

'That will not be necessary. I said you would be well provided for.'

'When do you intend to —?' She hardly knew how to put it.

'Make the change? There is nothing to be gained by putting it off,' he replied, blinking excitedly behind his glasses. 'Spring has come. The time is now. This very minute!'

Jane was scrupulously picking crumbs off the tablecloth, one by one, and placing them on her plate. 'You might wipe the dishes for me before you go,' she said sadly.

'Wipe the dishes? Why?'

'Just for the sake of sentiment,' said Jane, studying the crumbs. 'You used to do it, the first year we were married. Don't you remember? But it doesn't matter,' she added, as she looked up and saw the expression on his face.

'I think we'd better go out to the yard and get started before it's too dark,' said John Gwilt firmly.

'You know best, John,' she sighed. 'But — wouldn't it be wise to ask somebody's advice?'

John Gwilt frowned. 'Why should I ask anyone's advice? *Whose* advice? I know what I'm doing. Jane, this is not a sudden notion. I've been thinking about it seriously for a long time. Too long,' he said, rising abruptly and laying his hand on the table as if he were about to deliver a speech. 'Too long! I do not intend to put it off another minute!'

So they went out to the little yard at the back of the house, John carrying the spade and Jane a bucket of water. A garden, Jane called it, because she usually had a row of sweet peas clinging to a network of strings tacked on Dogan's fence, and a battalion of sunflowers presenting arms along the lane; but it was just a yard, closed in by the house, by the back fence, and by the neighbors' fences on either side; in a corner, by the gate the coal men used, stood the garbage cans and the mound of winter ashes from the basement; a plank walk zigzagged down the centre, more or less under the clothesline, for Jane's feet in wet weather: it divided the yard into two, an attempt at a lawn on Staines's side, and Jane's sweet peas, nasturtiums, and rhubarb on the other.

'This line,' said John Gwilt, with authority, 'will have to come down.'

'But, John ——' Jane's mouth dropped open. 'Where shall I hang the clothes? I must have a line!'

'You'll have to make some other arrangement.' He was lifting the planks and piling them beside the ashpile.

'I hope you are not going to be a very big tree — an oak, or anything like that,' Jane ventured. 'The garden is small enough.'

'Leave that to me,' said John, busy winding up the clothesline.

He tied it in a loop and left it hanging on the hook beside the kitchen door. 'I always wanted a tree in the back yard.'

'We have the honeysuckle in front ——'

John Gwilt grunted. 'Do you call that thing a tree?'

'Well, what kind are you going to be, John?'

'Leave that to me,' he repeated. (The truth was, he did not know.)

'Where do you want to be planted, then?'

'Right in the centre of the yard. Why do you think I took down the line? I want plenty of room to spread my branches.'

'I do hope you will be prudent,' Jane murmured. She sighed and began worrying about the clothesline.

John was busy measuring with his eye the distance from the fence on either side, but he was aware of his wife's thoughts. 'Remember,' he warned her. 'I won't have you fastening any clotheslines to my trunk. You'll have to find some other way of hanging out the wash.'

At this point, Fred Staines, the barber, put his head over the fence and saw his neighbors with bucket and spade.

'What are you putting in this year, Mrs. Gwilt?' he asked. 'I'm taking a shot at dahlias, myself.'

The Gwilts did not answer. John was grimly sinking the spade into the hard soil and Jane was standing by, watching, with her arms wrapped in her apron and crossed over her chest — it was a raw evening.

'You'll need to make it fairly deep,' she said.

'What on earth are you digging a hole there for?' asked Fred Staines, gaping over the fence. 'Are you burying something?'

'No, we're not burying anything,' said John Gwilt, in a tone that offered no encouragement.

'Well, that's good,' said the barber. 'I thought maybe Solomon was dead. What are you planting, then?' he persisted, after a pause.

'John,' said Mrs. Gwilt.

Mr. Staines uttered an exclamation of surprise and gazed blankly at the digger.

In a few words, Jane enlightened him. 'John,' she said, 'has decided to turn himself into a tree. He's tired of marching up and down the streets of Smeed with the mailbag.'

'Well, I'll be dog!' said Fred Staines. 'A tree has an easy enough life of it,' he admitted, as an afterthought.

John Gwilt leaned on his spade and looked up. 'Believe me,' he declared, 'the trees have the right idea.'

'It certainly is an original idea,' said the barber, staring at John. 'I wish I had done it sooner.'

John Gwilt turned again to his digging. 'I think the hole is deep enough,' he said to his wife, after a while. He stepped in. 'Yes, it comes halfway up my shins. And my roots will strike down deeper, of course.'

He sat on the new-thrown earth and pulled off his shoes and socks. The barber vanished.

'You're not going to undress, John?' asked Jane, in alarm.

'No, not until I get my bark.' But he rolled his trousers up to his knees.

'Ah!' he sighed, 'how good the earth feels to the feet! So cool! So cool!' He stretched his toes and said, 'All right, Jane, spade the soil in around my legs.' He stood up and balanced himself firmly on his soles and heels. I'll be a long time standing, he thought, and I might as well be comfortable from the start. 'Pack it down firmly and then water me and pack it down again.'

She was so awkward that John took the spade out of her hands and scraped the soil toward him. I suppose I made the hole wider than was necessary, he thought. 'All right, that will have to do. Pour the water — Ugh! it's cold!' He shuddered as she overturned the bucket. 'Never mind, pack the earth down some more.' He gritted his teeth. 'Look out, Jane! You'll graze my shin!'

Jane dropped to her knees and patted the earth with the palms of her hands, and as she patted she was seized with a sudden misgiving. Jane Gwilt was a reader of poetry. She sat back on her heels, holding her muddy hands stiffly in front of her, and said in a hushed voice: 'But, John, are you sure you are doing right? I thought that only God could ——'

'Let us not go into that!' John Gwilt said, with his teeth clenched; '*and please never quote those abominable verses.*'

'I hope you're not doing anything sinful, John, that's all,' said Mrs. Gwilt, with grave concern.

'You leave that to me,' said John Gwilt, a little more gently. He unhooked the spectacles from behind his ears and handed them to her. Before taking them, Jane wiped her hands on her apron. 'I won't need these any more,' he said. 'Keep them. The shoes you may send to the post office.' He grinned broadly and wagged his head. 'Send the shoes to the post office. Ha, ha, ha! The shoes belong to the post office. With my compliments. But I can do what I like with my feet!' He began to laugh a little hysterically. 'And I'm never going to make them walk again!'

'How does it feel, John?' The barber's head appeared over the fence again and beside it the head of Mrs. Staines.

'You have no idea how comfortable the cool soil is to the feet,' said John Gwilt happily.

Mrs. Staines asked how long he expected it would take.

'Oh, I can't tell you to the hour,' John replied. 'Not long.'

'Won't you get tired standing?'

'No more tired than I have been walking these twenty years and more. When I am well rooted, I won't be tired.'

He stretched and wriggled his shoulders and beamed. 'Did you ever hear of a tree getting tired? Listen!' he cried exultantly. 'I'll have hold of the earth, I'll be anchored to it, I'll be part of it! Do you understand? I'll draw its strength into my trunk and all my branches, into every twig and leaf! Oh, no, Mrs. Staines, I don't see myself getting tired!' He swelled his chest and smiled at her indulgently.

'What I can't understand,' said Fred Staines, with a puzzled frown, 'is how you're going to do it.'

John Gwilt blinked, folded his arms, and looked him square in the eye. 'I passed with honors in my correspondence course ——'

The barber looked at him incredulously. 'Do you mean to tell me they give courses in how to turn yourself into trees? If that doesn't beat all!' he exclaimed.

John Gwilt snorted and Jane answered: 'It's the Will Power course he means. How to Cultivate the Will in Twenty Lessons.'

'Mmn. So you're doing it by Will Power, eh?'

'When you are listening to Amos and Andy,' said John Gwilt, raising a solemn forefinger, 'and long after you are in bed and sound asleep, I'll be standing here, alone in the dark, willing myself into a tree.'

'To my way of thinking, it doesn't seem quite Christian,' Mrs. Staines observed, pursing her lips.

Jane sighed. 'There, John, I told you.'

'We needn't start that, Jane,' said John Gwilt, with a warning edge on his voice. 'Mrs. Staines, I don't think you'll find anything in your Bible against it. Besides,' he added, 'I am a pre-Christian.'

'John was always a great reader,' Jane explained, chastened. She looked regretfully at the glasses.

'I am sure we all wish you well, Mr. Gwilt,' said the barber's wife, charitably, but pursing her lips for all that, and adding, 'though I won't admit I understand it.'

'There are more things in heaven and earth, Horatio,' said John Gwilt, 'than are dreamt of in your philosophy.'

Mrs. Staines, slightly piqued, withdrew, and her husband called: 'Good luck, John! See how you're getting along, later.'

'I'll go in and fetch your hat, John,' said Jane. 'You haven't much hair, you know, and you might catch cold in the night.'

'Never mind the hat,' John said ungratefully. 'I'm not going to make myself look ridiculous. You'd better get your dishes done and leave me here to concentrate.'

'Very well, John. If you need anything, just call.'

John grunted and she gathered up his shoes and socks and went sadly into the house, leaving him standing there with his feet planted in the ground.

'What a balmy evening!' he exclaimed, stretching and taking a deep breath. Down the lane, someone was burning leaves, and he drank in the acrid smell with pleasure, until the thought occurred to him that it might be indelicate for him, a future tree, to enjoy the smell of burning leaves. A little ghoulish? he wondered, and turned his attention to a robin trilling on a telephone wire. 'Ah, spring!' he murmured, and then he pulled himself together and began willing.

As she washed the dishes, mournfully reflecting that she would have only half the number to do in future, Jane kept peeping out of the window, but John was standing quite still, rigid, with his arms folded and his eyes fixed on a knothole in the back fence, exerting his Will Power, and she did not like to disturb him.

When she did come out, an hour later, he said: 'Jane, you might bring me one of the kitchen chairs. I'm not used to it, you know, and I find I am getting a little fatigued.'

'But you'll grow crooked,' she protested mildly.

Nodding his head, he agreed that she was right. He frowned stoically and stiffened his spine.

'Is there any change yet?' Jane asked, with wifely solicitude.

John took stock of how he felt and replied that he thought his toes were striking root. 'It feels a bit like rheumatism,' he said.

'I'm afraid you'll catch your death of cold,' sighed Jane.

'A bit stiff, eh?' asked Fred Staines, appearing at the fence.

'Oh, nothing to speak of,' said John.

'You'll be stiffer before morning,' the barber remarked cheerfully. 'Early in the season, you know, and the paper says a drop in temperature.'

'I expect to be stiffer.'

'It isn't as if he was used to it,' Jane sighed. 'John was never given to sitting on flagpoles or anything like that, you know.'

The barber suggested that it might have been good training.

'I don't believe in wasting time on frivolity,' snorted John Gwilt. 'I never held with those marathon contests.'

'What are you going to do in winter?' asked the barber.

'It's a long time until winter,' said John Gwilt. 'I'll do what the other trees do. Hibernate. I won't,' he added pointedly, 'be stoking any furnaces. And I won't be plowing through snowdrifts in a heavy overcoat and galoshes.'

Jane began to wonder what was to be done with his winter undergarments and his other clothing, but she refrained from mentioning such things in the hearing of the neighbors.

Fred Staines leaned on the fence, smoking his pipe and gazing thoughtfully at the postman.

'What kind of a tree are you aiming to turn into?' he asked, at length.

'A Christmas tree,' said John Gwilt whimsically. 'Jane's going to deck me out in tinsel next Christmas and hang lollipops on my branches and festoon me with strings of colored lights, aren't you, Jane? And load me down with presents for Daisy and Billy Staines and the Bellows children. For once, I'll have arms enough to carry the Christmas parcels, and everybody *will come to me* to get them! Jane!' he said, warming with enthusiasm and throwing his arms wide. 'I want to give a grand party! Invite the Martins and the Bellows and the McCorkindales! And let all the youngsters join hands and dance around me in the snow!'

'This is no time for joking, John,' said Mrs. Gwilt, turning away with a sniff.

'But, my dear, I mean it! I want you to have a good time when I am meta——' He approached the word gingerly and then plunged recklessly in: 'metamorphosized.'

It sounds so much worse than plain 'dead,' thought Jane.

'And I want to be in the midst of the fun.'

'It should be a swell party,' Fred Staines observed. 'We'll drink your health, John.'

'In hot, steaming punch! I'll probably be asleep, you know, like the other trees; but I'll feel Christmas coming on — excitement in the air, bells, carol singers — and I'll wake up all of a tingle, as I used to when I was a youngster, and find my branches tangled in tinsel and lights — don't forget the lights, Jane: you can get them at the fifteen-cent store — and dolled up like the Arabian Nights in those pretty bubbles — red, blue, green, silver, gold, with a gleaming star on top!' His eyes blinked and sparkled, he threw his arms about, and Jane was a little taken aback: it did not seem like John. 'And see you all joining hands and dancing round and round ——'

'Round and round the maypole,' said Fred Staines, a trifle pityingly, as he knocked his pipe out on the fence; and Jane was humiliated. With his excitement snuffed, John Gwilt turned sulky.

'Well, good night,' said Fred Staines. 'Don't let the boll weevil get you, ha, ha!'

'The boll weevil doesn't attack trees,' said John Gwilt stiffly.

Jane went into the house and brought out a blanket. In spite of her husband's sullen protest, she wrapped it about his shoulders, and in spite of his protest he was grateful for the warmth. But he was obstinate about the hat.

Jane lingered irresolutely. At last she said, 'Good night, John,' and kissed him; and, not knowing whether she would ever see her husband in his familiar shape again, the wife went in to her lonely bed.

John Gwilt wrapped the blankets more closely about his shivering shoulders and took a deep breath to steady himself. Then, after listening intently and looking around fearfully, he lowered his body to a crouch, to rest his weary limbs.

Perhaps it would be more comfortable if I turned myself into a bush, after all, he thought weakly. But he had not been squatting a moment when out of the corner of his eye he glimpsed a flash of light. Jane Gwilt had gone into the bedroom. He straightened himself just as she came to the window to lower the blind. So when Jane looked out she saw her husband raised to his full height. She could not make him out very well in the dark, but the figure was upright and straight, proud and resolute. John Gwilt, after a momentary aberration, had returned to the dignity of his ambition. It would never do, he thought, for Jane to suspect that his Will Power was faltering. Women set such little store by these manly virtues.

So with faith in her husband unshaken, but quite forlornly, Jane waved to him and pulled down the blind. For a time, John stretched his neck and gazed at the narrow slit of light that showed beneath, and imagined Jane undressing and smearing her face with cold cream and kneeling in her nightgown to say her prayers. Then the light was extinguished and the house was in darkness. John Gwilt sighed. He thought of the warm bed and the contented ticking of the clock; he shuddered; a pang of nostalgia and wild regret sprang into his heart and then died as he stiffened his body and exerted his Will. 'What John Gwilt has begun, John Gwilt will end,' he said aloud.

He began consoling himself with the memories of twenty years, of burning feet and weary limbs, and shoulders aching from the weight of the mailbag. No more, he thought. Rest at last, he sighed happily. I might have found rest in death, of course, but why go to such extremes? I want to live. In my own quiet way. The resentment at Fred Staines's gibe still rankled, but he smiled and allowed himself to become indulgent. 'Calm and spacious,' he murmured. 'The ideal of Confucius. How seldom mankind attains it.'

Half asleep, he fell to dreaming of the long serene years that stretched before him; of springs, when the sap would begin to stir painfully, deliciously, in his limbs — like the tingling return of the blood when your foot has been asleep; when the twigs would thrust themselves out eagerly into buds, when the buds would burst into leaves; of summers, when he would spread his leaves against the sunlight and make a shimmering green shape against the blue sky and the piled up clouds, when his boughs would heave in the wind, and the rain would go sluicing down his broad trunk; of autumns, when he would be startled by the first sting of the frost and would turn suddenly to discover that the birds had gone and that the jingling of the crickets was slackening and that the year was running down; when his leaves would glow in a new color — I wonder if it will feel like sunburn? he asked himself — when he would gradually sink into the winter sleep, profound, deep, lost within himself, never regretting the leaves scattered over the grass, never feeling them go, less aware of their going than he had been of the thinning of his hair. There would always be new leaves.

The jazz band on the barber's radio ceased its monotonous drumming and wheedling; the light in the window went out; reappeared in the bathroom window; went out. Fred Staines had gone to bed. A motor car rushed by in the street and was quiet; a clock chimed and was quiet. The darkness gathered closer, and John Gwilt, huddling in his blanket, looked up at the cold, glittering stars.

II

In the morning, when Jane Gwilt awoke, she was for a moment bewildered at finding herself alone in bed. With a start, she remembered where John was, and her heart pumped and thumped as she threw back the covers and ran to the window. Has it happened? she wondered, or shall I see John stretched out dead? Or suppose something went wrong and he is changed into a fence post or a pillar of salt or something? What if his Will Power wouldn't work and he has run away in shame?

But there stood her husband as she had left him the night before, with his feet planted in the ground and the gray blanket around his shoulders. He looked more woebegone, perhaps, as he turned at the sound she made opening the window; his head rose red and bald out of the folds of the blanket; what little hair he had was damp and wispy, and as he was about to speak his body was wrenched by a violent sneeze.

Oh, dear, thought Jane, I should have given him a hot-water bottle. 'I'll be down as soon as I get something on,' she called.

Before coming out, she set the kettle boiling. It was a chilly morning and the sky was overcast. Rain, she thought; he'll catch his death.

'How do you feel, John?' she asked anxiously, laying her hand on his forehead.

John replied in a voice like felt, but he said, 'Fine. Fi——' and sneezed again.

'John, I think you'd better put this off until the weather gets warmer. It's going to rain and you'll catch your ——'

'No, I won't catch my death of cold!' retorted John Gwilt. 'And I have no intention of putting "this," as you call it, off. The transformation has begun.'

'Oh, John! How do you know?'

'*How do I know!*' He sneezed, and Jane hastened to mollify him.

'All right, John, I suppose you know. Is there anything I can do for you?'

'You could bring me a handkerchief.' He sneezed again. 'Get me a handkerchief, quick! Two or three of them!'

'John, John! I knew you'd ——'

He was about to explode, so she fled to the house.

'Can you take any nourishment?' Jane asked on her return. 'A bowl of corn flakes?'

'Who ever heard of a tree eating corn flakes!' John Gwilt demanded contemptuously.

Jane sighed. John blew his nose. 'Bring me some bacon and eggs. And coffee, quarts of coffee.'

The good wife carried out the card table and set it up in front of her husband. 'It won't be easy to eat standing,' she suggested, 'but the table will help.' She spread her luncheon cloth over it and laid out John's napkin, rolled in his own silver ring, and a knife and fork, salt and pepper and mustard pot, a pat of butter on a saucer, and a jar of marmalade.

As she stood back to appraise the table, she cast an apprehensive look at the lowering sky.

'No frills, Jane,' said John Gwilt. 'Hurry up with the bacon and eggs.'

Time was, thought Jane, when he couldn't get enough of my marmalade, and now he calls it frills; but I suppose trees have no taste for such things. She was gratified, however, to see her husband devour his breakfast with voracious appetite, in spite of his cold and the awkwardness of his position; he smeared his toast, and even his bacon, with the marmalade, drank the coffee-pot dry, and lighted his pipe.

Fred Staines came to the fence as Jane was clearing the table.

'Well, John,' he observed brightly, 'you'll soon be missing all these good things.'

John Gwilt threw off the blanket in a spasm of embarrassment and shrugged his shoulders. Taking the pipe out of his mouth, he said gruffly: 'I'll have better things. I find,' he added, looking a little wryly at the pipe, 'that I'm losing my human appetites.' He was disappointed in the pipe because of his cold.

'How does it feel after a night of it?' asked the barber. 'Pretty chilly, eh?'

'Might be worse,' said John Gwilt.

'Would you like anything else, dear?' asked Jane. 'You didn't read the *Sun* last night. I saved it for you ——'

'No thank you,' John said. 'When I leave the world, I leave the world.'

'Like going into a monastery,' Fred Staines remarked, tonsuring his own scalp with a forefinger.

'Oh, John isn't a Catholic,' said Mrs. Gwilt, with a little agitation.

'I don't care what happens to the entire human race,' John Gwilt said flatly. 'I agree with the scientist who said it was an accident, or a sort of epidemic attacking the beautiful body of Nature. I wash my hands of the human race.'

The last remark prompted Mrs. Gwilt to ask if her husband wished to make his morning toilet.

'A little dirt won't hurt me,' said John, examining his hands. 'After this, I am part of the earth.'

'If you would like me to shave you — if you think it would be easier' — Fred Staines suggested, rubbing his chin — 'it won't cost you anything.'

'I'm not an invalid,' said John Gwilt stiffly. 'And I'm not to be pitied because I'm turning myself into a tree. If you had any sense, you'd know I was to be envied.'

'Well, I can't say I envy you,' said Fred Staines, rather nettled.

John Gwilt intended to shrug disdainfully but sneezed instead and the barber said he had better be going to the shop.

'Shall I bring your mug and brush?' Jane asked.

'No, thank you, my dear,' said John Gwilt. 'I don't expect to be making any calls today.' He smiled benignly.

Like a wind that sets all the flags fluttering, the news spread about Smeed, and throughout the morning the neighbors trooped down the lane and stood at John Gwilt's fence, gaping at him and plying him with questions. It began to rain, but the gossips were loath to move, and they had a merry moment when Mrs. Gwilt appeared with an umbrella for her husband.

He waved her away, whispering hoarsely that the rain was just what he needed, but she prevailed (he did not want to make a scene) and he found the umbrella useful to shut out the throng at the fence.

'Gibber away, you fools!' he muttered to himself. 'There is more dignity in one tree than in a whole pack of chattering chimpanzees.' He refused to answer their questions or to acknowledge their taunts, but, holding the umbrella in front of his face and gazing intently at its ribs, he doggedly went on with his willing.

No less a person than the Postmaster himself, Harry Oikle, broke in upon his concentration.

The crowd fell back respectfully as the Postmaster pushed through, unbarred the gate, and strode across the yard to where John Gwilt was planted.

Oh, dear, thought Jane, I knew he should have shaved!

'Well, Gwilt,' said Mr. Oikle, with heavy indulgence, 'what's all this foolishness?'

John Gwilt raised his umbrella and blinked at the Postmaster, while Jane watched from the kitchen door, all of a tremble. For a second, he felt cowed, and, for a second, brave and triumphant; both impulses resolved themselves into a sneeze.

'Come, come, John,' said the Postmaster; 'pull on your socks and get off to work.'

'I have something better to do, Mr. Oikle,' said John Gwilt.

'Rubbish! You're making yourself the laughing-stock of the whole town, that's what you're doing.'

'Only fools laugh at wise men, Mr. Oikle,' said John Gwilt mildly.

The Postmaster surveyed him incredulously. 'So you consider yourself a wise man, do you?'

The gossips at the fence laughed and nudged one another and tapped their heads.

John Gwilt blew his nose resolutely, and carefully tucked the handkerchief into his pocket. Then he raised his chin, just a little impertinently, and blinked. Then he sneezed, and the crowd laughed again.

'I suppose you know what we do with wise men, Mr. Gwilt?'
said the Postmaster. He spoke with significant deliberation and
looked John steadily in the eye.

John Gwilt's eyes twinkled. 'I'll wait right here,' he said. 'I
won't budge an inch.' He raised his head and grinned at the Postmaster. 'But you'll never catch me.'

Mr. Oikle shrugged, but he left the yard with a puzzled face and
did not acknowledge the greeting of Caleb Hoop, editor of the
Smeed *Sun*, who had elbowed his way through the crowd and now
stood squinting at John Gwilt.

'What's the idea?' Hoop demanded, rolling a cigar between his lips.
John Gwilt looked back at him and made no reply.

'Doing it for a bet?'

Mr. Gwilt sniffed. 'What use has a tree for money?'

'Then why are you doing it?'

'Who wants to know?' asked John Gwilt, blandly.

'Don't you know who I am?' The visitor brought out a card.
'Hoop. Editor of the *Sun*.'

'Oh, I see.' John looked at the name. 'You want to put a piece
in the paper about me.'

'You guessed it. It isn't every day a man turns himself into a
tree. Naturally the public's interested. Look at the crowd out in
the lane there.'

Although he protested that he was not seeking publicity, Mr.
Gwilt could not help glowing with pleasure and he asked the editor
if he would like a photograph.

'The only photograph we have, dear,' piped up Mrs. Gwilt, who
had ventured out, 'is the snap I took at the picnic last summer ——'

'Fine!' the editor broke in, steering jaw and cigar in her direction.

'But,' said Jane, hesitantly, 'it's not a very good one, I'm afraid.
You see, I didn't hold the camera just right and Mr. Gwilt's head
was cut off.'

Mr. Hoop smirked. 'We'd need the head. Haven't you got anything else?'

'There's the wedding picture,' said John Gwilt.

'Oh, I wouldn't want to part with that!'

'It's all right, Mrs. Gwilt,' the editor reassured her. 'We'll send
it back O.K. A wedding picture would be just the thing. I'd like
to get you in, too.'

'Oh,' protested Jane, 'I haven't done anything.'

'You're the wife, aren't you?'

Jane blushed and said: 'I'll have to fetch it. It's in the album.'

'Got any shots of him as a little boy or anything?' the editor called after her. 'Bring the whole caboodle. Or I'll come in with you and look at the album in the parlor. It's kind of wet out here, anyway.'

'Wait a minute,' said John Gwilt. His wife hesitated while he sneezed and blew his nose.

'Never mind bringing the album, Jane.'

'There's the one of you on the rocking horse when you were five,' she reminded him. 'It's quite a cute one. He has a curl down the middle of his forehead,' she told the editor, 'and one over each ear.'

'Fine!' said the editor. 'Bring it along too!'

Mrs. Gwilt looked questioningly at her husband.

'No!' John cried. 'The wedding photo will be enough.'

Hoop stood munching his cigar and eyeing John Gwilt. 'Well, it's an original notion, anyway,' he remarked, not without admiration.

John Gwilt blinked at him and said, not without contempt: 'I make no claims for originality. You don't seem to have read your Greek history.'

'Well, the stunt hasn't been pulled off in Smeed before.'

'If you think this is a stunt, like sitting on a flagpole, you're mistaken, Mr. Hoop.'

'What do you call it then? A scientific experiment, like going up into the stratosphere or talking to the dead? What do you expect to find out?'

'I expect to find out something about dignity and peace,' said John Gwilt.

'Poise and repose.' The editor was thinking in headlines. He screwed his face into a coarse wink and nodded toward the house. 'Storm and strife, eh?'

Mentally, he jotted it down:

HARRIED HUBBY SEEKS SURCEASE

'Jane and I are quite happy,' said John Gwilt loftily. 'Domestic relations have nothing to do with my decision.'

'Just tired of life, eh? Just another poor mortal weary of the grind.'

'If I was tired of life,' said John Gwilt, 'I could blow my brains out.'

'That's true, too: it isn't as simple as straight suicide.'

'I love life,' said John Gwilt, 'but I don't like the life I have been forced to live for the past twenty years. I am a man of contemplative disposition.'

The editor nodded. 'Philosopher, eh?'

'Naturally, to a man of contemplative disposition,' said John Gwilt, gravely and deliberately, speaking for publication, 'there comes a time when he wearies of the hurly-burly ——'

'That's right,' said the editor. 'I always go fishing, myself.'

Throughout the conversation, he stood chewing his cigar, with his hands thrust deep in his raincoat pockets. The philosopher was a little disturbed because the editor was not taking notes. 'Do you,' he ventured, 'remember all your interviews?'

'Don't you worry about that, Mr. Gwilt,' said the editor. 'I'm an old hand at this game. I won't misquote you. What gave you the idea of turning into a tree?'

'Isn't it perfectly logical? I couldn't remain a postman and enjoy the contemplative life.'

The editor nodded. 'But couldn't you have retired?'

'I don't know if you newspapermen are at all inclined to the mystical,' began John Gwilt. He looked up, to see that the rain had cleared, shut his umbrella, and stood leaning on the crook. He blinked his watery eyes and continued, gazing far beyond the thick body of the editor. 'In the first place, I couldn't retire. I couldn't afford it. They don't give you a pension at forty-five. It would mean that Mrs. Gwilt would have to find some way of supporting me.'

'No self-respecting man could allow that,' said Mr. Hoop, looking at him quizzically.

'Certainly not.'

'And yet,' said the editor, cocking one eye at him, 'she will have to support you, after all.'

'That I deny,' said John Gwilt impressively. 'I shall be entirely self-supporting. Trees get their food and drink out of the earth and air — you should know that — and they grow their own clothes.'

'Ah!' Mr. Hoop interrupted. 'I see a solution for the unemployment problem. If we could plant a few hundred thousand men and change them ——'

'I am not interested in the unemployment problem,' said John Gwilt. 'It is only one example of human insanity. But I'm telling you I won't cost Jane a penny. Not if I live to be a hundred. And I'm not leaving my wife in the lurch,' he added, watching to make sure that his words were being marked. 'She is well provided for. There is plenty for one to live on. Nobody can accuse me of shirking my responsibility, even if I am changing my way of life.'

The editor wagged his head and struggled to light the ruins of his cigar.

'If I live to be a hundred,' John Gwilt repeated musingly. 'We got sidetracked on material things, Mr. Hoop, but I started to say something about the real reason for choosing to be a tree. I told you I loved life. I want to be alive, really alive; I want to live in the earth's way. We are all estranged. Do you understand what I mean? We are broken off from the earth. I want to be part of the earth's life. I'm tired of this helpless fluttering, all this hurrying and scurrying: it isn't dignified; it isn't sane; I want to stand still.'

'If you ask me,' said the editor, 'I think you're just plain tuckered out, Mr. Gwilt.'

'I'll go on living, for a hundred years — a thousand!' John Gwilt exclaimed, not hearing him. 'Never suffering the pains and miseries of growing old; enjoying the sun and the wind and the rain, too, for a change; the blue sky in the morning and the twinkling stars at night; watching the world go by; watching Smeed grow up around me. I only hope,' he said, in a wistful afterthought, 'that the town doesn't grow too rapidly in this neighborhood. I'd hate to be hemmed in by a horde of belching factories, choking my foliage with grime and soot.'

He leaned on his umbrella, lost in dreams, while the editor worried his cigar.

'You know,' said the editor presently, 'it mightn't be a bad idea for the town to set aside a sanctuary around you.'

'A sanctuary? Around me?' Tears sprang into John Gwilt's eyes.

'Yes, by golly! There's great possibilities in that idea. I'll have to get busy and do something. Get people talking. Start a fund. Good publicity for the *Sun*, good publicity for the town. You'll be

a great tourist attraction, Mr. Sycamore, or whatever you're going
to be! Smeed can't afford to slip up on a chance like this!'

John Gwilt was a little disturbed. 'I'm not fond of crowds, you
know,' he stammered.

'Listen, Mr. Gwilt,' said the editor, wagging the cigar at him,
'listen to me. You'd like to be a benefactor of your town, wouldn't
you? You'd like to go down in history, wouldn't you? Before I get
through with this story, the whole civilized world will be flocking
to Smeed to see you! Think of the business it'll bring to the town!
Think of the railways and the hotels and the filling stations and the
tourist camps! Think of the hot-dog stands, think of the souvenir
stores! By golly, Gwilt, you'll be the making of this town! You
never thought of that, did you?'

In his enthusiasm he injured the cigar beyond repair. John Gwilt
stood blinking at him, in a daze.

'Listen,' said the editor, 'we'll put a brass plate on your chest,
telling the whole story for posterity, names, dates and everything!
We'll have a big dedication ceremony, we'll get the Mayor out in
his silk hat, we'll have a picnic — beer — champagne — we'll do the
thing grand while we're at it! We'll get you to rustle your leaves
for the talkies! We'll have community singing. Declare a public
holiday, get all the Service Clubs, and the Chamber of Commerce,
the Merchants' Association, the Smeed Improvement League, the
Elks, the Moose, the Masons, the Odd Fellows, all the school
children. We'll get the band out in their busbies — both bands, by
golly! — the Salvation Army will want to come in on the celebration
— and have a bang-up parade — flags, banners, floats, cars buried
in flowers. We'll have the post office boys march with a big
wreath ——'

'What's the wreath for?' John Gwilt asked, uneasily.

'For you, of course. You're the hero, the guest of honor.'

'But I won't be — dead.'

The editor rubbed his chin. 'Well,' he compromised, 'we won't
have a wreath if you feel that way about it. I guess we can think
of something else. Drape you in bunting, or ribbon, or something.'

Perhaps Fred Staines's raillery about maypoles still pricked,
perhaps it was because he was at bottom a modest man — the
Christmas party would have been more or less a family affair — at
any rate, John Gwilt felt a little uncomfortable. 'Can't you just

leave me as I am? Won't the brass plate be enough without all that fuss?'

'Well, I tell you, we got to do the thing in style, you know.' Mr. Hoop rubbed his chin and chewed on the remains of his cigar. 'Hmn. Let me see now.' He smirked and nodded his approval of the idea that came to him. 'We'll have a picked chorus of high school girls, all in white, singing Joyce Kilmer's poem about trees ——'

Mr. Gwilt blinked desperately and said, 'No!'

'No?'

'No! I don't care for that poem.' John Gwilt shut his lips and stiffened his neck in obstinacy.

Hoop was confounded. 'You don't like it?' He took the cigar out of his mouth to gesture and recite:

> I think that I shall never see
> A poem lovely as a tree...

'It's too personal,' said John Gwilt.

'Speaking as a tree, you don't like it?'

'It's immodest,' said John Gwilt firmly.

'Lord, what a story!' the editor exclaimed under his breath.

SMEED'S MAN-TREE DEBUNKS KILMER

I'll hold that, of course, until things get warmed up. *Trees* is the nation's pet poem. I'll have them talking about Smeed from Cape Cod to San Diego!

'It's embarrassing,' John Gwilt was saying. He could not admit, even to himself, his secret qualm about the defeatism in the last line of the poem.

'You're a hard man to please,' said the editor, 'but I suppose we'll have to humor you. You're a sort of a — virtuoso.' Mentally he reserved his plan: when John Gwilt was actually a tree, there was very little he could do by way of protest, after all. He would stand in the centre of the ceremony, and if he didn't care for it — well, he might heave his branches about, but what difference would that make? The town was not to be deprived of its red-letter day because the guest of honor was inclined to be temperamental.

Although the rain had subsided, the sky was still overcast and the morning was gray and chilly. Feeling the damp in his bones, John Gwilt shuddered and stretched.

'You'll have to wait for warmer weather.'

'Oh, don't you worry, Mr. Gwilt; it'll take some time to get this thing into shape.'

'You can't very well have the celebration until — until the metamorphosis has taken place,' said John Gwilt whimsically.

'I'll say we can't! That's your job; we're depending on you. Our job is to get a fund to buy this property. You own it, don't you?' Mr. Gwilt nodded.

'Wouldn't care to donate it to the town, would you?'

'Well,' said Mr. Gwilt, doubtfully, 'I have to think of my wife.'

'Quite right, quite right. We'll buy it and make it a public square. Tear down the house.' The editor rubbed his chin. 'And we've got to have more room than this one small lot. May have to acquire two or three adjoining.' He made gestures of demolition toward the houses of Fred Staines and Bill Dogan. 'Pretty narrow, as it is. Yes, we'll have to do that, all right. It'll take two or three months, getting the money and making all the improvements. You'll be the central tree, of course, but we'll have to plant shrubs — lilacs and things — and lay out nice green lawns and flower beds. We might get the Rotary Club to put in a fountain. By golly, the more I think of the idea, the better I like it! Smeed needs something like this! I'll knock off an editorial on Breathing Spaces for the Growing City.'

Mr. Gwilt glowed with pride to imagine himself the centre of all these public improvements.

'Here is the wedding picture, John,' interpolated Jane, who had been listening patiently, anxiously, proudly, for some time.

Mr. Hoop reached out and took it. 'Thanks,' said he. 'Ah, fine! Just the thing!' He smacked his lips over the tortured couple in the photographer's studio. Mrs. Gwilt was in white, in a dress that looked as if it had been borrowed for the wedding; she held the bouquet self-consciously, paralyzed by the realization that a girl had flowers only twice in her life, when she was married and when she was buried, or as if they were property flowers, made of wax, thrust into her hands by a much-too-smiling photographer; and she held her head a little to one side and exhibited a strained, half-frightened smile, because the photographer rallied her and told her that all his brides smiled for him. Yet the delicate white ripple of the veil over her brow, and the hair escaping it in small curls, and her very awkwardness, made her appealingly pretty.

Perhaps if John Gwilt had taken the photograph from the editor's hand and had looked again at his young bride, he might have called for the spade and dug himself up, even if he had sprouted a root or two, and returned gladly to his bed and board and his daily round. Perhaps Mrs. Gwilt hoped that the photograph would restore him to his senses before it was too late, but John felt a little embarrassed, as a man does on being reminded of past foolishness — he was in the photograph, too.

'Maybe it would be better if you didn't print it, Mr. Hoop,' he suggested diffidently. 'It's rather personal, you know.'

Out of the corner of his eye he had glimpsed the stiff attitudes of the bride and bridegroom, and he blushed to remember himself as an extremely proper young man, slightly pompous and rhetorical, with thick, wavy hair and sideburns, and his coat buttoned up almost to his high, strangling collar. He was a trifle ashamed now of the self-confident way he stood, with one elbow poked out at an angle, and the way he held the bowler hat; ashamed of the bowler hat itself, and of the smirk of triumph — satisfaction, at any rate — on his face, and of the white carnation in his lapel. All this aplomb was humiliating to a man of meditative complexion who was about to transform himself into a stately tree.

The editor insisted that he take the photograph, and as he spoke put it in his breast pocket. 'You're like royalty, now; you're a celebrity, and you have no private life.'

Poor Mr. Gwilt could only be relieved that Jane had not brought out the photograph which betrayed him as an infant sprawling nakedly on a sheepskin, with his face screwed up to blubber.

'You will let me have it back?' implored Mrs. Gwilt, not without a tear.

'Oh, yes, ma'am, certainly,' Mr. Hoop promised. 'Don't you worry about that. We'll take good care of it. And you'll have a new clipping for your scrapbook. And, believe me, Mrs. Gwilt, when this story gets going, you'll need a dozen scrapbooks!'

He took his leave, and Mr. and Mrs. Gwilt stood looking at each other.

III

Jane sighed and gazed mournfully at her husband. 'John — wouldn't you change your mind, John?'

But John was determined, if only to save his face, to go through with it.

'It's too late,' said John.

'Then it *has* started? You feel something? You said — but I don't see ——'

'Well,' said John, 'it may only be the cold, but I do feel a little stiffening in the legs.'

'Will your legs grow together?' asked Jane.

'What do you expect? I'll have a trunk, like all the other trees.' Jane sighed.

'When I am a tree, I shall no longer be a man,' said John Gwilt, more harshly than was, perhaps, necessary. This may have been because he was stoically disciplining himself.

Jane Gwilt knew little about the life of trees; they seemed so remote from one another, so self-sufficient, that a woman could hardly be expected to understand them or sympathize with them. Yet they flourished. She could not help thinking of mermaids. She had often wondered about mermaids and how it was possible for them to have their cold, slippery, briny babies, and she concluded that mer-babies were born like fishes, however that was — were they hatched out of eggs? Of course Jane could never give utterance to such indelicate thoughts, and she could never in this world hint to John that, as a wife, she thought there was more comfort in a two-legged man than in a tree, be it ever so majestic.

'I suppose you would like some lunch,' she said apathetically.

'Well, my dear, for the most part, my system is still human.'

'I think a bowl of soup would do you good. Your cold is getting worse.'

His head was indeed stuffed and his eyes watered continually, and he was obliged to resort to his handkerchief a good deal.

'It's only eleven,' he said. He held his watch to his ear. It was ticking, but he wound it to make sure. 'A bowl of soup wouldn't do any harm, anyway,' he agreed, 'liquid diet'; and the faithful wife went into the kitchen.

John Gwilt stretched, did his best to breathe deeply, counting six in and eight out, snuffled, blew his nose, and began willing again. He ignored the two women, all that was left of the crowd, who stood looking over the fence and making remarks to each other.

'It's clearing up,' he said cheerfully when Jane brought the bowl of steaming soup. The gray wool of the sky had been pulled aside and a convalescent sun poked its head out of the rift, as from the folds of a blanket, and was scattering a feeble light over the town of Smeed, making John Gwilt's bald head glow ruddily and showing up the dark stubble on his cheeks. His wife, thin and straight in her brown raincoat, stood watching as he eagerly spooned the soup.

'Would you like anything else?' she asked, when he handed her the empty bowl. 'I must get my shopping done. What do you fancy for lunch? A couple of sausages and some grilled tomatoes?' Perhaps the thought occurred to her that an appeal to the inner John Gwilt might be a way to steer him from his folly. She went on: 'There's an R in the month. I could do up a nice oyster stew. Or there's liver and onions, with thick, brown gravy. Or bacon and lima beans. Fresh asparagus is in, of course ——'

'Why don't you get a chicken, Jane? This may be my last human meal. I may be past taking solids — even an hour from now. I don't know how quickly this thing works. After all, it's the first time I've done it.'

Mrs. Gwilt looked at him dubiously.

'A little more sun and I'll be well away. I feel a warm tingle now. Sap's running!'

'That may be the soup.'

'Well, Mrs. Gwilt, time will tell. You go and do your shopping. I must concentrate.'

For the greater part of the hour before Mrs. Gwilt returned from the shops and brought out the card table and a plate of sizzling sausages and tomatoes, with substantial slices of bread and a pot of coffee, John leaned on his umbrella, alternately dozing and exerting his Will Power. The children came trooping home from school down the lane, and climbed on the fence, shouting and jeering, but Mr. Gwilt maintained his dignity by putting up his umbrella and holding it in front of his face. Naturally this was a signal for the boys to begin pelting him with mud. John Gwilt winced and sweated, but the umbrella saved him from damage.

The process of change is always an ordeal, he thought. They laughed at Galileo. They threw bricks at the first silk hat — Not that I blame them for that, mind you, he added honestly.... I suppose all the other reptiles hooted at the first lizard to transform himself into a bird — probably tore him to pieces. Ah, well, the pioneers always suffer. When I am completely a tree, I shall not be the victim of rude gibes.

Eventually the children went home to their lunches, and Mr. Gwilt was able to eat his sausages in peace.

'I admit I am fond of sausages,' he said, with more banter than reproof in his voice, 'nice, sleek, brown, well-seasoned sausages; but you didn't take me seriously about the chicken, Mrs. Gwilt. Perhaps you're saving it for tonight?'

Mrs. Gwilt explained that in view of the circumstances a chicken would have been an extravagance.

'A common murderer gets a grand dinner before he goes to his doom, and you begrudge your husband a simple drumstick.'

John Gwilt may have meant to be droll; but it was an unfortunate allusion.

'If you consider you are going to your doom, you have only yourself to thank,' said his wife, a little grimly.

'Don't take me up so seriously!' John hastened to exclaim. 'I don't mean it that way.'

'Well, didn't you say that you might be past solids before the chicken was out of the oven? Could you expect me to spend money on a chicken that you couldn't eat? Money will be scarce enough,' Jane said, a little bitterly.

'All right,' said John Gwilt, chastened.

'I shall soon be taking nourishment through my roots,' he remarked, as he wiped his plate with a crust of bread, and Mrs. Gwilt was more cast down than ever, as if it were a reflection on her faithful years in the kitchen.

'Would you care to pass the time with a game of solitaire?' she asked unhappily. 'Shall I leave the table and bring the cards?'

'No,' was the firm answer.

'Would you like a book?'

'No,' replied John Gwilt. 'I must concentrate on my metamorphosis. Bring me the *Sun* when it comes.'

She left him, and he belched and remembered his lunch and fell to wondering about the nourishment of trees, whether there would be any taste to his food, or whether he would be unconscious of it,

as a man is unconscious of the blood in his veins; whether the rain
on his leaves would be like salt on the tongue, or would sting and
burn, or would strike chill.

He could not go far afield in these speculations, for, as he now
regretted, the diet of trees was a phase of the subject he had not
sufficiently studied. He felt that when the time came he would instinctively do the right thing.

John Gwilt blew his nose, and as he stowed away his handkerchief
in his pocket his fingers encountered a ring of keys and the keys
set him off on a long exploration into possession. The keys prompted
him to think of locks, and the locks, of doors, and from doors he slid
swiftly to windows and walls, floors, ceilings, roofs — houses and
all that was packed into them. He began by attempting a catalogue
of his own few belongings, but one thing reminded him of another
so precipitously that soon his mind was in a turmoil and the whole
confusion of the world — property, impedimenta, appurtenances,
appendages, paraphernalia, goods, chattels, tackle, gear, baggage,
furniture, harness, trappings, trinkets and gew-gaws — tumbled
about his ears as if the world had been blown sky-high and was
raining down upon him in bricks and sticks and stones and plaster,
and splintered steel and shattered glass. He gulped with horror
and, half cringing, stole a look at the sky; then he straightened his
back and fetched a deep breath and was thankful that he had chosen
to set himself free.

I have thrown off the world, he thought, as I used to throw off
my clothes when we played hookey from school and went swimming
in Miller's pond. He remembered with gratitude those young
spring days when he plunged into the chill water, holding his nose,
pretending he was a pearl diver in a limpid South Seas lagoon, and
afterward stood on the sprouting grass, curling his toes, digging
them into the turf, as he was doing now, and pulling his shirt over
a wet, shivering body. Until today, life had never been so fresh and
exciting.

Of course, the savages wear few clothes, he reminded himself,
as he rigged up a picture of John Gwilt out of shoes and socks, underclothes, shirt, trousers, vest, jacket, collar, tie, braces, garters,
laces, knots, buttons, studs, links, handkerchiefs, gloves, hat, overcoat, umbrella, galoshes, pipe, tobacco, matches, watch, chain,
locket, car tickets, library card, spectacles, keys, coins: but the

least complicated tribes deck themselves in beads and feathers and carry spears or bows and arrows, and go in and out of huts, and collect skulls and scalps and calabashes and wives.

There were other John Gwilts, too, he remembered: the John Gwilt of nightshirt; the John Gwilt of Lodge regalia — plumed hat, epaulettes, sash — but that had been a frivolity of his misspent youth.

How busy men are! thought John Gwilt: they are always doing and, to do, they need a multitude of *things* to help them, they need a multitude of things even to keep them alive. Men are workers and players, eaters and drinkers, goers, fighters, gatherers, movers; even when they are doing nothing, they need things to support them. Things! They are forever peering and prying, chopping, chipping, digging, scraping, hammering, shoving, piling, hoisting, tearing down, building up, making wheels go round. Things, things, things! Wheelbarrows and hearses. Howitzers, machine-guns, mousetraps, fly-swatters; crowns and sceptres, mitres and croziers, wigs and walking sticks; dogs on leashes, parrots in cages, goldfish in glass bowls, stuffed crocodiles, cases of coins and birds' eggs and butterflies, and toys from the tombs of Egypt — They used to say that Lawyer Trout's father kept a stuffed horse in his bedroom. It had been his favorite and it had won all those ribbons that were pinned on his office walls. When he came home reeking and reeling, as he often did, he used to climb up on the dead horse's back — he kept it saddled — and imagine he was vaulting hedges — whips and fishing rods, tennis racquets, snowshoes, balls, bats, clubs, sticks, corkscrews, dice, chips and chessmen, typewriters, adding machines, pens and pencils, books and playing cards, newspapers and tombstones.

What a clutter the human race drags around with it, from swaddling clothes to shroud, from cradle to coffin! And when the dead come back, they make tables dance and ring bells and send hats flying and scribble with pencils news about spirits smoking heavenly cigars, or push little wooden things around boards with numbers and letters printed on them. Numbers and letters, syllables and phrases, words and sentences, paragraphs and chapters, talk, talk, talk! letters and postal cards, and magazines and newspapers and books and sermons and speeches, and telephones and telegrams and phonographs and radios and talkies, jabber, jabber, jabber, din, din, din!

My God, thought John Gwilt, what a relief to be a quiet tree after all that uproar!

Almost the whole of human life is wasted on desiring and coveting, envying and hungering and getting, and holding on to the rubbish when it is collected, and fighting for it, killing for it — how insane! How infinitely superior, thought John Gwilt, are the quiet trees, who know nothing of greed, who stand where they are rooted and feed on the earth and air, the sun and the rain, who neither hunt nor kill, sow nor reap, hunger nor envy.

Man is man, thought John Gwilt. Even the greatest world re-nouncers are imprisoned in their strange, fragile spread-eagle shapes, arms and legs, needs and fears and jealousies. Even Gandhi, he thought, has his goat and his spinning wheel and wears spectacles. The most abstract philosopher, though he hide his shivering bones in nothing better than a hole, must have shelter; even if he stretch out naked on a bed of spikes, abhorring the flesh, or mortifying it with rods and scorpions, he must depend on *things*. Mahatma Gandhi, wearing nothing but a clout around his loins, eating a little fruit, and drinking a little milk, sleeping on the earth, comes as close as it is possible for any human being to come to the life of the trees. Yet for all this, and in spite of his ideal of the passive life, Gandhi restlessly jerks from place to place, from crowd to crowd, stirring up turmoil, as active as yeast.

It is impossible, reflected John Gwilt, to be a half-tree: how much better to be a full-spreading, proud, complete tree than an emaciated man without teeth! He felt glad that he was courageous enough to go all the way, and he pitied Gandhi for his compromise with humanity.

IV

Mr. Hoop was discreet. He spread the news across the front page of the *Sun* and illustrated it with an engraving, three columns wide, from the wedding photograph, but he said nothing about the public park or the brass tablet, and instead of yielding to his first impulse and printing the heading:

FOOTWEARY LETTER CARRIER TRANSFORMS
SELF INTO TREE

he compromised:

FOOTWEARY LETTER CARRIER WOULD CHANGE
SELF TO TREE

When the editor walked over to Gander Street to see how it fared with his protégé, he congratulated himself on his foresight. The erstwhile postman might make a laughing-stock of himself, but the *Sun* could not afford to risk ridicule. Yet it could not afford to miss a good story, however it turned out.

He found the poor man in a sorry plight. No sooner had the *Sun* appeared in the street than the whole town of Smeed, with one accord, on foot, on bicycles, on roller skates, in baby carriages, in automobiles, began rushing, as people rush to a conflagration, pell-mell, to the house of John Gwilt. When they discovered they could see nothing from the front and could not go through the house, which the distracted wife lost no time in locking and barricading, they rushed to the end of the street and poured into the lane. They pushed into Fred Staines's yard on the one side and into Bill Dogan's on the other, and some of the bolder spirits forced their way into Mr. Gwilt's own yard, to pester him with questions and pinch him to see if he were real. For a time, he kept his temper admirably, but at last he lost control of himself and began laying about him with his umbrella. This made the crowd laugh the more, and one hoodlum snatched the umbrella out of his hands and began fencing with it, poking John Gwilt in the ribs and dancing back and poking him again and dodging round him. Quaking with terror, Jane watched from the bedroom window, too frantic to think of calling the police. But Fred Staines and Bill Dogan both telephoned. The Chief came in person, big and black and threatening, and the crowd was driven, hooting, away.

'He's taking my umbrella!' cried John Gwilt, and when it was restored to him he stood clinging to it, half sobbing and half whimpering with rage and fright. 'Baboons, apes, jabbering chimpanzees! Thank God, I have enough sense to disown the whole mad tribe of them!' His teeth were chattering, and he was trembling so violently that when Mrs. Gwilt ventured out the Chief ordered her to bring a chair and a drop of brandy.

'Don't you worry,' the Chief said, patting him protectingly on the shoulder as he sank down on the chair. 'I'll send Fink to patrol the place until midnight. Here,' he said sympathetically, taking the tumbler from Jane's hand, 'swallow this.' John gulped and coughed and blinked and felt much better. 'I don't blame a man, wanting to get off his feet,' said the Chief.

'Call themselves the pride of Creation,' John Gwilt muttered. His eyes flashed and he paid no attention to his wife, who was timidly touching his still quivering hand.

'If a man wants to plant himself in his own back yard,' said the Chief to Hoop, in his bluff amiability, 'it's all right with me. So long,' he added heartily, 'as he is alive when he does the planting. We draw the line at corpses in people's back yards. And so long,' he went on impressively, 'as he keeps the peace. I can't, myself, imagine anything more peaceful than a nice tree. Harry Oikle,' he said in an aside to the editor, 'wants to have him committed.' He tapped his head. 'But I say if he's crazy, he certainly isn't at large! Eh?' He raised his voice for the benefit of all and sundry, as if making a proclamation: 'Now if Mr. Gwilt went to work and planted himself downtown, in front of Snooth's hardware, or at the door of the Baptist church, he might be blocking the traffic and disturbing the peace, but when he stays in his own back yard he's within his rights as a taxpayer, and it's the gapers and gawkers who are making a nuisance of themselves. We'll keep them away,' he said, turning to the dejected John Gwilt, 'until you get well settled. I'll have a man here first thing in the morning. Good evening. Evening, Mrs. Gwilt. You can quote me, Hoop, that law and order will prevail.' Promising to send Fink as soon as he had finished his supper, the Chief departed.

The editor examined John Gwilt with more disapproval than sympathy. 'Not a sprout yet,' he said, turning his cigar with his tongue.

John scowled at him, half inclined to hold Hoop responsible for all his misery.

'I think Mr. Gwilt has been too worried and upset,' said Jane.

John Gwilt sat glowering at the ground.

'How long is it going to take?' Hoop demanded.

Gwilt did not answer.

'The cold may be keeping him back, too,' suggested Jane timidly. 'I think he should give it up until the weather gets warmer, don't you, Mr. Hoop?' She began stroking her husband's head affectionately, but he threw off her hand. 'Come into the house and get rid of his cold,' she went on. 'Get a good rest, take a tonic and build himself up for it.'

John Gwilt muttered something under his breath and Hoop said encouragingly: 'A good night's rest will work wonders. Can you sleep standing up?'

John Gwilt admitted sulkily that he did not sleep well in the perpendicular, and the editor suggested a sleeping draught.

'Will you get out of here and leave me alone?'

The editor shrugged. 'O.K.,' he said cheerfully. 'Don't get too downhearted, old man, and we'll have that brass tablet on your chest yet. Gwilt Square will be the pride of Smeed, I'm telling you.'

'Sleeping draughts!' John grumbled when Hoop had gone. 'Is the man mad? What does he want to do, anyway, ruin my sap?'

Jane took special pains with her husband's supper, almost wishing she had got the chicken, but John was too agitated to eat, too feverish with indignation and cold, too weary in every bone and muscle. He was too depressed to notice that Fred Staines and Bill Dogan, annoyed because their young gardens had been trampled, looked over the fence at him in hostility; he sat with his face buried in his hands, and did not even see Fink patrolling up and down and keeping the townspeople moving along the lane. Jane brought out a chair and sat beside him for a while, but she did not stay long, for the evening was damp and chilly and John was unresponsive.

'Good night, John,' she said.

'Good night,' said John, almost bitterly. He looked up and sighed wearily. 'You'd better take the chair.'

'Oh, no, John!' she cried. 'You just sit there and rest. You must be worn out.'

But John Gwilt was obstinate. He rose and said: 'Take it. Do you think that gang of hoodlums can divert me from my purpose? I'm going to put them all to shame.'

Jane shook her head sadly. 'Good night, then,' she sighed. Fink carried the chairs to the kitchen for her and then returned and stood looking at John, as if he expected to catch him suddenly bursting into leaf. While he was on duty, he sauntered into the yard several times, but he was no hand at conversation, and John had nothing to say.

Darkness came as a great relief. John Gwilt was glad when Jane brought him a glass of hot lemonade and some aspirin and tucked the blanket around his shoulders and kissed him and went off, forlorn, to bed; he was glad to hear the Staineses come in from the movies and to see Fred put the car away and turn out the lights;

glad when Fink threw the flashlight ray in his eyes and said he was through for the night. Under cover of darkness, he felt safe; and he was able, at last, to make himself comfortable.

Night gathered quietly and protectingly around John Gwilt. He was too weary to exert his Will, so he listened absently to the *bong, bong, bong, bong* of the Town Hall clock and to the lonely *whoo-whoooo* of the trains, shivered and dozed and dreamed. Cold and hunger and a surge of utter helplessness and loneliness almost drove him into a panic, and several times he was on the verge of uprooting himself and stumbling into the house, defeated.

But resentment against the human race burned in him like a hot coal and kept him steadfast. 'I will turn into the dread Upas Tree,' he told himself savagely. 'I will destroy the whole town of Smeed with my fumes. Not a man, nor a woman, nor a child, nor a cat, nor a mouse, nor a blade of grass shall be left alive. I will shoot up into the air, a great white pillar, and I will fork out my branches like lightning and shake my wicked leaves, and the whole town shall fall down dead. No matter what they are doing, they shall die; let them be walking in the street, or reading the newspapers, or laughing in the movies, or eating ice cream, or digging in their gardens, or taking baths, or saying their prayers; no matter: nothing shall save them. They shall look up suddenly, surprised, and say, "What is that strange smell?" and gasp and shudder and collapse, and that will be the end of them. Smeed will lie dead about my roots, and it will have brought down its own doom upon it.'

John shuddered with mingled exultation and horror at his terrible vision, and then he was heartily ashamed of himself. Much as he had been tried by mankind, John Gwilt was far too tender-hearted to harbor for long such gloatings of revenge. 'It's the man in me,' he murmured. This was the last flare-up of his anger, he was ashamed, and, as he began to simmer down, he steadied himself by naming over in his mind all the trees he had ever seen or read about, and wondering which he would turn out to be.

The common trees he dismissed quickly, for he had a romantic as well as a contemplative disposition — ash, maple, elm, poplar, cottonwood, aspen, willow, sycamore, fir, pine, hemlock, tamarac, oak, basswood, birch, hickory, walnut, chestnut, rowan — beautiful as they might be — and he gave himself up to the luxury of imagining himself first of all an enormous spreading cedar and then a tragic cypress. But he rejected both cypress and cedar, and with them the twisted, sinister yew, and the olive — he did not care for olives and he could not justify himself producing them. Perhaps, he thought — it may have been because of his cold — I shall be a tall eucalyptus, fragrant on rainy nights; or a catalpa, with blowsy white flowers and broad leaves and curious, long beans; or a locust tree bearing the bread that nourished Saint John the Baptist in the wilderness; or an acacia; or a — no, neither oleander nor magnolia: they are too effeminate. I might be a handsome Lombardy poplar, shimmering like sequins in the sun, but I suppose that is effeminate, too, like a fancy-dress ball.

Suddenly, cinnamon, nutmeg, almond, fig, and date palm sprang into his mind all at once, and he smacked his lips as if he could taste his own spice and fruit. But he knew them as tastes and smells, and he was not quite sure of their shapes, so he reluctantly abandoned them and conjured up pictures of more familiar fruit trees.

I suppose I am hard to please, he said to himself, but I am afraid I can see no gratification in being an apple, a pear, a plum, or a cherry tree, or even a peach, or an orange, or a lemon, or a banana. Strictly speaking, the banana is not a tree at all, of course. I wonder if the guava is a tree or a bush? Bush, I think. But the mango is a tree, and so is the pawpaw — *papaia*, they call it in the Hawaiian Islands. Then there is the breadfruit, and the pandanus palm that is propped up with stilts, and the ironwood, and the kauri, and the fern trees, and the teak, the mahogany, the cork, and the rubber ——

My God! groaned John Gwilt, how can I ever make up my mind? I have read too much. I should have said, 'I will be a maple,' and let it go at that. But that would be too easy. It would be more worthy of John Gwilt to turn into something difficult to achieve. Like the pomegranate! How strange and exciting, to see a pomegranate tree in a back yard in Smeed! Or a cocoanut! Imagine a slender cocoanut tree skyrocketing over the rooftops of Gander Street! The town would stare in amazement, people would flock from all parts of the country to gaze up at my green fronds. Yes, he reflected, a little dampened, as he remembered what had happened to him a few hours before: they would flock; and I suppose the boys would play Tarzan of the Apes and shin up after my cocoanuts.

If I had money enough to carry me to Prester John's land, thought John Gwilt, I'd plant myself in his wilderness, a tree of the sun, or a moon tree, and no man dare molest me, for fear of dragons and crocodiles; and milk-white unicorns would sharpen their horns against my trunk, and sky-blue elephants would stand munching in the shade of my broad leaves. He sighed, knowing full well that he must stay in Smeed, and wondered if he might be a little intimidating without being malevolent: a holly tree, perhaps.

But you never know, I might turn out to be something quite strange — I might have no say in the matter at all — like a gingko, or a mandragora. He hesitated. Not too strange, I hope. It's the mandragora — or is it the mangrove? — that stands kneedeep in the stinking swamps, dragging its aerial roots in the mud and slime, half smothered in moss and infested with bats, myriads of furry bats hanging head downward in the branches and suddenly rising in furry clouds, blind and squealing. John Gwilt shuddered. Thank God, there is no such obscene swamp in the whole of Smeed! That's one thing I will say in its favor. He felt no better about the imba-uba of South America and the polygonums, riddled with the nests of wild bees and ants. Somewhere or other, he had read of a prickly, peppery tree called xanthoxylum and the name fascinated him, but he was afraid that no one in Smeed, not even Editor Hoop, would know what to call him. Would Hoop know the ylang-ylang if he saw it? Would he recognize the tall trunk and the showers of greenish-yellow blossoms drenching the neighborhood in fragrance? Ylang-ylang! It sounded like a Chinese gong.

'I'd laugh,' said John Gwilt, stretching out his arms and talking to the sky, 'if I turned into a banyan!' He fancied himself thronging the whole yard with his innumerable branches and trunks, like one of those many-limbed Hindoo gods. 'I might spread and spread,' he reflected, 'and crowd out the house, and crowd out Fred Staines's and Bill Dogan's houses!' He had some idea in his mind of great irresistible roots growing and pushing like a slow earthquake, burrowing in the ground and cracking the foundations of the houses, bringing down the fences; and of branches elbowing and shouldering, shoving the uprooted houses into the street and tossing the garages into the lane. 'They'd have to give me plenty of breathing space if I was a banyan tree!' he told the sky. But he decided that the town would not appreciate such an importunate plant. The Chief of Police might even consider it was disturbing the peace.

The same might be said of the baobab. All his life, John Gwilt had dreamed of going to Abyssinia, for no other reason than to gaze on the mystery and majesty of the baobab. Planted in John Gwilt's back yard, the baobab would spread itself in a massive mountain of wood, over John Gwilt's own lot, over Staines's, over Dogan's, over Smith's, next to Dogan's, and the field next to that again, and over the lot the other side of Staines — old man Moby's; reaching into the street and across it, and into the lane and across it, claiming land on both sides. It would demolish the houses and the fences, the garages and the gardens; cut off the traffic through Gander Street, knock down the poles, and snap the telephone and light wires. It would be worse than the banyan: it would be nothing less than an insurrection.

It would be bigger, John Gwilt thought, than the post office; indeed, it would be as big as the Washington Hotel. 'I have no right,' he murmured in awe, 'even if they did make me a public monument.'

At the same time, he was much too reverent of the tree to wish that he might transform himself into a baobab. Into *a* baobab? He believed that it was The Baobab: that there was only one in the world.

'I wish I could get to sleep,' he said to himself, as he hunched his aching shoulders and relaxed in a heavy sigh. 'Or I wish something would happen.' He moved his toes in the earth, but they seemed to be no longer than usual. He ran his thumbs over the tips of his fingers, but there was no change: they did not feel any more tender. He sighed again, pulled the damp blanket closely about his body, and stared straight ahead into the dark.

'I must get down to business,' he was saying, when a faint sound against the quietness of the night made him hold his breath. He listened intently and threw back his head to look up into the sky. It came again, a faint, far-distant honking, and John Gwilt could just make out the two thin lines — were they there, or did he imagine them? — joined together in a V, passing swiftly, high up against the stars. The wild geese were going north. John Gwilt trembled and the tears welled into his eyes. As he watched them melt into the sky, he almost wished that he had chosen to be a bird.

'Spring has come,' he said aloud, with a good deal of feeling, as if he were reciting a poem. He blinked and wiped his eyes with the back of his hand. 'I must be part of it. I must hurry and make up my mind.'

He breathed deeply, squinted at the stars, and listened, with the hope of discovering another flight of geese. But at that moment there came to his mind an image of the giant sequoia.

'Ah,' sighed John Gwilt, with great satisfaction, as if the matter were already settled, 'of all trees, perhaps I should choose to be the sequoia. Like the baobab, it is ancient, immortal. I should live forever, in splendid tranquillity. Why, there are sequoias flourishing today that were old when Julius Caesar was playing leapfrog, or whatever it was the little Roman boys played.'

It would not matter, he told himself, what happened to Gander Street. They could build factories or railway stations and send the dwellings in retreat farther and farther into the hills, but they would not dare destroy the giant sequoia. They would be proud of John Gwilt, the giant sequoia, and, even as Caleb Hoop predicted, keep a quiet sanctuary about him, and his vast bulk would go towering up and up until it overtopped the town and became a famous landmark. John Gwilt's story would be told from generation to generation and he would outlast the generations: he would be standing stalwart and serene when Smeed, grown from a town into a great city, was lying in ruins at his roots; when the whole world, and the whole race of mankind, was on the wind in dust and ashes.

Perhaps, thought John Gwilt, it would be wise to concentrate on being a sequoia and not just any tree. I might easily turn into some scrubby little maple and be betrayed. A giant sequoia they could not intimidate. Man will respect size, if nothing else.

He remembered the shabby little tree he had discovered only last spring, crowded, stifled by the pickle factory and the soap works, driven into a corner to die. In the midst of smoke and grime and noisome vapors, it was putting forth feeble green leaves, but not in song, leaves that were rather faint mumblings, broken notes, wretched memories of springs and summers long gone by, the mumblings of a tree in its dotage. As John Gwilt stood shaking his head and pitying the poor creature, Miss Estelle Benbow, the town authoress, came by and paused to see what held the postman.

'Ah, the poor little tree!' she cried. 'What a brave show.'

John Gwilt looked at her pink cheeks and the white curls under her wide hat, at her bracelets and rings, and said, rudely: 'Brave show, nothing! It's just a habit.'

Miss Benbow pouted. 'You have no fine feelings, postman.'

'I tell you the tree knows no better,' said John Gwilt. 'It is being pitiable and foolish. I'd rather see it dead.'

He marched off, leaving Miss Benbow gasping. But she wrote some verses about the brave little tree singing its cheery song, and they were printed in the *Sun*.

'People who write verses about trees should be clapped in the penitentiary,' said John Gwilt sourly. 'I hope she doesn't put me into a poem.' He stiffened with indignation. 'I must never allow myself to be dragged into the humiliation that tree suffered.'

John Gwilt began to wonder if he had been foolish to plant himself in his own back yard, foolish to trust even the sanguine schemes of Caleb Hoop. Might it not have been better if he had gone out into the hills where the trees led happier lives, or down to the sea? What a joy it would be to stand beside the ocean, one with the eternity of the water and the wind!

He fell to thinking about the old square down by the railroad track, and half wished he had gone there to keep the man in bloomers company. The man in bloomers was a statue, turned quite green and sadly blotched by Time's discourtesies, but he stood aloft, fixed in a swagger of imperturbability: he was even debonair, in his baggy bloomers and his hip boots, with his wide-brimmed hat flung aslant across his brow, and carrying his sword as if he were cutting his way through the treetops; debonair, though on gray days he smouldered with a livid phosphorescence, like a figure from the Day of Judgment. He was poised on a sort of box above a high swerving arch which was supported by four fluted pilasters, iron, but painted mahogany: from each pilaster, around the basin they straddled, ran a railing like a lead pipe issuing from the jaws of eight small lions' heads. They were all born in the same mould, those lions, all alike in their cast-iron consternation as they fruitlessly spewed the pipe from mouth to mouth. Once a fountain had spurted under the statue's feet, but now the basin was choked with dead leaves. The statue knew nothing of his lions, nor of the inscription on his box; all he knew was that he was pressing toward the towers of the Catholic church, with his sword heroically slash-

ing through the treetops; why, he knew not, unless he thought he
was rushing to save the church from the Indians. That he came
no nearer seemed to disturb him not a whit, no more than he was
disarranged by the collapse of the fashionable terrace on his left
into a cheap and unsavory boarding-house and the coming of the
Chinese laundry and the Negro barber shop to the row on his
right. Perhaps the square had never existed for him, even in its
heyday; perhaps he was lost in his quixotic dreams. Years ago,
the railway stole in behind his back and began a contemptuous
campaign of smoking him out, as the despised ambassador of a
silly, romantic age — swords and hip boots! His indifference was
sublime.

John Gwilt had a great affection for the shabby old square and he
loved the man in bloomers, if for no other reason than that he was
lost; lost, out of place and out of Time, forever advancing, with his
brave, foolish sword, and forever not arriving; so deeply hidden in
his dream of beauty and heroism that he could never know how
absurd he was.

Perhaps I should have gone and planted myself beside him,
thought John Gwilt. It is a public square already and will not
likely be disturbed. I might have got to know him better; he might
have told me his story; yet I am afraid nothing would turn his eyes
away from the quest: he might only want to cut me down. I am
sure, thought John Gwilt, he has never seen the Negro children
playing on the grass, or the old railway veterans sitting stiffly on the
green benches and gossiping about the days of links and pins, when
the men had to run along the tops of freight cars, and when, as they
say, the old girls used to gobble up the wood. He has certainly never
seen the crossing watchman wave his red flag, nor the slanting arms
of the gates go down; and if he has heard the *din din din din* of the
crossing bell, he has never turned his head; he has never known what
it meant; he pays no attention to the trains; he stands with his
back to them; he does not even know he is in Smeed, or where he is,
or in what century.

Yet I may be better off where I am. The square will grow dingier
and dingier, that's sure. It was forlorn enough in winter, he remembered, when the trees were bare and the veterans were indoors dying.
The square was cut into segments by two diagonal paths and the
monument stood in the centre, where they crossed: the forsaken

benches were all but buried in filthy snow, and they seemed to go swirling endlessly around the statue, caught in some turgid vortex.

I should be asleep, but I should dream about it; and I am not sure that I could put up with being so close to the trains, chuffing and rumbling at all hours of the day and night, hoo-hooing and ding-donging, and belching out their black smoke. I'd like an out-look a little more cheerful than those drab red-brick terraces; thinking of their past dignity would only make them seem more dismal. And I don't believe I care for willows. They're all willows in that square, and I might have to follow suit. Of course a tree is a tree, but some I like better than others, and the willow always struck me as insipid: its foliage in spring is like a sort of delicate diarrhoea.

No, the square by the railroad track, man in bloomers or no man in bloomers, would have been a mistake.

Fresh qualms now assailed Mr. Gwilt. Was it too much to expect that a sequoia would flourish in Smeed? He realized now how foolish had been his dreams of shooting up into a lofty cocoanut tree or wriggling and pushing into a banyan. One of Smeed's winters, with its shrill winds and drifting snows, would be enough to annihilate anything as fragile as a green palm. Was the sequoia, for all its size, more robust? It belonged to a warmer climate. And he could not be sure that the soil of Gander Street, or of any street in Smeed, was rich enough to nourish a sequoia. He had a notion that the soil was largely responsible for the tree: he might have been wrong, but he could never shake off the fancy that the copper beech, for example, drew a sinister blood from the earth, as if it were fed by the bodies of murdered men. What was in the soil of John Gwilt's back yard? Could there possibly be the makings of a sequoia?

Poor John Gwilt fell into despair, and tried to haul himself out by saying that he could only try, and by keeping his mind on the memory of a photograph he had seen in the *National Geographic Magazine*, the colored photograph of a sequoia in the Yosemite, superbly dwarfing a group of trail-riders on horseback.

He was worn out, and he succumbed at last to dozing, and at last wandered into an uneasy sleep. Soon he discovered that he was a massive chestnut tree, alight with blossoms, great clusters of blossoms, every one a tingling, burning taper. There he stood on the

hilltop, ablaze for all the world to see, and all the world was packed
in a dense throng, looking at him, thousands and thousands of awe-
struck faces, lit by the blossoms, gazing up at him. Suddenly the
press divided, as if it had been cloven by a stroke of lightning, and a
solemn procession moved through the channel: Mayor Hollyberry
in his frock coat and silk hat, and Editor Hoop with his cigar, and
Postmaster Oikle, carrying a mailbag, John Gwilt's own bag, and
the Chief of Police, and Fink, and Mrs. Gwilt. Jane was all in black,
dressed like a bride, in a long trailing veil, but even the veil was
black. The procession stopped and the Mayor took off his silk hat
and handed it to Mrs. Gwilt, who put her bouquet in it and set it on
the ground and said she was sorry but she must go and get a bowl of
soup. The band, which seemed to be sitting in John Gwilt's
branches, played a mighty flourish, as the circus band does when
the star of the trapeze is turning somersaults. John Gwilt felt the
blast through all his limbs and his blossoms shook violently. Then
Editor Hoop took a large brass plate out of the mailbag and reached
up to hold it against John's broad trunk while the Mayor, his forehead glistening with sweat, began driving in the screws. Every
thrust of the screwdriver pierced John Gwilt with agony. He
groaned and the band echoed his groans; he trembled and the
crowd of people began to tremble. Suddenly everyone burst into
shrieking laughter and John Gwilt discovered, to his horror, that he
was no longer a tree but a little man standing stark naked on the
hilltop, in front of a jeering multitude. He tried to turn but could
not; he tried to run, but his feet were fast in the earth; he pulled and
tugged until blood and sweat poured off him, but he could not
budge; he shivered with cold and shame, though his chest burned;
and the crowd swayed and rocked and jeered.

V

In the morning, Jane found her husband in very low estate. He
rolled his eyes lugubriously at her and croaked, 'Food, for God's
sake!' in a voice so thick and hoarse that she could hardly distinguish the words. After a dish of porridge and great draughts of
scalding coffee he felt a little better, but confessed that he had a
pain in the chest.

Jane was aghast. Her mouth dropped open and she uttered the
dread word 'Pneumonia!'

'John!' she cried, 'I knew you'd get your death! I'll call Doctor Dwindle at once.'

She started toward the house, but John had enough spirit left to summon her back and catch her by the wrist and say, looking threateningly into her eyes, 'You will do nothing of the sort.'

Jane whimpered and implored, but John was adamant. He did give her the satisfaction, however, of agreeing to wear a mustard plaster.

As she laid it against his chest and tied a string around it to keep it from sliding down, John Gwilt thought ironically of the brass tablet. He buttoned his shirt and waistcoat, saying he would soon be past these mortal frailties.

'But, John! There are no signs yet! It isn't going to work! You'll die out here on your feet from sheer pigheadedness. Please, please, for my sake, give it up. Let's go away somewhere for a holiday ——'

'I will not give it up,' said John Gwilt. 'Listen, Jane,' he added, a little more kindly, 'I have to go through with it now. Can't you see how people would laugh? Besides, I've thrown up my job.'

'You could get another. Something that would be easier on your feet.'

'Jane Gwilt, I made up my mind I would be a tree, and a tree I intend to be.'

Jane shook her head dolefully. 'You will die before you get even a single leaf.'

'Wait and see, my dear, wait and see.'

John Gwilt spoke hopefully, but in his heart he was growing discouraged, and when Hoop's young assistant, Jasper Bone, arrived, grinning from ear to ear, he was almost ashamed to meet his gaze. The result of the interview was a facetious story in the *Sun* about the mustard plaster.

Jane tried to keep the paper from him, but John insisted on seeing it and was outraged. 'I'll show them!' he exclaimed, grinding his teeth. 'They'll laugh on the other side of their faces when I stand in dignity before them.'

The nightmare troop of Smeedians, irresistibly drawn by the wretched figure of the little man leaning on his umbrella, was kept at a distance by the police; the sun shone and warmed his aching bones; so, save for his cold, and the gnawing doubt, and his chagrin at the *Sun*, and the visit of the Reverend Doctor Daniel Doody, John Gwilt had a fairly comfortable day.

'I know,' Doctor Doody boomed, like a bell, 'I know' — what a sinful pleasure that man took in his voice! — 'I know you seldom come to church, Mr. Gwilt, but your good wife does, and we still look upon you as a member of the congregation.' He smiled blandly and wagged a fat white finger at the sinner. 'Never a sheep strays, Mr. Gwilt, but we know where he wanders.'

'Very considerate,' said John Gwilt coldly.

'At a time like this,' Doctor Doody boomed, 'we must let by-gones be bygones, grieved as we may have been at your — shall we say? — indifference.' He paused for breath and effect. 'May we not attempt — we cannot let you pursue this — shall we say? — folly, without making some effort to stay its headlong course.'

Jane, standing humbly by, wiped her eyes with her apron.

'My good man,' said Doctor Doody, laying his hand on John's shoulder, 'will you not abandon this — er — madness?'

'It is not madness,' said John Gwilt, puffing up his chest and stiffening his neck, 'and I will not abandon it.'

Doctor Doody shook his large head reproachfully. 'For the sake of your dear wife and family, will you not yield to reason?'

John Gwilt felt the mustard plaster slipping, but he put his hand to his breast and stood firm.

The Reverend Doctor Doody tried another tack. 'Do you think, Mr. Gwilt, that what you are doing is right in the sight of the Lord?' He finished with a smack of the tongue and his features took on an expression of commanding sternness. 'Are you not afraid of the consequences of such obstinacy, of such defiance, of such — must I say it? — of such utter depravity?'

'I am not afraid of your bogeymen!' cried John Gwilt, blinking excitedly. 'You may not know, Doctor Doody, but I have read a good deal. I am a pagan, a pre-Christian. If there is a God, and he has any sense, I am sure he would far rather have one self-respecting tree than a whole menagerie of jabbering chimpanzees.'

Doctor Doody gasped and drew his head back as if he had been struck. He opened his mouth to speak, but John Gwilt gave him no opportunity.

'I suppose you know that trees were made before men? Your Bible will tell you that. Have you never heard of the Tree of Life and the Tree of Death in the Garden of Eden? Have you never heard of Ygdrasil, which towers above the stars?'

'You are compounded of ignorance, Mr. Gwilt, ignorance and impudence,' said Doctor Doody arrogantly, 'or you would know that the tree is an inferior form of life. In spite of all his sins, man is the Lord of Creation ——'

'Yes,' said John Gwilt, holding himself erect, with one hand on his chest and one grasping the umbrella, and looking beyond the Reverend Doctor Doody, 'man can talk platitudes. And he can run about on legs, here, there, and everywhere. For what reason? Ants can do the same, and they have more legs. He has power, I will admit: the power of destruction. He can chop us down and saw us into lumber' — John Gwilt winced — 'and he can invent guns to blow himself to pieces. But you can't tell me that makes him superior. No, Doctor Doody, a tree can never have any respect for a man. I tell you, man is an impudent upstart. Trees were created before men, and trees will flourish when the whole race of man has destroyed itself.'

John Gwilt breathed heavily and his brow was wet; he pressed his hand against his chest and gasped, but his eyes snapped.

'You're quite the orator, Mr. Gwilt,' Doctor Doody said, out of a twisted mouth. As a preacher, he resented being preached at by a layman, and his broad face was scarlet. He turned an outraged back on John Gwilt and faced the weeping Jane. 'Mrs. Gwilt,' he intoned solemnly, holding his wrath in check, 'either your husband is sunk in the depths of depravity or he is a raving lunatic. I hope, for your sake, it is the latter. In either circumstance, there is nothing I can do to turn his steps from this rash course.'

'He may be delirious,' said Jane, in a stifled voice, 'he has such a terrible cold.'

'Reason with him, my dear woman, plead with him; there may yet be time to snatch him from perdition.'

Without another look at the lost soul, he stamped solidly and haughtily out of the yard.

John Gwilt felt that he had won a triumphant victory. 'Jane,' he said, tenderly, 'you mustn't listen to that old windbag. You're a musician. Don't you remember what Beethoven said? Well, Beethoven said he'd rather have a tree than a man, any day, and I think there's more weight in the words of a great genius like Beethoven than in the mouthings of a hundred puffed-up parsons like Doctor Daniel Doody. Cheer up, Jane; you'll be very proud and happy when you're able to come out in the afternoon and sit in the shade of my spreading branches.'

Jane sniffed and said it would be a comfort.

'I'm sure I'd rather have you, my dear, than a blue elephant,' he added thoughtfully.

When John Gwilt was finishing his supper, a sparrow lit on the table and then flew up and perched on his shoulder, winking its tail and cheeping into his ear.

'Why, look who's here!' cried John, hugely delighted. 'Look who's here, Jane! It's a sign! He isn't afraid! He seems quite at home!'

Jane said dolefully that he was probably looking for a place to build a nest.

John picked up a piece of cake and crumbled it in his fingers. 'Come, chuck, chuck!' he wheedled. He was overjoyed when the sparrow jumped into his hand and began pecking at the crumbs. 'Knows me already!' cried John. 'It's a sign, Jane! It's a sign!'

Jane shook her head and sniffed and began piling the dishes on the tray.

'Think of the birds coming to see me! Coming to live with me! I always liked the little fellows. Perhaps we can entice a pair of bluebirds, or an oriole! Jane, you'll have to get rid of Solomon: he'll scare all the birds away.'

It was Jane's turn to take a firm stand. She had set the tray on the ground and was folding up the card table. Three of its legs pointed menacingly at John as she bridled and exclaimed, 'I will do no such thing!' John was a little taken aback at her vehemence. 'Nothing of the kind, you selfish man! I will not sit down and allow you to deprive me of every comfort. Get rid of Solomon! How dare you think of such a thing!'

'All right, my dear,' John Gwilt said soothingly and resignedly; 'as you say. I only thought you might like the odd oriole — something gay and pretty — in the garden. Better than a surly old tomcat. However,' he added, not without malice, 'if the town buys the place and turns it into a park, you'll have to move anyway.'

Jane was alarmed. She had not begun to think of such a contingency. 'What am I going to do?' she protested. 'Where am I going to live if they tear down the house?'

'You'll be better off than you ever were before, my dear. You'll have the money, and, after all, you wouldn't be able to look after this place by yourself.'

'Whatever happens, I keep Solomon,' was Jane's final word, as she marched into the house with the tray.

When she came back to get the table, she found her husband talking to Fred Staines.

'What's the matter with the old Will Power?' Fred Staines asked, with a friendly sneer.

Buoyed up by the visit from the sparrow, John Gwilt replied: 'The Will Power's all right. Takes a little time, that's all.'

'The only change I can see,' said Fred Staines, his elbow on the fence, 'is you've got yourself into a swell cold.' John did not deign to answer. 'And you've made a fine laughing-stock of yourself.'

'Time will tell who's the laughing-stock, Fred Staines, you or me,' said John Gwilt placidly. 'Long after you're lying horizontal in the ground, worn out by a life of senseless chasing after will-o-the-wisps, long after the Odd Fellows have put you away, and long after your granite headstone has tumbled down, I shall be standing upright, holding out my strong branches to the summer showers, or catching the sun on my glittering leaves.'

Naturally, Fred Staines lost his temper.

'You're crazy!' he shouted. 'And furthermore, you're making a public nuisance of yourself, stuck up there like a scarecrow and attracting all the rubbernecks in the country. I'm not going to have them trampling down my garden, let me tell you! I won't stand for it!'

'I'm keeping to my own side of the fence,' said John Gwilt, with dignity. 'You keep to yours. I can't help it if those yahoos come trooping and whooping. I don't want them. I didn't advertise myself as an exhibition.'

Jane could not forbear asking who had spread the news in the first place, telling it to every Tom, Dick, and Harry who came into the barber shop. Whereupon Fred Staines threw up his hands and vanished.

With a fresh mustard plaster burning on his chest and his shoulders drooping under the blanket, with every bone and muscle aching, John Gwilt that night fell into an unquiet sleep. He dreamed that he was standing in the yard, talking to the Reverend Doctor Daniel Doody, when he suddenly heard an explosion like the sound of a gun, followed by a dreadful roar, like the roar of a terrific wind or a terrific fire. Aghast, he turned and saw that his own house was ablaze. The flames were leaping out of the windows and running up the blistering boards, and the roof was crowned with fire and smoke. He shrieked 'Jane!' and started to run. But his feet were rooted in the earth. He tugged and pulled until the sweat poured from him, but the more he pulled the deeper his toes shoved themselves into the ground; they did not seem to belong to him at all; they resisted him, they pulled against him, savagely and with growing strength. Then he realized that he was no longer a man but a tree. Yet he could see the dreadful conflagration, he could hear its roar, and he could feel the heat. His leaves began to shrivel and he strained his boughs in agony. Jane, he thought, is surely dead, burned to a cinder. But at that moment he saw Jane spring out of the flames into the arms of the Reverend Doctor Doody. As they rolled over on the ground, the roof crashed in. John Gwilt sagged with relief. But Jane jumped up, frantically clutching Doctor Doody's coat-tails and screaming: 'John's in there! John's in there! Save him! Save him!' Poor John Gwilt strained and stretched in his anxiety to tell her that he was alive, standing safe in the yard, but he could not utter a word, and he heard the parson tell Jane: 'You have my deepest sympathy, but I am afraid it is as it should be. Your husband merited no better end.'

John Gwilt woke with a violent start, to see his wife standing in front of him with a flashlight in one hand and a steaming glass of lemonade in the other. She wore rubbers on her bare feet and had thrown a raincoat over her nightgown; her hair was in curl papers.

With the glare of the light in his eyes, John was by no means certain, for a moment, whether he was awake or still dreaming, or whether his dream had been a reality.

'Drink this, John, dear,' the apparition was saying. 'It will do you good. How's your poor chest? I had a nightmare and woke up, and I just had to come out and see if you were all right.'

John blinked at Jane, and then turned his head to make sure that the house was still standing.

'Been dreaming, myself,' he admitted. His hand trembled as he took the glass and began sipping the lemonade.

'How do you feel?'

'Just the same.'

'How's the plaster?'

'Must be all right. It burns. This drink is good.' He had been shaken by the dream, and as he handed his wife the empty glass John Gwilt looked at her closely. For a moment he was perilously close to saying: 'I give up, Jane. Help me out of this.' He hesitated, and felt an excitement in the pit of his stomach as a man does when he is faced with an important decision; his heart thumped. He opened his mouth to speak, and shut it again and drew a deep breath.

'Now go back to bed, Jane,' he said at last. 'Too cold out here for you. What time is it, anyway?'

Jane said it was only half-past one and she would like to sit with him a while, she was so lonely; but he told her she needed her rest, and so did he, and she sighed and kissed him and padded off toward the house.

'Of course anything might happen,' said John to himself, as he reflected on his ugly dream. Pushing the blanket aside, he felt in his pocket for pipe and tobacco pouch. Maybe I shouldn't smoke, he thought; perhaps it was an omen that I'm going to fall asleep and set myself on fire. Nevertheless, he went on stuffing his pipe. You have to take these chances, he added, as he struck the match and puffed.

As he smoked, the horror of the dream died away, and with it the memory of the jeering neighbors and the facetious young reporter who made vulgar jokes in the *Sun* about his mustard plaster, and even the irritation of the sanctimonious Doctor Doody. He slipped into a placid revery.

Perhaps I have turned, he thought: I feel so peaceful, and not nearly so tired as I was. But he realized that this could not be, for he was smoking, and he had never heard of a tree that smoked tobacco. Yes, he could feel the pipestem in his teeth and the smoke in his throat; he still had arms, and hands and fingers; he still had a stubbly chin that he could stroke; he could feel the cool air about his naked head; and, now that he came to think of it, he was still conscious of the mustard plaster burning on his chest. He moved his arms, he bent his knees, he twisted his neck. 'Ah, well,' he sighed as he blew out a little cloud of smoke, 'it takes time, takes time.'

No doubt he should have been exerting his Will, but he was content to smoke and muse. 'Funny little fellow,' he murmured, thinking genially of the sparrow. 'I wonder if I shall be able to understand their language. She wouldn't put Solomon out of the road. Poor Jane, she has to have some pleasure, and she *is* fond of that old cat. I wonder why I never thought of suggesting that she metamorphosize with me. Hasn't enough W.P. I could have willed for the two of us, I suppose. We could have been like that old Greek couple, Philemon and Baucis. But she'd never do it, never in this wide world.'

He imagined himself towering high above the rooftops, high above the telephone wires, his glorious green crown dominating Gander Street. Jane would be hard put to it to believe that this leafy magnificence was her husband; she would be awed, a little afraid, prouder of John than she had been at any time since the day she had met him at the picnic many years ago, and he had impressed her with his wisdom and his vocabulary.

Now and again, on a drowsy summer afternoon, he would hear a child's *dee-deedle-dum-dum* coming through the parlor window, and he would hear the tap of Jane's pencil on the piano keys. He would watch his wife affectionately. He would preside over her goings and comings: see her lock the front door behind her as she went to church on Sunday mornings; see her, on weekdays, emerge with her market basket; see her going off for a ride in Fred Staines's motor car; try to catch what she was saying to Mrs. Staines over the fence. He would bear her no grudge if she tied the clothesline around his trunk, and he would love to see her hanging out the wash, with clothespins in her mouth. He wondered whether the fluttering garments would stir any feelings within him. 'You goose!' he would exclaim, when he saw her running out to save the clothes from a sudden shower: 'I could have told you it would rain! You people have no weather sense at all!' But she would not hear him. It would make him happy to see her crouching over the garden plot and prodding the earth with the trowel, sifting in the seed and then shoving stakes through the colored envelopes and sticking them in the ground so that she could distinguish carrots from cucumbers and nasturtiums from sweet peas. How lovingly he would watch the straggling rows of green shoots! — though he would be irritated with Jane for not planting under a taut string.

I shall see her grow old, he thought complacently, though affectionately: poor Jane! and one day I shall see them carry her down the front steps in her coffin; and Doctor Doody will pray lugubrious prayers and say mournful things about her. Thank God! there is no coffin for me and I shall have no funeral. Perhaps, he reflected a little sadly, I shall never know what happens to her. When they tear down the house and lay out the sanctuary ... I wonder if she will ever come to see me? I think I would rather just go on living with Jane, just the two of us. ...

He switched his thoughts abruptly back to Solomon. 'I hope he doesn't make a pest of himself,' he said. 'I'd love to have a few birds. Nice ones, like orioles, or those little nuthatch fellows that creep up and down. My God! I hope the woodpeckers don't find me out! Much as I admire them. ...' He nearly broke into a cold sweat at the thought. 'However, perhaps when you're wood, you don't mind so much. But I'll have to speak to Jane about starlings; something will have to be done about the starlings: I can't stand their filthy habits.'

He knocked his pipe out against his knee and put it back in his pocket. Yawning and stretching, he caught sight of the stars over the rooftops and stood for a long time gazing at them. 'I'm going to see a lot of the stars from now on,' he said, and he wished he had paid more attention to the sky maps Hoop's paper printed once a month.

All I know is the Big Dipper, he realized, with profound regret. I'm not even sure about the little one. Which is Orion, and where is Hercules with his club? I can't even tell Mars from Venus! Mars is red, of course. Well, no use regretting it now. I'll have to find out the shapes of the constellations for myself and think up my own stories and my own names for them. Why not? Why should the Greeks name everything, anyway? I'll have plenty of time, night after night.

The stars are better than music, he thought, for you can stare at them hour on hour, and they remain; while sound, rise it ever so piercingly, before you have grasped its pattern, is quickly hushed into a tremor, into silence, into nothing. Music shocks, seizes you and shakes you, and drops you, bewildered and disappointed, but the stars, the stars remain.

He sighed. But have trees eyes? Of course. Maybe they are all eyes, and every leaf is an eye as well as a tongue. He grinned at the fancy. We *must* see! Perhaps we see better than men. What a time I'm going to have, with the moon, and eclipses, and meteors!

I shall become familiar with the phases of the moon, thought John Gwilt, and study the changes of the Equinox. I shall grow weatherwise: the trees, like the birds, must be able to foresee the coming of winter.

I think I shall always love spring best, he mused. We are at our happiest then, after the long, frozen, naked winter, and before the full-blown summer. How miraculous we are! Whether it be a broken maple, half-strangled between a fence and a brick wall, or a magnificent colonnade of Lombardy poplars shielding a convent from the street, it is impossible, in the spring, to believe that the city can put forth trees: the city is so sterile in steel and stone and cement and hard-baked brick, and the trees are so frail: they touch the heart, they are so frail, sprouting up through the cracks in the brutal stones, and the light shines through them.

He fell to thinking of their shapes and colors: a haze of green, a splash of green, a spatter of red and gold against the wash of clouds, gray clouds, thinning away to white, dissolving into the luminous blue sky. The maples are pink and gold, he thought, and the elms are intricate webbings of twigs showing through a thin veil of green; the chestnuts unclench fat fists on thick black arms; out of the twisted thorns, the leaves burst in agony; and the birch trails her tatters, and the balm of Gilead, dripping with catkins and leaves like green glass, is a glittering chandelier....

John Gwilt began to nod, his head fell forward on his breast, and he dozed off, standing patiently in the midst of the sleeping town, alone under the far-flung stars.

VI

In the morning, he greeted Jane with a complacent smile, indeed a knowing smile, and said 'Good morning, my dear!' with such gaiety that it was a wonder she did not become suspicious at once.

But Jane was not good at reading smiles, and she could not forbear murmuring, a trifle disparagingly, 'Three nights and not a twig.'

'You seem disappointed, my dear.'

'Oh, John!' she cried remorsefully, 'how can you say such a thing! I never wanted you to do this.

'Then why say "Three nights and not a twig" in such a disgusted tone, my dear?'

'I just meant,' said Jane, 'that it should be enough to convince you that — it isn't going to work.'

'Yes,' John said cheerfully, 'you are beginning to lose faith in me; like all the others. You're tired of waiting on me, bringing me my breakfast, and laying on the mustard plaster. Well, my dear, I don't blame you. It does get to be trying, especially with all the neighbors sneering and jeering.'

'I don't begrudge you anything I do for you, John; you know that. I never did.'

'Well, Jane, your troubles are over.'

Jane's mouth and eyes popped open; she stepped back as if he had struck her. 'You don't mean — you've — sprouted?'

'The metamorphosis has begun,' said John Gwilt, with enormous satisfaction.

Perhaps Jane thought he looked too preposterous, standing there wrapped up in his blanket, with three days' growth of beard and a nose red with cold, and his bald head so damp and pink, and that bland, idiotic smile on his face. Perhaps she simply did not wish to believe. She stared at him incredulously and began to reproach herself for not calling Doctor Dwindle earlier.

'It began with the feet,' said John Gwilt happily. 'I have no feet now, Jane. Roots. And what roots! They stretch out and out, deep and deep, far down into the dark earth. Oh, what a satisfaction there is in strong, deep roots! I feel so tremendously solid and secure! I feel immortal! Nothing can shake me, no wind can throw me down!'

Jane burst into tears, and her husband drew her toward him and put his arms around her and comforted her.

'My legs have grown together,' he said. 'I am a tree to the waist. Look, my trousers have burst.'

He drew the blanket aside and revealed his trunk. 'Not as big around as it will be, of course, but feel it: isn't that satisfying?' he slapped the thigh that was now wood, covered with bark, and enjoyed the hardness of it.

Jane snuffled.

'I've lost my fatigue,' he crowed. 'I'll never walk again.'

Jane sniffed.

'You'd better take these clothes to the house,' said John Gwilt. 'It won't be long now. There's no use splitting them all.'

He took the blanket off, neatly folded it, and handed it to his wife. Jacket and waistcoat followed; then he undid the buttons and slipped off his shirt. He piled all the garments and the cold mustard plaster into Jane's arms and bade her take them away, together with the broken trousers.

'What good are they to me?' she asked mournfully.

'Well,' said John, 'give them to Shuffling Sam, if you like. I'm through with them.'

She stood looking at him so pensively that he grinned and chucked her under the chin. 'Cheer up, Jane,' he said. 'No more socks to darn. No more buttons to sew on.'

'That's one consolation,' she sighed, trying to be bright. 'I hope,' she said, with sudden misgiving, 'you won't expect me to keep your leaves sewed on?'

'When they come off, they come off,' he assured her affably.

On her return, she asked him if he would like some breakfast.

'I think not, my dear. I am still half a man, but I have no stomach.' He observed that he was suffering a little discomfort, just a slight uneasiness, as if his system were not quite used to the arboreal diet he was now drawing through his roots. 'And I feel a little light-headed,' he added blithely.

So John Gwilt stood, in his back yard, the naked torso of a man down to his waist, and, below that, the solid trunk of a tree well rooted in the ground, and Jane Gwilt stood looking at him disconsolately.

'I think I am branching!' said John Gwilt, with a smirk. 'Don't my original arms look longer to you, Jane?' he inquired, with an edge of pride on his voice. 'And look! I am in bud!'

As he spoke, the tips of his fingers burst into little green leaves.

'Oh, dear! It's true, then!' cried Jane. 'And now I am a Hindoo, married to a tree!'

She did not know what was required under the circumstances, so after fluttering about her husband, half hysterical, for a moment, she fled into the house to consult the Bible.

John was examining his young shoots with curiosity and affection, trying to decide what sort of tree he was, when Mr. Hoop arrived.

'Gosh all fishhooks!' he roared, dropping the cigar out of his mouth in amazement. He shoved his hat to the back of his head as he rubbed his brow and stared at John Gwilt with popping eyes.

He recovered quickly and gulped, 'Got a 'phone in the house?'

John smiled and nodded, and the editor ran across the yard and pushed into Jane's kitchen without knocking.

It was not long before the photographer arrived and John Gwilt was smiling for the camera, extending his leafy fingers on his chest, shaking hands with Mr. Hoop ('Don't bruise my leaves!' he cautioned. 'They are very young and tender'), standing in an affectionate pose with red-eyed Jane, and with his arms spread out like branches.

All rancor against the human race had melted away from John Gwilt's heart, and he looked upon the world, and the town of Smeed, with the benignity that a tree might be expected to bestow upon an inferior form of life. When the *Sun* appeared, emblazoning his strange history on the front page, with headlines, and with photographs of all the poses, the crowds that came to stare at him were so great that the fence was broken down, and Chief Pettibone and Sergeant Fink were called upon to organize the people of Smeed into queues and keep them moving in a loop from the lane through the yard and out on the other side. Yesterday the steady tramp, tramp, tramp of his neighbors filing past and gaping at him, the gawking and sniggering of some and the superstitious open-mouthed awe of others, would have driven him frantic, but today, half tree, he smiled and nodded, and even uttered a few words to show that he was alive and, indeed, enjoyed the reception. I have never had so much attention paid me in all my life, he thought happily.

At first he was a little nervous about his young leaves, and while he did not mind holding up his fingers, he steadfastly refused to shake hands. He did not like people pinching the human part of him, but he found that a kick did not hurt his trunk. On the whole, he escaped very well; the police were efficient, and Jane, standing on one side of him, and Hoop on the other, kept the more boisterous of the jostling line within bounds.

'I will shake hands with *you*, Fred,' said John Gwilt to his friend

the barber. 'We have always been good neighbors, even if you did
think me a little queer ——'

'Oh, no!' Fred Staines protested.

'Careful, Fred. Don't bruise my leaves.'

'Good-bye,' said Fred, a little embarrassed. 'Good luck, John.'

'Will you do something for me?' John Gwilt asked benignly.
'Promise me that when the weather is dry and you're out watering
your garden, Fred, you'll turn the hose on me?'

'I couldn't do less for a friend,' Fred Staines promised.

As the crowd passed, Mr. Hoop was busy estimating its numbers
and dismally regretting that so much public interest was going to
waste. If he stays as he is, thought Editor Hoop, I'll make myself
his manager, put a tent over him, and charge admission.

*Half man and half tree! Have you seen him? Have you seen him?
He's alive, alive, alive! Come on ovah! Come on ovah! Instructive!
And entertaining! The chance of a lifetime here! Come on ovah! See
the tree man! Half man and half tree here! The most stupendous! the
most colossal, the most amazing miracle ever beheld by the eyes of man!
Have you seen him? Have you seen him?*

I'll put a tent over him and have some banners painted, advertise
him far and wide, all over the country, and *what a clean-up Caleb
Hoop will make!*

But nothing came of his scheme; for next morning, when Jane
Gwilt looked out of the bedroom window, she was confronted by a
fully grown sycamore, upright, symmetrical, beautifully branching,
many times taller, many times more handsome than the little postman she had married and lived with so long. She ran down to the
yard in her nightgown and threw her arms around his trunk and
kissed his rough bark and wept, the while he stirred his branches
and shook his young green leaves as if they were so many little bells.

BLIND MAN'S BUFF

By LIBBY BENEDICT

(From *Time and Tide*)

IT'S easier to tell the story now, because so many years have passed. It's a story that really happened to me, or at least to the person that has become me. Usually when a writer tells a story in the first person, he or she fakes at being a dockhand or a waitress instead of himself or herself. But this story is really mine, so completely mine that I shouldn't know how to begin translating it into another person's life.

I was very much in love with the young man who formed the other corner of the odd triangle, and he was very much in love with me. I was twenty-four, he still below thirty. And although we were both representative of that very iconoclastic and supposedly free class that was so extant a little less than a decade ago, the emotion that grew rapidly between us drew us just as rapidly into thoughts of marriage and permanence.

We were really very well mated, the person that he was then and the person that I was then, and we got along very well together. He was a sensitive individual, extremely keen and able, rather completely self-taught, and in a position of such responsibility that he thought it wise to give his age as more than it was.

He was ambitious, but somehow disposed to doubt his capacities. Even in conversation he was inclined to swing to a joke before any pinnacle, side-tracking the development of his own thoughts. In all things he provided preliminary protection for himself, rather than face the possibility of injury. He surrounded himself with numerous friends, among whom he had a reputation for great goodness of heart and generosity. He lent money, and he did not do it for the sake of having someone grateful to him, but only for his own sake. Among women he had the reputation of being somewhat of a Don Juan, because he liked making appointments at the last minute and always knew a sufficient number of girls to find one who was not busy.

My own inadequacies of that period do not really need to be dwelt on. There were many. I had a turbulent, turgid emotional capacity, complicated by a senseless sense of rigidity. I wanted everything or nothing. I was very deficient in granting the right of another person to exist as he was. I wanted always to drag him over to some centre line I thought superior.

However, neither his deficiencies nor mine were to blame for the unfortunate ending of our love affair. Perhaps he came closer to being responsible because the blind man was his friend, but that is hardly a point from which to hurl condemnation.

The blind man had become blind at the age of seven. He had been playing with some other children near the piers of the city in which they lived, a port town where much oyster fishing was done. Some child threw an oyster shell which pierced his eye. He lost the other as the result of the infection that set in in the optic nerve.

What he had done with his life was magnificent. He had not only finished his regular schooling, he had also graduated from a high grade conservatory of music, and was an excellent piano teacher and musician. My admiration for him, and for the extreme naturalness and normality of his existence, is today as unbounded as it was then.

His whole existence was very normal, even to his manner of speech. When he referred to any part of the vast field of literature with which he was familiar, he always said, 'I read.' Actually he used Braille very little; everything was read to him. He had picked up, from hearsay, some knowledge of the characteristics of certain famous painters, and could discuss them with startling intimacy. When talking to his friends, he frequently said, 'You're looking well today,' or 'You look pale,' and was invariably right. I once heard him even say that he preferred to see a girl's leg in a black silk stocking rather than in a light hose. There must have been some element of self-deception or compensation in all this, but so normal was his own bearing that one actually did not think of it.

His friendship with the man I knew was of long standing. For several years my friend had worked night shift on a newspaper, and after hours he would go to the blind man's home and read to him. It was characteristic of him.

With all the normality the blind man had, it would still have been too much to expect that an acute sense of possessiveness and jealousy should not have arisen in him in regard to this faithful friend.

Particularly now, when the man I knew had left the other city and come to New York. They could be together now only several times a year, and the most important of these times were the visits the blind man made to New York.

It was, therefore, some time before I met the blind man, because his semiannual visit to New York did not occur until long after I had met the other. Whether he had heard of me before he came I don't know. But he had certainly heard of me before we met at lunch.

At once a rebellion started in me for the obvious preference the two had for each other. Yet it was less the affection my friend showed the blind man that annoyed me than it was the possessiveness the blind man showed over him. I did not really mind being left at the table while he was taken over for a moment to meet a well-known artist who was sitting a few tables away. But I did object to the blind man's unending use of 'we,' particularly when a negative development followed, 'We're going to be very busy this week, I'm afraid. I'm not sure that we'll be able to see you again.'

I shall never know how much aware my friend was of what was happening at that lunch. Cataclysmic events never let their full import be seen immediately; the moments at which they actually happen are only peep-holes through which the torrent is distantly glimpsed. The deluge comes afterward.

I don't know, either, whether the blind man knew all that was happening, or even whether he knew all that he wanted to happen. Certainly in my presence he sensed a danger he had not sensed with any of the other girls his friend knew. It was not a danger in which my volition played a part, but a danger created by my very existence. Perhaps the man's preoccupation with me was obviously greater than it had been with anybody else. Perhaps he had confessed it to the other. And at the possibility of having to share his friend, or to lose him, all the agony of his blindness, so successfully hidden in his manner of speech and general mode of life, began to come out.

I, too, was aware of its agony. From the very first moment of his intrusion, I knew I could not strike back. For he was blind.

Yet even that day there were moments of naturalness and happiness when I forgot his handicap. I certainly did not think of it when we talked about music. I forgot it so completely that once, when he asked for an ash tray, I simply held it out to him and waited for him to take it, quite as if he could see.

But when he said, 'We can't see you tomorrow night. We have an appointment,' I grew glum and bitter.

Yet I could not direct my bitterness against him. I began to direct it against the other. I had, as I have already said, a great turgidity of emotion. I could be violently nasty in infinitesimal ways, and I was. It was to the seeing man that I sent a furious 'I don't know when you'll see me again. I'm going to be terribly busy myself.'

It was hardly the way to treat love. Yet even today I am convinced that saner behavior would have made no difference. The direction was set, and nobody could turn back.

How we tried! Every day for a week he telephoned me, and every day, struggling on my side to retain a hold on what we had, I let him postpone the appointment. It had to be that way. He always had to make it contingent on the blind man's plans, and always the blind man managed to arrange something else. Several times I had to 'phone the apartment, and always the blind man said: 'Sorry we can't see you tonight. We have another appointment.'

Yet finally an arrangement was made. And for a whole day beforehand I told myself the past week had been only imagination. Now the three of us would clasp hands and remain friends forever. We would have dinner together, we would sit for hours talking. There would be plenty of time to establish the understanding we all needed.

I was to call first at my friend's apartment, where the blind man would be waiting for me, and we would both wait for the other.

While we waited everything was really congenial and my hopes were high.

Then the other man came in. The first words the blind man said to him were:

'I've made an appointment for nine o'clock. So-and-so is going to Europe tomorrow and there's a farewell party at ——'s.'

'Whom did you make the appointment for?'

'You and me. It's an intimate group, and they don't want strangers.'

There would really be no purpose in describing the dinner or the silences. I don't remember where we ate or what we ate. I remember only the parting, on a corner when I was to enter the subway to go home. And even of that parting there is nothing that I remember. All I know is that if I were to pass that corner today I should still see the three of us standing there.

We left ourselves there and went on, became other people, got married. I am sure we are both happier as we are. But we were not as we are the night we said good-bye on that corner. And those people, as I said, are still standing there.

A TOOTH FOR PAUL REVERE [1]

By STEPHEN VINCENT BENÉT

(From *The Atlantic Monthly*)

SOME say it all happened because of Hancock and Adams (said the old man, pulling at his pipe), and some put it back to the Stamp Act and before. Then there's some hold out for Paul Revere and his little silver box. But the way I heard it, it broke loose because of Lige Butterwick and his tooth.

What's that? Why, the American Revolution, of course. What else would I be talking about? Well, your story about the land down South that they had to plow with alligators reminded me.

No, this is a true story — or at least that's how I heard it told. My great-aunt was a Butterwick, and I heard it from her. And every now and then she'd write it out and want to get it put in the history books. But they'd always put her off with some trifling sort of excuse. Till finally she got her dander up and wrote direct to the President of the United States. Well, no, he didn't answer himself exactly — the President's apt to be a pretty busy man. But the letter said he'd received her interesting communication and thanked her for it, so that shows you. We've got it framed, in the trailer — the ink's a little faded, but you can make out the man's name who signed it. It's either Bowers or Thorpe, and he wrote a very nice hand.

You see, my great-aunt, she wasn't very respectful to the kind of history that does get into the books. What she liked was the queer corners of it and the tales that get handed down in families. Take Paul Revere, for instance — all most folks think about, with him, is his riding a horse. But when she talked about Paul Revere — why, you could just see him in his shop, brewing the American Revolution in a silver teapot and waiting for it to settle. Oh, yes, he was a silversmith by trade — but she claimed he was something more. She claimed there was a kind of magic in that quick, skillful hand of his — and that he was one of the kind of folks that can see just a little bit farther into a millstone than most. But it was when she got to Lige Butterwick that she really turned herself loose.

For she claimed that it took all sorts to make a country — and that meant the dumb ones, too. I don't mean ijits or nincompoops — just the ordinary folks that live along from day to day. And that day may be a notable day in history — but it's just Tuesday to them till they read all about it in the papers. Oh, the heroes and the great men — they can plan and contrive and see ahead, but it isn't till the Lige Butterwicks get stirred up that things really start to happen. Or so she claimed. And the way that they do get stirred up is often curious, as she'd tell this story to prove.

For, now you take Lige Butterwick — and before his tooth started aching he was just like you and me. He lived on a farm about eight miles from Lexington, Massachusetts, and he was a peaceable man. It was troubled times in the American colonies, what with British warships in Boston Harbor and British soldiers in Boston and Sons of Liberty hooting the British soldiers — not to speak of Boston tea parties and such. But Lige Butterwick, he worked his farm and didn't pay much attention. There's lots of people like that, even in troubled times.

When he went into town, to be sure, there was high talk at the tavern. But he bought his goods and came home again — he had ideas about politics, but he didn't talk about them much. He had a good farm and it kept him busy — he had a wife and five children and they kept him humping. The young folks could argue about King George and Sam Adams — he wondered how the corn was going to stand that year. Now and then, if somebody said that this and that was a burning shame, he'd allow as how it might be, just to be neighborly. But, inside, he was wondering whether next year he mightn't make an experiment and plant the west field in rye.

Well, everything went along for him the way that it does for most folks with good years and bad years, till one April morning, in 1775, he woke up with a toothache. Being the kind of man he was, he didn't pay much attention to it at first. But he mentioned it that evening at supper, and his wife got a bag of hot salt for him. He held it to his face and it seemed to ease him, but he couldn't hold it there all night, and next morning the tooth hurt worse than ever.

Well, he stood it the next day and the next, but it didn't improve any. He tried tansy tea and other remedies — he tried tying a string to it and having his wife slam the door, but when it came to the pinch he couldn't quite do it. So finally he took the horse and rode into Lexington town to have it seen to. Mrs. Butterwick made him — she said it might be an expense, but anything was better than having him act as if he wanted to kick the cat across the room every time she put her feet down hard.

When he got into Lexington, he noticed that folks there seemed kind of excited. There was a lot of talk about muskets and powder and a couple of men called Hancock and Adams who were staying at Parson Clarke's. But Lige Butterwick had his own business to attend to — and, besides, his tooth was jumping so he wasn't in any mood for conversation. He set off for the local barber's, as being the likeliest man he knew to pull a tooth.

The barber took one look at it and shook his head.

'I can pull her, Lige,' he said. 'Oh, I can pull her, all right. But she's got long roots and strong roots, and she's going to leave an awful gap when she's gone. Now, what you really need,' he said, kind of excited, for he was one of those perky little men who's always interested in the latest notion, 'what you really need — though it's taking away my business — is one of these-here artificial teeth to go in the hole.'

'Artificial teeth!' said Lige. 'It's flying in the face of Nature!'

The barber shook his head. 'No, Lige,' he said. 'That's where you're wrong. Artificial teeth is all the go these days, and Lexington ought to keep up with the times. It would do me good to see you with an artificial tooth — it would so.'

'Well, it might do *you* good,' said Lige, rather crossly, for his tooth was jumping; 'but supposing I did want one — how in tunket will I get one in Lexington?'

'Now you just leave that to me,' said the barber, all excited, and he started to rummage around. 'You'll have to go to Boston for it, but I know just the man.' He was one of those men who can always tell you where to go and it's usually wrong. 'See here,' he went on. 'There's a fellow called Revere in Boston that fixes them and they say he's a boss workman. Just take a look at this prospectus' — and he started to read from a paper: '"Whereas many persons are so unfortunate as to lose their fore-teeth" — that's you, Lige — "to their great detriment, not only in looks but in speaking, both in public and private, this is to inform all such that they may have them replaced by artificial ones" — see? — "that look as well as the natural and answer the end of speaking to all intents" — and then he's got his name — Paul Revere, goldsmith, near the head of Doctor Clarke's wharf, Boston.'

'Sounds well enough,' said Lige, 'but what's it going to cost?'

'Oh, I know Revere,' said the barber, swelling up like a robin. 'Comes through here pretty often, as a matter of fact. And he's a decent fellow, if he is a pretty big bug in the Sons of Liberty. You just mention my name.'

'Well, it's something I hadn't thought of,' said Lige, as his tooth gave another red-hot jounce, 'but in for a penny, in for a pound. I've missed a day's work already, and that tooth's got to come out before I go stark, staring mad. But what sort of man is this Revere, anyway?'

'Oh, he's a regular wizard!' said the barber. 'A regular wizard with his tools.'

'Wizard!' said Lige. 'Well, I don't know about wizards. But if he can fix my tooth I'll call him one.'

'You'll never regret it,' said the barber — and that's the way folks always talk when they're sending someone else to the dentist. So Lige Butterwick got on his horse again and started out for Boston. A couple of people shouted at him as he rode down the street, but he didn't pay any attention. And going by Parson Clarke's he caught a glimpse of two men talking in the Parson's front room. One was a tallish, handsomish man in pretty fine clothes and the other was shorter and untidy, with a kind of bulldog face. But they were strangers to him and he didn't really notice them — just rode ahead.

II

But as soon as he got into Boston he started to feel queer — and it wasn't only his tooth. He hadn't been there in four years and he'd expected to find it changed, but it wasn't that. It was a clear enough day, and yet he kept feeling there was thunder in the air. There'd be knots of people talking and arguing on street corners, and then, when you got closer to them, they'd kind of melt away. Or if they stayed, they'd look at you out of the corners of their eyes. And there in the Port of Boston were the British warships, black and grim. He'd known they'd be there, of course, but it was different seeing them. It made him feel queer to see their guns pointed at the town. He'd known there was trouble and dispute in Boston, but the knowledge had passed over him like rain and hail. But now here he was in the middle of it — and it smelt like earthquake weather. He couldn't make head or tail of it, but he wanted to be home.

All the same, he'd come to get his tooth fixed, and being New England he was bound to do it. But first he stopped at a tavern for a bite and a sup, for it was long past his dinnertime. And there, it seemed to him, things got even more curious.

'Nice weather we're having these days,' he said in a friendly way to the barkeep.

'It's bitter weather for Boston,' said the barkeep in an unfriendly voice, and a sort of low growl went up from the boys at the back of the room and every eye fixed on Lige.

Well, that didn't help the toothache any, but being a sociable person, Lige kept on.

'May be for Boston,' he said, 'but out in the country we'd call it good planting weather.'

The barkeep stared at him hard.

'I guess I was mistaken in you,' he said. 'It *is* good planting weather — for some kinds of trees.'

'And what kind of trees were you thinking of?' said a sharp-faced man at Lige's left, and squeezed his shoulder.

'There's trees and trees, you know,' said a red-faced man at Lige's right, and gave him a dig in the ribs.

'Well, now that you ask me ——' said Lige, but he couldn't even finish before the red-faced man dug him hard in the ribs again.

'The liberty tree!' said the red-faced man. 'And may it soon be watered in the blood of tyrants!'

'The royal oak of England!' said the sharp-faced man. 'And God save King George and loyalty!'

Well, with that it seemed to Lige Butterwick as if the whole tavern kind of riz up at him. He was kicked and pummeled and mauled and thrown into a corner and yanked out of it again, with the red-faced man and the sharp-faced man and all the rest of them dancing quadrilles over his prostrate form. Till finally he found himself out in the street with half his coat gone galley-west.

'Well,' said Lige to himself, 'I always heard city folks were crazy.'

But politics must be getting serious in these American colonies when they start fighting about trees!'

Then he saw the sharp-faced man was beside him, trying to shake his hand. He noticed with some pleasure that the sharp-faced man had the beginnings of a beautiful black eye.

'Nobly done, friend,' said the sharp-faced man, 'and I'm glad to find another true-hearted loyalist in this pestilent, rebellious city.'

'Well, I don't know as I quite agree with you about that,' said Lige. 'But I came here to get my tooth fixed, not to talk politics. And as long as you've spoken so pleasant, I wonder if you could help me out. You see, I'm from Lexington way — and I'm looking for a fellow named Paul Revere ——'

'Paul Revere!' said the sharp-faced man, as if the name hit him like a bullet. Then he began to smile again — not a pleasant smile.

'Oh, it's Paul Revere you want, my worthy and ingenuous friend from the country,' he said. 'Well, I'll tell you how to find him. You go up to the first British soldier you see and ask the way. But you better give the password first.'

'Password?' said Lige Butterwick, scratching his ear.

'Yes,' said the sharp-faced man, and his smile got wider. 'You say to that British soldier, 'Any lobsters for sale today?' Then you ask about Revere.'

'But why do I talk about lobsters first?' said Lige Butterwick, kind of stubborn.

'Well, you see,' said the sharp-faced man, 'the British soldiers wear red coats. So they like being asked about lobsters. Try it and see.' And he went away, with his shoulders shaking.

Well, that seemed queer to Lige Butterwick, but no queerer than the other things that had happened that day. All the same, he didn't quite trust the sharp-faced man, so he took care not to come too close to the British patrol when he asked them about the lobsters. And it was lucky he did, for no sooner were the words out of his mouth than the British soldiers took after him and chased him clear down to the wharves before he could get away. At that, he only managed it by hiding in an empty tar-barrel, and when he got out he was certainly a sight for sore eyes.

'Well, I guess that couldn't have been the right password,' he said to himself, kind of grimly, as he tried to rub off some of the tar. 'All the same, I don't think soldiers ought to act like that when you ask them a civil question. But city folks or soldiers, they can't make a fool out of me. I came here to get my tooth fixed and get it fixed I will, if I have to surprise the whole British Empire to do it.'

And just then he saw a sign on a shop at the end of the wharf. And, according to my great-aunt, this was what was on the sign. It said 'PAUL REVERE, SILVERSMITH' at the top, and then, under it, in smaller letters: 'Large and small bells cast to order, engraving and printing done in job lots, artificial teeth sculptured and copper boilers mended, all branches of goldsmith and silversmith work and revolutions put up to take out. Express Service, Tuesdays and Fridays, to Lexington, Concord and Points West.'

'Well,' said Lige Butterwick, 'kind of a jack-of-all-trades. Now maybe I can get my tooth fixed.' And he marched up to the door.

III

Paul Revere was behind the counter when Lige came in, turning a silver bowl over and over in his hands. A man of forty-odd he was, with a quick, keen face and snapping eyes. He was wearing Boston clothes, but there was a French look about him — for his father was Apollos Rivoire from the island of Guernsey, and good French Huguenot stock. They'd changed the name to Revere when they crossed the water.

It wasn't such a big shop, but it had silver pieces in it that people have paid thousands for since. And the silver pieces weren't all. There were prints and engravings of the Port of Boston and caricatures of the British and all sorts of goldsmith work, more than you could put a name to. It was a crowded place, but shipshape. And Paul Revere moved about it, quick and keen, with his eyes full of life and hot temper — the kind of man who knows what he wants to do and does it the next minute.

There were quite a few customers there when Lige Butterwick first came in — so he sort of scrooged back in a corner and waited his chance. For one thing, after the queer sign and the barber's calling him a wizard, he wanted to be sure about this fellow Revere, and see what kind of customers came to his shop.

Well, there was a woman who wanted a christening mug for a baby and a man who wanted a print of the Boston Massacre. And then there was a fellow who passed Revere some sort of message under cover — Lige caught the whisper, 'powder' and 'Sons of

Liberty,' though he couldn't make out the rest. And finally there was a very fine silk-dressed lady who seemed to be giving Revere considerable trouble. Lige peeked at her round the corner of his chair, and somehow or other she reminded him of a turkey-gobbler, especially the strut.

She was complaining about some silver that Paul Revere had made for her — expensive silver it must have been. And 'Oh, Master Revere, I'm so disappointed!' she was saying. 'When I took the things from the box, I could just have cried!'

Revere drew himself up a little at that, Lige noticed, but his voice was pleasant.

'It is I who am disappointed, madam,' he said, with a little bow. 'But what was the trouble? It must have been carelessly packed. Was it badly dented? I'll speak to my boy.'

'Oh, no, it wasn't dented,' said the turkey-gobbler lady. 'But I wanted a really impressive silver service — something I can use when the Governor comes to dinner with us. I certainly *paid* for the best. And what have you given me?'

Lige waited to hear what Paul Revere would say. When he spoke, his voice was stiff.

'I have given you the best work of which I am capable, madam,' he said. 'It was in my hands for six months — and I think they are skillful hands.'

'Oh,' said the woman, and rustled her skirts, 'I know you're a competent artisan, Master Revere ——'

'Silversmith, if you please,' said Paul Revere, and the woman rustled again.

'Well, I don't care what you call it,' she said, and then you could see her fine accent was put on like her fine clothes. 'But I know I wanted a real service — something I could show my friends. And what have you given me? Oh, it's silver, if you choose. But it's just as plain and simple as a picket fence!'

Revere looked at her for a moment and Lige Butterwick thought he'd explode.

'Simple?' he said. 'And plain? You pay me high compliments, madam!'

'Compliments, indeed!' said the woman, and now she was getting furious. 'I'm sending it back tomorrow! Why, there isn't as much as a lion or a unicorn on the cream jug. And I told you I wanted the sugar bowl covered with silver grapes! But you've given me something as bare as the hills of New England! And I won't stand it, I tell you! I'll send to England instead.'

Revere puffed his cheeks and blew, but his eyes were dangerous.

'Send away, madam,' he said. 'We're making new things in this country — new men — new silver — perhaps, who knows, a new nation. Plain, simple, bare as the hills and rocks of New England — graceful as the boughs of her elm trees — if my silver were only like that, indeed! But that is what I wish to make it. And, as for you, madam' — he stepped toward her like a cat — 'with your lions and unicorns and grape leaves and your nonsense of bad ornament done by bad silversmiths — your imported bad taste and your imported British manners — puff!' And he blew at her, just the way you blow at a turkey-gobbler, till she fairly picked up her fine silk skirts and ran. Revere watched her out of the door and turned back, shaking his head.

'William!' he called to the boy who helped him in the shop. 'Put up the shutters — we're closing for the day. And William — no word yet from Doctor Warren?'

'Not yet, sir,' said the boy, and started to put up the shutters. Then Lige Butterwick thought it was about time to make his presence known.

So he coughed, and Paul Revere whirled and Lige Butterwick felt those quick, keen eyes boring into his. He wasn't exactly afraid of them, for he was stubborn himself, but he knew this was an unexpected kind of man.

'Well, my friend,' said Revere, impatiently, 'and who in the world are you?'

'Well, Mr. Revere,' said Lige Butterwick. 'It is Mr. Revere, isn't it? It's kind of a long story. But, closing or not, you've got to listen to me. The barber told me so.'

'The barber!' said Revere, kind of dumbfounded.

'Uh-huh,' said Lige, and opened his mouth. 'You see, it's my tooth.'

'Tooth!' said Revere, and stared at him as if they were both crazy. 'You'd better begin at the beginning. But wait a minute. You don't talk like a Boston man. Where do you come from?'

'Oh, around Lexington way,' said Lige. 'And, you see ——'

But the mention of Lexington seemed to throw Revere into a regular excitement. He fairly shook Lige by the shoulders.

'Lexington!' he said. 'Were you there this morning?'

'Of course I was,' said Lige. 'That's where the barber I told you about ——'

'Never mind the barber!' said Revere. 'Were Mr. Hancock and Mr. Adams still at Parson Clarke's?'

'Well, they might have been for all I know,' said Lige. 'But I couldn't say.'

'Great heaven!' said Revere. 'Is there a man in the American colonies who doesn't know Mr. Hancock and Mr. Adams?'

'There seems to be me,' said Lige. 'But speaking of strangers — there *was* two of them staying at the parsonage, when I rode past. One was a handsomish man and the other looked more like a bull-dog ——'

'Hancock and Adams!' said Revere. 'So they are still there.' He took a turn or two up and down the room. 'And the British ready to march!' he muttered to himself. 'Did you see many soldiers as you came to my shop, Mr. Butterwick?'

'See them?' said Lige. 'They chased me into a tar-barrel. And there was a whole passel of them up by the Common with guns and flags. Looked as if they meant business.'

Revere took his hand and pumped it up and down.

'Thank you, Mr. Butterwick,' he said. 'You're a shrewd ob-server. And you have done me — and the colonies — an invaluable service.'

'Well, that's nice to know,' said Lige. 'But, speaking about this tooth of mine ——'

Revere looked at him and laughed, while his eyes crinkled.

'You're a stubborn man, Mr. Butterwick,' he said. 'All the bet-ter. I like stubborn men. I wish we had more of them. Well, one good turn deserves another — you've helped me and I'll do my best to help you. I've made artificial teeth — but drawing them is hardly my trade. All the same, I'll do what I can for you.'

So Lige sat down in a chair and opened his mouth.

'Whew!' said Revere, with his eyes dancing. His voice grew solemn. 'Mr. Butterwick,' he said, 'it seems to be a compound, agglutinated infraction of the upper molar. I'm afraid I can't do anything about it tonight.'

'But ——' said Lige.

'But here's a draught — that will ease the pain for a while,' said

Revere, and poured some medicine into a cup. 'Drink!' he said, and Lige drank. The draught was red and spicy, with a queer, sleepy taste, but pungent. It wasn't like anything Lige had ever tasted before, but he noticed it eased the pain.

'There,' said Revere. 'And now you go to a tavern and get a good night's rest. Come back to see me in the morning — I'll find a tooth-drawer for you, if I'm here. And — oh, yes — you'd better have some liniment.'

He started to rummage in a big cupboard at the back of the shop. It was dark now, with the end of day and the shutters up, and whether it was the tooth, or the tiredness, or the draught Paul Revere had given him, Lige began to feel a little queer. There was a humming in his head and a lightness in his feet. He got up and stood looking over Paul Revere's shoulder, and it seemed to him that things moved and scampered in that cupboard in a curious way, as Revere's quick fingers took down this box and that. And the shop was full of shadows and murmurings.

'It's a queer kind of shop you've got here, Mr. Revere,' he said, glad to hear the sound of his own voice.

'Well, some people think so,' said Revere — and that time Lige was almost sure he saw something move in the cupboard. He coughed. 'Say — what's in that little bottle?' he said, to keep his mind steady.

'That?' said Paul Revere, with a smile, and held the bottle up. 'Oh, that's a little chemical experiment of mine. I call it Essence of Boston. But there's a good deal of East Wind in it.'

'Essence of Boston,' said Lige, with his eyes bulging. 'Well, they did say you was a wizard. It's gen-u-wine magic, I suppose?'

'Genuine magic, of course,' said Revere, with a chuckle. 'And here's the box with your liniment. And here ——'

He took down two little boxes — a silver and a pewter one — and placed them on the counter. But Lige's eyes went to the silver one — they were drawn to it, though he couldn't have told you why.

'Pick it up,' said Paul Revere, and Lige did so and turned it in his hands. It was a handsome box. He could make out a growing tree and an eagle fighting a lion. 'It's mighty pretty work,' he said.

'It's my own design,' said Paul Revere. 'See the stars around the edge — thirteen of them? You could make a very pretty design with stars — for a new country, say — if you wanted to. I've sometimes thought of it.'

'But what's in it?' said Lige.

'What's in it?' said Paul Revere, and his voice was light but steely. 'Why, what's in the air around us? Gunpowder and war and the making of a new nation. But the time isn't quite ripe yet — not quite ripe.'

'You mean,' said Lige — and he looked at the box very respectful — 'that this-here revolution folks keep talking about ——'

'Yes,' said Paul Revere, and he was about to go on. But just then his boy ran in, with a letter in his hand.

'Master!' he said. 'A message from Doctor Warren!'

IV

Well, with that Revere started moving, and, when he started to move, he moved fast. He was calling for his riding boots in one breath and telling Lige Butterwick to come back tomorrow in another — and what with all the bustle and confusion, Lige Butterwick nearly went off without his liniment after all. But he grabbed up a box from the counter just as Revere was practically shoving him out of the door — and it wasn't till he'd got to his tavern and gone to bed for the night that he found out he'd taken the wrong box.

He found it out then because when he went to bed he couldn't get to sleep. It wasn't his tooth that bothered him — that had settled to a kind of dull ache and he could have slept through that — but his mind kept going over all the events of the day — the two folks he'd seen at Parson Clarke's and being chased by the British and what Revere had said to the turkey-gobbler woman — till he couldn't get any peace. He could feel something stirring in him, though he didn't know what it was.

''Tain't right to have soldiers chase a fellow down the street,' he said to himself. 'And 'tain't right to have people like that woman run down New England. No, it ain't. Oh, me — I better look for that liniment of Mr. Revere's.'

So he got up from his bed and went over and found his coat. Then he reached his hand in the pocket and pulled out the silver box.

Well, at first he was so flustrated that he didn't know rightly what to do. For here, as well as he could remember it, was gunpowder and war and the makings of a new nation — the revolution itself, shut up in a silver box by Paul Revere. He mightn't have believed there could be such things before he came to Boston. But now he did.

The draught was still humming in his head, and his legs felt a mite wobbly. But, being human, he was curious. 'Now, I wonder what *is* inside that box,' he said.

He shook the box and handled it, but that seemed to make it warmer, as if there was something alive inside it, so he stopped that mighty quick. Then he looked all over it for a keyhole, but there wasn't any keyhole, and if there had been, he didn't have a key.

Then he put his ear to the box and listened hard. And it seemed to him that he heard, very tiny and far away, inside the box, the rolling fire of thousands of tiny muskets and the tiny, far-away cheers of many men. 'Hold your fire!' he heard a voice say. 'Don't fire till you're fired on — but if they want a war, let it begin here!' And then there was a rolling of drums and a squeal of fifes. It was small, still, and far away, but it made him shake all over, for he knew he was listening to something in the future — and something that he didn't have a right to hear. He sat down on the edge of his bed with the box in his hands.

'Now, what am I going to do with this?' he said. 'It's too big a job for one man.'

Well, he thought, kind of scared, of going down to the river and throwing the box in, but, when he thought of doing it, he knew he couldn't. Then he thought of his farm near Lexington and the peaceful days. Once the revolution was out of the box, there'd be an end to that. But then he remembered what Revere had said when he was talking with the woman about the silver — the thing about building a new country and building it clean and plain. 'Why, I'm not a Britisher,' he thought. 'I'm a New Englander. And maybe there's something beyond that — something people like Hancock and Adams know about. And if it has to come with a revolution — well, I guess it has to come. We can't stay Britishers forever, here in this country.'

He listened to the box again, and now there wasn't any shooting in it — just a queer tune played on a fife. He didn't know the name of the tune, but it lifted his heart.

He got up, sort of slow and heavy. 'I guess I'll have to take this back to Paul Revere,' he said.

Well, the first place he went was Doctor Warren's, having heard Revere mention it, but he didn't get much satisfaction there. It took quite a while to convince them that he wasn't a spy, and when he did, all they'd tell him was that Revere had gone over the river to Charlestown. So he went down to the waterfront to look for a boat. And the first person he met was a very angry woman.

'No,' she said. 'You don't get any boats from me. There was a crazy man along here an hour ago and he wanted a boat too, and my husband was crazy enough to take him. And then do you know what he did?'

'No, mam,' said Lige Butterwick.

'He made my husband take my best petticoat to muffle the oars so they wouldn't make a splash when they went past that Britisher ship,' she said, pointing out where the man-of-war *Somerset* lay at anchor. 'My best petticoat, I tell you! And when my husband comes back he'll get a piece of my mind!'

'Was his name Revere?' said Lige Butterwick. 'Was he a man of forty-odd, keen-looking and kind of Frenchy?'

'I don't know what his right name is,' said the woman, 'but his name's mud with me. My best petticoat tore into strips and swimming in that nasty river!' And that was all he could get out of her.

All the same, he managed to get a boat at last — the story doesn't say how — and row across the river. The tide was at young flood and the moonlight bright on the water, and he passed under the shadow of the *Somerset*, right where Revere had passed. When he got to the Charlestown side he could see the lanterns in North Church, though he didn't know what they signified. Then he told the folks at Charlestown he had news for Revere, and they got him a horse, and so he started to ride. And all the while the silver box was burning his pocket.

Well, he lost his way more or less, as you well might in the darkness, and it was dawn when he came into Lexington by a side road. The dawn in that country's pretty, with the dew still on the grass. But he wasn't looking at the dawn. He was feeling the box burn his pocket and thinking hard.

Then, all of a sudden, he reined up his tired horse. For there on the side road were two men carrying a trunk — and one of them was Paul Revere.

They looked at each other and Lige began to grin. For Revere was just as dirty and mud-splashed as he was — he'd warned Hancock and Adams all right, but then, on his way to Concord, he'd got caught by the British and turned loose again. So he'd gone back to Lexington to see how things were there — and now he and the other fellow were saving a trunk of papers that Hancock had left behind, so they wouldn't fall into the hands of the British.

Lige swung off his horse. 'Well, Mr. Revere,' he said, 'you see I'm on time for that little appointment about my tooth. And by the way, I've got something for you.' He took the box from his pocket. And then he looked over toward Lexington Green and caught his breath. For on the Green there was a little line of Minute Men — neighbors of his, as he knew — and in front of them the British regulars. And, even as he looked there was the sound of a gunshot, and suddenly smoke wrapped the front of the British line and he heard them shout as they ran forward.

Lige Butterwick took the silver box and stamped on it with his heel. And with that the box broke open — and there was a dazzle in his eyes for a moment and a noise of men shouting — and then it was gone.

'Do you know what you've done?' said Revere. 'You've let out the American Revolution!'

'Well,' said Lige Butterwick, 'I guess it was about time. And I guess I'd better be going home, now. I've got a gun on the wall there, and I'll need it.'

'But what about your tooth?' said Paul Revere.

'Oh, a tooth's a tooth,' said Lige Butterwick. 'But a country's a country. And, anyhow, it's stopped aching.'

All the same, they say Paul Revere made a silver tooth for him, after the war. But my great-aunt wasn't quite sure of it, so I won't vouch for that.

MR. MERGENTHWIRKER'S LOBBLIES [1]

By NELSON S. BOND

(From *Scribner's Magazine*)

THAT year instead of the raise I damn well deserved they handed me the resounding title of Assistant City Editor, which meant that in addition to all my regular duties I was now responsible for the boners of the leg men. The only good break I got — if you'd call it that — was a 'private office' with my name on the door. A dingy little hole just off the City Room, littered with last year's papers, and elaborately furnished with three overflow files from the Morgue, a swivel chair with one missing caster, and a yellow oak desk neatly scalloped with cigarette scars.

The faint tap on the door gave me a chance to get my feet off the desk before I shouted, 'Come in!' The door swung open hesitantly and I saw him.

'Yes?' I said.

He stood there, blinking at me apologetically. A tiny man, hardly more than five foot one, or maybe two, with sand-colored hair and eyes. His clothing was plain but neat. And he was nervous. His hands twitched and wriggled constantly; darting in and out of pockets, brushing imaginary pieces of lint from his lapels, fumbling at his watch chain — always on the move. He was restless on the hoof, too — shuffling and fidgeting like he had termites in his trousers.

'Are — are you the man who takes the news?' he said.

'Who, me?' I answered elaborately. 'Hell, yes! I'm the whole damned newspaper. I write the front page, lay out the ads, draw the cartoons, dig up the dirt, and sell papers on the street. Why, me and Bill Hearst — say, what do you want, anyway?'

His meek, twidgety gaze needled me. He stood there gaping as though my every word was Gospel. He jerked when I shot the question at him, and his pale eyes grew a little frightened.

'Why, I — I just wanted to tell you,' he faltered, 'that there's going to be a murder. This afternoon.'

You meet all kinds of crackpots in this racket. I grinned at him
sort of cheerfully, and nodded.

'Nice going, Mr. ——'

'Mergenthwirker,' he supplied. 'Henry Mergenthwirker.'

'Nice going, Mr. Mergenthwirker,' I said. 'You socked it right
on the button that time. There *is* going to be a nice little murder
this afternoon. Blood and brains all over everything. I'm just
writing the headlines now. "D.A. SLAYS MATE IN ——"'

'Oh, no!' gasped the little man. 'Not the District Attorney!
Nothing like that! It's a girl up in the Bronx. A secretary named
Hazel Johnson. She's going to be killed with a hammer!'

Honestly, that stopped me for a minute. He looked so darned
sincere, his tiny hands fluttering around his coat lapels like bewildered moths; his tawny eyes wide and horrified. I thought:
'Perhaps this is one of those psychological cases. A potential murderer compelled to confess his crime before it happens. Perhaps it
has happened already, and he is trying to establish an alibi.' I
looked at him sharply.

'What's the gag?' I said. 'You know the girl?'

'Me?' he said. 'No, I never saw her in my life.'

'Then how do you know about the murder?'

He smiled beatifically.

'*They* told me,' he said. He gestured vaguely toward the door
with one hand.

'They? Who?'

'My lobblies,' explained the little man patiently. He pointed,
proudly, I thought, toward the doorway again. 'The big one's
name is Japheth, but the little one is named after me. They tell
me everything.'

'Now, wait a minute, buddy,' I said. 'Are you trying to tell me
there's somebody in this room beside you and me?'

He rinsed his hands in a gesture of quick despair.

'Oh, *don't* tell me you can't see them!' he wailed. 'So *few* people
can!' He stamped his foot in sudden exasperation. 'It's all because
they *will* change color! If they'd only stay *put!* But, no! They're
forever ——'

This time I got it. I rose swiftly and grabbed the little fellow by
the shirt front.

'Listen, Mr. Whatsis,' I told him. 'I've got things to do, but worrying about your D.T.'s isn't one of them. Now, scram! And on the way out, tell the boys in the City Room that it went over like a lead balloon.'

I pushed him, indignantly protesting, through the door, and waited until the pit-a-pat of his footsteps disappeared down the hallway. Then I strolled out into the City Room, with one eye peeled for the grins. A couple of the boys were matching nickels over by Duff Godshall's desk. I sauntered over carelessly.

'O.K., boys,' I said. 'Let's have the wisecracks!'

'Tails!' said Duff. He took a nickel off the back of each of the other fellows' hands; then looked at me curiously. 'Wisecracks?'

'I suppose none of you boys ever heard tell of a guy named Mergenthwirker?' I asked caustically.

Three heads shook in unison.

'It's a gag,' guessed Bill McGhee. 'Early in the day to start drinking, Len.'

'Oh, skip it!' I said wearily. 'Anyway, it didn't work, in case you're interested. Come on, who's matching who in this game?'

I had just pulled a couple of nickels from my vest pocket when the boss shoved open his door and let out a blat to high heaven.

'Hawley! Godshall! Get Maguire and light out for the Bronx. There's a hammer killing up there! A broad named Johnson!'

The funny part about it was that there was no mystery connected with this hammer job. They caught the guilty man an hour after they found the body, and he confessed right off the bat. What I mean is, there wasn't one thing to connect my nutsack visitor with the case. So the affair bothered me. I looked up the name 'Mergenthwirker' in the telephone book and the city directory, but it wasn't in either of them. I don't know just what I would have done if it *had* been. After all, you can't go to the bobbies and say, 'Look here, a guy named Mergenthwirker has two green familiars who told him there was going to be a murder.' So I puzzled over the thing for a week or so, and then it gradually dropped out of my mind. It might never have occurred to me again if I hadn't dropped into Tony's joint one night for a drink.

Tony's bar, as usual, was jammed with half-lit reformers, solving national problems in three easy lessons, so I ducked for the back room. It's a dimly lit little hole, with only about four tables. As I

entered, I saw this guy Mergenthwirker sitting at the best table —
the one beneath the only light — with a beer glass before him. The
places on his left and right had beer glasses, too, but no one was
sitting there. The sandy little man looked up as I entered.

'Oh, hello!' he said in a pleased voice. Evidently he didn't bear
me any ill will for kicking him out of my office. 'Won't you join us?'

I would. I moved around to the chair on his left and started to
pull it out. Mergenthwirker leaped up suddenly, slopping his beer
all over the table.

'Oh, not there!' he cried. 'You'll sit on Henry!'

I took the chair across from him. Tony came out with my beer,
mopped up the mess on the table, and left. The little man smiled
at me apologetically.

'It's so *dark* in here,' he said. 'I guess you didn't see Henry, did
you?'

'No,' I said bluntly, 'I didn't. Listen, buddy, I've been looking
for you. How did you know about the Johnson murder?'

There was an astonished, half-aggrieved look in his pale eyes.

'Why, my lobblies,' he said. 'My lobblies told me.'

I jerked my head toward the empty chairs.

'Henry, here, and ——'

'— and Japheth! Yes, certainly! They tell me all sorts of
things. For instance' — he leaned far over the table eagerly —
'did you know the Second National was going to be robbed Tuesday?'

'The Second National?'

'Yes!' he said excitedly. 'Four men in a blue Olds will hold it
up at 3.30 P.M. Only the police will catch them. They're going to
smash up their car trying to escape!'

'Got all the details, haven't you?' I said.

'I *always* have all the details,' he complained. 'I had all the
details before, but you' — he smiled forgivingly — 'well, it doesn't
matter. Will you call Tony, please? Japheth wants more beer.'

I gulped and stared at Japheth's glass . . . or maybe I stared first
and then gulped. The glass was empty! And I would swear on a
stack of proof sheets that I had been watching the little man every
instant since I came in. And he did *not* drink that beer himself!

'Does he' — I began cautiously — 'does he drink very much
beer?'

Mergenthwirker sighed.

'Barrels! Both he and Henry. But what can I do? If I don't buy it for them, they make scenes.'

'Scenes?' I repeated vaguely.

'Yes,' he confided. 'You know — pinch people on — on busses, and whisper things to girls. Especially pretty girls. *Young* girls.' He smiled shyly, and a faint blush crept over his colorless cheeks. 'Henry's the worst. He just doesn't seem to care *what* he says to young girls. Once he even ... I mean, there was that girl in Atlantic City ...'

Tony came just then with four glasses of beer. As he renewed ours, I noted that now Henry's, as well as Japheth's, glass was empty. And this time I *knew* Mergenthwirker had not touched the beer. I paid for the round, and Tony waddled away.

'Mergenthwirker,' I said seriously, 'either you're nuts or I am. You call Japheth and Henry "lobblies." What do you mean by that?'

'Why, that's what they are, of course,' he said, his eyes round with surprise.

'But how ... or where ... did you get them?'

'I've always had them,' he said — proudly, this time. 'Ever since — oh, since I was very young. Japheth came first, but he was lonely, so after a while the little one came, too. We named him Henry, after me. Of course, he was *very* young when he came, and he had some perfectly awful habits at first. But he's starting to get over them now.'

'Habits?' I said. 'What kind of habits?'

'Oh — lobbly habits!' said Mergenthwirker airily. 'Things like pwidgeting and rikking trilks and ... eh, what's that?' He leaned to his right, listened intently, then nodded.

'Japheth says you wouldn't understand,' he told me. 'Do you mind?'

'Not at all,' I said. I was hot and cross and irritable and my watch told me it was time to grab some shuteye. 'Say, Mergenthwirker,' I said, 'I've got to run along now, but I wish you'd drop in at the office again some day soon. Bring — bring the lobblies with you.'

'Thank you, I will,' said the little man. I rose from the table, reaching for my hat.

'Oh, Japheth and Henry say thank you for the drink,' added my companion. I glanced at the table swiftly. Once more the beer glasses were empty....

At three o'clock the next afternoon I hoked up a phony excuse to plant two of the boys and a cameraman in the Second National Bank. At 3.30 on the dot a blue Olds sedan drew up, four men stepped out, whisked briskly into the bank, covered the joint with a tommy gun, scooped up the gravy, and moved along. At 3.57 their car, closely followed by my three men and the police, clipped an elevated post on Sixth. And at 4.10 my sheet pulled the first 'beat' this burg has seen in the past six years — a complete pictorial account of the Second National robbery!

I had just finished receiving the boss's congratulations — *sans* bonus — when Mergenthwirker came in. He was beaming delightedly.

'So!' he said triumphantly.

'So,' I agreed slowly, 'you were right. I don't know how or why — but you were.'

'It's my lobblies,' Mergenthwirker boasted. 'They know everything.'

'Man,' I told him, 'with Japheth and Henry to help you, you could be the richest guy this side of Hades. Do they know the results of horse races, lotteries, football games?'

'Why — why, I suppose so,' said Mergenthwirker. 'I never stopped to think ——' His brows furrowed momentarily. 'My *goodness!* I *could*, couldn't I!'

'Looks as if,' I grunted. 'Here, won't you and the boys sit down?' The little man was dancing with nervousness.

'Oh, *no!*' he said excitedly. 'Oh, *my!* I never even *thought* of using Henry and Japheth to —— Will you come over and have a drink with us? Talk it over?'

'Why not?' I said. We went down in the elevator, Mergenthwirker jabbering six to a dozen, to the vast amusement of the elevator boy. On the street he grabbed my arm and held me back.

'Let *them* go ahead,' he whispered hoarsely. 'Perhaps they wouldn't exactly like it if they knew I was planning to — to *use* them like that. I'll have to break it sort of gently, and see what they think. I wouldn't want to ——'

His words were drowned in the belligerent squawk of one of those huge, lumbering trucks that the city still allows on its main thoroughfares. The traffic light had just turned red, holding us to the curb, but a few pedestrians ahead were still scrambling, with affronted awkwardness, for the safety zone. Mergenthwirker screamed shrilly, his tiny hands digging painfully into my arm.

'Henry!'

Suddenly he left me, and darted into the middle of the street with arms outthrust before him as though to push some slighter body out of danger. A horn growled, brakes squealed viciously, somewhere a whistle shrilled, and the spattering of many voices tightened into a murmuring knot in the center of the street. Suddenly numbed with fear, I elbowed my way through the crowd. Mergenthwirker, his body grotesquely twisted, lay crumpled on the asphalt. I leaned over him and lifted his head on my arm. His eyes fluttered open, recognized me.

'Henry' — he gasped. 'Is he all right?' His head turned stiffly, his eyes searching the press of babbling bystanders. 'Ah! There — I thought so. Then he *is* safe. . . .' He closed his eyes contentedly.

'Take it easy, guy,' I said. 'There'll be an ambulance here directly.'

'Ambulance!' He stared at me; his tawny eyes were wide and then they were suddenly deep with growing fear. 'For me? Oh, no — that can't be! I can't die! Japheth! Henry! What will they do without me? My lobblies — my lovely, beautiful lobblies! Nobody to talk with . . . nobody to buy them beer . . . and Henry is *so* young! What ——'

'Listen,' I said, 'they'll be all right. I'll take care of them.'

There was a slow ripple through the crowd. Far down the street I heard the wailing siren of an ambulance. The little man's eyes flickered briefly, and a great weariness pressed upon their lids.

'Thank you! Thank you very much,' said Mr. Mergenthwirker. . . .

THE CHEAT'S REMORSE [1]

By MORLEY CALLAGHAN

(From *Esquire*)

PHIL was sipping a cup of coffee in Stewart's one night, sitting at the table near the radiator so the snow would melt off his shoes and dry, when he saw a prosperous-looking hairy, blue-jowled man at the next table pushing a corned-beef sandwich on rye bread away from him slowly as if the sight of it made him sick. By the way the man sighed as he concentrated on the untouched sandwich anyone could see he was pretty drunk. He was clutching his food check firmly in his left hand as he used the other to tug and fumble at a roll of bills in his pocket. He was trying to get hold of himself, he was trying to get ready to walk up to the cashier in a straight line without stumbling, pay his check with dignity, and get into a taxi and home before he fell asleep.

The roll of bills that hung in the man's hand underneath the table as he leaned his weight forward staring at the cashier started Phil thinking how much he needed a dollar. He had been across the country and back on a bus, he was broke, his shirts were in a hand laundry on Twenty-sixth Street, and a man he had phoned yesterday, a man he had gone to school with, and who worked in a publisher's office now, had told him to come around and see him and he might be able to get him a few weeks' work in the shipping room. But they wouldn't let him have the shirts at the laundry unless he paid for them. And he couldn't bear to see a man he had grown up with who was making a lot of money unless he had at least a clean shirt on.

As he leaned forward eagerly watching the man's thick fingers thumbing the roll of bills stiffly, trying to detach a bill while he concentrated on the goal which was the cashier's desk, the thing that Phil had hardly been daring to hope for happened: a bill was thumbed loosely from the roll, the fat fingers clutched at it, missed it, and it fluttered in a little curve under the table and fell in the black smudge on the floor from the man's wet rubbers.

[1] Copyright, October, 1937, by Esquire-Coronet, Inc.

With a dreamy grin Phil kept looking beyond the man's head, beyond all the tables as if he were sniffling the rich odors from the food counter. But his heart gave a couple of jerks. And he had such a marvelously bright picture of himself going into the laundry in the morning and getting the shirts and putting on the light blue one with the fine white stripe that he had paid four dollars for a year ago in Philadelphia.

But the drunk, having noticed him, was shaking his head at him. He was staring at Phil's battered felt hat and his old belted coat and his mussy shirt. He didn't like what he saw. It didn't help to make him feel secure and in full possession of himself. The dreamy look on Phil's face disgusted him.

'Hey, dreamy,' he said, 'what's eating you?'

'Me?'

'Yeah, you, dreamy.'

'I wasn't looking at you. I'm making up my mind what I want.'

'Excuse me, dreamy. Maybe you're right. I've been making mistakes all evening and I don't want to make any more,' he said.

While he smiled very humbly at Phil a girl in a beige-colored coat spotted with raindrops and snow, a girl with untidy fair hair that needed curling at the ends, and with good legs and a pale face, came over and sat down at his table. An unpunched food check was in her hand. She put her elbows on the table and looked around as if she were waiting for someone. The dollar bill on the floor was about two feet away from her foot.

The drunk rose from the table with considerable dignity and began to glide across the floor toward the cashier, his check held out with dreadful earnestness, his roll of bills tight in the other hand now. And when he had gone about twenty feet Phil glanced at the girl, their eyes met in a wary appraisal of each other, they looked steadily at each other, neither one moving, her eyes were blue and unwavering, and then, in spite of herself her glance shifted to the floor before she had time to move.

Phil got scared and lurched at the bill, one knee on the floor as he grabbed at it, but she knew just where the bill was and her foot swung out and her toe held it down with all her weight, absolutely unyielding as he tugged at it, and he knew there was no chance of his getting even a piece of it unless he tore it. While he kept holding the edge of the bill he stared helplessly at her worn shoe that was wet, and then he looked at her ankle and at the run in her stocking that went half way up the calf of her leg. He knew she was bending down. Her face was close to his.

'I guess it's a saw-off,' he said, looking up.

'Looks like it,' she said, her toe still on the bill, her face tense with eagerness.

'Maybe you want to run after him with it?'

'That wasn't in my mind,' she said. She smiled a little in a bright, hard, unyielding way.

If she had taken her toe off the bill while they talked he mightn't have done the thing he did, but she made him feel she was only waiting for him to straighten up and be friendly to draw the bill closer to her; and the expectation of having the dollar and getting the shirt had given him quite a lift too, so he said, shrugging good-humoredly, 'What do you think we should do?'

'What do you think yourself?'

'Tell you what I'll do,' he said. 'Figuring maybe we both saw it at the same time and that we both need it, how about if I toss you for it?'

She hesitated and said, 'Seems fair enough. Go ahead.'

They both smiled as he took a nickel from his vest pocket, and when she smiled like that he saw that she was quite young, there was a little bruise under her eye as though someone had hit her, but her face seemed to open out to him in spite of the pallor, the bruise and her untidy hair, and it was full of a sudden, wild breathless eagerness. 'Heads I win, tails you win,' he said, getting ready to toss the coin.

'Let it land on the table and don't touch it and let it roll,' she said, nodding her head and leaning forward.

'Watch me, lady,' he said, and he spun the coin beautifully and it rolled in a wide arc on the table around the little stand that held the sugar, mustard, vinegar, and horseradish sauce. When it stopped spinning they leaned forward so quickly their heads almost bumped.

'Heads, eh? Heads,' she said, but she kept on looking down at it as if she couldn't see it. She was contemplating something, something in her head that was dreadful, a question maybe that found an answer in the coin on the table. Her face was close to his, and there were tears in her eyes, but she turned away and said faintly:

'Okay, pal. It's all yours.' She raised her foot and smiled a little while he bent down and picked up the bill.

'Thanks,' he said. 'Maybe you're lucky in love.'

'Very likely. More power to you,' he said, and she walked away and over to the cashier, where she handed in her unpunched food check.

He watched her raising the collar of her beige coat that was spotted from the rain and snow. A little bit of hair was caught and held outside the collar. While she was speaking to the cashier he was looking at the coin flat in the palm of his hand, looking at it and feeling dreadfully ashamed. He turned it over slowly and it was heads on both sides, the lucky phony coin he had found two years ago. And then he could hardly see the coin in his hand: he could see nothing but the expression on her face as she watched it spinning on the table; he heard her sigh, as if all the hope she had ever had in her life was put on the coin; he remembered how she had stiffened and then smiled: he felt that somehow her whole fate had depended on her having the bill. She had been close to it, just close enough to be tantalized, and then he had cheated her.

She was going out, and he rushed after her, and he saw her standing twenty feet away in the door of a cigar store. It was snowing again. She had walked through the snow; her bare shoes were carrying the snow as she stood there in the wet muddy entrance looking up and down the street. Before he could get near her she put her hands deep in her pockets and started to walk away rapidly with her head down.

'Just a minute, lady. Hey, what's the hurry?' he called.

Unsmiling and wondering she turned and waited. 'What's the matter with you?' she said.

'Do me a good turn, will you?'

'Why should I?'

'Why not if it don't hurt?'

'That depends on what it is,' she said.

'Take the buck, will you, that's all,' he said.

She tried to figure him out a moment, then she said: 'What is this, mister? You won it fair and square enough. Okay. Let it go at that.' Her face looked much harder, suddenly much older than it had in the restaurant.

'No, I didn't win it on the level,' he said. 'Here, miss, take it, please,' and he reached out and held her arm, but she pulled away from him, frowning. He grew flustered. 'That was a phony coin I tossed, don't you see? I'll show it to you if you want to. You didn't have a chance.'

'Then why the big heart now?' she said.

'I don't know. I was watching you go out and I got a hunch it was worse for you than it was for me. You had a bigger stake in it ——' He went on pleading with her earnestly.

Mystified, she said. 'Look here, if you cheated me you cheated me and I might have known it would be phony anyway, but ——'

'I thought I needed the buck badly, but I felt lousy watching you go out. I needed to get my laundry tomorrow. I needed a clean shirt. That's what I was thinking watching the guy fingering the roll. And it was tough to see you come in on it. I didn't stop to think. I just went after it.'

She was listening earnestly as if his remorse truly puzzled her, and then she put out her hand and gave him a pat on the arm that made him feel they knew each other well and had been together all evening, and that she was very old and he was just a green kid.

'Listen, you figure a clean shirt'll help you?' she said.

'I figured it would give me a head start, that's all.'

'Maybe it will. Go ahead. Get the shirts.'

'No, please, you take it.'

'A clean shirt won't help me, nor the price of one,' she said harshly. 'So long,' she said, with that bright, unyielding smile.

She walked away resolutely this time, as if she had made some final destructive decision, a decision she had dreaded and that she mightn't have made if he hadn't cheated her and she had got the dollar.

Worried, he went to run after her, but he stopped, startled and shaken, perceiving the truth as she had seen it, that a dollar in the long run was no good to her, that it would need a vast upheaval that shook the earth to really change the structure of her life. Yet she had been willing to stop and help him.

But the clean shirt became an absurd and trivial thing and the dollar felt unclean in his hand. He looked down the street at the tavern light. He had to get rid of the dollar or feel that he'd always see her walking away resolutely with her hands deep in her pockets.

THE BROTHERS [1]

By JOHN CHEEVER

(From *The Yale Review*)

THEY always planned to come up the driveway of Amy's farm in the late afternoon, and in those years no habit of theirs was more seldom broken. On Saturdays Kenneth's office closed at one, and since Tom wasn't working then, he met him downtown and they lunched together in a restaurant near the market, drinking a lot of beer and talking with the old barman about the horses that had run that season. After lunch they walked into the Italian quarter looking for something to buy as a present for Amy. Many of the marketmen knew by sight the two young Yankees, who came there every Saturday afternoon, and they joked with them about their girls or their car or their knowledge of Italian. After joking and haggling for half an hour that afternoon, they came away with a gallon of wine and walked back to Dock Square, where their Ford was parked.

The brothers never argued about who would drive, for during the four years they had lived together, they had fallen into such a routine that it was inconceivable that one or the other of them should question it. This week it was Tom's turn. They drove down Atlantic Avenue and crossed the harbor on the ferry. Aboard the boat they went to the engine room and talked with the stokers, who had learned to expect them with the same assurance as the marketmen. When the signals came to reverse the engine, they climbed up from the hold and started the Ford again, driving out through Maverick Square to the turnpike that runs between Boston and Newburyport.

It was a fine day in September. Some of the roadside stands and lunch carts were already shuttered against the winter, and a light wind was bringing down the first leaves. The country that lay along the road was one of the exhausted regions of New England with its broken walls and gutted houses. But it was the New England of their fathers, and although they never talked of it, they loved it in spite of what time and industry had done to its timber and its fields. Their affection for it was a part of the singular life they led together, from which they jealously excluded the rest of the world, as if sharing it with others would be some betrayal of their pleasure. It belonged to their private fund of experience, like the crowded streets of the Italian quarter and the conversation of the stokers and the wharves of the East Shore, where they sometimes watched the freighters load; or the fugitive saloons along Howard Street, where they were known by all the barmen and waitresses.

They stopped in Topsfield and had a couple of beers, and Kenneth bought a carton of cigarettes. There they turned off the turnpike into an empty road, and Kenneth took the car sixty-five and seventy miles an hour. The country of the Merrimack Valley was familiar and reassuring, and it was less than a half hour after leaving Topsfield that they drove in at the stone gates of Amy's farm. The light of the afternoon was going, and the shadows of the maples reached a long way out across the fields. Through the trees they could see the faded white walls of the farm, and then they could hear the police dog beginning to bark.

When Amy heard the Ford rattling over the ruts of the driveway, she laid down her book. Four years ago the brothers had come down to her farm for the first time, and since then their week-end visits had become one of the most regular and dependable things in her life. She had grown to know them and love them and to acknowledge whatever part the fact that they were homeless, and she was widowed, with a daughter but no son of her own, might have in fostering their relations. Once they had brought their mother down with them, and Amy knew the story of their mother and father and the separation. She had been able to gauge the bitterness of their feeling about it not so much by anything they had said, as by the strength of the brothers' attachment for each other that had grown out of the divorce.

Amy remembered their little capricious mother with her dyed hair and her strident stagy voice. She had smoked all the time. She was restless, and fond of travel. She was also vain. It was evident that when she was young she had had a hard kind of beauty, and refused to realize that she had lost it. Amy could see that love had never penetrated her immense vanity — that she had never loved

her husband or her sons. At the time when her sons began to look
to her for companionship, they found their mother completely absorbed in despising her husband. They had told Amy a good deal
about their parents — how their father tired in the end of giving his
wife the adoration and flattery that had sustained their relation, and
she took his silence for abuse; how their love came to an absolute
end, and in its place they began to nourish a hatred that was more
various and absorbing than their love had ever been, so that all
family gatherings became very uncomfortable, for if there was not
an open quarrel at the dinner table there was a silent tension worse
than the tears and the screaming. The boys were young enough to
be greatly upset by the growth of this hatred, and in trying to make
something out of their own lives, to bring some peace and order into
the household, they became deeply attached to each other.

By the time Kenneth was twenty and Tom seventeen, it was clear
that their parents couldn't live together any longer. There was one
night when their mother became hysterical. They did not pity her.
They did not sympathize with her. They saw her standing at the
head of the stairs with her hair down over her shoulders, screaming
and screaming and screaming. After that their father had gone to
live in a hotel, and preparations were made for a divorce. The
divorce proceedings, with the stale smell of cigars in the courthouse
corridor, brought the brothers still closer together, and when it was
all over and their home had been emptied and put up for sale, they
took a small apartment in the city, where Kenneth had found a job.
Shortly afterward, their father had died, and their mother had gone
to California to live with an elderly, well-to-do aunt.

It was during the months following the divorce that Amy met
the brothers. Before they had begun to visit her, such social life as
they had was in the saloons along Howard Street. She welcomed
them to the farm, and as she liked having them about and thought
their companionship would be good for her daughter, they had a
standing invitation to come back there whenever they wanted to.
She knew how deeply men enjoy a familiar room, and she had given
them that room. When she walked down the hallway with them
and saw the lamps in the kitchen and smelled the baking bread and
heard the rattle of crockery, she was as conscious of their pleasure
as if she were walking through the streets of a strange town and
were observing all this from the cold.

She wondered whether anything would come of the brothers' visits beyond mere friendship. They were good-looking and attractive and liked being with women, though they were obviously not dependent on them. She would be glad, she thought, if her daughter were to marry one of them, but she doubted if this would happen, for Tom and Kenneth were so engrossed in the life they had managed to shape together out of the wreck of their expectations, and so devoted to each other, that they seemed to think of Jane and herself only as casual week-end companions. She did not resent this, and she was as happy as if it were her own sons she was expecting when she heard the klaxon and saw their Ford coming up the drive.

The police dog loped down the dusty road and began to bark at the wheels of the car.

'Hullo, Fritz,' Tom called to him.

'Hullo, boy. Hullo, there.'

Then they stopped the car in front of the barn, and Amy walked across the drive and embraced them as they got out.

'Hullo, strangers.'

'Hullo, darling.' ·

'Hullo, hullo.'

'It's awfully good to see you,' she said. 'Where've you been keeping yourselves? I thought you'd forgotten all about me — all about me. Account for yourselves. What have you been doing? Why weren't you down last week? What's your excuse?' She took the arms of both and held them warmly.

'Well you see, Amy, it was this way. The car ——'

Her laughter interrupted Kenneth. 'You can't blame it on the car again,' she said.

'But really, Amy. We tried to put in a new head gasket, and we got the head off and ——'

'Well, it's good to have you back again,' she said, 'even if you do forget me. You both look fine. You're getting thinner, Tom. I don't know where Jane is,' she said as they started across the lawn. 'She's been talking about you all week, and now that you've come, she's not here, of course. Well, tell me what you've been doing. I haven't seen a strange face for two weeks.'

Arm in arm the three walked up the lawn and crossed the porch to the other side of the house, which had a view of the broad, slow river and the hills. The sun had gone down, and the light in the west was beginning to whiten and harden, and against this the hills were very dark.

'Well, is there any news from the city?' Amy asked. 'I haven't read a paper all week. Walter still sends down the *Times*, but I don't look at it. I shouldn't have known if war had been declared all over Europe. And I shouldn't have cared, I suppose,' she added.

After the excitement of greeting was over, she looked around for Jane and wondered where she was. She had always been there to meet them when they came.

'Well, have the big Powers declared war?' she asked.

'There hasn't been any declaration,' Kenneth said, 'but the newspapers keep drumming up the war scare. Where is Germany marching? Where is Italy marching? Where is Russia marching? Battles in Spain and riots in lots of places.'

He also wondered where Jane was. He knew she wasn't in the house for she would have been playing the phonograph, or he would have heard her slamming a door. But he didn't miss her.

'I don't read the papers any longer,' Amy said. 'I don't know why . . .'

She was interrupted by the sound of a rider. They turned and saw Jane galloping her horse across the field and into the road.

'Oh, there's Jane,' Amy said. 'I wondered where she was.'

'I wouldn't want to be in Europe this winter,' Kenneth said.

'Neither would I.'

Between their sentences they could hear Jane's distant, clear voice — she was talking affectionately to the mare as she unsaddled her and led her into the stall. Then they heard her whistling as she crossed the lawn and came up the porch steps.

'Hullo.'

'Hullo, Jane.'

'Hullo, you strangers, you deceivers. Where've you been all the time?'

She embraced both of them and sat down on the porch railing beside Kenneth.

'It's awfully good to see you again,' she said, 'awfully good. We don't see many strange faces, you know. We're gradually losing contact with the world. Believe it or not, but I walked down to the village on Wednesday night to see the train come through. And Mother's stopped reading the *Times*.'

'Oh, see the star,' Amy said, pointing into the afterglow. 'Right there at the tip of that tree. See it? The winter stars will be coming up in a little while now. Brrrr!' She pretended to shiver and drew her jacket around her shoulders. 'I hate to think of it. Maybe I can go to New York for Christmas.'

'How is the car running?' Jane asked.

'Good,' Kenneth said slowly. 'We still get seventy out of it. It rattles like hell.'

'I'd like to go to New York for Christmas,' Amy said.

'I'd like to go to Canada,' Kenneth said.

'Really?'

Jane began to sing 'Star Dust' in a low fresh voice. Then they heard someone slamming a door, and the cook began to ring the dinner bell.

'Goody, goody,' Jane said, getting up from the railing and taking Kenneth's arm. 'Take me in to dinner, Mister? Just for practice. Just in case I ever should get to a city.'

After dinner they went into the living-room and talked, and the brothers took turns dancing with Jane to the music of the old phonograph. Jane enjoyed having them both to dance with, but she liked Kenneth so much more than Tom that she would have preferred him alone even to the company and the flattery of the two. She had been unable to explain or describe her preference very clearly, but she knew that she thought continually about Kenneth and that the dependence she felt upon his indifference or attention, and the jealousy she felt at each interested word he exchanged with Amy or Tom, were growing stronger.

'Want to go down to Larssen's?' Kenneth asked.

'Sure,' Tom said. 'That sounds good. How about it, Jane?'

'That sounds awfully good,' she said. 'That sounds wonderful. Will it be all right if the boys take me down to Larssen's, Mother?'

'Of course it's all right,' Amy said. 'I'm going to bed anyhow.'

Jane took the brothers' arms. 'We're going down to Larssen's,' she sang, 'we're going down to Larssen's, we're going down to Larssen's.' She went up and kissed Amy. 'See you in the morning, darling. Good night.'

'Good night, Amy.'

'Take good care of her, won't you?'

When they left the house the police dog thought they were going for a walk, and he began to gambol around them and to jump up on Jane. 'No, Fritz,' she said. 'We're not going to take a walk. We're going down to Larssen's and drink applejack, and you wouldn't want to come, even if we wanted to take you. No, Fritz; down.' When the dog saw that they were taking the car, he quieted down and went back to the house.

Jane sat between the brothers and Tom drove, racing the car down the rough, twisting drive in second. The night was cool and still and misty and there was a moon in the southeast, filling the mist with light. Tom drove as fast as the car would go, and turned the corners without slowing so that he could feel the body lean and the tires grip the road. They drove out into the hills beyond the river, where Larssen had his farm. The old Swede opened the door when he saw their headlights. 'Hullo, Mr. Manchester! Hullo, Mr. Manchester!' he called across the drive. 'You got a girl with you? Oh, hullo there, Miss Henderson! Come right in. Come right in.' They followed him through the kitchen down into the cellar, where he sold his applejack.

'I guess you'd better bring us a quart,' Kenneth said.

Larssen returned in a few minutes with a quart of clear, raw applejack and three jelly glasses.

'Want me to leave the door open,' he asked, 'so you can hear the radio?'

'Sure,' Kenneth said. 'That would be good.'

'How's business?' Tom asked.

'Not so good,' Larssen said sadly; 'not so good.' He talked for a little while about how bad his business was and then he went upstairs, leaving the door open, so that they could hear some faint dance music coming from a club in New York.

Jane had not remembered the desolation of the place, and it surprised and disappointed her. With the exception of theirs, the tables were empty, and the light was weak, and Larssen's smelly clothes and his long pale face had repelled her. The liquor was hot and raw, and she had to light one cigarette from another to kill the taste. The fact that the boys didn't seem to be at all conscious of her uneasiness only made it worse. She felt uncomfortably as if she were intruding into something that was only for men, like a smoker or a burlesque show. Above everything, she felt how accustomed the boys were to sitting across from each other at table with no one between them.

They gave this impression strongly, for their own relations were singularly personal and sensitive, and appeared to have nothing to do with their easy but impersonal relations to other people. The things that were important to them they did together, and by the same token they respected each other's privacy in casual affairs. In the city both had their girls, and they took them out separately, and if Kenneth knew Tom had a girl in the apartment, he would spend the night in a hotel. All this was a part of the tacit understanding that seemed to enclose their lives.

If the brothers had been alone, they would have felt no obligation to talk or they would have talked intermittently about the world that was their own — the freighters, docks, highways, saloons, burlesque girls — or about a late afternoon when they had driven into Scranton, or another when they had waited for the ferry at Levis, or an evening when they had eaten supper at a Child's in Trenton or had played a jazz record in their apartment. Even now their talk kept awkwardly returning to things that left Jane out. Kenneth would mention a boxer or a dancer she did not know, and Tom, realizing that Jane did not understand what they were talking about, would change the subject.

Jane saw clearly the indifference with which Kenneth listened to her and the eagerness with which he listened to his brother, but after several drinks she felt an overwhelming desire to win his interest. Just watching his hand reach across the table for the ash tray excited her. She was a little drunk, and she felt powerful and shrewd and beautiful.

When the bottle was half emptied they corked it up, and Kenneth put it under his coat, and they left the cellar. They said good night to Larssen and went out the back door into the yard. Jane went first, Tom following her. Kenneth stood in the doorway for a little while, talking with Larssen.

It was cooler than it had been when they entered the house, and the air tasted of frost. The moon was over a cornfield, the shocks black and distinct against the light. Against this light Tom could see Jane going straight out into the field. She walked quickly and nervously, and then she turned and looked back at Kenneth standing in the bright doorway. Tom saw her throw herself violently onto the ground, and then he heard her call, 'Kenneth, Kenneth, Kenneth!'

Kenneth ran over to where she was lying and picked her up and supported her in his arms.

'I've sprained my ankle or something,' she said softly. 'It's stupid of me. I must have stumbled in a hole. It's stupid of me but it hurts, it hurts.'

'What's the matter, Jane?' Tom asked.

'I stumbled,' she said. 'It isn't serious or anything. I just stumbled in a hole. It hurts a little.'

'Miss Henderson hurt herself?' Larssen called.

'It's nothing,' she said, and hobbled over to the car.

Then Tom started the Ford, and they drove quickly back to the farm.

Leaving Jane and his brother at the front door, Tom took the car to the barn. When he came into the living-room they were sitting together by the fire, and Jane was talking animatedly. She had forgotten all about her ankle, and by her voice Tom could tell she was very happy. 'Good night,' he said. 'I guess I'll go up.' He started up the stairs, but before he had reached the landing Kenneth called to him.

'Going up now?'

'Yeah. I'm sleepy.'

'Well, I'll be up in a minute,' Kenneth said. 'I'll see you upstairs.'

'Why don't you stay down?' Jane asked, putting her hand on Kenneth's arm. 'It's early. And you can sleep tomorrow morning. And think of me. I won't see you again till next week. That's seven days. Seven days of walking around the house thinking of things to say to you when you do come. Stay down a little longer. Think of me.'

Tom went to their room and undressed and climbed into bed. But a few minutes later he heard Kenneth coming up the stairs and into the room.

'Asleep, Tom?' Kenneth asked in a low voice.

'Hullo.'

'Want a cigarette?'

'No, thanks.'

Kenneth lit a cigarette and sat on the edge of the bed.

'I suppose it's this autumn weather,' he said, 'makes me think of winter. You know we'll be skiing in a couple of months.'

'Yeah,' Tom yawned.

'I'd like to go up to Canada,' Kenneth said. 'Colby was telling me about a run up there I'd like to try. It's about sixty miles out of Montreal. It runs between Ste. Agathe and a town called Shawbridge.'

Tom said nothing.

'If I could get a couple of days off at New Year's, we could go up then. We could go up by train. I guess it would be easier. Gee, remember the last time we were in Quebec? And we opened that warm bottle of Burgundy and it sprayed all over the room, and we tried to sop it up with copies of *L'Avenir National* and the landlady gave us hell. ...'

In the morning Tom woke up before his brother and left the room without waking him. He breakfasted with Amy and then went down to the river and pulled the canoe off the float. He sat in the stern, paddling slowly and twisting the paddle with each stroke to correct the direction of the canoe, and while he traveled upstream he thought seriously about Kenneth and Jane and himself. He was not greatly worried, though he was disturbed. He loved his brother, and this love was the strongest thing in his comprehension; but it was a love that held no jealousy and no fear and no increase, and in the beginning it had been as simple as walking into the sun. What disturbed him was Jane's desire for Kenneth and Kenneth's indifference to her, for it seemed that Kenneth had acted with a complacency and an absorption that were not like him. It was the first time it had occurred to Tom that their devotion to each other might be stronger than their love of any girl or even than their love of the world.

He purposely went far up the river in order to stay away from the farm. During his absence Jane and Kenneth would be alone, and perhaps everything would be straightened out. He rested his paddle, letting the wind and the current swing him about and carry him slowly back towards the familiar hills. When he came into view of the landing he saw someone standing there. So far off he would have been unable to recognize anyone else, but he knew the way Kenneth wore his hats and his jackets and the way he shot his cigarette butts or stooped to tease the dog.

Standing by her bedroom window, Jane had seen Tom go up-stream in the canoe. Then she waited for Kenneth either to walk to the landing after his brother, or to stay around the house and look for her. When he had taken the path to the river, she began to cry and to call him a fool and a weakling. She saw his devotion to his brother and his indifference to her as some meanness in his character. She ate breakfast by herself and took a book and some cigarettes and went off angrily into the woods behind the farm, staying there until she could tell by the height of the sun that she would be late for dinner.

Amy said it was probably the last time they would be able to eat Sunday dinner on the porch. As it was, the flies kept lighting on the roast, and she had to keep waving her hand over the platter. Tom sat next to her and helped serve. Beside the brothers there was another guest — George, an undergraduate from Cambridge whose parents Amy knew. When they sat down, Jane's place was empty. But she came in a few minutes later, looking composed and happy, and sat down by George and flirted and joked with him in a loud voice. He was pleased with the flattery; but the rest at the table grew silent and embarrassed at her laughter and talk. Then, as soon as the meal was finished, Jane dropped her attentions to George and got up and walked off by herself.

Kenneth fell asleep after dinner, and Tom pitched horseshoes with George in a lot behind the barn. Towards the end of the afternoon the air turned sharp and cool, and they could feel it on their faces and hands and on the cold iron of the horseshoes. When Tom returned to the house, Amy was arranging an armful of painted maple leaves.

'See what I've found,' she said. 'Aren't they lovely?' The leaves were red and yellow and orange, and they rustled under her hands. A fire was burning on the hearth, and the air of the room was warmer and heavier than the air of the fields. Tom sat down beside Kenneth, and they began to talk about the new Ford motors.

When Jane came in and found the brothers there, she put on a loud phonograph record and asked Kenneth to dance. 'I've got rubber soles on,' he said, pointing to his sneakers. 'I can't dance with these shoes on. — They'll never be anything like the old fours,' he said, turning back to his brother. 'You used to be able to get at those motors. I could take the head off the old sedan in five minutes.'

Jane went out onto the porch and looked up at the sky, furious with jealousy. The sun was going down in a mass of thunderous clouds, beyond the river and the hills. She could walk with him and show him this, she thought — as if the sky were her own land. She would show him how dark the hills and the buildings between them and the sky could become at that instant before dark; like a burnt match, like a burnt piece of wood.

She was standing by the railing looking up at the sky when she heard them coming out onto the porch. At first she thought it might be Kenneth alone, but when she turned she saw that Tom and George were with him. George was carrying a coat for her. 'It's cold out here,' he said. 'You'd better put this on.'

'Thanks,' she said indifferently, taking the coat and hanging it over the porch railing. Then she spoke before she had planned or weighed her words.

'Want to go for a walk with me, Kenneth?'

He looked up vaguely, unaware, it seemed, of the painful importance she attached to the question. 'I don't know,' he said. He turned involuntarily to his brother as he had turned to him for years. 'Want to go for a walk, Tom?'

'No, I don't think so,' Tom said quickly. He knew what her question had meant.

'I don't think I want to go,' Kenneth repeated after his brother.

Jane stood still for a moment, and then slipped on her coat and walked over to George, leaning so close to him that her body touched his.

'You'll walk with me, darling,' she said, 'won't you? You'll walk with me?'

'Sure,' he said. 'Sure I'll walk with you.'

She took his arm, glancing back over her shoulder at the brothers. She measured Tom with jealous hatred, and he felt it more sharply than he would have done if she had stood there screaming and reviling him with foul, bitter curses. He wanted to explain to her, to talk to her, to follow her, but there was nothing he could do, or say, even to himself. She looked young and lovely and angry as she walked down the porch with George, holding tightly to his arm. Tom watched them go under the maples and down the dirt road.

About an hour after dark, the cook brought supper into the living-room. It was cold outside, and the wind had risen and sounded stormy. But there was no rain, and from the windows they could see the moon and the clouds, colored like a bruise, filing across the moon. George and Jane had not come back from their walk. They were probably in the hayloft, Tom guessed, and it all seemed useless and foolish, for he had felt Jane's deep dislike of George. They hadn't returned when Tom and Kenneth got ready to leave.

The brothers said good-bye to Amy, who went to the door with them, standing on the stoop with a coat thrown over her shoulders.

'Good-bye,' she said. 'Come down next week-end if you can make it. Please. Good-bye.'

As they started the car, they could see her standing against the light in the hall, and then she called the dog and turned and went into the house.

The grease in the transmission was cold, and Tom knew his hands would feel cold on the wheel before they got back to the city. At Topsfield they turned into the turnpike again and drove down the familiar road. But no road of Europe or any other country could have seemed stranger to Tom. He had decided to go away.

Still thinking of Jane's glance, he saw no earthly reason in their going on together and in cherishing their habitual round, their aimless comings and goings, the little certainty they had rescued from the wreck of their home. He felt a sharp thrust of responsibility for them both — they must live and not wear out their lives like old clothes, in a devotion that would defeat its own purpose. The responsibility was intense as any desire.

On the following night he took a bus to New York. His explanation was simple. 'I can't find work here. I may as well try some other city. I have twenty-five dollars. I'm not sure where I'll go. Maybe New York. Maybe Buffalo. Maybe Syracuse. I'll write as soon as I get settled.'

Kenneth went down and saw him off. They drank a couple of whiskeys on Howard Street. Kenneth realized why he was leaving by that time, but knew it would be as foolish to argue with him as to argue with an infatuated man. They talked casually on the way to the bus stop and then shook hands, and Kenneth stood on the curb watching the bus pull out.

He went down to the farm alone that week-end for the first time in his life. Jane was there, but she showed no interest in him. His attraction for her had been the result partly of jealous pride, partly of loneliness. She was making arrangements to go and live with Amy's sister in Chicago, and had become indifferent to anything that happened on the farm.

When Amy asked him why Tom had gone, he could give her only Tom's own explanation of his departure. 'He's gone to New York looking for work. Or maybe Buffalo. Or maybe Syracuse. He hadn't decided when he left. He said he'd write when he gets settled.' Amy took his arm and they walked down the porch together, and he was lonely and miserable then. An instant after speaking, he felt as if something had been torn from his own body.

He spent the afternoon playing touch football, and did not come back to the house until time for dinner. He was very quiet at the table, and they were all self-conscious, not wanting to speak of Tom, who was in their minds. When dinner was over, he went into the musty living-room with the others. He didn't want to drink. He didn't want to race the car. Absently he watched the fire roaring up the flue. The others were reading, but they looked up furtively when he took his jacket and got up and went out of the house.

He went down the drive, and at the gateposts he turned off toward the river, walking straight across the fields with the brush and grass whipping at his trousers. It was one of the first great nights of autumn, and the wind tasted of winter and of the season's end, and moved in the trees with the noise of a conflagration. He made a mechanical clutching gesture with his hands as if something were slipping through them. He saw the dark hills, darker than the sky, and the grass and the trees and the river, as if he had never seen them before. Now he felt the pain that Tom had brought down on both of them without any indignation; they had tried to give their lives some meaning and order, and for love of the same world that had driven them together, they had had to separate. He walked through the fields clutching involuntarily at the air, as if something were slipping from his grasp, and swearing and looking around him like a stranger at the new, strange, vivid world.

WHAT HURTS IS THAT I WAS IN A HURRY

By VLADIMIR CHERKASSKI

(From *Short Story Manuscripts of 1937*)

ONE day as you hurry past a pond you hear a cry for help. Near-by a human being is drowning. You see his arms struggling to remain afloat. There is a rowboat you can use to save him. If you do that you will miss your train. Therefore you leave him to drown and hurry on to the station? Is that possible?

Another day you are on a station platform. As the train approaches a girl leans over as if to throw herself to the tracks. You watch indifferently, impartially, so to speak. The train has come in but the girl has lost her courage. She backs away in horror. You become curious and remain to watch. She is a half-starved creature, very young and therefore very sensitive about her indigence. Her face is covered with dust. You know she has not washed for a few days. Her lids half conceal her dull eyes. There are yellow blotches under them. She is a little girl not more than five three, exhausted, haggard, and thin. Her brown coat is dirty and loose around her wasted body. You reflect that under ordinary circumstances, that is, under circumstances of wholesome food and socially healthful activities, she is life-loving and cheerful, a strong, fleshy girl, eager and companionable, with bright, open eyes — fast moving, all seeing — responsive to a comical situation or a practical joke, laughing so heartily that with her hands on her stomach she bends over, stamps her feet, turns around, and pretends to be barely able to stand up. You look upon this emaciated girl and you reflect thus because you do not care what happens to her, now. Is that right?

She and you are alone on the station platform. She moves over to you timidly, and says:

'Mister, will you — take me — for a quarter?'

You look down at her with indifference, with some contempt, even. Poor, wretched girls like her look ugly.

'For a nickel,' you answer, 'I would give you to a dog.'

She covers up her face with her hands and walks away shaking
with tears. Soon the next train approaches. She steps over to the
edge of the platform and makes ready to fling herself. But she
wavers. You know, you feel certain that she has tried many times
to kill herself, but each time she lacked courage. You feel that
also this time her courage will fail, so you walk over, put your hand
on her shoulder, and as the train rushes in you push her somewhat
— she is so slight. She falls to the tracks, and the iron wheels
crashing against iron rails grind her bones and mash her flesh and
blood. Is this possible? Could you do such a thing?

One night last fall I was returning from the movies. I alighted at
the First Avenue Subway Station, and noticed the girl sitting on a
bench in the rear of the opposite platform. She attracted my attention because she was alone there and asleep, sitting with one leg
bent under her, and leaning heavily on the arm-support, her head
low, resting on her hand, as if pretending she was awake; she looked
pathetic — a homeless, unattached human being.

I watched her some minutes. She stirred, changed the leg she
sat on, and leaning over this time backwards, and dropping her
head to one side, went to sleep at last, more resolutely. The station
was deserted on both sides, it being near midnight, and I stood
riveted to the cold concrete, looking across the tracks at the girl.
I felt regret and sorrow, as if somehow I was instrumental in her
misfortune, as if the fact that I as yet worked, inevitably drove her
into the streets. Feelings come to one often without foundation.
That was a late cold night and I was returning from a wish-fulfill-
ment movie. (One need only be a freedom-loving soul. Watch the
birds. They avail themselves of the limitless expanse of the heavens.
You can avail yourself of the limitless vastness, the limitless abund-
ance of the earth. Give heed to the locomotive whistle! Perch
yourself on the caboose. Go on, travel, breathe in deeply, feel the
ecstasy of freedom!)

I was thinking of something else, feeling shivers in my spine. In
my mind there were thoughts with ugly, revoltingly cruel consequences, perhaps, because I myself anticipated the homelessness of
the sleeping girl. Perhaps so, but my mind was poisoned, and bitter.

One summer night you pass a lonely block. You notice a dog
sleeping in a doorway. The air is comfortably cool after a hot day
and you wish to stay out-of-doors as long as you can. You whistle

to the dog, but he does not stir. You go over and shove him with your foot. He wakes and whines plaintively. He is a poodle dog, American and impure, with a short hairy face, and black spots on his ears. You shove him again, in the ribs, to see if he would bite, but he only whines. He rises and lies down again a foot away, and thus works himself into your sympathy. You bend over and pick him up in your hands. He is skinny, and smells with dog-perspiration. He thrusts his head forward and licks your face. His tongue is wet and velvety and the dog-breath is pleasant. You love this dog. You set him down, pull out a chocolate, and feed him. He eats it, wags his tail, licks your hands, and becomes very much animated. You take out all your chocolates, three of them, and feed them to the dog. He swings his tail for more. 'All right,' you say, 'the show is over,' and you leave him and walk toward home. The dog follows you. At first you are amused and pleased, but he follows you for ten blocks, and as you approach your home you become annoyed. What would you do with a dog in a small bachelor's apartment? You try to scare him away. You pretend to be angry, to throw stones at him, to seem to kick him and strike him with your hands. Nothing helps. The dog runs away and whines, but as you begin to walk on he follows you. Then you think, 'If he is male, I'll take him.' You call him. He is so happy that he crawls to you on his belly, sweeps the sidewalk with his wagging tail, and when he reaches you he indicates complete, unconditional surrender and loyalty by turning over on his back. You cannot see well in the faint light of the street lamp, so you pick him up and find that he is female. You feel disgusted and you fling him to the pavement. The dog is hurt. He yelps and shrieks. With one hind leg lifted into the air he skips away on his remaining three. He yelps shrilly a long time, not with complaint, not indignation, but with genuine pain and sorrow.

As I watched the sleeping girl I thought of this and felt love for her — not the love of lust, she did not look pretty — but the love of one regretting his better fortune in the presence of one so unfortunate. I decided to go out and re-enter the subway on her side. I wished, figuratively, to shove her with my foot and to feed her candy.

Outside I met someone I knew, a young man who until five months previously had been working at my side. For three years the economy ax had been swinging, like the pendulum in Edgar Allan Poe's tale. It struck decisively without concern over melodrama or tragedy. The office atmosphere was tense, fearful. Some of us had lost other jobs before. They'd had their taste of impending evictions, of social degradation and shame, the pain of exposure before the public eye, before one's friends and relatives, in the parks, on the bread lines. This young man, someone I had learned to like for his good humor and self-confidence, tried to avoid me. 'Emanuel!' I cried when I saw him. He responded, pretended to be surprised to see me. Do not ask a young man whether he has found another job. If he has he will tell you readily enough. I did not ask him. He felt all right, he said. His eyes had become bad, of a sudden, since he stopped working. He could not read for half an hour without inducing a headache. Never had eye trouble when he worked. Funny! He wondered whether he could hold a job even if he got one. His cousin, the eye doctor, thought there was nothing wrong with his eyes.

Emanuel was bound for Avenue B. He was staying with his sister. She was all right. Her husband had had a job a week now. The old parents were staying with his brother in Philadelphia. I lived on Avenue A. There we parted.

My flat was damp and cold. I lighted the gas heater and sat for an hour reading a chapter from H. G. Wells's 'Outline of History.' Later I made tea. It was near two in the morning when I undressed and went to sleep. I had forgotten about the girl.

The next morning I overslept. I shut off the alarm at half-past seven and went back to sleep till a quarter to nine. At the office I was due at nine. I jumped out of bed furious with myself. 'I've lost my job for sure this time.' I dressed as fast as I could, brushed my teeth; unwashed, unshaven, without breakfast I dashed out, and ran full speed to the subway. I missed a train and walked to the rear of the platform, where there were hardly ever any passengers waiting. The girl was still sitting on the bench. My God!

She looked more feeble than the night before, but awake. She sat, bent at the stomach. That was the impression she made. I felt as if the emptiness in her stomach made her bend that way. She must have been hungry a long time, many days. The lipstick was dried and cracked on her parched lips.

Trains passed every seven minutes at that hour, and we were

alone at our end. The girl looked at me, down at my feet. She tried to lift her eyes. Her lids either felt too heavy or she had not the courage. I stood close to her, not more than five feet away. I felt embarrassed standing there, knowing she was hungry and suffering. I had never seen a young person look so timid, sitting bent like that, with a face so drawn, and with no courage to open her eyes and look straight at objects or at people, stealing furtive glances. I felt so uncomfortably embarrassed that I turned around so I would not see her.

I thought I heard her whisper. I listened intently, and then heard a timid, childish voice, as if she had just been through a session of prolonged crying, and was now sighing in spasms, almost as if in pain.

'Mister,' she said. I turned slowly. She rose, came over to me, and standing very close, looked downward, as if trying to ask permission to do something I had expressly forbidden. She said:

'Mister, which way to New York?'

I was taken back. She could not have meant to ask me that. I tried to think what she really meant to ask, but answered her matter-of-factly:

'You are in New York now. Where do you wish to go?'

She turned and walked back. She bent her head and fingered the arm support of the bench, nervous, gathering courage. I pulled out my watch. It was nine-fifteen. I felt furious. I needed twenty minutes to get to the office.

The girl remained where she was, fingering the wood as before, now and then turning, as if desperately trying to face me, but each time turning back nervously. I walked over to her.

'Where do you wish to go?' I asked. She faced me and, looking away, said:

'To Thirty-fourth Street. There are shoe factories there, aren't there?'

'Take the first train here,' I said. 'Go two stations to Union Square. There walk out and go upstairs and change for the uptown train. I am going in the same direction. You can follow me if you like.'

She remained silent while I reflected and said: 'I believe that there are no shoe factories uptown. There are several in the Williamsburgh and East New York sections of Brooklyn.'

The girl turned abruptly as if hurt and walked away, leaving me feeling uncomfortable. Presently she started back, taking single steps and stopping, advancing at me sideways.

The next train would arrive in a few minutes and I was resolved to board it. I intended to try to keep my job. I could have told her briefly to go to a police station and there to ask directions to some relief agency. I knew that no aid was available for single persons, but one could try asking for work. One ought to try to do something. I was naïve, as much as that. She must have tried everything and was down to her last capacity as a girl, and she seemed to be gathering courage to try that. It must be very hard, especially for a sensitive girl. I cannot know how she would feel. I am a man. But I can think of difficult situations I, myself, faced, and then assume that her situation was more difficult.

I remember one time I had determined to register for a course at the University. I am very much interested in history and was attracted by a course in the History of Civilization. When I reached the college campus something strange happened to me. I was appalled by the tall buildings of the college, the strange foreign architecture. I felt so small and alien to so seemingly grand an institution that I had no courage to enter. This must seem silly and exaggerated. I remained outside for two hours gathering courage to go in and ask for the information booth, but all that time I felt more and more insignificant, more and more alien. I left never to return, never to register for the course in the History of Civilization. I assume that the problem the girl faced was infinitely more difficult.

I wished to help the girl. I did not mean to humiliate her, or to hurt her in any way. I loved her, and loving her felt intimate with her. But God knows I was too upset and too much in a hurry to think clearly or to act delicately. I reached into my pocket for a dollar bill.

That was foolish. If I did nothing more I would have done indeed little. True, on a dollar, sleeping in the subways, she could keep herself in food, somehow, two or more days, and feel miserable to have accepted alms. (I am convinced that many girls find it more humiliating to accept alms than to sell themselves. I am not worrying which of the two ways is *easier*. I think, however, that to accept alms is *harder*.) After she had spent the dollar she would again find herself near her last capacity. It is a cruel thing to say, but it was up to her to resolve to live in shame or to resolve to kill herself. What other avenue there is, I do not know.

Here is what I often think I should have done. I should have offered to take her for a dollar. She needed to be broken in. I might have been sympathetic and nice and given her courage to go on with her new trade. Someone else might have been vulgar and discouraging in his conduct. Or I might have asked her to live with me. She could sleep in the kitchen and eat my food. That's what I mean. I earned fifteen dollars a week just then. The rent for my two-room, heatless apartment was twelve dollars a month. I could have managed.

This is idle talk. Now I am not working. The economy ax is still swinging. I can write a story about myself, too.

The dollar bill was crumpled in my hand. I walked over to her and said, 'Take this.' She looked at my hand, at first eagerly, then she burst into tears and ran away toward the very end of the long platform. I felt stung.

Let her cry, I thought. She has got to eat. I'll force the dollar bill into her coat pocket.

I had no time to be patient, and walked quickly toward her, but as I approached she ran back past me and sat on the bench, and continued to cry. I was not stopped. I walked over to her.

'Take this,' I said. 'I won't ever miss it.'

She made no movement to accept, although my hand was close to her own. On the contrary, she withdrew her hand and thrust it into her coat pocket. Her crying, however, subsided, and she said, 'I have carfare.'

I know, I thought. You have been holding on to the last of it for a long time.

'Take this. Buy yourself food.' I was beginning to speak as if I myself had just been crying. The situation was tense for me. I felt stupid and faltered, 'You look hungry.'

'No,' she said. 'I won't take — your money — like this.'

She was becoming more docile, I thought. 'I won't take — your money — like this' made me feel she was at last determined. Considering how pitiful she looked, I know I could not have been a party to that.

I leaned over the edge of the platform and saw the train lights approaching. The train would arrive in less than a minute. I felt impatient and agitated. I was throwing away my job.

'Take this, for God's sake!' My obvious irritation startled her, and for the first time she opened her eyes and looked at me. Her eyes were light brown, small, and round, I remember. She backed away from me. I tried to force the dollar bill into her pocket, but she held her hands in them. We struggled. 'Please!' She cried.

The train was moving in. I felt so provoked, I could have struck her across her face, but she screamed, tore herself loose, and ran away to the end of the platform. She stumbled and fell to her knees crying, but made no attempt to rise. I started after her.

Then I was resolved. The doors of the train were open. Nearer the other end, the entrance, all the passengers were already in. A few that had alighted were rushing out. I ran inside the train just as the doors were closing, leaving the girl. At once I felt apprehensive.

The girl was in my mind all day. I could think only of her and what she was likely to do. Upon recollection I was sure I had seen her in that place at different times for over two days. She may have been gathering courage for a great deal more than soliciting men. She was at the very least two days without food, unwashed, cold, and alone.

I often think — that is, when I am unemotional and trying to reason this out — that I should have tried to co-operate with her, to have tried to take her. What else was there for her to do? The Salvation Army? They would put her up for a week and turn her out. She had probably already tried that. There is also the Municipal Lodging House for Women. I can see her standing outside without the necessary sense of degradation, or the sheer courage, to accept such charity. And even if she had entered those portals, would she, then, have been sustained in nourishment? I have heard many stories, and I have believed the worst of them.

The problem that faces me — that is, in the supposition I had acted in co-operation — is where in this god-damned world of sympathy — that's how strong I feel about it — will you get the nerve to strike a dying human being, especially one you can love, and possibly save?

That is how I feel when I do not reason this out, when I feel this in my own heart. I dare not think what really has happened.

Let us suppose I had acted in co-operation.

Suppose one evening you walk leisurely back and forth on Irving Place. You see a girl before you. You look her up and down. You scrutinize her hips. That is how one makes a choice. A man wants to know she is buoyant. Then you face her to see if she appeals to you in the front. One likes a young face, another a full bosom, or blue eyes, or fleshy lips. Every man according to his own preference. This is a hard-boiled business.

You go up to her room on East Sixteenth Street. That is a likely location. A few minutes later you hate her. The indelicacy, the abandon of some of these creatures! You put up with it because you have to have it, or at any rate, that is the idiotic notion you have put into your head.

These thoughts preoccupied me all day. I had to have an answer and I tried to figure one out. You have flung the dog to the pavement and broken its leg. Why have you done this? Because you realized the enormity of its abjectness? That it was female? But you liked the dog. You liked the moist tongue on your hands and cheek, the dog-breath. You shoved it with your foot and it whined and wagged its tail. You gave it candy and it followed you and surrendered. You thought you had driven it away, but it had returned stealthily to follow you, skipping on one hind leg and whimpering. It found the house you lived in and never left it. Its broken leg never grew well. It found access to the cellar and lay down behind some empty boxes and firewood. There it died, and when the odor of the decomposed body alarmed all the tenants, the Board of Health sent over a truck. The body was removed, and the spot where it lay was covered up with a great quantity of white powder. The odor vanished; the germs were killed; the white patch remained. All was forgotten. Is that right?

As the day wore on I got to feeling better. The boss smiled at me. He even complimented me on my work. He was expressing sympathy at my impending dismissal. He hated to do it. He had been seeing me daily for seven years. I had been a likable companion and had become, to him, a habit, a necessity. He added pressure on the ax. It swung more certainly; it cut and severed.

That day I did not know all this. That was the reason I gradually rid myself of the unpleasant thoughts and really began to feel and to reason optimistically, finding an answer. I threw overboard all caution and schemed and planned for the girl.

I left the office at five o'clock happy with determination. In twenty minutes I would be at the First Avenue subway station. That, when I arrived, she should, perhaps, no longer be there, would have struck me as impossible. When I found she was not there I was shocked.

I sat down on the bench and sat there, no longer thinking or reasoning. I was kept down by the weight of frustration.

Later the colored porter came with a pail of water and sprinkled the platform. Then he returned with an enormous brush and began to sweep. From under the bench I sat on, he swept out a small piece of cloth. It was the girl's handkerchief. He shoved it with the rest of the dirt. The cloth absorbed the water he had sprinkled and it looked black with dirt. Having swept the platform, he shoved the refuse into a scuttle and walked away with it.

I got up and walked mechanically to the edge of the platform, as if to see whether a train was approaching. Looking down at the tracks I saw a white patch there. Something in my stomach twisted and I felt sick.

Was that your answer? You must not miss your train, therefore you leave a human being to drown? You wish to co-operate, therefore you put your hand on her shoulder and push her somewhat?

I do not know what really had happened. I know, however, that in my own mind I had come prepared with a humble answer. Come with me. Sleep in my kitchen. Eat my food.

DEAR MR. FLESSHEIMER[1]

By WHITFIELD COOK

(From *The American Mercury*)

D EAR MR. FLESSHEIMER:
It seems funny, me writing to you this way. And I honestly don't know how to begin. You don't know me. I'm the husband of Peggy Buell that works in your display department. She's really Mrs. Dave Goggins, only she thinks it's better for a girl in business to use her unmarried name. I don't know whether you even knew she was married. But I guess you did. I guess you know a lot about her, Mr. Flessheimer. You see, I've been hearing things.

I'm not one to believe in gossip. But certain information has come to me which I cannot close my eyes to. And then Peggy has finally said, yes, it's the truth. At first she said, no, no, it's all a lie, it's just those jealous little bitches in the office telling lies about me. But now she says, yes, it's the truth, so what? And I don't know so what. So that's why I'm writing to you, Mr. Flessheimer. I'm not blaming you, you understand. I know these sort of things just happen sometimes. And with a high-spirited girl like Peggy, it would especially happen.

I put myself in your shoes, and I can see that it was all as natural as falling off a log. You saw Peggy when she was a stenographer in your office. And you noticed that she had beautiful hair like gold and a good figure. You can't help noticing those things with Peggy. And naturally you thought, this would be a good girl to have model our corsets and those new Smoothie Brassières we're putting out. Well, I can understand that, Mr. Flessheimer. It was just good business. And then when you talked to Peggy about it, she was only too delighted, because it meant a raise and because she always hated pounding a typewriter anyway. At the end of a day her hands would hurt. When we were first married, I'd always kiss each of her fingers when she came home from work. That was only when we were first married, of course.

Well, I can remember that day you had told her you wanted her

[1] Copyright, 1937, by The American Mercury, Inc.

to model Flessheimer undergarments. I'd had a pretty good day too. That was when I was still selling Fix-It Stocking Menders out in the suburbs from house to house. I figured I'd made $2.20 in commissions that day. So when Peggy told me about her good news, it seemed we ought to celebrate. So we did. We got Mrs. La Fleur to put the baby to bed in her apartment. Mrs. La Fleur lives in the apartment below us, and she used to take care of little Joe while Peggy and I were working. Then I went out and bought a steak. A real big one and potato chips. And a pint of gin. And a jar of shrimps. Because Peggy is living-crazy about shrimps. And was she pleased! When I got back to the apartment, she'd opened a can of stewed tomatoes and mixed them up with bread crumbs the way I like them. And I could smell the coffee cooking. And Peggy had on a soft pink thing and looked so comfortable with her shoes off. And the room looked cozy with just the lamp going on the table we eat on.

Well, it was a good dinner. The steak just melted in your mouth. I cooked it, because Peggy isn't so good at cooking. And we stuffed ourselves like kids and loved it. And we had a lot of fun. We laughed a lot about goofy little things. You know how you do sometimes, Mr. Flessheimer? We laughed because we ate so much and because Peggy said my new mustache was crooked and because we broke a plate we'd never liked anyway. And we laughed because the Inadoor bed didn't come out right. Gee, we had fun.

And Peggy was so lovely that night. Sort of like a dream or something. And yet so real and warm in my arms. And she seemed to love me an awful lot. More than she ever had before, I think. And more than she ever has since, Mr. Flessheimer.

You know how sometimes everything seems swell, and you think everything's going to be all right? Well, that's how it was that night. Only afterwards things didn't go so good. First of all, people seemed to stop wanting Fix-It Stocking Menders, so I left that concern to take a job with an insurance company. Only people didn't seem to want insurance, either. And after a month, the company let me go. And I want to say, Mr. Flessheimer, that it wasn't because I couldn't sell it, like the company said, but because people just didn't want it. Then I spent several weeks looking around for a job. I had some pretty interesting things lined up, but they all seemed to fall through.

Well, I was getting pretty nervous about not working and wondering when I would get a job. But we got along all right. Peggy was getting some new clothes through her modeling work. Sometimes she modeled dresses, she said, and the company'd give her the samples. That was the first I knew your company sold dresses as well as undergarments. So anyway, Peggy managed to look very smart and chipper in spite of having a husband that was doing nothing. And that made me feel good, because I do like Peggy to look nice and classy. I tell her when she's dressed up, like in that black number with the big white bows, she could walk right into the Follies and knock them dead.

Then I did land a job for a few weeks. As a soda jerker. Not a very dignified job, eh, Mr. Flessheimer? But it was just to fill in. Till I got something more in my line. I'd never done anything like it before, except that I did use to dish out ice cream at our Christian Endeavor sociables when I was a kid back in Brooklyn. So I was pretty awkward, as you can imagine. I kept breaking glasses and things. Well, I didn't stay there long. I guess you're thinking the poor coot certainly has had bad luck, aren't you, Mr. Flessheimer? And that's right. I certainly have.

So I was out of work again. And I began answering ads and going around to see people who might have something for me. A real-estate firm offered me a job as office boy. But after all, I'm a husband and a father, and it seemed to me I ought to be able to get something better than just being an office boy. But jobs *are* scarce. I have found that out all right. I have walked the streets for months. And I have worked hard on every prospect that came along. Like Pete Malley saying maybe his father-in-law could take me on selling oil-burners. I thought sure he was going to take me on. But he didn't. And then for so many jobs you have to have experience. And I've only had experience being a salesman. And with the salesman jobs there is always some catch, like you have to have a car or go into another state or have a following. It's pretty discouraging, I can tell you. I wrote to my old insurance company and I said please would they take me back. I said I'd promise to sell one policy a week. I said I'd *promise*. They never answered. Finally I went back to the real-estate firm and told them I'd take that job as office boy. But they already had somebody.

II

Well, the long and the short of it is I haven't worked in ten months. But I haven't been just doing nothing. Since Peggy's been so busy with her modeling, I've been sort of looking after the apartment and the baby. I decided that since I had such a lot of time to myself, I could take care of little Joe, and that would save the three dollars a week we gave to Mrs. La Fleur. And anyway I wanted to get the boy away from her influence, which I don't think is so hot on account of her being French. And you know what the French are, Mr. Flessheimer. I guess you have been right in France and seen them there, eh?

And I like taking care of Joe. Because I sure am crazy about that kid. He's three and one-half now and the damnedest cutest little scamp you have ever seen. He has big brown eyes like Peggy's. And light hair. And you should hear him talk. He's a scream. I wouldn't be surprised if he turns out to be a Number-One comedian when he grows up. Really I wouldn't. You see, I love Joe more than Peggy does, Mr. Flessheimer, though that's an awful thing to say about a mother, and she has grown pretty fond of him. But it's been sort of difficult for her. You know what she's like. She's got to be free and on the go. And she didn't want Joe. The first one she didn't want either. That was on the way before we'd been married three months. And was she sore. She wanted to do something. But by the time we had managed to borrow enough money, it was too late. And she had to go through with it. But we lost it. Born dead. A girl. And then when Joe was on the way, she was upset all over again. But she calmed down and didn't complain much because she knew how much I wanted a baby and because I told her I wouldn't let her be tied down by it and how I'd help her as much as I could. And I was working then, and everything looked rosy.

I guess Peggy'd kill me if she knew I was telling you all this, because then maybe you wouldn't think she was so attractive any more.

Well, Joe was born in April. A fine eight-pound boy. When I could see Peggy, I went to the hospital with a big bunch of lilacs for her. She looked tired but beautiful. She was the most beautiful woman in the ward. I put the lilacs beside her on the bed. And she stared down at them. I said, I'm glad it's a boy. She didn't say anything. And then I saw tears run down her face. And she turned her head away. I didn't know what to do. I just stared at the lilacs. And I could smell them and the hospital smell, too. And I knew that Peggy still didn't want Joe. And I didn't know what to do. Because it made me feel dirty and ashamed to think of anybody not wanting a baby after it was there and everything. It didn't seem right.

Well, it was last June that I first heard a rumor that Peggy was running around with you. I didn't believe it. I just laughed it off. A husband should know better, Mr. Flessheimer. He should always be on the look-out. Especially when he has a wife who is a high-spirited girl like Peggy. And especially, I guess, when he is no Arrow Collar Ad, being short and thin like me, with only a thirty-four chest and losing hair before I'm thirty.

I did notice Peggy's manner to me had changed a little. She seemed vague and kind of absent-minded when I talked to her. And she never told me anything any more about her work. But I just put it down to the hot weather coming on.

Then one night we went to the movies. And when we came out of the show, Peggy ran into a girl friend of hers who I had never seen before. And they talked for about ten minutes, and Peggy never introduced me. Well, that made me sore. And on the way home I said, why didn't she introduce me? And Peggy said she forgot. But I thought all of a sudden that she was ashamed of me. And I knew that was it. Was I sore! And I kept getting sorer all the way home. And when we got into the apartment I let loose. So you are ashamed of me, I said. Just because I do all your lousy work for you and take care of the baby and empty slops, you think I'm nobody and not good enough to meet your friends. You are not so almighty wonderful yourself, I said. I could take Joe and walk out on you right now, I said. And Peggy screamed at me, go ahead, walk out, walk out. There's other fish in the sea. Plenty of them. And I'd be glad if I never saw you again. You are not showing me such a hot life. I quieted down. Aw sweetheart, I said. She started crying. Don't you think I want to get somewhere, she said. And be somebody. Don't you think I want nice things, she said. I knew what she meant, and I couldn't stand seeing her cry. Aw sweet-heart, I said.

I couldn't sleep that night, thinking about what had come over Peggy. I'd sit up and look at her sleeping beside me and shiver all over to think what it would be like without her.

A couple of weeks later I heard some more talk about you and Peggy. And this time I decided I better ask her. We were going to borrow Fred Sullivan's car and go to the country on the next Sunday. I decided I could ask her then, and she wouldn't get mad maybe in the country.

Sunday was one of those warm hazy days. And boy, were we glad we were getting out of the city. We drove up the Post Road into Connecticut. And we found a hill with a lot of pine trees on top. And we sat up there and had a picnic lunch. And Joe had never been in the country before, and he sure had the time of his life.

After lunch Peggy and I lazed around under those pine trees and watched the kid playing. And it was cool under them because the sun just came through in little bits. I reached out my arm and took Peggy's hand in mine. I waited a minute. And then I said, honey, I heard something I want to ask you about. And she said, yeh? And I said, I heard something about you and Mr. Flessheimer. I heard he was taking you places and buying you clothes. And that's when she said it was all a lie and something the girls in the office was spreading around to damage her good name. And I believed her. I suddenly felt good and happy inside. And I began humming 'When Day Is Done.' And then I wanted to make love to Peggy, but she wouldn't let me. But I didn't really care, I was so lazy and happy.

III

Well, we hung around in the country till it began to get dark and Joe got sleepy and cross. And then we drove back to the city. And that was the last day the three of us had any fun together. After that, things were sort of different. Peggy wasn't home much. She worked hard, and lots of times she'd say it rested her to stay downtown and eat with the girls and go to a movie maybe. And I couldn't blame her. She was the one who was working, and she had some fun coming to her, I guess. Even on Sundays sometimes she'd go over to a girl friend's for the afternoon. And why shouldn't she, she said? You can't expect me to be tied to a two-by-four apartment, she said. You and Joe do what you like on Sundays, don't you? She meant by that me taking Joe every Sunday to Bronx Park to see the animals. I said she could come along. I said it would be swell to have her come along. But she said, no, she did not have a yen for animals.

So you see how things were going, Mr. Flessheimer. And then one Sunday evening about supper time the phone rang, and it was some woman's voice. And she said, never mind who this is but it is a friend, a friend who does not want to see you hoodwinked any longer. Do you know where Peggy is right now, she said? Why yes, I said, at Nell Pabst's house. Some of her girl friends are having a little party. Well, she ain't, said this voice, she is with Mr. Flessheimer. And she is with him every Sunday. And sometimes on weekdays she does not do any work but goes right to Mr. Flessheimer's apartment. She's cheating on you, she said, and then hung up.

Well, I thought maybe it was a joke or just some mean person. But I called up Nell Pabst. And Peggy was not there, and there was not a party.

I didn't know what to do. I put Joe to bed, and then I waited up. By midnight Peggy wasn't home. I undressed and sat in the dark waiting. I got scared and I smoked one cigarette after the other. And I kept thinking what that woman had said about Peggy going to your apartment. And I thought, after all she is a wife and mother and she would not do things like that.

And at five in the morning Peggy came in. And she had more than a few drinks under her belt. And she had on a beautiful white dress that glistened all over that I had not seen before. She slammed the door and turned on the center chandelier. And the light hurt my eyes. And I had to squint. And I felt silly sitting there in all that light in my underclothes. Peggy said, well, you're a pretty picture. And I asked her where had she been. You know where I been, she said. Yes, I know all right, I said. You been at Mr. Flessheimer's. She just kicked off her shoes and sat on the bed. Haven't you, I said. You bet, she said. Peggy, I said, is it true about you going around with Mr. Flessheimer and going to his apartment and all that? Peggy said, of course it's true, you goddam fool, so what? I could not say anything. Peggy fell back on the bed and went right to sleep with her clothes on. I turned out the light. I stood and looked down at her. I couldn't really see her but I could hear her breathing heavy. And I thought she couldn't know what she was doing. She couldn't know.

Well, when Peggy got up a few hours later, she had a fine hangover. And she didn't say anything about what we had talked about when she came home. And I hoped maybe she had forgotten it, because I didn't want to say anything about it either. It made me sick.

But she hadn't forgotten it. Because when she left she said she wouldn't be home for dinner that night. And I asked her where was she going. And she said, to Mr. Flessheimer's and what are you going to do about it? I didn't answer her. She said, I'll tell you what you are going to do, wise guy. Nothing. And some day Mr. Flessheimer is going to take me to Miami or Paris maybe. And you are not going to do anything then either. Not if you know what's good for you. I got a right to live my own life. See?

Well, I guess she was joking when she said that about Miami and Paris. But it scared me. And I kept thinking what if it was true. I couldn't stand it, I couldn't stand it!

IV

Listen, Mr. Flessheimer, I have not got any friends. You know, real close ones like you can talk to. Bert Munn he was the one real close pal I had, but he went to Texas and he never writes. So I have not got any one. Only Peggy. And I need her, Mr. Flessheimer. I need her more than you do. And I think Peggy could be happy with me if you'd only let her alone and not turn her head. Honest I do, Mr. Flessheimer. Something's bound to break for me one of these days. There must be a job for me somewhere. And sooner or later I'll find it. And then maybe Peggy will treat me nice like she used to. Because she's a good girl at heart. Honest she is.

So I'm writing this to you, because I don't know what else to do. If this was the movies, I'd go out and shoot you. But I don't want to shoot you. And even if I did, I don't know where I'd get a gun. Or if I had a lot of money, I could try to beat you at your own game. Or if I had a lot of sex appeal maybe I could hold her that way. But I guess I have not got a lot of sex appeal. But anyway I love Peggy. I love her so much.

Jesus, Mr. Flessheimer, I can't write any more. I'm all choked up. I hope you get what I'm trying to say. I don't know what to do. I don't know which way to turn. Please, please, Mr. Flessheimer, don't take Peggy away from me. Just give me a break, will you?

Sincerely,

Your humble servant,

DAVE GOGGINS

NIGGERS ARE SUCH LIARS[1]

By RICHARD PAULETT CREYKE

(From *Story*)

JEB and Everett suspected that Anderson, the nigger that cooked for the camp, went in swimming in the lake late at night after all the boys were in bed. They never spoke of it to the other fellows, but they were forever kidding him about it. Anderson, however, always denied it, complaining: 'Nothin' of the so't. You knows ah cain't swim. An' anyway, niggers ain't 'lowed to go in dere.'

The boys didn't believe him, though, and Jeb had kept a mischievous eye ever on the alert for a chance to show up Anderson and have some fun at the same time. Now that the time had come, and, speaking in that manner which in a thirteen-year-old boy always means trouble, he had advised Everett to come with him and be in on the fun. But he wouldn't confide his plans.

It was about three o'clock in the afternoon when the two boys, together with Anderson, went down to the small pier adjacent to the cabin which they, with eight other boys, had rented to keep camp for a month. Jeb was stripped down to his swimming trunks, but Anderson was sporting his red-brown Sunday suit, colorful in itself but forming a drab background against his intense blue tie. The canoe and the rowboat were both tied up to the pier. Jeb winked to Everett and started to climb down into the canoe. Anderson, who was strutting toward the rowboat, stopped.

'Hyeah!' he exclaimed. 'Ain't nobody gonna git me in dat thing. Wha's 'a matter wi' de rowboat?'

Jeb was prepared to meet that objection, but he found it hard to keep from laughing. 'I promised some fellers I'd bring the canoe over this afternoon, an' I ain't goin' 'cross twice.'

'Dem things is pow'ful easy to spill.'

'There's nothing wrong with it,' said Jeb. 'Come on if you want to get across. I ain't got all day.' He picked up the paddle and took his seat.

Anderson still looked uneasy, but he finally gave in. 'All right,' he said, 'but you be mighty ca'eful.'

Everett chuckled as he untied the rope. Then he stood on the pier and watched the canoe closely; he had a pretty good idea of what was up. Jeb was stroking smoothly now, and the canoe was skimming along over the not-too-blue waters of the lake. Anderson was holding onto the sides for all he was worth. When the canoe was about a hundred yards out from the shore Everett saw that Jeb was beginning to stroke slower and slower. Then he took the paddle out of the water. Now for the fun.

Anderson's big thick lips began to move. Everett laughed and looked across the lake to see if anybody was looking. There were only three or four people in the water at the time, and none of them seemed to be paying any attention. But Doc Hilton, the Red Cross instructor, looked as though he was watching pretty closely from his perch on top of the bathhouse. But then he wouldn't say anything; he was a good sport.

Jeb was pointing over to the boathouse when Everett looked back at the canoe. Anderson stopped talking and turned around. Jeb stood up. Anderson turned back quickly and started to yell. Then he got up and started toward Jeb. Everett couldn't see exactly what happened, but in another second the canoe was turned over. Jeb managed to make some sort of a dive, but Anderson fell on his back. Everett laughed. Now Anderson would have to show them that he could swim. And his best Sunday suit — Jeb certainly did fix it up!

Anderson's head appeared above the water. He started flapping his arms and hollering. Then he went under again. Jeb popped up about twenty-five yards away and started swimming back toward the canoe, looking all around the surface of the water. Then he turned aside and picked up the paddle.

Where was Anderson? Everett stopped laughing. He hadn't come up yet. Maybe he was swimming under water, just to fool them. The boy looked across the lake. Doc Hilton was hurrying down from his watch.

In the water, Jeb was climbing onto the overturned canoe. He looked around the lake and then peered down into the water. Everett heard him call, 'Anderson! Hey, Anderson!'

Doc had gotten into the Red Cross boat by now. With him was

one of the fellows who had been on the bathhouse porch. Jeb was screaming. Everett hurried to untie the rowboat and started out to Jeb. Anderson hadn't come up yet. Nobody could swim under water that long — especially with all his clothes on. Besides, Anderson had always said he couldn't swim. Of course you wouldn't be sure of that; niggers are such liars —

Jeb was still screaming: 'Hey, Doc! Hurry up.'

When Everett got within shouting distance he called out, 'What's happened to Anderson?'

Jeb shouted back: 'I don't know. Can't see him anywhere.... Hey! Anderson.'

Everett drew up alongside the canoe. Jeb was nervous, awful nervous — he could see that. There was gooseflesh all over his legs and chest. 'What'd you do to him? Why hasn't he come up?'

'I don't know. I jes' turned over the boat and — say, Ev, you don't s'pose ——' He stopped, as though he was afraid to say any more. But Everett knew what he was going to say. He was thinking the same thing.

Jeb called out to the boat approaching from the opposite shore: 'Doc, it's Anderson. He's in the water somewhere. I — what'll I do?'

'Nothing!' Doc called back. 'Keep still.'

The boat drew up. 'Now both of you boys stay where you are,' Doc ordered. He turned to the fellow in the boat with him. Everett saw it was Roy Talbot, one of the senior life-savers. 'All right, Roy,' he said, 'you know what to do.... Here, Everett, grab hold of this boat and don't let it get away.' He dived straight down into the water on the side where Anderson had disappeared. Roy followed right after him.

Everett grabbed hold of Doc's boat. There was no longer any doubt in his mind. He wondered if they'd be able to find Anderson. 'Do you think ——?' He decided not to say anything about it. Jeb wasn't listening, anyway; he was staring at the water where the men had dived in. Everett watched them as they kept diving down and coming up. They kept almost perfect time — one going down as the other came up. It seemed like an awfully long time. It must be a real job to find a man in water as deep as that — and it *was* deep, too. He'd heard Doc say that in some places it was over forty feet deep — and with a slimy mud bottom that was dangerous because of the old logs and other débris stuck in it.

Jeb had tried to speak with Doc once, but he wouldn't listen. Then he sat down in the boat. He was still glaring down into the water. After a while he said, 'I'll hold that boat for you for a while, Ev, if you want me to.' His voice sounded dry. Everett said it was all right; he didn't mind.

Finally Doc came up with Anderson. Then Roy came up and they laid the body in the Red Cross boat. Just to look at it made Everett feel like he was going to be sick. The awful white of the eyes against the black skin. And the Sunday suit and once-slick hair covered with ugly green mud. 'All right,' Doc said; 'you boys follow me in to shore.... Roy, get to work on Anderson. I'll row in.'

Roy pulled off Anderson's water-soaked coat and tie and started giving him artificial respiration. Both boats started for the shore. There was no sound other than the noise of the oars as they struck the water and Roy's grunts as he threw his weight forward on Anderson's lungs.

When they were getting out of the boats, Doc turned to the boys. 'Don't either of you go away. I want to see you.'

Everett almost wanted to laugh; that was so funny. As if either of them was thinking about going anywhere. 'All right,' said Jeb. 'But Doc, is he —?'

'I'll talk to you later. Now both of you go in the bathhouse and keep quiet. Keep quiet, understand? Don't talk to a soul.'

Everett saw Doc go over and relieve Roy, who had laid Anderson out on the beach and continued to work on him. Then he and Jeb went into the bathhouse. They heard a car start up and race down the road to town. The other boys who were in swimming had gathered around, and Doc was yelling for them to get back and give him air.

Then Mr. Clayton, the man who kept the bathhouse, said, 'Come on in here, boys.' They put on the sweaters he gave them. 'I'll send somebody across to your camp for some of your clothes.'

Everett said, 'Thanks.' He looked at his companion. Jeb was staring down into the floor. He was half-way crying, and looked sad in the heavy blue sweater that was much too big for him. And he was a lot whiter than Everett had ever seen him before. They both had a lot of time to think. But Everett couldn't make it out. He wanted to find out exactly what had happened, yet he knew Jeb didn't want to talk about it. But whatever it was, it was meant to be a joke. That's what he bad been there for — to see the fun. But Anderson had — he must have gotten a stomach cramp. That was it, he —— No, it was too long after dinner ——

Mr. Clayton brought their clothes. They dressed....

It was half an hour later by Mr. Clayton's clock when they heard a car come up the road. Someone called, 'Where is he?' Jeb looked up. In another moment his father burst into the bathhouse.

'Jeb! Are you all right, Jeb?'

Jeb jumped up to greet him. 'I guess so — Gosh! dad, I'm glad you've come.'

'How about you, Everett?'

'Yes, sir. I'm all right. It's Anderson. He ——'

'Yes, I know,' Mr. Turner said quickly. 'We brought Doctor Harrison out with us. Now you both stay here; I'm going out. But whatever happens talk to no one till I get back. No one, understand?' He hurried outside.

Jeb turned and talked to Everett for the first time. 'Everett, do you — will dad —?' He was trembling a little. 'I mean — what do you think he'll do?'

'What? Why — nothing. It wasn't your fault. You — it was a jo ——'

'I know, but it was too my fault.'

'But Anderson, he ——'

'I turned it over. I knew I was gonna turn it over when I left shore. I had it all planned ahead ——' He started. 'Oh! That makes it worse, don't it?'

'What?'

'When — it's all planned. When — when you've thought it all out.'

'What do you mean?'

'I mean when you kill somebody, isn't it worse —?'

Everett cut in. 'Kill somebody?' He hadn't thought of it that way.

'Yes. If it's — you know, like in detective stories. If it's first degree, they ——'

'But you didn't kill him.'

'Yes, I did.'

'But he isn't — I mean — you're not sure.'

'But even if he's not they'll say I tried. I can't ——'

Mr. Turner came back into the house. He, too, looked pale.

Jeb spoke up. 'Dad ——'

'Yes, son?'

'Dad, is he — dead?'

'That's what the doctor says.'

Jeb sank into a chair. 'Then I — that means I ——'

'Keep quiet!' Mr. Turner said sternly. 'Don't get any fool ideas into your head. That goes for you too, Everett.'

The others came in quietly. They must have given up Anderson — It seemed to Everett that there were an awful lot of them. But there weren't, of course. Doctor Harrison was talking to Doc Hilton. 'It couldn't possibly have been anything else. No sign ——'

Doc Hilton nudged him to keep quiet. 'I think we'd better go into the back room and talk this over. All right, Clay?'

'Sure. Go ahead, Doc,' Mr. Clayton said.

Doc called, 'All right, boys.'

Jeb and Everett went into the back room, and Mr. Turner and Roy and the two doctors followed them. Doc Hilton wouldn't let anybody else in. 'Will you see that nobody hangs around this door, Clay?' He shut the door. 'Now,' he said, 'let's get at this thing.'

'I hope you understand ——' began Mr. Turner.

Doc looked straight at him. 'I'm sure we all understand.'

Jeb was standing as close to his father as he could get.

'You say you saw the whole thing from your watch?' asked Mr. Turner.

Doc answered, 'Yes.'

'Well, suppose you ——'

'I'd rather have Jeb tell us first.'

'All right. Jeb, tell us what happened.'

'I — I don't know, Dad.' He was fighting hard to keep from crying.

'None of that, now. I want the truth. How did you happen to have Anderson in the boat with you?'

'Well, Anderson, he ——'

Everett spoke up. 'I can tell you ——' He stopped. He was sorry he had spoken. Maybe Jeb — but no, Jeb was planning to tell the truth. He was just having a hard time getting the words out.

'Were you with him?' asked Mr. Turner.

'No, sir. I was standing on the pier. Jeb was rowin' Anderson across the lake so's he could hook a ride to town.'

'I see.'

Jeb broke in. 'And when we got in the middle of the lake I turned the boat over.'

His father looked shocked. 'You don't mean you deliberately turned it over?'

'Yes, sir.'

'What made you do that?'

'It was a joke. I swear it was only a joke. We wanted to show Anderson — and he had his best clothes on and all ——' Jeb broke off.

Doc Hilton was watching Jeb's father. As Mr. Turner turned, their eyes met. Doc wrinkled up his forehead. Then, after a moment, he nodded.

Mr. Turner looked worried. He was biting his lip. Then he turned to Jeb and said sternly, 'Didn't Anderson try to turn over the canoe?'

'No, sir. He tried to stop me.'

'Yes, but ——'

Doc interrupted. 'But Anderson turned around just then. I saw the whole thing from my watch. Didn't he do that to turn over the boat?'

'No, sir. I ——'

Mr. Turner didn't let him finish. 'But Anderson must have turned over the boat when he turned around. That's the way you figure it, isn't it, Doc?'

'But I ——' Jeb began.

'You don't always know how these things happen, son.'

'And then when Anderson turned around you got up to try and steady the boat, didn't you?' asked Doc.

'No, sir. I got up to ——'

'And Anderson tried to fight you off, and in the struggle he overturned the boat.'

'No.' Jeb was crying. Everett felt sorry for him, but he thought it best not to say anything.

'Anderson's one of those smart niggers,' said Mr. Turner. 'Wanted to go in swimming where niggers aren't allowed. Probably thought it would be a good joke.'

'That's about it,' said Doc. The two men's eyes met once more.
'Now look here, son. You're sure he didn't hurt you any?'

'But listen!' cried Jeb.

'Be quiet!' ordered his father.

'But you won't listen to me. That's all a lie. It wasn't Anderson's fault. I planned it this morning. And Everett was watching to see the fun.' He turned to his friend. 'Weren't you, Ev?'

Everett was about to speak, when Mr. Turner said hurriedly, 'I guess the shock's upset him a little.'

'No, sir,' said Everett. 'He's right. I ——'

'Both of you boys keep still. Now, then, Doctor' — he turned to Doctor Harrison — 'you said he had been seized with a stomach cramp, didn't you?'

'Well, I ——'

Doc Hilton interrupted. 'I'm sure that's what you said, Doctor.'

'Well — I'd say that's what it was.'

'But it — was a long time — after dinner ——' Jeb was crying hard now.

'Now tell me, Jeb, could Anderson swim?'

'I don't know, but ——'

Everett decided to help Jeb out. 'We always thought he went in swimming after dark. 'Course, he always said he couldn't swim. But then, niggers are such liars ——'

'Precisely. You can't trust them at all,' said Mr. Turner. 'Certainly he could swim. Went in every night. The boy said so.'

'I didn't say ——'

'That's enough now.'

'I guess Anderson thought he was pretty clever,' said Doc Hilton. 'I guess he was just a little too clever — or not quite clever enough.' He laughed nervously, then he looked around at the other men. They were very tense. He seemed to have forgotten Roy was there. He moved a little nearer to him. 'That's about the case, isn't it, Roy?'

'Seems pretty clear to me, sir.'

'But,' sobbed Jeb, 'you wanted the truth.'

'That's enough, now,' said his father. 'No need to drag this thing out.'

'I guess that's all we need to know,' said Doc Hilton. 'I don't reckon there'll be any confusion if there's an inquest. It's an open and shut case. And Mr. Turner can take care of the boys. How about it, Doctor?'

'I'm satisfied.'

'That's fine, Doctor,' said Mr. Turner.

The other men went out and left Mr. Turner alone with the boys. 'Now I want you to get this, both of you. You're not to talk about this to anyone.'

Jeb looked up at him. 'What's going to happen to me, Dad?'

'I'm going to take you both back to town with me this afternoon.'

'I mean — what are *they* going to do to me?'

'Who?'

'Anybody — everybody — on account of my killin' Anderson.'

'Get that idea out of your head. You did nothing of the sort. It was Anderson's fault. He turned the boat over.'

'But Anderson wouldn't do it. Why would he turn the boat over when he couldn't swim?'

'But he could swim. He was just lying to you when he said he couldn't. All niggers lie. They're born that way. Now when we get home I'll tell you exactly what to say about this. Meanwhile, keep quiet.'

'Then — then they're not going to do anything to me?'

'Not if you remember to say exactly what I tell you to. Now can you do that?'

Everett nodded.

Jeb cried out, 'But, Dad. I killed him!'

Mr. Turner turned red and started shouting: 'Damn it! Forget it!' Then he quieted down a little. 'Now come along; you've got to go back with me.' He went out after the others.

Everett got up. 'Come on, Jeb; we've got to go.'

Jeb remained seated, and silent.

'Jeb!'

Jeb spoke without looking at Everett. 'They're not going to do anything to me.'

CHRIST IN CONCRETE [1]

By PIETRO DI DONATO

(From *Esquire*)

MARCH whistled stinging snow against the brick walls and up the gaunt girders. Geremio, the foreman, swung his arms about, and gaffed the men on.

Old Nick, the 'Lean,' stood up from over a dust-flying brick pile, and tapped the side of his nose.

'Master Geremio, the devil himself could not break his tail any harder than we here.'

Burly Vincenzo of the walrus mustache, and known as the 'Snoutnose,' let fall the chute door of the concrete hopper and sang over in the Lean's direction: 'Mari-Annina's belly and the burning night will make of me once more a milk-mouthed stripling lad. . . .'

The Lean loaded his wheelbarrow and spat furiously. 'Sons of two-legged dogs . . . despised of even the devil himself! Work! Sure! For America beautiful will eat you and spit your bones into the earth's hole! Work!' And with that his wiry frame pitched the barrow violently over the rough floor.

Snoutnose waved his head to and fro and with mock pathos wailed, 'Sing on, oh guitar of mine. . . .'

Short, cheery-faced Joe Chiappa, the scaffoldman, paused with hatchet in hand and tenpenny spike sticking out from small dice-like teeth to tell the Lean as he went by, in a voice that all could hear, 'Ah, father of countless chicks, the old age is a carrion!'

Geremio chuckled and called to him: 'Hey, little Joe, who are you to talk? You and big-titted Cola can't even hatch an egg, whereas the Lean has just to turn the doorknob of his bedroom and old Philomena becomes a balloon!'

Coarse throats tickled and mouths opened wide in laughter.

Mike, the 'Barrel-mouth,' pretended he was talking to himself and yelled out in his best English . . . he was always speaking English while the rest carried on in their native Italian: 'I don't know myself, but somebodys whose gotta bigga buncha keeds and he alla times talka from somebodys elsa!'

Geremio knew it was meant for him and he laughed. 'On the tomb of Saint Pimplelegs, this little boy my wife is giving me next week shall be the last! Eight hungry little Christians to feed is enough for any man.'

Joe Chiappa nodded to the rest. 'Sure, Master Geremio had a telephone call from the next bambino. Yes, it told him it had a little bell there instead of a rose bush. . . . It even told him its name!'

'Laugh, laugh all of you,' returned Geremio, 'but I tell you that all my kids must be boys so that they some day will be big American builders. And then I'll help them to put the gold away in the basements for safe keeping!'

A great din of riveting shattered the talk among the fast-moving men. Geremio added a handful of 'Honest' tobacco to his corncob, puffed strongly, and cupped his hands around the bowl for a bit of warmth. The chill day caused him to shiver, and he thought to himself, 'Yes, the day is cold, cold . . . but who am I to complain when the good Christ himself was crucified?

'Pushing the job is all right, (when has it been otherwise in my life?) but this job frightens me. I feel the building wants to tell me something; just as one Christian to another. I don't like this. Mr. Murdin tells me, "Push it up!" That's all he knows. I keep telling him that the underpinning should be doubled and the old material removed from the floors, but he keeps the inspector drunk and . . . "Hey, Ashes-ass! Get away from under that pilaster! Don't pull the old work. Push it away from you or you'll have a nice present for Easter if the wall falls on you!" . . . Well, with the help of God I'll see this job through. It's not my first, nor the. . . . "Hey, Patsy number two! Put more cement in that concrete; we're putting up a building, not an Easter cake!"'

Patsy hurled his shovel to the floor and gesticulated madly. 'The padrone Murdin-sa tells me, "Too much, too much! Lil' bit is plenty!" And you tell me I'm stingy! The rotten building can fall after I leave!'

Six floors below, the contractor called: 'Hey Geremio! Is your gang of dagos dead?'

Geremio cautioned to the men: 'On your toes, boys. If he writes out slips, someone won't have big eels on the Easter table.'

The Lean cursed that 'the padrone could take the job and shove it . . .!'

Curly-headed Sandino, the roguish, pigeon-toed scaffoldman, spat a clod of tobacco juice and hummed to his own music.

. . . 'Yes, certainly yes to your face, master padrone . . . and behind, this to you and all your kind!'

The day, like all days, came to an end. Calloused and bruised bodies sighed, and numb legs shuffled towards shabby railroad flats. . . .

'Ah, *bella casa mio.* Where my little freshets of blood, and my good woman await me. Home where my broken back will not ache so. Home where midst the monkey chatter of my piccolinos I will float off to blessed slumber with my feet on the chair and the head on the wife's soft full breast.'

These great child-hearted ones leave each other without words or ceremony, and as they ride and walk home, a great pride swells the breast. . . .

'Blessings to Thee, oh Jesus. I have fought winds and cold. Hand to hand I have locked dumb stones in place and the great building rises. I have earned a bit of bread for me and mine.'

The mad day's brutal conflict is forgiven, and strained limbs prostrate themselves so that swollen veins can send the yearning blood coursing and pulsating deliciously as though the body mountained leaping streams.

The job alone remained behind . . . and yet, they too, having left the bigger part of their lives with it. The cold ghastly beast, the Job, stood stark, the eerie March wind wrapping it in sharp shadows of falling dusk.

That night was a crowning point in the life of Geremio. He bought a house! Twenty years he had helped to mold the New World. And now he was to have a house of his own! What mattered that it was no more than a wooden shack? It was his own!

He had proudly signed his name and helped Annunziata to make her x on the wonderful contract that proved them owners. And she was happy to think that her next child, soon to come, would be born under their own rooftree. She heard the church chimes, and cried to the children: 'Children, to bed! It is near midnight. And remember, shut-mouth to the *paesanos!* Or they will send the evil eye to our new home even before we put foot.'

The children scampered off to the icy yellow bedroom where three slept in one bed and three in the other. Coltishly and friskily they kicked about under the covers; their black iron-cotton stockings not removed ... what! and freeze the peanut-little toes?

Said Annunziata, 'The children are so happy, Geremio; let them be, for even I would a Tarantella dance.' And with that she turned blushing. He wanted to take her on her word. She patted his hands, kissed them, and whispered, 'Our children will dance for us ... in the American style some day.'

Geremio cleared his throat and wanted to sing. 'Yes, with joy I could sing in a richer feeling than the great Caruso.' He babbled little old country couplets and circled the room until the tenant below tapped the ceiling.

Annunziata whispered: 'Geremio, to bed and rest. Tomorrow is a day for great things ... and the day on which our Lord died for us.'

The children were now hard asleep. Heads under the cover, over ... moist noses whistling, and little damp legs entwined.

In bed Geremio and Annunziata clung closely to each other. They mumbled figures and dates until fatigue stilled their thoughts. And with chubby Johnnie clutching fast his bottle and warmed between them ... life breathed heavily, and dreams entertained in far, far worlds, the nation-builder's brood.

But Geremio and Annunziata remained for a while staring into darkness, silently.

'Geremio?'

'Yes?'

'This job you are now working....'

'So?'

'You used always to tell me about what happened on the jobs ...who was jealous, and who praised....'

'You should know by now that all work is the same....'

'Geremio. The month you have been on this job, you have not spoken a word about the work.... And I have felt that I am walking into a dream. Is the work dangerous? Why don't you answer...?'

Job loomed up damp, shivery gray. Its giant members waiting. Builders quietly donned their coarse robes, and waited.

Geremio's whistle rolled back into his pocket and the symphony of struggle began.

Trowel rang through brick and slashed mortar rivets were machine-gunned fast with angry grind Patsy number one check Patsy number two check the Lean three check Vincenzo four steel bellowed back at hammer donkey engines coughed purple Ashes-ass Pietro fifteen chisel point intoned stone thin steel whirred and wailed through wood liquid stone flowed with dull rasp through iron veins and hoist screamed through space Carmine the Fat twenty-four and Giacomo Sangini check.... The multitudinous voices of a civilization rose from the surroundings and melded with the efforts of the Job.

To the intent ear, Nation was voicing her growing pains, but, hands that create are attached to warm hearts and not to calculating minds. The Lean as he fought his burden on looked forward to only one goal, the end. The barrow he pushed, he did not love. The stones that brutalized his palms, he did not love. The great God Job, he did not love. He felt a searing bitterness and a fathomless consternation at the queer consciousness that inflicted the ever mounting weight of structure that he HAD TO! HAD TO! raise above his shoulders! When, when and where would the last stone be? Never... did he bear his toil with the rhythm of song! Never... did his gasping heart knead the heavy mortar with lilting melody! A voice within him spoke in wordless language.

The language of worn oppression and the despair of realizing that his life had been left on brick piles. And always, there had been hunger and her bastard, the fear of hunger.

Murdin bore down upon Geremio from behind and shouted:

'Goddamnit Geremio, if you're givin' the men two hours off today with pay, why the hell are they draggin' their tails? And why don't you turn that skinny old Nick loose, and put a young wop in his place?'

'Now, listen-a to me, Mister Murdin ——'

'Don't give me that! And bear in mind that there are plenty of good barefoot men in the streets who'll jump for a day's pay!'

'Padrone — padrone, the underpinning gotta be make safe and ——'

'Lissenyawopbastard! If you don't like it, you know what you can do!'

And with that he swung swaggering away.

The men had heard, and those who hadn't knew instinctively.

The new home, the coming baby, and his whole background, kept the fire from Geremio's mouth and bowed his head. 'Annunziata speaks of scouring the ashcans for the children's bread in case I didn't want to work on a job where.... But am I not a man, to feed my own with these hands? Ah, but day will end and no boss in the world can then rob me of the joy of my home!'

Murdin paused for a moment before descending the ladder.

Geremio caught his meaning and jumped to, nervously directing the rush of work.... No longer Geremio, but a machine-like entity.

The men were transformed into single, silent, beasts. Snout-nose steamed through ragged mustache whip-lashing sand into mixer Ashes-ass dragged under four by twelve beam Lean clawed wall knots jumping in jaws masonry crumbled dust billowed thundered choked....

At noon, Geremio drank his wine from an old-fashioned magnesia bottle and munched a great pepper sandwich ... no meat on Good Friday. Said one, 'Are some of us to be laid off? Easter is upon us and communion dresses are needed and...'

That, while Geremio was dreaming of the new house and the joys he could almost taste. Said he: 'Worry not. You should know Geremio.' It then all came out. He regaled them with his wonderful joy of the new house. He praised his wife and children one by one. They listened respectfully and returned him well wishes and blessings. He went on and on.... 'Paul made a radio — all by himself mind you! One can hear Barney Google and many American songs! How proud he.'

The ascent to labor was made, and as they trod the ladder, heads turned and eyes communed with the mute flames of the brazier whose warmth they were leaving, not with willing heart, and in that fleeting moment, the breast wanted so, so much to speak, of hungers that never reached the tongue.

About an hour later, Geremio called over to Pietro: 'Pietro, see if Mister Murdin is in the shanty and tell him I must see him! I will convince him that the work must not go on like this ... just for the sake of a little more profit!'

Pietro came up soon. 'The padrone is not coming up. He was drinking from a large bottle of whiskey and cursed in American words that if you did not carry out his orders —— '

Geremio turned away disconcerted, stared dumbly at the structure and mechanically listed in his mind's eye the various violations of construction safety. An uneasy sensation hollowed him. The Lean brought down an old piece of wall and the structure palsied. Geremio's heart broke loose and out-thumped the floor's vibrations, a rapid wave of heat swept him and left a chill touch in its wake. He looked about to the men, a bit frightened. They seemed usual, life-size, and moved about with the methodical deftness that made the moment then appear no different than the task of toil had ever been.

Snoutnose's voice boomed into him. 'Master Geremio, the concrete is rea — dy!'

'Oh, yes, yes, Vincenz.' And he walked gingerly towards the chute, but, not without leaving behind some part of his strength, sending out his soul to wrestle with the limbs of Job, who threatened in stiff silence. He talked and joked with Snoutnose. Nothing said anything, nor seemed wrong. Yet a vague uneasiness was to him as certain as the foggy murk that floated about Job's stone and steel.

'Shall I let the concrete down now, Master Geremio?'

'Well, let me see — no, hold it a minute. Hey, Sandino! Tighten the chute cables!'

Snoutnose straightened, looked about, and instinctively rubbed the sore small of his spine. 'Ah,' sighed he, 'all the men feel as I — yes, I can tell. They are tired but happy that today is Good Friday and we quit at three o'clock ...' And he swelled in human ecstasy at the anticipation of food, drink, and the hairy flesh-tingling warmth of wife, and then, extravagant rest. In truth, they all felt as Snoutnose, although perhaps with variations on the theme.

It was the Lean only who had lived, and felt otherwise. His soul, accompanied with time, had shredded itself in the physical war to keep the physical alive. Perhaps he no longer had a soul, and the corpse continued from momentum. May he not be the Slave, working on from the birth of Man — He of whom it was said, 'It was not for Him to reason?' And probably He who, never asking, taking, nor vaunting, created God and the creatable? Nevertheless, there existed in the Lean a sense of oppression suffered, so vast that the seas of time could never wash it away.

Geremio gazed about and was conscious of seeming to understand many things. He marveled at the strange feeling which permitted him to sense the familiarity of life. And yet — all appeared unreal, a dream pungent and nostalgic. Life, dream, reality, unreality, spiraling ever about each other. 'Ha,' he chuckled, 'how and from where do these thoughts come?'

Snoutnose had his hand on the hopper latch and was awaiting the word from Geremio. 'Did you say something, Master Geremio?'

'Why, yes, Vincenz, I was thinking — funny! A — yes, what is the time — yes, that is what I was thinking.'

'My American can of tomatoes says ten minutes from two o'clock. It won't be long now, Master Geremio.

Geremio smiled. 'No, about an hour ... and then, home.'

'Oh, but first we stop at Mulberry Street, to buy their biggest eels, and the other finger-licking stuffs.'

Geremio was looking far off, and for a moment happiness came to his heart without words, a warm hand stealing over. Snoutnose's words sang to him pleasantly, and he nodded.

'And Master Geremio, we ought really to buy the seafruits with the shells — you know, for the much needed steam they put into the ——'

He flushed despite himself and continued. 'It is true, I know it — especially the juicy clams ... uhmn, my mouth waters like a pump.'

Geremio drew on his unlit pipe and smiled acquiescence. The men around him were moving to their tasks silently, feeling of their fatigue, but absorbed in contemplations the very same as Snoutnose's. The noise of labor seemed not to be noise, and as Geremio looked about, life settled over him a gray concert — gray forms, atmosphere, and gray notes. ... Yet his off-tone world felt so near, and familiar.

'Five minutes from two,' swished through Snoutnose's mustache.

Geremio automatically took out his watch, rewound, and set it. Sandino had done with the cables. The tone and movement of the scene seemed to Geremio strange, differently strange, and yet, a dream familiar from a timeless date. His hand went up in motion to Vincenzo. The molten stone gurgled low, and then with heightening rasp. His eyes followed the stone-cementy pudding, and to his ears there was no other sound than its flow. From over the roofs somewhere, the tinny voice of *Barney Google* whined its way, hooked into his consciousness and kept itself a revolving record beneath his skull-plate.

'Ah, yes, Barney Google, my son's wonderful radio machine... wonderful Paul.' His train of thought quickly took in his family, home and hopes. And with hope came fear. Something within asked, 'Is it not possible to breathe God's air without fear dominating with the pall of unemployment? And the terror of production for Boss, Boss and Job? To rebel is to lose all of the very little. To be obedient is to choke. Oh, dear Lord, guide my path.'

Just then, the floor lurched and swayed under his feet. The slipping of the underpinning below rumbled up through the undetermined floors.

Was he faint or dizzy? Was it part of the dreamy afternoon? He put his hands in front of him and stepped back, and looked up wildly. 'No! No!'

The men poised stricken. Their throats wanted to cry out and scream but didn't dare. For a moment they were a petrified and straining pageant. Then the bottom of their world gave way. The building shuddered violently, her supports burst with the crackling slap of wooden gunfire. The floor vomited upward. Geremio clutched at the air and shrieked agonizingly. 'Brothers, what have we done? Ahhhh-h, children of ours!' With the speed of light, balance went sickeningly awry and frozen men went flying explosively. Job tore down upon them madly. Walls, floors, beams became whirling, solid, splintering waves crashing with detonations that ground man and material in bonds of death.

The strongly shaped body that slept with Annunziata nights and was perfect in all the limitless physical quantities, thudded as a worthless sack amongst the giant débris that crushed fragile flesh and bone with centrifugal intensity.

Darkness blotted out his terror and the resistless form twisted, catapulted insanely in its directionless flight, and shot down neatly and deliberately between the empty wooden forms of a foundation wall pilaster in upright position, his blue swollen face pressed against the form and his arms outstretched, caught securely through the meat by the thin round bars of reinforcing steel.

The huge concrete hopper that was sustained by an independent structure of thick timber, wavered a breath or so, its heavy concrete rolling uneasily until a great sixteen-inch wall caught it squarely with all the terrific verdict of its dead weight and impelled it downward through joists, beams and masonry until it stopped short, arrested by two girders, an arm's length above Geremio's head; the gray concrete gushing from the hopper mouth, and sealing up the mute figure.

Giacomo had been thrown clear of the building and dropped six floors to the street gutter, where he lay writhing.

The Lean had evinced no emotion. When the walls descended, he did not move. He lowered his head. One minute later he was hanging in mid-air, his chin on his chest, his eyes tearing loose from their sockets, a green foam bubbling from his mouth and his body spasming, suspended by the shreds left of his mashed arms pinned between a wall and a girder.

A two-by-four hooked little Joe Chiappa up under the back of his jumper and swung him around in a circle to meet a careening I-beam. In the flash that he lifted his frozen cherubic face, its shearing edge sliced through the top of his skull.

When Snoutnose cried beseechingly, 'Saint Michael!' blackness enveloped him. He came to in a world of horror. A steady stream, warm, thick, and sickening as hot wine bathed his face and clogged his nose, mouth, and eyes. The nauseous syrup that pumped over his face, clotted his mustache red and drained into his mouth. He gulped for air, and swallowed the rich liquid scarlet. As he breathed, the pain shocked him to oppressive semi-consciousness. The air was wormingly alive with cries, screams, moans and dust, and his crushed chest seared him with a thousand fires. He couldn't see, nor breathe enough to cry. His right hand moved to his face and wiped at the gelatinizing substance, but it kept coming on, and a heart-breaking moan wavered about him, not far. He wiped his eyes in subconscious despair. Where was he? What kind of a dream was he having? Perhaps he wouldn't wake up in time for work, and then what? But how queer; his stomach beating him, his chest on fire, he sees nothing but dull red, only one hand moving about, and a moaning in his face!

The sound and clamor of the rescue squads called to him from far off.

Ah, yes, he's dreaming in bed, and far out in the streets, engines are going to a fire. Oh poor devils! Suppose his house were on fire? With the children scattered about in the rooms he could not re-

member! He must do his utmost to break out of this dream!
He's swimming under water, not able to raise his head and get to
the air. He must get back to consciousness to save his children!

He swam frantically with his one right hand, and then felt a face
beneath its touch. A face! It's Angelina alongside of him! Thank
God, he's awake! He tapped her face. It moved. It felt cold,
bristly, and wet. 'It moves so. What is this?' His fingers slithered
about grisly sharp bones and in a gluey, stringy, hollow mass,
yielding as wet macaroni. Gray light brought sight, and hysteria
punctured his heart. A girder lay across his chest, his right hand
clutched a grotesque human mask, and suspended almost on top
of him was the twitching, faceless body of Joe Chiappa. Vincenzo
fainted with an inarticulate sigh. His fingers loosed and the body-
less-headless face dropped and fitted to the side of his face while
the drippings above came slower and slower.

The rescue men cleaved grimly with pick and axe.

Geremio came to with a start ... far from their efforts. His brain
told him instantly what had happened and where he was. He
shouted wildly. 'Save me! Save me! I'm being buried alive!'

He paused exhausted. His genitals convulsed. The cold steel
rod upon which they were impaled froze his spine. He shouted
louder and louder. 'Save me! I am hurt badly! I can be saved, I
can — save me before it's too late!' But the cries went no farther
than his own ears. The icy wet concrete reached his chin. His
heart was appalled. 'In a few seconds I shall be entombed. If I
can only breathe, they will reach me. Surely they will!' His face
was quickly covered, its flesh yielding to the solid, sharp-cut stones.
'Air! Air!' screamed his lungs as he was completely sealed. Savagely, he bit into the wooden form pressed upon his mouth. An
eighth of an inch of its surface splintered off. Oh, if he could only
hold out long enough to bite even the smallest hole through to air!
He must! There can be no other way! He is responsible for his
family! He cannot leave them like this! He didn't want to die!
This could not be the answer to life! He had bitten half way
through when his teeth snapped off to the gums in the uneven conflict. The pressure of the concrete was such, and its effectiveness
so thorough, that the wooden splinters, stumps of teeth, and blood
never left the choking mouth.

Why couldn't he go any farther?

Air! Quick! He dug his lower jaw into the little hollowed space and gnashed in choking agonized fury. 'Why doesn't it go through? Mother of Christ, why doesn't it give? Can there be a notch, or two-by-four stud behind it? Sweet Jesu! No! No! Make it give. ... Air! Air!'

He pushed the bone-bare jaw maniacally; it splintered, cracked, and a jagged fleshless edge cut through the form, opening a small hole to air. With a desperate burst the lung-prisoned air blew an opening through the shredded mouth and whistled back greedily a gasp of fresh air. He tried to breathe, but it was impossible. The heavy concrete was settling immutably, and its rich cement-laden grout ran into his pierced face. His lungs would not expand, and were crushing in tighter and tighter under the settling concrete.

'Mother mine — mother of Jesu-Annunziata — children of mine — dear, dear, for mercy, Jesu-Guiseppe e 'Maria,' his blue-foamed tongue called. It then distorted in a shuddering coil and mad blood vomited forth. Chills and fire played through him and his tortured tongue stuttered, 'Mercy, blessed Father — salvation, most kind Father — Savior — Savior of His children help me — adored Savior — I kiss Your feet eternally — you are my Lord — there is but one God — you are my God of infinite mercy — Hail Mary divine Virgin — our Father who art in heaven hallowed be thy — name — our Father — my Father,' and the agony excruciated with never-ending mount, 'our Father — Jesu, Jesu, soon Jesu, hurry dear Jesu Jesu! Je-sssu....!' His mangled voice trebled hideously, and hung in jerky whimperings.

The unfeeling concrete was drying fast, and shrinking into mono-lithic density. The pressure temporarily desensitized sensation; leaving him petrified, numb, and substanceless. Only the brain remained miraculously alive.

'Can this be death? It is all too strangely clear. I see nothing nor feel nothing, my body and senses are no more, my mind speaks as it never did before. Am I or am I not Geremio? But I am Geremio! Can I be in the other world? I never was in any other world except the one I knew of; that of toil, hardship, prayer ... of my wife who awaits with child for me, of my children and the first home I was to own. Where do I begin in this world? Where do I leave off? Why? I recall only a baffled life of cruelty from every direction. And hope was always as painful as fear, the fear of displeasing, displeasing the people and ideas whom I could never understand; laws, policemen, priests, bosses, and a rag with colors waving on a stick. I never did anything to these things. But what have I done with my life? Yes, my life! No one else's! Mine — mine — MINE — Geremio! It is clear. I was born hungry, and have always been hungry for freedom — life! I married and ran away to America so as not to kill and be killed in Tripoli for things they call "God and Country." I've never known the freedom I wanted in my heart. There was always an arm upraised to hit at me. What have I done to them? I did not want to make them toil for me. I did not raise my arm to them. In my life I could never breathe, and now without air, my mind breathes clearly for me. Wait! There has been a terrible mistake! A cruel crime! The world is not right! Murderers! Thieves! You have hurt me and my kind, and have taken my life from me! I have long felt it — yes, yes, yes, they have cheated me with flags, signs and fear.... I say you can't take my life! I want to live! My life! To tell the cheated to rise and fight! Vincenz! Chiappa! Nick! Men! Do you hear me? We must follow the desires within us for the world has been taken from us; we, who made the world! Life!'

Feeling returned to the destroyed form.

'Ahhh-h, I am not dead yet. I knew it — you have not done with me. Torture away! I cannot believe you, God and Country, no longer!' His body was fast breaking under the concrete's closing wrack. Blood vessels burst like mashed flower stems. He screamed. 'Show yourself now, Jesu! Now is the time! Save me! Why don't you come! Are you there! I cannot stand it — ohhh, why do you let it happen — it is bestial — where are you! Hurry, hurry, hurry! You do not come! You make me suffer, and what have I done! Come, come — come now — now save me, save me now! Now, now, now! If you are God, save me!'

The stricken blood surged through a weltering maze of useless pipes and exploded forth from his squelched eyes and formless nose, ears and mouth, seeking life in the indifferent stone.

'Aie — aie, aie — devils and Saints — beasts! Where are you — quick, quick, it is death and I am cheated — cheat — ed! Do you hear, you whoring bastards who own the world? Ohhh-ohhhh aie-aie — hahahaha!' His bones cracked mutely and his sanity went sailing distorted in the limbo of the subconscious.

With the throbbing tones of an organ in the hollow background, the fighting brain disintegrated and the memories of a baffled lifetime sought outlet.

He moaned the simple songs of barefoot childhood, scenes flashed desperately on and off in disassociated reflex, and words and parts of words came pitifully high and low from his inaudible lips, the hysterical mind sang cringingly and breathlessly, 'Jesu my Lord my God my all Jesu my Lord my God my all Jesu my Lord my God my all Jesu my Lord my God my all,' and on as the whirling tempo screamed now far, now near, and came in soul-sickening waves as the concrete slowly contracted and squeezed his skull out of shape.

BLACK WIND AND LIGHTNING[1]

By MICHAEL FESSIER

(From *Esquire*)

H E WAS just a little guy — about the size of a clarinet-player. His face was all wrinkled up like a California dried peach that hadn't been sulphured enough. He'd bought a nickel's worth of beer and had dunked a quarter's worth of pretzels in it.

'In me,' he said, 'you observe a man who has seen all things and done all things. You'd probably be dumbfounded if I were to tell you.'

I was wiping off the bar and thinking what a hell of a business it was that made you stand the company of a little tomato like that, all for a penny profit on a glass of beer.

'I dumbfound very easy,' I said, 'so if you'd just as soon, don't tell me.'

'On the other hand,' he said, shaking his beer so's it'd bubble, 'you strike me as a peculiarly unenlightened person, and perhaps it is my duty to acquaint you with some of the more easily digested facts of the universe.'

'All right, kid,' I said. 'That crack goes with the beer — just like the pretzels. We like our customers to be happy, but there's a limit. The next time you open your duck farm, it's on you. I like to bounce wise guys.'

'In your own inimitably obnoxious manner you have arrived at a sound conclusion,' he said. 'I am — as you ungrammatically state — a wise guy.'

'Right,' I said, 'and wise guys never are very smart, and if you were smart you'd drink your beer and go out and look at the stars before I give you a fistful of 'em inside your conk.'

'Stars,' he sniffed. 'Pooh! Verminous bits of light like cigarette butts on a cracked ash tray!'

'I'm sorry you don't like our stars, mister,' I said, 'but we do our best. Maybe you came from a place where they have bigger and better stars. Colored ones!'

'Comets,' he said. 'Now you take comets...'

'I don't need any comets,' I said. 'I got a comet.'

He looked interested.

'Have you?' he said. 'Really?'

I started cleaning out the coils.

'Aw, nuts!' I said.

'There's nothing exceptional about owning comets,' he said. 'I own several.'

'Is that so?' I said. 'What color?'

'Purple,' he said. 'All of them.'

'I'll be a son-of-a-gun,' I said.

'If you insist,' he said, 'although it isn't a bit necessary, I assure you. Not necessary in the least.'

'What isn't necessary?' I asked.

'Your being a son-of-a-gun,' he said. 'It strikes me as a perfectly ridiculous procedure.'

'Oh, it doesn't bother me,' I said. 'It's just a state of mind. Where do you keep your comets?'

'In the endless reaches of spaceless eternity,' he said. 'My purple comets thunder through the limitless void.'

'That's nice,' I said. 'What causes things like that?'

He drank the last of his beer.

'You probably won't understand,' he said, *'but there came a time when there was no more light and the dark gray clouds gathered and there was black wind and lightning.'*

He stared at me a minute.

'Then came catastrophe!' he said.

'Oh,' I said. 'That's how it is. Another beer?'

'Yes,' he said. 'That's how it is. No, thanks, I'll have no more beer. You are beginning to bore me. Good-day, sir.'

He got off the stool and marched out of the place. After the door swung to behind him I thought of a couple of good cracks I'd liked to have made. It wasn't more'n a half-hour before I looked up and he was coming in again.

'Oh, so you're back,' I said, and tried to remember the wise cracks so's to pull 'em on him.

The guy got onto a stool and reached for a pretzel.

'I've never been in here in my life,' he said. 'I'll have a beer.'

It was the voice that did it. I looked closer at him.

'By golly,' I said. 'I would of sworn you were the other guy. He must be your brother.'

'I haven't got a brother,' he said. 'I'll have a beer.'

I drew a beer and stared at the guy. He did look a little different than the first guy, but not much. The main difference was in the voice.

'Maybe your father got around more'n you think,' I said. 'There was a guy in here you could of used for a mirror.'

'Have it your own way,' he said, dunking a pretzel in his beer.

'He was a nut,' I said. 'Goofy as hell.'

'So?' he said.

'Yeah,' I said.

I laughed, just thinking of the other guy.

'Says he owns a flock of comets,' I said.

The guy looked up.

'Did he?' he asked. 'Where?'

I tried to remember what the other guy'd said.

'In the endless reaches of spaceless eternity,' I said. 'His comets thunder through the limitless void. Purple ones.'

The little guy almost spilled his beer.

'He did!' he said. 'He said that?'

'Yeah,' I said. 'But don't get in an uproar about it. He's just a nut.'

The little guy pounded his fist on the bar.

'Who was he?' he yelled. 'Where is he?'

'I don't know,' I said. 'What's biting you?'

'I've been robbed!' he said. 'Now I know why I have been restless of late!'

'Robbed of what?' I asked.

'My comets!' he screamed. 'My beautiful purple comets!'

'Oh, my God!' I said. 'Another one! The town's full of 'em! It must be a convention!'

'Don't stand there and dribble nonsense from that foul mouth of yours!' he yelled. 'Do something! Help me! Where did that man go?'

'He went out the door,' I said, 'and you'd better follow him if you want to stay healthy. A man can stand just so much.'

He got up and glared at me.

'*There came a time when there was no more light,*' he said, '*and the dark gray clouds gathered and there was black wind and lightning.*'

He reached over and speared his glass of beer and drank it.

'*And then came catastrophe,*' he said.

He turned and walked out.

I reached down and got my private bottle of whiskey and had a swig for myself. I needed it.

The next night there'd been a prize fight near the joint and there were a lot of customers. The boss was there helping me serve 'em. I worked down toward the end of the bar and two guys eased up to it and sat down.

They were the two guys that'd done all the talking about purple comets. Seeing 'em together, I couldn't tell any difference between them. They looked just as much alike as two walnuts.

'I'll have a beer,' the first guy said.

'Same,' said the other.

'Did you make him give your comets back?' I asked.

'What comets?' the first guy said.

I pointed to the second guy.

'Those comets of yours,' I said. 'You said he'd swiped 'em from you.'

'What are you talking about?' asked the second guy. 'Losing your marbles or something?'

'What do you think you're pulling off?' I said. 'You two tomatoes trying to pull my leg or what?'

I was speaking pretty loud and some of the customers came over to listen.

'This beer-jerker's losing his buttons,' the first guy told one of the customers. 'Talking about comets and things.'

'Purple ones!' said the second guy.

'What's biting you, Jack?' the customer asked me.

'Nothing,' I said. 'Only these two wise guys came in yesterday and put on a song and dance about some comets they owned.'

'What are you talking about?' the second little guy said.

'Those purple comets you birds were kidding me about,' I said. 'You know damn' well what I mean. I mean those purple comets that thunder through the limitless void in the endless reaches of spaceless eternity!'

The customers started laughing and the boss came down to see what it was all about.

'What's going on?' he asked me.

'Nothing,' I said, 'only a couple of guys who need a poke in the puss are trying to make a fool out of me.'

I turned to the first guy.

'You know damned good and well you came in here and started jabbering about black wind and lightning and comets thundering through spaceless voids,' I said.

The two little guys looked at one another and then looked at the boss.

'My brother and I just got off the train from Boston,' the second guy said. 'We've never been in New York before, so we've never been in here before and, of course, haven't ever seen this man before.'

I made a grab at him.

'You dirty little liar!' I said. 'I'll bust your beak!'

The boss grabbed me.

'What's this business about purple comets and black wind?' he said. 'What's biting you?'

'Nothing,' I yelled. 'Only this guy said he owned 'em and the other guy said he'd been robbed and ——'

The boss was a big guy. He grabbed me and started shoving me along while the customers slapped one another on the back and roared.

'I warned you for the last time about drinking on the job!' he said. 'So now you've got a lot of time to drink in, because you're canned!'

He gave me a shove toward the door. I turned and was going to argue, but all the customers started laughing at me and saying things about black wind and hot air, so I decided to let it go at that.

I looked back just before I went out. The two little guys had their arms around one another and they were almost falling off their stools, they were laughing so hard!

TURKEY HUNT[1]

By ALBERTA PIERSON HANNUM

(From *Story*)

FOR the full time of year, things were looking lean. The corn-field was nothing but a slantwise piece of ground torn up by its roots, with here and there a stalk lying dry and tramped on by soldier shoes. The open log barn cried alike for plundered horse and hay, the woods standing close by the back fence seemed not so friendly now with the cow-bells silent in it. The unpainted slab house looked starved; perhaps the few hens scratching, more from habit than hope, in the barren yard, made it seem so. A lone pig rooted near the doorstep.

'Hit's got to live till butcherin' time,' said the woman in the house, looking out at it. 'Hit's our meat for the rest of the winter.'

'Don't you go to be troubled, Clarinda. This war'll be over by winter, then I'll be home to stay, and fill that old smoke house full to bustin' with wild meat — and hit's better'n hog meat any day.'

'Oh, Davy!' The woman, who was not very old, seventeen — and looking not a day over — turned away from the sorry outdoors toward her husband, and was heartened. He was in Lee's gray, to be sure, but he was here: hers for a day and a night, anyway.

'Oh, Davy, hit's so good to have you. I wish you never would go back to that old war.'

'Sh — what a thing to say! They *need* me down yander.'

She had a quick and unworthy thought, this girl wife did, that she and the babe needed him too. And with the thought came back that sucked dry feeling around her heart which had so much been there since he had gone off warring. But she hid her fears under a little prayer and said: 'Shore, that's what I know. We'll kill us a chicken and have dumplin's you can think about till you git home ag'in.'

'Dumplin's?'

She nodded triumphantly. 'I got a smidgen of flour hid away under the bed tick.'

[1] Copyright, 1937, by Story Magazine, Inc.

And they were very gay while she wrung a scrawny fowl's neck and plucked its feathers off. David plagued and deviled her and took on generally till she declared they wouldn't be worth shucks, neither chicken nor dumplings! Contentedly the while, Matt, the baby, pushed a low stool back and forth across the floor. Once, after sober consideration, he backed up to it and sat down — smack — missing it entirely, his legs spread wide, and his eyes. How they laughed! With Davy catching the surprised little fellow up in his arms and hugging him.

An hour later found him still holding the child, jigging it up and down on his knee, with the sun full on them both, and Davy knowing to his bones the content of an August noon in the mountains, clear and hot and good to feel.

'Now,' said Clarinda. The chicken he had been smelling for an hour was piled brown and brave on a platter, and the dumplings were floating in the best bowl.

Over the baby's rumpled towhead their eyes met in full appreciation of the feast: the riotous gaiety that goes with deliberate improvidence, the full consciousness of a security that cannot last, and that sudden sucked dry feeling in both their breasts. The baby wriggled down from his father's loosened hold and made a gleeful lurch toward the table. But before ever he reached it, before either of them could dart to haul him back, a sound broke up the whole plan of the feast. The dull, even sound of men marching down a dirt road.

Clarinda stood paralyzed, remembering whispered outrages in other neighborhoods at the hands of Kirk's marauders. David slid to a shadow by the door where he could look down the road and see dust rising about as high as the berry bushes alongside, and men in blue above it. Just a hantel of them — rag-tag and bobtail, for the war had been going on two years now. They might be furriners, or they might be neighbors (mountain men were divided in their sympathy), but whichever they were, they were Federals.

With a step backward, keeping his eye all the while on the road coming toward the house, he felt for the laurel hooks on the wall where his gun rested.

'Davy!' It was protest against all violence; it was fear; it was indignation at this interruption of their time together. 'Hide in the loft.' At the same time, with presence of mind, she grabbed up a chicken that was just stepping over the threshold. It squawked in fright as she flung up the lid of a chest by the fireplace and dropped it in. 'That's one chicken they won't git,' grimly. She gave up, as lost, another which had evaded her clutch and now was flying and running distractedly in front of the advancing terror, its wings flapping. Then, imploringly, 'Davy!' as he continued to stand illy concealed in the door shadow.

The first of the straggling file of blue was even with the furthest corner of the yard by now. For an instant David experienced the same sensation that he might have in a smoke-filled woods while he waited behind a tree for some instinct of war to guide him in his next move. But that deadly casualness did not last the instant out. For the baby, catching sight of the strange men, flung both his arms about his father's legs and clung to him for dear life. David looked down. He saw the little tad venture to show his face for another peek at the moving, looming awfulness out front, then wriggle back to safety. Davy felt him, close and depending. He dropped his hand to the flaxen head. A second chicken with beady, scared eyes and a red comb was being dropped by Clarinda's resolute hands into the chest.

'Take away my plate, and you and the youngin eat.' He swung up the ladder into the loft.

Even though the soldiers could turn in any place now — for the fence out front was broken and scattered — she took time to go with him, with her eyes, into his hiding. Then, her young mouth old, she hurried the platter of chicken and all but a small dish of dumplings into the cupboard. Mechanically she sat shoveling dough bits into the youngin's mouth while he lolled against her, pushing the table edge luxuriantly with bare toes. His gaze upon her was contented; the strange men were forgotten.

Up in the loft David lay on the floor, propped up by one elbow, peering out through a crack in the logs. He did not recognize any of the intruders, so calculated they were furriners. Beside him was his gun, ready to pick up and aim down the loft hole if they showed any meanness when they came in.

But he heard an order cracked out. The marching column double-quicked on past the house, with the pig ambling out to see why, and the midday sun hurrying to hit the muzzles of briskened arms. David was surprised. Evidently this was not just a foraging party

— perhaps they had been cut off from their company. Nevertheless they appeared, through the dust they were raising, ready to drop and hungry. Not nearly so hungry as all of Lee's men looked, however.

Had this observation occurred to him at any other time except now — under fire, in camp, retreating, advancing — it would have stuck in his gizzard. But the feel of his least one was still warm with him, and the fellowiness of the last hour with his wife-woman had made fighting for some far away and absent cause not worth more than a slight rise of emotion which dropped again quickly. Abstractedly then, he followed the enemy by with no especial ill-will.

Until one, with his blue coat open and his whitish shirt showing, reached out and with a deft sideswiping of hand and foot pulled the pig into the middle of the column. There was the sound of muffled laughter and pig squeals. The rear guard marched close and irregularly down the road, with the meat that was to have lasted Davy's homefolks all winter marching with it.

Through the crack the glint of sun on muzzle made a blazing smear in front of the watcher's eyes.

From below came a quick scraping of chair and cautious: 'Davy, they're gone. But better you stay up thar a piece — I'll keep the chicken hotted.'

There was no answer. A moment earlier David had risen, on high toes had stepped across to the low window hole, and dropped with his gun to the ground.

Stealing from house to barn to cedar to fence corner, he made the woods in safety. Keeping in its shelter, he skirted the upper side of the looted cornfield, then dropped abruptly with it and the road and the blue men marching, to a cloistered level spot. Looking back, he could not now see the chimney of his house, although he was not many yards away.

Here the company halted. Immediately that the word was given, there was a willing scramble for firewood and a good deal of scuffing over who would stick the hog. One big soldier good-humoredly pawed the others off, grabbed the squealing animal, and straddled it, while another, with his sleeves up and his knife out, cleared himself a working space and deftly jabbed into the middle of a grunt.

Taking quick stock of the trees about him, David chose a tall sycamore with a magnificent spread. He was up it in a minute. Now he could see his chimney smoke, his whole house and yard sitting bare in the sun. Looking the other way he could see the barbecue blaze shimmering in the noon heat. The man with his sleeves rolled up now had his right arm up to the elbow inside the male brute's belly-slit. From his place of vantage David looked on. That was a job of work for Clarinda this winter when he was far away and the weather bitter and food for the youngin scarce. She would not pull and yank like that, but stick her brown arm in and work and loosen carefully. He did not reflect further. A single word was in his mind. War. Without any excitation of feeling, he gave a wild turkey call.

Two of the men lying on their backs at a distance from the butchering scene raised their heads and listened. After a time, David repeated it. A third soldier on yon side the fire wheeled around. 'Turkey! Boys, it's a feast!' He picked up his gun and made for the woods, with laughter and advice thrown after him.

Up in the sycamore the Confederate smiled and, with his own weapon leveled, watched the eagerness yet prudence of the other's approach. To guide him came softly again the wild game cry. It was not a big woods, nor uncommon deep, and so, sun-speckled. From sun to shadow, sun to shadow, the man in blue came on, and when he got near enough for David to see that he was a pleasant enough old fellow with food in his beard, he fired. The Yankee dropped with a bullet hole in his chest and his gun teetering across his body. He lay groaning. Davy turned his face homeward. There in the yard was Clarinda looking distractedly for him. Again sounded the turkey call, this time as if from a greater distance.

The two men flat on their backs down in the camp raised up as before and one of them got on his feet.

'Old Jo must have missed. Guess I'll have to go bring down that gobbler myself.'

The pig now was swung up on an improvised spit over the fire, and there was even more joshing this hunter than there had been the first. The Federal army's heart was growing bigger, as its nostrils filled with wood smoke and the first smacking of hog juice on the flame.

When the second man, turkey-hunting and looking up, came into David's particular patch of sun, he almost stumbled over the writhing body of the comrade. But before he could cry out or take aim or even wholly regain his balance, the second shot rang out. He swayed, and toppled, and fell against a tree in a half-sitting posture, quite dead. It struck David as an odd sight to be in a bright patch of the sun. A chicken came wandering in to share it with him. It seemed unsteady on its legs, a little dazed. He recognized it as the one which had fled wildly down the road. Forlorn thing. With kindly, absorbing pleasure he watched it snatch up in its beak an insect from out of the earth. Then, as if his cue had been given, he started, and gave at once the cry of a grouse.

Down around the fire a man with his coat open and white shirt showing, looked up sharply, dropped his armload of fresh wood abruptly. He said something in a low tone to the men nearest him, and five of them followed as he entered cautiously into the woods. David knew by this that they guessed it was no ordinary game bird that was calling from the thicket. And he experienced a confused and peculiar joy. When the white-shirted leader — the one who had marched away with the pig — came within hearing, David gave the soft cluck, cluck, cluck of the ruffled grouse which precludes its flight.

Evidently the other was as acquainted with the ways of the woods as he, for the Yankee stopped and listened, as if for the rustle of wings which should follow; when none came he proceeded even more guardedly. He was within range now, but David did not fire. His hesitation was due more to an inbred code of respect than to any present studying over the matter — the fellow was no addle-pate, and he deserved a chance.

David waited. He could see now that the white-shirted one still had down on his cheeks, and zest in him for everything. Suddenly he raised his head and their eyes met. There was the shock for a second of an actual contact. Then, the vibration still in his arms, his legs, his chest, David presented his musket. But the lock hung up and it would not fire. He jerked and yanked. The whole world was a confusion of blue cloth and shining metal. There was no moisture in David's mouth, and he could not swallow. He heard distinctly the preliminary click of the Federal trigger. There flashed in his mind all the things a man about to die should think of, but there was no time.

The splintering, crackling sounds were the sycamore branches breaking as he fell down through them, and the sound of the impact of the body on the earth was a peculiar mingling of something dead and something deeply living.

The boy in blue stood with his carbine hanging loosely from his right hand, his mouth open, the oppression so great within him he could not breathe properly.

'See,' he pointed tragically as the others came up, 'see what I've done!'

In amazement, derision, four of them heard him. But the fifth, an old man who had lived long and knew much, was silent. He kicked the chicken away from the new puddle of entrails.

THE WHOLE WORLD IS OUTSIDE[1]

By MANUEL KOMROFF

(From *Esquire*)

COME, children, I think the time has arrived. Reach me the woolen shawl and I will try to sit up. Come here beside me. Your mother wants to hold you close and she has a lot of things to tell you.... And you must listen carefully to what she says.'

The children brought the woolen shawl to the edge of the bed and the dying woman wrapped it about her shoulders. Peter, who was ten years old, was the first to get up on the bed and nestle beside his mother. He was two years older than his sister Ellen, but in many ways he was still an infant. His mother stroked his head, and he rested it upon her shoulder and close to her face. Ellen hesitated a moment and then came to the other side of her mother and curled up among the blankets.

'Now you know what we spoke about yesterday?'

The children nodded.

'And Peter will take the dollar and you will go and visit your Auntie Pauline and play with Jerry. Won't that be nice?'

The children nodded, for they knew that Jerry, the high-strung wire terrier, was always ready to play and he could catch a rubber ball in his mouth. For some reason or other they had seen much less of Jerry than they would have liked. It was a rare occasion when their mother visited her sister.

'Yes, you will be able to play with Jerry as long as you like, and you will sleep there and Jerry will sleep with you, so you will not be afraid, will you?'

'No,' they said together.

'Your mother will not be with you and so you will have to be big children. And at night if you want a glass of water or something you will not disturb your auntie when she is sleeping. Just light the light and then you will see how to get it for yourself just like grownups do. You know. And your Auntie Pauline will love you and you must remember to be sure to love her also. And she will be very good to you I know, and you must also be good and do what she tells you. She will send you to school. You want to go to school and play with other children, don't you?'

'Yes, Mummie,' said Peter, while Ellen nodded her flaxen-braided head.

'You remember, children, where your Auntie Pauline lives?'

'Fairwoods,' they replied.

'And you know how to go there?'

They nodded.

'Go, Peter, and take the dollar and bring me the box from the top bureau drawer.'

Peter left his mother's side and got the dollar bill from its hiding-place and brought the box she asked for.

'You will be sure not to lose the dollar? Let me see where you put it. That's good. And Ellen, you see where he put it so he knows what pocket it is in.'

She opened the small box that he brought to the bed.

'Here, now this is very important. See what it says on this card. I will read it for you. Mrs. Pauline Monroe, 227 Hillside Avenue, Fairwoods, New York. Now don't lose it. That is where you are going, and you show this to a man in Grand Central Station and give him the dollar and he will put you on the train. And when you get off at Fairwoods you show it to the man at the station and he will bring you to the house. Now, Peter, put the card in your pocket. And Ellen dear, here is a letter for you to give your Auntie when you get there. You see the same name and address is on it. You can keep it in your coat pocket. . . . You must be careful when you go to the station and not cross the street until the light changes. And Peter, you will hold Ellen's hand.'

'Yes, Mummie.'

'Now I have something very nice for both of you. Here, Peter, is your Daddy's watch and chain. You will take care of it. I will wind it up and set it for you and tomorrow you can wind it yourself. It is now two o'clock.'

She wound the silver watch, and placing it in his pocket attached the end of the chain to a buttonhole in his vest.

'There now. And do you remember what your father's name was?'

'George,' they both said at once.

'Yes. You will always remember his name was George. And here,

Ellen, is your Grandma's locket, but before I put it on I want to place this ring on the chain. Some day the ring may fit you.'

She drew the ring from her finger, and placing it on the chain clasped it about Ellen's neck.

'There, it looks very pretty. Now that is all your Mummie has to give you. She would like to give you a lot more, but the best thing she can give you now is to let you go back to school. She has kept you home too long and you have taken good care of her. If only attention and devotion were a medicine it would have cured her. And now you will go back to school and your Auntie Pauline and Uncle Fred will look after you much better than anyone. And your Mummie will go away on a long, long journey.'

'Far?' asked Ellen.

'Yes, very far.'

'And will you visit us?'

'I will try. Somehow or other I will try. But you will be good children anyway, and when you grow up you will understand everything. And Peter, you must promise me that you will look after your sister and always take good care of her, and she will love you as I have loved you and that love will make you a strong and big man. If you stay together there is no strength in the world that could defeat you. And so you must promise me that you will never quarrel no matter what the cause may be. You promise, don't you?'

'Yes, Mummie.'

'And you, Ellen dear. Soon you will be a little lady, and you will try and see that your brother does not catch cold or do foolish things.'

She nodded her head.

'Now there is nothing more to say because it would be too much for you to remember. Only one thing. Try and be brave. Don't be afraid. And if you are not afraid then you will be brave. It is sometimes very hard to be brave.... Now give your Mummie a good hug and a nice kiss, and go put on your hats and coats.'

She embraced her children and kissed them passionately. Her strength was gone, and she dropped her head back into the pillow. She watched them put on their coats and hats, and when they were ready to go she said in a feeble voice: 'Try and be brave. Your Mummie tries very hard to be brave and she wants you to try also.'

'Yes, Mummie,' they said together.

'Now go, and leave the door a tiny bit open; just a crack. And Peter, take your sister's hand when you are outside. The whole world is outside, and may God love you and watch over you.'

The fingers of one hand were close to her mouth, but the other hand she reached out from under the quilt and waved very slowly.

The children stood at the door and also waved to their mother. They saw her smile and they smiled back, not a full broad smile, only a little stifled smile. Slowly they backed out and Peter closed the door, leaving just a crack.

As they walked down the stairs Ellen suddenly stopped, waved her arm, and called, 'Good-bye, Mummie.'

'She can't see you from here,' said Peter. 'Come.'

As soon as the door had closed the woman in bed could restrain herself no longer. Cast iron would have melted long before this. She put her fingers in her mouth and sobbed, and a tiny rivulet in zigzag path streamed down her face and into the pillow. And now the last hold was torn away and it seemed easy to stretch her limbs and close her eyes.

It was a dozen blocks to Grand Central Station, and these the children walked hand in hand. They were now walking in the great world that is outside. Now and then they paused to look into the shop windows where toys or novelties were displayed, and when they had paused long enough Peter said, 'Come.'

Once they stopped before a movie house and looked at the big colored poster showing a man embracing a woman. This was a kind of love; but they hated this love and thought it quite unnecessary. It was not like the love their mother had for them. They did not tarry long.

At the station Peter paused beside a news-stand and bought a strawberry lollypop with five pennies that he happened to have in his pocket. He gave it to Ellen as though she were a child and he the parent.

They walked to the information desk and displayed the card.

'So you want to go to Fairwoods?'

'Yes.' Peter showed the dollar.

'Who is this person in Fairwoods?'

'Our Auntie Pauline.'

The clerk called a colored porter, who brought them to a ticket window and bought them two one-half tickets to Fairwoods. There was a little change from the dollar, which Peter put in his pocket.

'This way,' said the porter.

As they crossed the big hall Peter drew out the silver watch and compared it with the station clock. Ellen looked at him to see if he was doing this worldly business properly. And while she looked at him she sucked on the strawberry lollypop.

While walking down the platform the porter spoke to the children.

'Where your mother is?'

'She has gone away.'

'On a trip?'

'Yes.'

'Where did she go?'

'She went where people go when they go to die.'

'Lordie, Lordie. Is that so!'

'Yes, sir. She did not want to tell us, but we know.'

And Ellen nodded her head to say that this was true.

Jerry nearly jumped out of his skin when he discovered the children walking up the drive hand-in-hand. He knew now that he would have someone to play with. He ran out on the lawn and found his rubber ball and brought it close to the house.

'Why, it's the children, you darlings!' cried Mrs. Monroe, and she gave them each a hug and a kiss.

'Your mother sent you, I suppose, for she knows how fond we are of you.'

The children were silent.

'She is well?'

Peter nodded as though everything were all right.

She rang the bell and asked the maid to bring some slices of cake and fruit, for while she had no children of her own she knew that children were often hungry at odd hours.

The children were anxious to play with Jerry, and therefore they hurried through with the cake and fruit. Then followed a full hour of joyous running up and down on the lawn and tossing the ball in the air for Jerry to catch, and throwing it far off to have Jerry chase it madly and bring it back.

Suddenly Peter remembered the letter and reminded Ellen. She went to the hall closet and drew it from her coat pocket and gave it to her Auntie Pauline.

'What is this?'

'A letter from Mummie,' she said simply.

She opened the envelope and read: 'Pauline, here are the children. I cannot take them with me and they are too old to leave on a doorstep. I returned your last few letters unopened because there really was no use. You cannot approve of anything and I am sick and tired of listening to your smug remarks.

'Yes, Pauline, I married a drunkard. But while he lived we were happy, very happy. This is something you have never known, and I doubt if you are capable of knowing it. Your husband has given you diamonds and furs and mine has left me but poverty and a widow's veil. But I had the children and we have managed as best we could. For God's sake, Pauline, the kids are innocent. Do not hold against them what you would hold against me. Try not to criticize death. If you love them they will bring you much happiness. More I could not leave anyone. Your sister, Laura.'

Ellen was standing beside her aunt and watched as she read the letter.

'Do you know what is in this letter?'

She nodded her braided flaxen head. Yes, she knew.

It was then as she nodded her head that her aunt noticed that the child was wearing the old chain and locket that once her own mother wore. She kissed the child and went quickly to the telephone to call her husband.

'Fred, Fred. I'm glad I got you before you left the city. The children are here. Yes.... About an hour ago.'

'I am glad you made it up with your sister at last. I've missed those kids,' he called from the other end.

'No, I haven't made it up. Listen to me. The children are here. They are here for good. Just a minute and you will understand. Please take a taxi right away and go over. No, there is no telephone. And call me back. Do anything necessary. Good-bye.'

Fred Monroe arrived at the apartment, but the visitor Death had crept in before him. The door was still open just a tiny crack.

There were a lot of things to be done, and it was fairly late that evening when Uncle Fred got back to Fairwoods.

'Yes,' he said, 'I did everything necessary. Are the children asleep?'

'I put them to bed an hour ago.'

'Uncle Fred,' came a small voice from an upstairs bedroom.

'Yes, darling. Coming.'

The children were not asleep at all. And their uncle was very happy to see them. They climbed all over him and hugged him and laughed and told him about a new trick that they taught Jerry.

After a time Ellen, still quite cheerful, asked, 'Did you see Mummie?'

Their uncle did not want to reply.

'She told us to be brave,' Peter said. 'And so we know all about it.'

'What do you know?'

'We know she went away, far away. She was going to visit God. Did she go?'

'Yes. She went.'

That seemed all that needed to be said. The children soon went back to bed, closed their eyes, and slept. They slept soundly and dreamed of very nice things, the kind of things that hang on Christmas trees and things that come out at Easter time, like rabbits and chocolate eggs and that sugar crystal egg that has a whole village scene inside with a shepherd and a little 'bitzie' lamb.

The sun rose up to call out the morning of a new day. Jerry, that four-legged piece of nervous energy covered with a coat of wire hair, was already standing in the kitchen waiting for his biscuit soaked in fresh milk. He shook himself to get the sleep out of the marrow of his bones and lapped up the food with great noise. The drops of milk were still dripping from his blunt muzzle as he stood waiting for the children to get up and play.

Soon they were all in the yard with the rubber ball. They never seemed to tire of this game. Ellen paused for a moment and asked her brother, 'Mummie isn't coming back?'

He shook his head.

'Not at all?' she asked.

'No. She won't come back.'

'What does it mean when they say the whole world is outside?'

'I don't know.'

He handed her the ball and they went on playing.

THE GIRL [1]

By MERIDEL LE SUEUR

(From *The Yale Review*)

SHE was going the inland route because she had been twice on the coast route. She asked three times at the Automobile Club how far it was through the Tehachapi Mountains, and she had the route marked on the map in red pencil. The car was running like a T, the garage man told her. All her dresses were back from the cleaner's, and there remained only the lace collar to sew on her black crepe so that they would be all ready when she got to San Francisco. She had read up on the history of the mountains and listed all the Indian tribes and marked the route of the Friars from the Sacramento Valley. She was glad now that Clara Robbins, the 'Math' teacher, was not going with her. She liked to be alone, to have everything just the way she wanted it, exactly.

There was nothing she wanted changed. It was a remarkable pleasure to have everything just right, to get into her neat fine-looking little roadster, start out in the fine morning, with her map tucked into the seat, every road marked. She was lucky too — how lucky she was! She had her place secure at Central 'High,' teaching history. On September 18, she knew she would be coming back to the same room, to teach the same course in history. It was a great pleasure. Driving along, she could see her lean face in the windshield. She couldn't help but think that she had no double chin, and her pride rode in her, a lean thing. She saw herself erect, a little caustic and severe, and the neat turn-over collar of her little blue suit. Her real lone self. This was what she wanted. Nothing messy. She had got herself up in the world. This was the first summer she had not taken a summer course, and she felt a little guilty; but she had had a good summer just being lazy, and now she was going to San Francisco to see her sister and would come back two days before school opened. She had thought in the spring that her skin was getting that papyrus look so many teachers had, and she had a little tired droop to her shoulders and was a little bit too thin. It was fine to be thin but not too thin. Now she looked better, brown, and she had got the habit of a little eye shadow, a little dry rouge, and just a touch of lipstick. It was really becoming.

Yes, everything was ideal.

But before long she was sorry she had come through the Tehachapi Mountains. Why hadn't someone told her they were like that? They did her in. Frightening. Mile after mile in the intense September heat, through fierce mountains of sand, and bare gleaming rock faces jutting sheer from the road. Her eyes burned, her throat was parched, and there was mile after mile of lonely road without a service station and not a soul passing. She wished, after all, that Miss Robbins had come with her. It would have been nice to be able to say: 'What an interesting formation, Miss Robbins! We really should make sketches of it, so we could look up the geological facts when we get back.' Everything would have seemed normal then.

She drove slowly through the hot yellow swells, around the firm curves; and the yellow light shone far off in the tawny valleys, where black mares, delicate-haunched, grazed, flesh shining as the sun struck off them. The sun beat down like a golden body about to take form on the road ahead of her. She drove very slowly, and something began to loosen in her, and her eyes seemed to dilate and darken as she looked into the fold upon fold of earth flesh lying clear to the horizon. She saw she was not making what is called 'good time.' In fact, she was making very bad time.

She had been driving five hours. She looked at her wrist watch and decided she would stop, even if it was only eleven-thirty, and have lunch. So when she saw a little service station far down, tucked into the great folds of dun hill, she was glad. Her car crept closer, circling out of sight of it and then circling back until her aching eyes could read the sign — Half Way Station — and she drew up to the side and stopped. Her skin felt as if it were shrivelling on her bone. She saw a man — or was it a boy? — with a pack, standing by the gas pump probably waiting to catch a ride; she wouldn't pick him up, that was certain. These hills were certainly forsaken.

She went in at the door marked Ladies. The tiny cubicle comforted her. She opened her vanity case and took out some tissue, made little pads, and put them over her eyes. But still all she could see was those terrifying great mounds of the earth and the sun thrusting down like arrows. What a ghastly country! Why hadn't someone told her? It was barbarous of the Automobile Club to let her come through this country. She couldn't think of one tribe of Indians.

She really felt a kind of fright and stayed there a long time, and then she got a fright for fear she had left her keys in the car and with that boy out there — she could see his sharp piercing glance out of his brown face — and she had to go pouncing all through her bag, and at last she found them, of all places, in her coin purse, and she always put them into the breast pocket of her suit. She did think people were nuisances who had to go looking in all their pockets for keys. Habit was an excellent thing, and saved nobody knew how much time.

But at last she drew a deep breath, opened the door onto the vast terrible bright needles of light, and there she saw through the heavy down-pouring curtain the boy still standing there exactly as he had been standing before, half leaning, looking from under his black brows. He looked like a dark stroke in the terrible light, and he seemed to be still looking at her. She fumbled the collar at her throat, brushed off the front of her skirt, and went into the lunch room.

'My, it's certainly hot,' she said to the thin man behind the counter. She felt strange hearing her voice issue from her.

'It is,' said the proprietor, 'but a little cooler in here.' He was a thin shrewd man.

She sat down in the booth. 'Yes,' she said, and saw that the boy had followed her in and sat down on the stool at the lunch counter, but he seemed to be still looking at her. He looked as if he had been roasted, slowly turned on a spit until he seemed glowing, like phosphorus, as if the sun were in him, and his black eyes were a little bloodshot as if the whites had been burned, and his broad chest fell down easily to his hips as he ground out a cigarette with his heel.

The thin man brought her a glass of water. 'What will you have, ma'am?' he said with respect. 'I'll have a lettuce sandwich,' she said. 'I'm afraid we ain't got any proper lettuce, ma'am,' he said, bowing a little. 'We can't get it fresh out here. We have peanut butter, sliced tongue ——'

'All right,' she said quickly, 'peanut butter and — well — a glass of beer.' She felt that the boy was somehow laughing at her. She felt angry.

'This the first time you been in these parts?' called out the thin man from behind the counter. 'Yes,' she said, and her own voice sounded small to her. 'It is.' The boy at the counter turned his head, still with it lowered, so that his eyes looked up at her even though she was sitting down in the booth, and a soft charge went through her, frightening. She felt herself bridling, and she said in a loud cool voice: 'This is a very interesting country. Do you know anything about the formation of these curious rocks that jut out of the hills? — they are so bare and then suddenly this rock ——'

Was she imagining it only, that the boy seemed to smile and shifted his weight?

'No'm,' said the thin man, drawing the beer. 'I can't say I ever thought about it.' She felt as if something passed between the two men, and it made her angry, as if they were subtly laughing at her. 'I know it's hard to grow anything here, unless you got a deep well,' he said.

'Oh, I can imagine,' she sang out too loud; she felt her voice ringing like metal. The boy seemed not to be touched by what she was saying, but he attended curiously to every word, standing silent but alert like a horse standing at a fence waiting for something. So she began to tell the lunch room proprietor the history of the country, and he seemed amazed but not impressed. It made her feel vindicated somehow. Still the boy drooped alert on the stool, his half face turned towards her, his huge burned ear springing from his head. She stayed half an hour and so cut her time still further, but she felt much better and thought she would make up for it. She got up and paid her bill. 'I'll send you a book about the Indians,' she said to the thin man.

He smiled. 'That will be very nice,' he said. 'Thank you, I'm sure,' and the two men looked at each other again, and she was amazed at the anger that gushed like a sudden fountain in her breast. She sailed out and got into the car.

The thin man came after her. 'Oh, by the way,' he said, 'the lad in there has had an awful time this morning catching a ride. He's got to get up to the bridge, about fifty miles.' She felt they were putting something over on her. 'I'll vouch for him,' the thin man said. 'He lives here, and I know his folks now for eighteen years. He's been to the harvest fields, and it would be something for him to ride with an educated lady like you,' he added cunningly. The boy came out and was smiling at her now very eagerly. 'Now they want something,' she thought, and she was suddenly amazed to find out that she despised men and always had.

'I don't like to drive with a strange man,' she said, stubborn.

'Oh, this boy is harmless,' the thin man said, and that look passed between the two of them again. 'I can vouch for him — good as gold his family is. I thought maybe anyhow you might give him a mite of education on the way.' A pure glint of malice came into the thin man's eyes that frightened her. He hates me too, she thought. Men like that hate women with brains.

'All right,' she said. 'Get in.'

'Get right in there,' the thin man said. 'It's only a piece.'

The boy rose towards her, and she drew away, and he sat down in a great odor of milk and hay, right beside her, stifling. Without speaking she threw the clutch in, and they plunged up the bald brow of the hill and began to climb slowly. The sun was in the central sky, and the heat fell vertically. She wouldn't look at him and wished she could get out her handkerchief — such a nauseating odor of sweat and something like buttermilk. She couldn't help but be conscious of the side of his overall leg beside her and his big shoes, and she felt he never took his eyes off her, like some awful bird — and that curious little smile on his mouth as if he knew something about her that she didn't know herself. She knew without looking that he was bending his head towards her with that curious awful little glimmer of a smile.

He said in a soft cajoling voice: 'It's pretty hot, and it's nice of you to take me. I had a hard time.'

It disarmed her. She felt sorry for him, wanting to be helpful. She always wanted to help men, do something for them, and then really underneath she could hate them. 'Oh,' she said, 'that was all right. You know one hates to pick up just anyone.'

'Sure enough,' he said. 'I heard in Colorado a fellow got killed.'

'Yes,' she said; but she was on her guard. His words seemed to mean nothing to him. He was like the heat, in a drowse. 'My, you must have been in the sun,' she said.

'Yes,' he said. 'I've been as far as Kansas — looking for work.'

'The conditions are pretty bad,' she said.

'There ain't no work,' he said simply.

'Oh,' she said, 'that's too bad,' and felt awkward and inane. He seemed in such a sun-warmed ease, his legs stretching down. He had his coat in his arms and his shirt-sleeves were torn off, showing his huge roasted arms. She could see the huge turn of the muscles of his arms, out of the corner of her eye.

They went climbing in gear up that naked mountain, and it began to affect her curiously. The earth seemed to turn on the bone rich and shining, the great mounds burning in the sun, the great golden body, hard and robust, and the sun striking hot and dazzling.

'These mountains,' she began to tell him, 'are thousands of years old.'

'Yeah,' he said, looking at her sharply. 'I'll bet.' He lounged down beside her. 'I'm sleepy,' he said. 'I slept on a bench in L.A. las' night.' She felt he was moving slowly towards her as if about to touch her leg. She sat as far over as she could, but she felt him looking at her, taking something for granted.

'Yes,' she said, 'it would be an interesting study, these mountains.'

He didn't answer and threw her into confusion. He lounged down, looking up at her. She drew her skirt sharply down over her leg. Something became very alert in her, and she could tell what he was doing without looking at him.

They didn't stop again. The country looked the same every minute. They rose on that vast naked curve into the blue blue sky, and dropped into the crevasse and rose again on the same curve. Lines and angles, and bare earth curves, tawny and rolling in the heat. She thought she was going a little mad, and longed to see a tree or a house.

'I could go on to San Francisco with you,' he said, and she could feel her heart suddenly in her.

'Why would you do that?' she said, drawing away, one hand at her throat.

'Why shouldn't I?' he said insolently. 'It would be kind of nice for both of us.' He was smiling that insolent knowing smile. She didn't know how to answer. If she took him seriously it would implicate her, and if she didn't it might also. 'It would be kind of nice now, wouldn't it?' he said again with his curious soft impudence. 'Wouldn't it?'

'Why, of course, I'm going to San Francisco anyway,' she said evasively.

'Oh, sure,' he said, 'I know that. But it isn't so hot going alone. And we get along, don't we?' He didn't move, but his voice drove into her.

'Why, I don't know,' she said coldly. 'I'm only taking you to the bridge.'

He gave a little grunt and put his cap on his head, pulling the beak over his eyes, which only concentrated his awful power. She pulled her blouse up over her shoulders. She had never noticed before that it fell so low in front. She felt terribly. And to her horror he went on talking to her softly.

'You wouldn't kid me, would you? You know I like you, I like you. You're pretty.'

She couldn't say a word. She felt her throat beating. He was making love to her just as if she was any common slut. She felt her throat beating and swelling.

He kept on his soft drowsy talk, 'The times is sure hard.' His words seemed to be very tiny falling from the enormous glow of his presence, wonderful, as if he had been turned, naked, roasted in the sun. You could smell his sunburnt flesh. And you could smell the earth turning on its spit under the mighty sun. If only he were not so near; the car threw them close together, and she tried to go easy around the curves so that his big body would not lounge down upon her like a mountain. She couldn't remember when she had been so close to a man. It was as frightening as some great earth cataclysm. She prided herself on knowing men. She was their equal in every way, she knew that.

If only she could see something familiar, then she could get back her normal feelings about men. She felt as if she were in a nightmare.

'I worked when I was twenty,' he went on softly. 'Made good money, blew it in on Saturday night. Made big money when I was twenty — Jesus, I've got something to look forward to, haven't I?'

She sat over as far as she could. 'Where did you work?' she managed to say. She prided herself on always getting information about people. They talked about Roosevelt and the New Deal. She always had strong views, but for the first time in her life she felt as if what she was saying was no good, like talking when some gigantic happening is silently going on. She didn't know what was happening, but she felt that every moment he won, was slowly overcoming her, and that her talk gave him a chance silently to overcome her. She was frightened as if they were about to crack up in a fearful accident. She relaxed on the seat, and the heat stroked down her body. She wished she wasn't driving a car. The great body of the earth seemed to touch her, and she began looking where the shadows were beginning to stroke down the sides of the mounds as if she might sleep there for a little while. An awful desire to sleep drugged her, as if she hadn't slept for years and years. She felt warm and furred and dangerously drugged.

It was as if a little rocket exploded in front of her face when he said, 'Let's don't talk about that,' and he leaned closer than he had. 'Let's talk about you.' She could see suddenly his whole face thrust to her, the gleaming strong teeth, the roasted young cheeks, and he had long single whiskers growing out like a mandarin. She laughed a little. 'Who do you think I am?' she asked nervously. 'Why, I guess you're a pretty good-looking girl,' he said. 'You look pretty good to me.' She bridled at this common language, as if she were nothing but any girl you pick up anywhere.

'Why, I'm a schoolteacher,' she cried.

He didn't seem surprised. 'O.K.,' he said, laughing into her face.

'Why, I could almost be your mother,' she cried.

'Aw, that's a new one,' he said, and he put his great hand straight on her arm. 'Never heard of a girl wanting to make out she was old before.'

She had an awful desire to make him say more; she was frightened. Swift thoughts, habitual thoughts, came into her head, and they seemed like frail things that the heat pounded down. Was it because they were so far out in these strange, rising, mounded hills?

'Are those cigarettes?' he said pointing to the pocket beside her. 'Let's stop and have a smoke.'

'Oh no,' she cried. 'I haven't time. I'm behind now. I've got to make up a lot of time.'

'O.K.,' he said. 'We can smoke here.'

'All right,' she said, handing him the package. 'You keep the package.'

'All right,' he said, and took one out and put the package into his pocket.

The sun moved to her side and fell on her shoulder and breast and arm. It was as if all her blood sprang warm out of her. The sun moved slowly and fell along her whole side.

'Oh,' he said, 'I know you like me.'

'How do you know?' she said, offended, trying to see the road. She felt fatuous indulging in this adolescent conversation. She let her skirt slip up a little. She knew she had good legs, tapering down swiftly to her ankles. But he didn't seem actually to be looking at her; a heat came out of his great lax body and enveloped her. He seemed warmly to include her, close to himself.

'What kind of a wheel is that?' he said and put his large thick hand beside her own small one on the wheel. 'Oh, it turns easy,' he said. 'I haven't driven a car since I left home. A good car is a pretty sweet thing,' he said, and leaned over and began to fondle the gadgets on the front, and she looked fascinated at his huge wrist joint covered with golden hair bleached in the sun. She had to look, and saw that his hair was black on his skull but also burnt around the edges. Looking at him she met his gaze and felt her face flush.

They fell down the valley, yellow as a dream. Then hills lifted themselves out on the edge of the light. The great animal flesh-jointed mountains wrought a craving in her. There was not a tree, not a growth, just the bare swelling rondures of the mountains, the yellow hot swells, as if they were lifting and being driven through an ossified torrent.

The Tehachapis rolled before them, with only their sharp prime-val glint, warm and fierce. They didn't say anything about that in the books. She felt suddenly as if she had missed everything. She should say something more to her classes. Suppose she should say — 'The Tehachapi Mountains have warmed and bloomed for a thousand years.' After all, why not? This was the true information.

She stopped the car. She turned and looked directly at him. 'What is your name?' she asked.

Puzzled, he leaned towards her, that tender warm glint on his face. 'Thom Beason,' he said. The hot light seemed to fall around them like rain.

'Listen,' he said gripping her hands, twisting them a little. 'Let's get out. Wouldn't it be swell to lie down over there in the hills. Look, there's a shadow just over there. It's cool in those shadows if you dig down a little ——'

She saw his wrists, his giant breast, his knees, and behind him the tawny form and heat of the great earth woman, basking yellow and plump in the sun, her cliffs, her joints gleaming yellow rock, her ribs, her sides warm and full. The rocks that skirted the road glistened like bone, a sheer precipice and dazzle of rock, frightening and splendid, like the sheer precipice of his breast looming towards her so that she could feel the heat come from him and envelop her like fire, and she felt she was falling swiftly down the sides of him, and for the first time in her life she felt the sheer sides of her own body dropping swift and fleet down to her dreaming feet, and an ache, like lightning piercing stone, struck into her between the breasts.

She let her head fall over their hands and pulled back from him in hard resistance. She could not go to his breast that welcomed her — all my delicacy, my purity, she thought. He will not see me. I must not change. I must not change. The tears came to her eyes, and at the same time a canker of self-loathing, terrible, festered in her.

The moment had passed. He withdrew from her. 'O.K.,' he said. 'You don't need to be scared. Only if you wanted to. O.K. Let's go. You can make up your time. We're only about a half hour from the bridge where I blow.'

She began driving very fast, very well. He withdrew completely from her, just waiting to get out. It hurt her, as if there had been before her some sumptuous feast she had been unable to partake of, the lush passional day, the wheaty boy, some wonderful, wonderful fruit.

'I'll swan,' he said. 'There's old Magill going with a load of melons. Hi!' he shouted.

She wished he was gone already. She wildly began thinking what she could say to him. She thought she would say, casually — 'Well, good luck.' She felt easier knowing what she was going to say. She stopped the car. He got out and stood by the car. She wanted to do something for him. She really would have liked to give him something. She thought she would buy him a melon. 'How much are they?' she said nodding towards the melons and hunting for her pocketbook. He ran over. 'You pick out a good one,' she called after him.

He came back with a large one with yellow crevasses. His strong talons curved around it, and he kept pressing it, leaving a dent

which swelled out after his fingers. He held up the great melon
with its half-moon partitions, grading golden towards the sun.
She fumbled with her purse to pay for it, and suddenly she saw
that he was holding it towards her, that he was giving it to her, and
she was ashamed and held the quarter she had taken out, in her
hand. He was smiling at her as if he felt sad for her. She smiled
foolishly and sat pressing her wet hands together.

'Well, good-bye,' he said. 'And good luck.'

'Good-bye,' she said. Now she could not say good luck. He had
beat her to it. Why should he wish her good luck when she had
it? . . .

He turned and ran towards the wagon, climbed in, and did not
look back. She drove around the curve, stopped, turned down the
mirror, and looked at her face. She felt like a stick and looked like a
witch. Now she was safe — safe. She would never never change,
pure and inviolate forever; and she began to cry.

After five minutes she saw a car rounding the mountain to her
right. It would pass her soon. She got out her whiskbroom, brushed
her suit, brushed off the seat where he had sat, opened the back
window to air out the smell of buttermilk and hay, started the car,
and drove to San Francisco because that was where she was going.

SHE ALWAYS WANTED SHOES[1]

By DON LUDLOW

(From *The New Masses*)

IT WAS hot in the little cemetery. The heat lay like brushed wool over the parched crosses. It nursed the moisture ruthlessly from the small mound of fresh earth. Nothing moved but the ants and a fly, lost away from the vineyards and the sweet ooze of drying grapes. The man sitting on the ground did not move. His hair drooped over his forehead like thirsty wheat. His gaunt hands were at rest beside him.

'She always wanted shoes,' he said.

Forty miles to the east the Sierras were bitter, jagged. West the Coast Range rolled dark, hidden in the smoke screen of hot distance. An ant crawled over the cuff of his blue jeans, searching. The fingers of the man's right hand convulsed and buried themselves in the damp, yellow soil of the mound.

'Even not seeing the circus wasn't so bad,' he said. 'She was only four then, but she didn't even cry when I told her the field boss wouldn't pay till Monday. She was a good little kid. She asked if we would just take her down to look from the outside — she said she wouldn't beg to go in.

'She couldn't see much, only the pictures, and the legs of the horses and ponies under the edge of the stable tent, but she was happy and laughed and talked about it for a long time. She was pretty healthy then; it was that winter when we went down to Imperial Valley she began to get sick.

'To make up for the circus we took her to a show. There were kids dancing on the stage and she liked it a lot. For over a week she was singing and dancing and trying to turn handsprings all over the tent. She wanted to be a dancer, and asked if she could have shoes like they had if she learned to dance real good. We told her yes.

'After the season was over we sold the tent to a family that was going to stay on the ranch all winter. We decided to quit tramping and went down to Los Angeles and rented a house.

[A number of the ranchers in Kern County allowed non-resident families who had worked for them in the summer to remain on the ranch property during the winter when there was no work. One family consisting of a father, a mother, and little girls, three and four years old, and a baby of seven months, had pitched its tent on some rolling ground near a road, about twenty-five feet from two other family tents. There were no trees in the vicinity. Some hundred feet from the tents a toilet had been constructed by thrusting four tree branches in the ground and lapping burlap around. During irrigation periods, about once a month, water could be secured from the pump five hundred feet away, but for the rest of the time it was necessary to haul it in large milk cans from a pump two miles away. The family of five was living in a tent nine feet wide and fifteen feet long. The canvas was dirty; many holes had been patched, but it was not waterproof, and during the storm just before the visit the beds had become wet. Pieces of carpet had been placed along the walls to keep out the wind. The earth had been swept, and carpets, so worn and thin they looked like the ground itself, had been put down. At one end of the tent was a screen door with a canvas curtain. In the tent were two beds crowded up against each other. The other furnishings consisted of a wood stove, a rocking chair, and a table made from boxes. A kitchen built of pieces of sheet iron and canvas had been added to the tent, but the rain was pouring in through the cracks. The mattresses on the beds were home-made, gray, and lumpy. The beds had no sheets. One bed had one pair of thin blankets and on each bed was a heavy 'pieced' quilt. Two kerosene lamps were on the table. A bright-colored calendar was stuck on the wall. A line extending the full length of the tent was used as a clothesline. The mother wore a sleeveless cotton dress and was shivering with the cold. The two little girls wore sweaters, but their noses were running, their faces dirty. The mother said they were all recovering from colds. The baby was in one of the beds with a quilt piled around him, and cheesecloth protecting his face from the many flies. — From *Transients in California*, a study compiled by the Division of Special Surveys and Studies of the California Relief Administration, and released in August, 1936.]

'The house we rented in Los Angeles cost twelve dollars a month. She was pretty happy then, living in a house. (She wasn't two yet when the drought dried us off the farm back home.) She had a lot of fun turning the electric lights on and off and running water from the faucets in the sink.

'I got a job in the oil fields, and we told her she could go to school pretty soon. She liked that, and spent almost all the time talking about when she would start going. She tried to spell out words on the signboards, and looked in all the store windows for pencil-boxes and slates and things. She asked if all the kids that went to school wore shoes. I said, "I think so."

'But the job at the oil fields lasted only a few days. I'd kind of lost my strength somehow since we left the farm, and I let a pipe slip. I didn't blame them much for canning me — you've got to be pretty strong to work around the fields — but I was discouraged. It scares you when you find you're not as strong as you think you are. I guess it was because I didn't get over a stroke of sun I got in the cotton fields, and you don't eat any too regular following the crops. Moving from place to place all the time takes a lot of gas and oil, and while waiting for the crops to ripen you have to keep on eating.

'We waited too long trying to find another job — I guess mostly because she didn't want to leave the little house and go to the fields again. So when we reached the Valley, we didn't have money to rent a place to live.

'It was pretty hot on the way down, and she got sick and threw up a lot. She didn't complain, though. She just laid her head against her mother's shoulder and looked out at the desert going by. There wasn't any place for her to lie down, because the back of the car was filled up with all our junk. Maybe the exhaust from the car had something to do with it; the manifold gaskets were leaking, but I was afraid to tighten the nuts any more for fear of twisting off a bolt.

'She cried the first night we were in Imperial. She was asleep when we found a place to stop. It was an old shanty, beside an irrigation ditch, made out of brush and paper cartons woven together. She was asleep when we found the place — and when she woke up, we had her lying on the mattress in the shanty. The wind was blowing and rattling the brush, and the candle was flickering and making shadows on the walls. She liked nice things even though she was little, and the place scared her. When we told her it was only the weeds making the noise, she stopped crying, but she wouldn't eat anything, and all night she kept crying in her sleep that the weeds were getting her.

'After that winter she never was the same again; she didn't sing and dance any, and she didn't laugh very much. Her face got old-looking, and her lips and under her eyes got kind of blue. She began talking older, too; about jobs and groceries and things. She seemed to forget she was a little kid.

[In Imperial County, many families were found camping out by the side of irrigation ditches, with little or no shelter. One such family consisted of the father, mother, and eight children; the father hoped there would be some work in the valley later in the year. The mother had tuberculosis and pellagra, and it was because of her health that the family came to California. One of the children had active tuberculosis. The family had no home but a 1921 Ford. The mother was trying to chop some wood for the fire. The barefooted children, scantily clad, played on the ground, which was covered with cantaloupe husks.

A meat and vegetable stew was being cooked in a large, rusty tin can over a grate supported by four other cans. A cupboard and a table had been constructed of boxes. There were no toilet facilities, nature's needs being attended to behind bushes. Some water was brought from the ice plant in El Centro for drinking purposes, but for cooking and washing, water from the irrigation ditch was used. The family had been sleeping on the ground. The blankets were kept during the daytime in the car. There was no possible shelter. The night after this visit was made, there was a heavy rainfall. This family said they had been accustomed to a better standard of living in the East. The mother told the worker on the survey that she had been known as the best housekeeper in her home town. — From *Transients in California*.]

'It was pretty tough on her that winter. The field hands were making only a few dollars a week, and some days we didn't have much but bread and lettuce to eat. She didn't complain, though. Sometimes she'd forget, when she was playing with the other kids, and run in and ask for bread and butter and jelly. Then she'd look kind of embarrassed and say, "I mean just anything to eat, Mother." She understood pretty well for a little kid.

'Along towards spring she caught cold after a rain that soaked through the wall of the shanty. We were scared because her chest was hurting. We didn't have anything to put on it but onion juice and lard. We took her to the doctor in town. He said she was all right except she ought to have more milk, and eggs, and orange juice, and she should have hot mush every morning. He charged us two dollars. I made only four that week, so seeing him didn't do much good.

'After that the health officers came and told everybody they had to get out of camp because one of the kids had caught some contagious disease. They didn't tell us where to go, but we had to get out, so we started north for the spring oranges.

'In the orange groves I made enough to get a tent, and an army cot for her to sleep on. She was getting thinner, and the blue under her eyes was getting deeper. Pretty soon she couldn't walk. I put her in the car and took her to the county hospital. They asked, "Is this an emergency case?" I said, "I don't know." They said, "Is she hurt?" I said, "No, she is sick." They asked, "Who is your doctor — who sent you here?" I told them, "We haven't got any, we just came." They said, "We can accept only emergency cases without a doctor's orders."

'On the way back she asked, "Am I going to die?" I said, "No, you are going to get well and go to school." She smiled at me and said, "When I go to school I can have shoes, can't I?" I said, "Yes."

[For many years the laws of California provided that county supervisors should be responsible for the relief of needy persons who had lived a year in the state and three months in the county, but in 1931 this law was changed to provide that the county need care only for those who had been three years in the state and a year in the county, and who during this time had not received relief. Thus, all the newcomers were excluded from public aid, including medical care in the county hospitals or clinics. — From *Transients in California*.]

'I sat on the ground beside her cot and told her stories on the days when I wasn't working; but when she got sicker I'd forget to talk and just sit looking at her. I went to the library to get books to read to her. They asked me for my address and telephone number. When I told them we lived in a tent, they said, "We must have a deposit." I stole books by putting them inside my shirt while they thought I was reading.

'She liked to have me read stories about kids. While I was reading she would get color in her cheeks and look almost well again. Once in a while she would smile a little.

'Then she died.

'I carried her in my arms to the hospital. I forgot about the car. She was very small.

'They said, "What is the matter with her now?" I told them, "She is dead."

'They said, "Oh!"

'They called for a stretcher and took her away.

'When we looked at her in the coffin, they had made her lips smile. They had put a new dress on her.

'There was a preacher there. He looked at me and said, "She is with God."

'There was a lady with him. She said, "Poor little thing, it is all for the best."

'I felt through the covers they had over her. They had put shoes on her feet.'

LITTLE BRIDE [1]

By DOROTHY McCLEARY

(From *Harper's Bazaar*)

WELL, now, Mr. Ludlow's waiting, dear,' said her mother. 'Best run along.'

'Yes, I suppose so,' said Ida, picking up her mother's big brush and starting to brush her hair. 'Just wait till I get my hair brushed.'

'Couldn't my little girlie do that up in her new room?'

'In Mr. Ludlow's room?' asked Ida. 'How on earth could I, Mother? Mother, look, can I always dress and undress down here?'

'Why, my dear little girl ——'

'*This* is my room, you know that.' Ida went and crowded herself into her little mahogany childhood chair.

'Ida, you're a puzzle.' Mrs. Chanders sat up in bed and drew her flannel dressing-sack around her shoulders. 'Come here, dear.'

Ida came and sat on the side of the bed.

'Now what would Mr. Ludlow think if he could hear you?' said Mrs. Chanders. 'His little wife, that he thinks the world and all of!'

'I know it. I guess I'm mean, but ——' Ida raised her eyes to the ceiling. Just that ceiling between here and his room. Down here everything blissfully as of old. Up there —— 'He looked nice this afternoon, didn't he?' She felt of her two rings.

'Lovely. Just lovely,' said Mrs. Chanders with a little sigh of relief. 'Did you hear what Mrs. Doremus said to me, just afterward? She said, "Why, Mr. Ludlow's what I'd call *distinguished*-looking, really distinguished-looking, with his dress suit and that nice mustache and all!"'

'She did?'

'She certainly did. And from Mrs. Doremus, you know, that's something! She mingles right and left with the very best, she can judge, she's ——'

'Look what he gave me, Mother.' Ida felt in her dressing-gown pocket and brought out a little piece of tissue paper. 'Imagine! He handed me this while we were at the supper, and I looked into it and I thought I'd die.'

'Mercy — whatever?'

'Just look here, will you?' Ida opened the paper.

'A bill!' exclaimed Mrs. Chanders. 'For some little spending money for you! Oh, isn't Mr. Ludlow the thoughtfulest ——'

'Bill?' cried Ida. 'It's a hundred-dollar bill!' She unfolded it and spread it on her mother's lap.

'Why, *Ida Chanders* — Ludlow!'

'Yes,' said Ida. 'I didn't know there were such things. It's a real hundred all right. I showed it to Lily, and I thought she'd die right there.'

'Bring mother her glasses, dear!'

The two pored over the bill, examined it on each side, felt of it, read the 100 aloud. '"This certifies that ——"' read Mrs. Chanders. 'Well, well! And look here, Ida, dear old Benjamin Franklin, if you please! Mercy, so little to be so big. Why, he gives you out a hundred-dollar bill the way we'd give out a quarter!'

'And so fresh and new.' Ida rumpled it to hear it crack. 'I wish Papa could have seen this. Did he ever see a hundred-dollar bill?'

'Oh, I don't know — maybe not exactly *see* one; but your father handled sums of money at various times; don't forget that.'

'I know what Papa'd say if he was alive today.' Ida giggled. 'He'd say: "Brand-new, eh? Make it yourself, Mr. Ludlow?"'

'Yes. Yes, indeed.' Mrs. Chanders sighed. 'Always such a joker, your papa. This would have been our twenty-eighth — no, let me see — this would've been our *thirtieth* anniversary, Ida,' said Mrs. Chanders in a hushed voice.

'Yes, sir, so it would,' said Ida, tightening her hand over her mother's. 'Why, I can remember it just as well as if ——'

'Remember it?' asked her mother, shocked. 'What are you talking about?'

'I mean I can picture it — you've told me about it so many times; I can't believe I wasn't standing right there, beside you and Papa ——'

'Well, of all things! That would have been a fine how do you do, wouldn't it?'

'I don't mean *really*,' said Ida, caressing her mother's cheek, 'just in my imagination.'

'No, indeed, you weren't even heard tell of, my dear, for two whole years.'

'Two years,' said Ida meditatively. 'I can't imagine you and Papa without me along.'

'Oh, we had our times!' Mrs. Chanders smiled archly. 'My gracious, we wouldn't have wanted a great girl trailing after us from the word go, would we?'

'I know, but ——'

'No, the first year or so I was just a little bride, dear — no cares, no responsibilities. That's what you are now, Ida, a little bride. Just you make the best of it, for time flies!'

'But I belong in *this* family,' protested Ida, smoothing down her mother's pillow. 'I'm part of this family, not ——'

'Well, of course, but now Mr. Ludlow ——'

'Oh, he's just an outsider,' said Ida scornfully.

'Why, Ida Chanders!'

'I don't care, he's just an outsider,' repeated Ida. 'And now I'm married to him and I can't get out of it. But it makes prickles run all up and down me to think I'm married to him.'

'But, my dear little girl' — Mrs. Chanders looked helplessly at Ida — 'you talk like a baby, dear. You're not a baby any longer. A big girl twenty-seven years old to talk so!'

Ida looked down askance at the strange hundred-dollar bill, so out of place on the white counterpane. 'Why couldn't things go on as they were!' she said bitterly. 'He had his room — wasn't that enough for him?'

'Why, my child!'

'Little did I think,' said Ida angrily, 'when he came here, seven years ago ——'

'Yes, and don't you forget he's kept us alive these seven years. He's put bread in our mouths. He's kept this roof over our heads. Why, poor Mr. Ludlow, and how we made fun of him there at the first — it's a mean shame, Ida! We ought to've been whipped for it; indeed we ought! Making fun of his poor little ——'

'I've married Mr. Ludlow,' said Ida in a low voice to herself. 'I've gone and married Mr. Ludlow. I must have been crazy.'

'Ida, Ida, this distresses Mother beyond words!' Mrs. Chanders reached out and put her arm around Ida's shoulders. 'Why, dearie, I'd thought how nice, how lovely — for us all. As I said to Mrs. Doremus, my little girlie married and settled, but still close at home where I can keep an eye on her ——'

Ida covered her face with her hands. 'When I think of all the times I've cleaned his room and hung up his nightshirt' — she winced — 'and made his bed! Why it just — I never thought, then, that I'd — and his mattress goes right down in the middle! You know that yourself. There he sleeps, night after night, in the middle of his bed! It's *his* room, Mother, it's Mr. Ludlow's room, never *mine*.'

'Well, what do you propose, Ida darling? Do you want me to fix up the old back room for you and Mr. Ludlow? But I can tell you he won't like that one little bit. Why, he loves that room of his so; he said to me just last night, "Mrs. Chanders ——"'

'I hate him!' Ida burst out.

Mrs. Chanders put her hand over Ida's mouth. 'Do you know what you're saying?' she asked coldly. 'Ida, if I were you I'd kneel right down this minute and ask God to forgive you for what you've just said. Forsooth, Ida!'

'Oh, when you say "forsooth"!' Ida wrenched herself up and away from her mother.

'A pretty way to act on your wedding night!'

'Now *you've* turned against me,' cried Ida. 'Oh, heavens!' She ran to the window and got between the lace curtains and the pane. 'Oh, dear, look at the tree out there! I'd rather be that tree than me. I'd rather be Soda, or Mrs. Chesney's dog, or anything but me. I'd rather be a tramp, and go hungry ——'

Mrs. Chanders got out her handkerchief from under the pillow and began to unfold it.

'A new moon!' said Ida, pointing to it in a fury. 'Yes, there *would* be a new moon tonight, just when I ——'

'Wish on the new moon,' said Mrs. Chanders tearfully. 'Wish for a happy new life. That's what we must do.'

'No!' Ida turned her back on the moon. 'Mother, I'm not going up there, tonight.'

'What's that?' cried Mrs. Chanders.

'You can't *make* me go up there.'

'Have you taken leave of your senses?' Mrs. Chanders blazed out.

'Oh — Mother!' Ida broke into tears and hid her face in the window curtains. 'Why did I? Why did I? Why did you let me?'

Mrs. Chanders tugged impatiently at the bedclothes and looked about for her bedroom slippers. 'Ida, must Mother get out of her warm bed and ——'

'Oh, it's easy enough for you!' said Ida. '*You* don't have to leave your own room. *You* don't have to go up there and knock on a stranger's door ——'

'Knock on the door!' cried Mrs. Chanders. 'Oh, no, not now you don't have to knock on the door, not any more. Just walk right in, dear.'

'Into *his* room,' said Ida bitterly. 'No. I can't do it.' She took up her Mother's hairbrush again and ran it over her hair. 'I took my things all up there and everything. Now I've nothing.' She looked down at the top of the bureau, the left side of which had been hers; now her mother's belongings were spread out wide over it.

'Well, when a little girl's married ——'

'Married? I might as well have married old Mr. Bachrach next door,' Ida said miserably, 'for all the *married* I feel.'

'Oh, but it's too soon, my little pet. Of course, it's too soon to realize — just a few hours ago! Why, you're still in a daze, that's it.' Mrs. Chanders nodded brightly. 'Just you wait. Wait till you hear yourself introduced around as *Mrs.* Jasper Ludlow! Then you'll know. Oh, that *Mrs.!* I remember still how it made me feel when I first heard it — Why, there's no describing it. *Mrs. Chanders!* My darling, I felt like somebody out of a play! One minute just Miss Pease, little Sylvia Pease, and the next minute — *Mrs. Chanders*, for always.'

'But you were marrying *Papa*,' said Ida sadly. 'No wonder.'

'Marriage is like a new life, my dear. Oh, the companionship! And after a lonely girlhood ——'

'Going everywhere together, you mean?' asked Ida.

'Nothing can take the place of marriage!' exclaimed Mrs. Chanders, clasping her hands. 'Marriages are made in heaven!'

'I'll bet you mine wasn't.' Ida bit her lip.

'But why else do you suppose it was put into Mr. Ludlow's head to come here seven years ago, to just this house? Why, indeed? That was all part of a plan, pet. God's great plan. No, we mustn't question. Sometimes we don't know what He means, but if we're only patient and do His will it all works out in the end . . . you'll find out ——'

'I couldn't have got out of it, you mean?' Ida looked fearfully at her ringed hand. 'If I'd said no, it wouldn't have done any good, according to all that.'

'Mr. Ludlow would never have taken no for an answer, dear.' Mrs. Chanders laughed merrily. 'Nobody like him, with that serious way of his, would ever ——'

'Lily says he hasn't any sense of humor,' said Ida.

'Oh, nonsense! *Lily* says. Who's Lily, pray, to pass judgment? Lily has too much sense of humor, always with that silly grin on her face. What do you see in Lily?'

'Oh — she's fun, that's all.' Ida shrugged her shoulders.

'One *very* nice thing about your marrying Mr. Ludlow — Lily'll get put out in the cold where she belongs. He won't stand for Miss Lily five minutes!'

Ida laughed. 'I took Lily up and showed her his nightshirt once, just after he first came, and his socks laid out to dry on the chair-rungs, and I thought she'd *die* of laughter.'

'Aren't you ashamed of yourself, Ida Chanders? Poor Mr. Ludlow!'

'"Old maid," Lily said he was, "just an old maid!" That's why I hated like poison to let on to her about my going to marry him. I didn't tell her till way last week — I knew how she'd laugh.'

'You ought to be ashamed of yourself.'

'Well, you used to make fun of him yourself, and you can't deny it.'

'Oh, perhaps just a little, there at the first. He was such a different type than any man we'd been used to. Poor Mr. Ludlow — Ida, if he knew some of the things we said about him down here ——'

Ida began to giggle.

'But such a *gentleman!*' said Mrs. Chanders vigorously. 'Oh, so considerate, so quiet, and never so much as a pin out of its place in his room. I tell you it speaks pretty well for his mother, poor soul

— too bad she couldn't have been alive and with us today to see
her boy taking unto himself a little wife. My, my —— Did you
hear him call me "Mother" at the supper?'

'Oh, for goodness sake. He *didn't!*'

'Called me "Mother" just as nice as you please. I was handing
him the chicken salad. "Have you had some, Mother?" he said
right out. I think Mrs. Doremus heard him.' Mrs. Chanders sup-
pressed a smile.

'*Heavens!*' said Ida. 'He's got no right to call you that; you're
not old enough to be his mother.'

'Oh, that's not the point, dear. It's just a little mark of — well,
to show he feels close to me because of you. See, dear? We're all
three drawn very close together now.'

Ida looked hard at her mother's face. 'All the same, if you'd been
in my place *you* wouldn't have given in and married him.'

'I?' cried Mrs. Chanders. 'Horrors, no! A man ten years
younger than me?'

'If he'd been the right age, would you?'

'Oh, you silly child!' Mrs. Chanders laughed and blushed.
'What kind of ideas are you putting into your old mother's head?
No, dear, no more marrying in *this* house. I had my own dear hus-
band, that's enough.'

'No, but I mean honestly and truly, you think he's kind of —
funny, don't you?'

'*Mr. Ludlow?*' asked her mother, in a shocked voice.

'Yes, old Roly Poly.'

'I think he's a very, very fine man,' said Mrs. Chanders, 'a man
in ten million.'

'Sh!' said Ida suddenly. 'Listen.'

They heard Mr. Ludlow's door quietly open; then his slippered
feet made their way down the stairs and tiptoed past the room.
'Going to the bathroom,' Ida whispered.

Mrs. Chanders nodded and they both smiled, knowing just how
he would look, in his brown bathrobe with its monk's hood, his
mug and gold-handled toothbrush in one hand. 'Really you ought
to be getting along up there now, Ida. What must he think?'

'I'll go in my own good time,' said Ida, fingering the hundred-
dollar bill. 'Mother, tomorrow you and I'll go downtown and get

this changed and then we'll divide it in half — you fifty, me fifty.'

'No, precious, Mr. Ludlow meant that for all yours, that's for a little nest egg for you.'

'What's mine's yours,' said Ida, running her hand lovingly along her mother's soft arm. 'What are you going to get with your half? New dress? A nice pretty coat? You could get a dress *and* a coat!'

'No, no, one or the other's enough!' protested Mrs. Chanders. 'Listen, he's running the shower!'

'Yes, sir ——'

'What's got into him? I never knew him to take a bath at night before.'

'Oh, my, what a day we'll have tomorrow!' Ida cuddled up excitedly against her mother. 'Let's go down first thing after breakfast, to Kaufman's, and change our money — get two fifty-dollar bills. And then we'll sit in the rest room for a minute and just *look* at our money, what do you say? Then we'll get some nice things and then we'll go and walk into the Wallace Hotel and eat our lunch!'

'My dear child! Ought we?'

'We'll have shad roe!' cried Ida ecstatically.

'Shad roe!' Mrs. Chanders gave Ida a big hug.

'Then we'll come out and we'll say, "Now what'll we do?" And then we'll go to a good moving picture.'

Mrs. Chanders's face was bright with anticipation. 'Anybody'd think to hear us talk it was *me* that's got married.'

'And do you know what next?' said Ida, weaving her fingers into her mother's hand. 'From way downtown, by the monument there, we'll come home in a taxi! How's that?'

'Oh, if Mrs. Doremus could only catch sight of us!' cried Mrs. Chanders.

'What a day we'll have!' said Ida. 'And all before old Roly Poly gets back home.'

'Can't you bring yourself to call him Jasper, dear? You must, you know. It isn't right ——'

'Old Roly Poly,' said Ida.

'Sh! No more of that, now,' said Mrs. Chanders.

'Lily says Jasper's just exactly the right name for him. But, Mother, I can *never* call him by it. I'll say "you" if I have to call him anything. I told Lily I liked the name Jasper, but I hate it worse than poison. *Jasper!* Ugh! Why, you couldn't call him Jasper yourself, could you?'

'Well, I — Jasper,' said Mrs. Chanders, trying it on her own tongue, 'Jasper. Yes, we must both learn to say it, dear, or he'll think it very strange.'

'Jasper,' they said in unison, then fell to giggling.

The bathroom door-latch shot back, and they heard Mr. Ludlow's tread again in the hall.

'Go now, dear, go,' said Mrs. Chanders, laughing as she gave Ida a little push with her elbow. 'It's disgraceful ——'

'Oh, I can't go now, I'd have hysterics! Listen,' she whispered, 'wait till he gets to the step that creaks — he'll be to it in a minute ——'

They held their breath to listen, lying arm clasped in arm.

'Now, Ida, you must' — Mrs. Chanders labored and wet her lips over her words — 'you know, Ida, mother's girlie must hold herself a little aloof ——'

They lay tensely, waiting for Mr. Ludlow to sound the creaking board.

THE LAST MEETING [1]

By WILLIAM MARCH

(From *The Atlantic Monthly*)

I

JOHN came into the dingy, outmoded restaurant and waited for a moment until his eyes became adjusted to the semi-darkness of the place. He raised his thin face and stared steadily above the heads of the dispirited people who sat before him eating their lunches. After a moment his glance rested on the vacant table set in an alcove, and he noted with relief that it was screened somewhat by the palm that stood beside it, a spurious affair of paper and hemp which sprouted from dusty moss as false as its own raveling fronds. He went to the table and sat down, grateful all at once for the slight privacy which the alcove and the disintegrating shrub afforded. He took off his hat and his gloves and placed them on the chair beside him.... That, he thought quickly, would force his father to sit opposite him; there would be the width of the table between them, at least.

A middle-aged waitress, as faded as the background against which she moved, came up to serve him. She brushed crumbs and cigarette ash into her tray with a fretful, preoccupied gesture and spread a napkin over the stains that other diners had left behind them on the cloth. When she had finished, she fetched a bill of fare from a near-by table and put it before him. She stood looking at him incuriously with eyes which had once been fine.

'I'm waiting for a guest. I won't order until he comes.'

The waitress nodded and filled his glass with water. Then she walked in heavy-footed silence and sat on a bench near the entry to the pantry. Another waitress bearing a tray of empty dishes passed and they spoke to each other, laughed briefly, and then turned their heads away.

John looked at his watch once more. It was five minutes past one, and already his father was late, but the thought consoled him a little and he smiled bleakly. 'Why should I expect him to be on time, or to do what he says?' he thought.... 'I imagine he's changed very little in the past five years.' He turned his head at an angle and looked at the door, conscious of the muffled, hammerlike sound of leather heels beating against the boardwalk. But he heard these things dimly, as if from another world, for he was at this moment concerned mostly with his own resentment.... His father had a colossal cheek to force himself on him this way! That was the sheerest cheek, and no mistake about it, after the way he had behaved in the past!... There was nothing his father had not done in the old days to shame them all, and it was because of him that he had left home just as quickly as he was able to make a living for himself. Since that time he had endured things, he felt, merely for the sake of his mother and his sisters, who had not been able to escape so easily: the arrogant demands for money which he could not afford, the drafts on his bank account which pride, at first, had made him honor, but which necessity had at length forced him to protest. Recently there was the embarrassing matter of the check which the bank official had questioned and which John had explained....

'But this is so obviously *not* your signature, Mr. Coates. It isn't even an effective attempt. It's plain to anybody that this is a bungling forgery.' The official had stopped on an annoyed, ascending note as if he had meant to end his sentence with the words 'my good fellow,' but had thought better of it. John had looked coldly at the official, thinking, 'I'd be obliged if you wouldn't patronize me quite so obviously, because I'm an English gentleman, the same as yourself, or at least you have no way of knowing that I'm not.' He got up, hooked his umbrella over his forearm, and drew on his gloves, smiling with frigid amusement. 'I'm afraid I must disagree with you, Sir Robert. That bungling forgery, as you describe it, is my signature, and I'll be obliged if you'll debit my account with the ten pounds.'

II

John shook his head, remembering this recent scene, and glanced again at his watch. It was a quarter past one, and he decided that he would not wait much longer. When his father had telephoned from the railway station that morning, explaining that he had just got in, he had felt a quick, depressed sensation in his stomach and his one thought had been that he must keep his father away from his office and his friends at all costs. He had been panic-stricken for a moment, not quite knowing what to do, and he was surprised at the exactly right note of heartiness he put into his voice when he did answer.

'How long will you be in town, Father? You must have lunch with me, at least!... Shall I come to the station to meet you, or do you think you can find your way about?'

And his father had explained in his light, mocking voice which somehow gave the impression that he smacked his lips daintily over his words as if they were tangible things to be tasted: 'I know my way about quite well, Mercutio. I lived here as a young man, long before I married your mother or before you were born.... You didn't know that, I take it.'

'No,' said John. 'No, I didn't know that.'

There had been a moment of silence in which John sat drawing the profile of a man with exaggerated sideburns. He framed his picture in a triangle as precise as he could make it. 'Is there any particular reason for your trip, Father? Is it on business?' He drew a circle about the triangle and then obliterated his sketch with four quick, brutal lines.

'No. No, it hasn't anything to do with business, except in a remote way. I merely wanted to visit the place again, to see some of the old friends I remember.' There was a short silence and in a moment his father added, 'I have been sick, as your mother probably wrote you. I have been quite sick.'

It was then that the older man suggested lunch at Ravino's, and John agreed hastily before his father reconsidered his choice. He knew of the place vaguely as being close to the boardwalk in the more down-at-the-heel end of town, but he had never been in it. At any rate he was not likely to meet any of his friends there, and for that he was grateful; but he was puzzled, nevertheless, that a man of his father's florid tastes should have chosen such an obscure place. He rested his elbows on the cloth before him and cupped his thin, aristocratic face in his hands. He closed his eyes for a few seconds, but opened them with nervous prescience at the exact instant his father came through the door with aged jauntiness and stood poised inside the room as if he had expected a burst of applause. John pushed back his chair and stood up, thinking, 'How thin he is! How he has changed since I saw him last!' but he made no sign of recognition. Then their eyes met across the room and his father came rapidly toward him, his hand stretched forward as if this were a thought-out entrance in one of his forgotten, romantic plays. He was, John noted, wearing a soft, pale green hat which was years too young for him, and his light top coat was too pronounced both in its cut and in its checked lavender and fawn pattern.

'Well, this is really very nice! You're looking well, Mercutio. I'm glad to see you.'

John said: 'I wish you wouldn't call me that, Father. I don't use the name any more. I've taken the name John since I left home.' But to himself he thought: 'How spruce he looks in his finery — how spruce and how ridiculous!... And how very conscious he is of the effect he's making on people at the other tables.'

'There's nothing wrong with the name Mercutio. It's a very distinguished one, as a matter of fact.'

'Possibly so, Father; but I don't like it, I'm afraid.'

'I've played the rôle hundreds of times. It's a very good name, and very unusual.'

'I find it slightly absurd, I'm afraid.' He sat down again, smiling with the correct shade of cordiality at the coffee stains on the cloth which the waitress had failed to hide.

'Oh, very well. Very well.' The older man hung up his coat and hat and sat opposite his son while he removed his lemon-colored gloves. He stuffed them into the pocket of his topcoat and rested his hands on the cloth. John moved his eyes and examined his father's hands, noting dispassionately that they were as brittle and bloodless as cracked porcelain, and of the same yellowish white; that the nails were swollen a little and the tips of his fingers were blue. It was then he knew that his father was going to die, that before long he would be free of him forever. He looked up from the table, thinking these things, and read the framed signs that hung on the wall: Ravino's Still Hocks; Ravino's Dry Amontillado Very Choice; Ravino's Sparkling Moselles For All Occasions, his lips moving slowly to form the words. When he spoke, his voice was calm, devoid of all emotion.

'How did you amuse yourself this morning, Father? I hope you found something interesting to do.'

'I walked about looking at the old places I remembered, but they've torn so many of them down.'

'Yes. Yes. That's quite true.'

The petulant waitress came toward them and waited while they ordered their luncheons. She adjusted another napkin on the table and filled the two glasses to their brims, her free hand resting professionally on her hips. When she had finished, she bent forward and switched on the lamp that stood on the table, and instantly the older man's face emerged sharply from the blurring duskiness of the alcove. It was then John saw that his father's hair and eyebrows had been dyed a hard, brittle black and that against his parchment skin there were spread two unmistakable, fan-like reaches of theatrical rouge.

'I went this morning to call on some of the old friends I remembered, but they're mostly dead now. The ones who are alive didn't seem to place me.' He laughed with disbelief. 'I didn't think the people here would ever forget me, a small place like this. . . . I played three summers here in repertory, and I was something of a sensation. I tell you, my boy, I packed them in. Things were much different in those days. I was known as Cyril Mullarney then, but my manager made me take my own name when I made my first appearance in London.'

Cyril sighed, leaned back in his chair, and glanced up at the waitress. He sat up straight and examined her more closely, his eyes half closed. He had seen her before somewhere, he was sure of that, but he could not quite remember the occasion He shrugged his shoulders and dismissed the matter from his mind. 'Yes,' he continued, 'this place has changed since my day. When I was a young man, Ravino's was the exclusive place to go, but look at it now! Everybody came here in those days: all the fashionable people. There were private dining-rooms upstairs where we held our parties. It was all very gay.'

They selected their food while the heavy-footed waitress noted their orders on a pad. She returned almost at once and put the food on the table before them, and again Cyril looked at her speculatively. He raised his finger and stroked his lip with the mannered, graceful gesture that he had used in so many of his old successes.

'I've known you at some time in my life,' he said positively. 'I can't place you now, but it must have been many years ago.'

The waitress, whose vocabulary had of late been modeled after the American movies she had seen, threw back her head and spoke from the corner of her mouth. 'Sure you have. Sure. So what?'

'I remember now,' said Cyril. 'It all comes back to me. It was the last season I played here. You wrote me a note and met me at the stage door. You had a girl friend, and I brought along a man from the company named Arthur Holden. I was called Cyril Mullarney in those days, don't you remember? We came to this very place for supper.' He laughed with delight, his porcelain cheeks stretched tightly across the bones of his face.

The waitress turned and stared. 'So what?' she repeated sullenly. 'So what, big shot?'

'I even remember your name,' continued Cyril proudly. 'It's Annie Wheatley.'

John leaned back in his chair, so that his face was more completely screened by the dusty palm. 'It isn't necessary for him to talk so loudly,' he thought. 'He's grotesque enough as it is.'

The waitress said: 'I never saw you in my life before, and what's more if you don't take your hand off my knee I'll call a police officer.' She looked contemptuously at the old man, and then turned to John, seeing his embarrassment. 'Scram!' she said. 'Scram, big shot!' She laughed disdainfully and winked, as if she and John shared a common secret. All at once Cyril became very gay. It wasn't possible for her to have forgotten him. She must remember him. His pictures had been in all the papers and on the boards before the theatre. He had had dozens of letters from his female admirers, just as he had received the note from her.

The waitress drew back. 'Scram!' she said. 'Scram!' She walked away, disappearing into the obscurity of the service pantry.

'She hasn't forgotten me!' said Cyril. 'She remembered me very well.' He lifted his dying hands again, and again he turned the turquoise and silver ring on his finger.

'Have you been sick long, Father?'

'She remembers me very well, you can be sure of that.'

'Did the doctor say what the trouble is?'

'A doctor's concern is to frighten you so badly that you'll pay his outrageous bills, Mercutio.'

'Did your doctor succeed in frightening *you* that badly, Father?'

'No,' said Cyril in delight. 'No, I can't say that he did.'

III

There was a long silence between them while they ate, but at last Cyril spoke again: 'Being sick so long has left me short of funds. It's only temporary, of course, until I get an engagement for the summer.' And John, chewing steadily, looked up and nodded. His father was coming into the open now. They were getting down to the real reason for his visit. But his father need expect nothing from him this time; he refused to be bled any more.

The waitress came out of the pantry with her friend, a woman as frayed as herself. They stood whispering together while the waitress touched her hair and her cheeks and nodded her head to indicate the direction in which her friend was to look. It was as if she said: 'Yes, he's really got rouge on!... There! There, back of the palm. You can't see him very well from here!' The second woman picked up a handful of silver and walked carelessly, too carelessly, in the direction of the alcove. She stopped at a near-by table and began to rearrange it. She raised her eyes in anticipation of what she would see, but she got no farther than John's cold stare fixed steadily upon her face. She lowered her head, gathered up her silver in confusion, and retreated.

All at once John felt an unaccustomed fury within himself. He beckoned to the waitress who had served them, and who still stood by the door awaiting her friend's incredulous corroboration of what she had just been told. She started to turn, but he crooked his finger imperiously and she came toward the alcove. She waited at his elbow.

'This fork that you gave me is dirty,' he began in his cold, passionless voice. 'You can see that it hasn't been cleaned properly.'

She took the fork and examined it, turning it over and over in her hands, not quite knowing what to say. 'I don't clean the forks,' she said at length. 'I'll tell them about it in the kitchen.'

John smiled steadily. 'You don't clean your fingernails either, it seems, but that, I take it, is a matter of personal choice, Miss Wheatley.'

The woman's neck turned red. She glanced quickly at her soiled hands and as quickly put them behind her back.

'I don't know the class of people who come here as a rule,' said John. 'Possibly they don't mind. I'm afraid I find it slightly' —

he paused and smiled again, weighing his words — 'slightly nauseating,' he said at last.

'Yes, sir.'

Cyril had stopped eating and was looking from his son to the
waitress as if not quite understanding what was taking place.

'You *are* Miss Wheatley?' said John.

'Yes, sir.'

'You may give me the check, please.' He took the slip and folded
it into squares. 'The gentleman to whom you were so rude is my
father, if that interests you.' Then he got up and helped his father
with his coat, proud that no sign of his fury escaped to the watching
world. Cyril looked at his son's grave face and at once his own face
became grave, as if he could adjust himself instantly to the atmosphere about him, could be depended upon to fall immediately into
any situation and read his lines appropriately, even though he had
not known what had gone before.

When he had settled with the cashier, John held the door for his
father and followed him to the pavement outside. He was, on the
whole, pleased with his handling of the waitress and with the manner in which he had put her at once in her place. He had been cool,
dispassionate, and completely master of his hands, his voice, and
his face, and the thought would have, on another occasion, pleased
him; at the moment, the problem of his father, and what he had
better do with him, negatived his earned satisfaction.

His father reached out suddenly and took his son's arm, and
John stiffened slightly at the touch, but he lifted his head and smiled
his steady, uncompromising smile as they walked along the promenade, talking of things which they both knew to be of no importance, the penetrant breeze from the sea lifting Cyril's coat and
swirling it about his knees. After a moment John glanced at his
father and then turned his head, for in the sunlight the dyed hair
and eyebrows were fiercely revealed, and the spread rouge stood
out like crimson patches on yellow cloth. He wondered, then, just
what it was his father demanded of him this time and how long he
purposed staying. He was willing to do his duty within reasonable
limits, but his personal life, he felt, was his own, and he had no idea
of sharing it with his father or of introducing him to his friends.
Making a place for himself in this stolid, unfriendly town had not
been easy, but he had succeeded at last by the unaltering force of

his character, and he was accepted now. He would not have that new security jeopardized. . . .

IV

They turned after a moment and went into a small park. They sat together on a bench and watched the sea flashing with silver in the chill April sunlight. They had exhausted their protective talk and they were both silent for a time, neither quite knowing what to say. Again John glanced at his father, and again he turned his head away. He would let the future take care of itself, he decided. He would sit here for a decent interval and then go about his business and dismiss the whole matter from his mind. Perhaps it had been a mistake to see his father in the first place. He would not make that mistake a second time. Certainly he would refuse his father the money which he would, inevitably, ask.

Cyril, as if understanding his son's thoughts, began to talk again, his eyes fixed on the sea with desperate craftiness. 'I'm disappointed with my trip on the whole, Mercutio. It has been quite disappointing. My expenses have been very high of late.' He turned the turquoise ring on his finger and added, 'My sickness, of course. . . . I had thought to raise money among my old friends here, but it seems not.' He drew his coat about his thin body and shivered with distaste, as if at some humiliating memory.

'I'm sending home all the money that I can possibly afford. I keep very little for myself.'

'Yes, yes, Mercutio. I'm not denying that. But I'm used to so many things, and I can't give them up now. It's different with you.'

'There's one thing, at least, that you must give up,' said John, smiling fixedly. 'You must give up signing my name to checks. That is forgery, as you know.'

'You take those things too seriously,' said Cyril. 'I knew you'd send me the money. It wasn't forgery, really. I merely signed the check with your name to save time.'

'Yes,' said John. 'Yes, I know.'

'If I could raise twenty pounds I think I'd call the visit off and go back home tonight,' said Cyril wearily. 'The whole thing has been a bitter disappointment.'

'I'm sorry, but I haven't twenty pounds, Father.'

Again there was a long silence, and then Cyril, as if trying a new attack, began to talk about the daughter who had married the year before and moved to Bristol, while John listened uneasily, suspicious of his father's sudden interest in her welfare. It appeared that the family rarely heard from her, and it almost seemed as if she were trying to forget that they existed, or that she was ashamed of them now. He had been thinking before his illness of visiting her, to assure himself that she was quite happy in her new home and that her husband treated her with consideration, for he knew her pride, and if her marriage was not successful she would never say a word about it, being much like himself in that respect.... At any rate, he would like to make sure.

'There's no necessity for that, Father. I hear from her regularly. She wrote me last week. She's quite happy.'

Cyril raised his hand and stroked his lips with his forefinger, his eyes narrowed in shrewdness. 'I'd like very much to read her letter,' he said after a long pause. 'I'd like to assure myself at first hand.'

John said, 'I'm afraid I haven't the letter with me. I left it in my desk at the office'; but almost before the words were off his tongue he knew that he had blundered.

'Shall we go to your office together and get it?' said Cyril gently. 'It will give me a chance, as well, to see where you work, and to meet your employers.'

John shook his head quickly, lifted his umbrella, and began jabbing at pebbles in the path. 'Why do I permit him this power over me?' he thought. 'I'm a grown man. He couldn't exploit me this way unless I permitted it.' He held the umbrella against his legs and furled the silk more tightly with his cold hands. When he had finished he fastened the snap and looked steadily outward at the sea, knowing himself defeated. It would be better, he said at last, if he went alone for the letter, and if his father waited for him there in the park. The office was being redecorated, and everything was in confusion. He got up and straightened his necktie, calculating how much money he could possibly spare, wondering if his father would be content with less than the twenty pounds that he demanded. 'I'll take a taxi,' he said. 'I'll be back very soon.' He turned and walked away, afraid that Cyril might overrule the plan, but his father sighed, leaned back against the bench, and began to rotate the silver and turquoise ring on his finger.

V

When he reached his desk, John counted the money that remained in his pockets and examined his bank balance again, although he knew to the shilling the amount that he possessed. He shook his head helplessly. He would have to ask the cashier for another advance, no matter how greatly he disliked doing so. He concluded his arrangements at length, and wrote Cyril a note: 'Dear Father: I am enclosing eighteen pounds. It is all I have at the moment. I hope that you have had an enjoyable trip. Please give the family my regards when you see them tomorrow.' He blotted the sheet on which he had written his message, folded it exactly over the notes, and slipped it into the envelope containing his sister's letter. Then he buttoned his topcoat, glanced at himself in the mirror above the washstand, and went out of his office.

His father was sitting on the bench where he had left him, but he got up expectantly at John's approach and braced himself against the seat, swaying slightly. John handed him the envelope, and Cyril, feeling its added bulk, smiled and nodded in approval, his parchment skin pulled so tightly over the bones of his face that he seemed to be a dead man revived for an occasion of gaiety after years in his grave rather than one who was only now going to death after a long and happy life.

'The waitress's name was *Blanche* Wheatley; not Annie. The girl she brought for Holden was named Annie.'

'Yes,' said John.

'You were very rude to her, Mercutio. Unnecessarily rude.'

'Yes,' said John.

Cyril had become very animated, very arrogant now that he was in funds again. He excitedly shaped the new jade-green hat more becomingly to his head, half-turned toward the town, and glanced longingly at two girls who passed arm in arm down the promenade.

John said: 'I'm afraid that I must be getting back to work. I'll say good-bye now.'

'You mustn't blame me too bitterly later on,' said Cyril. 'You mustn't expect to change me at my age.'

John said: 'No. No, of course not.'

He watched while his father turned from the small park and passed on to the promenade, hesitated, and then walked in the direction that the girls had taken, his fingers touching and retouching his new hat, his silver ring, and his dyed moustache as though he thought himself still the actor of romantic rôles to whom a world of women wrote their amorous, pleading notes. Then all at once his father's retreating figure trembled and shattered before John's eyes, and he knew, then, that the defenses he had built up so laboriously in the past years had failed him at last, and without warning, and that he was stretched again on the rack of old issues which could never be settled for him in this world. He turned and walked toward the bandstand, his eyes unfocused against the blurred and wavering sea, his hands closed so tightly that he could feel the bite of his nails against his flesh. . . .

He would be all right in a minute or so, but he was, he thought scornfully, behaving at this moment precisely like the emotional French, who weep and embrace in the streets: he was a man with no more dignity than those Americans who call noisily to acquaintances across dining-room floors. . . .

'Father! Father!' he said.

He hooked his umbrella over his forearm, raised his thin, delicately chiseled face, and closed his eyes. He pressed his hands against his face and willed not to remember. 'Father! Father!' he said. . . . And then a long time later: 'Father!' . . .

TO THOSE WHO WAIT [1]

By ELICK MOLL

(From *Scribner's Magazine*)

From darkness, from the darkness, coming.... From despair without meaning and death that was without burial. From too much pity and too much dread. From hunger that was not alone our hunger, and brotherhood that was a two-edged sword between us, against our rest, against all hope of rest....

In land that will be again our land. In days that will again be light for seeing — not for too much seeing; for knowing — not for too much knowledge. In darkness that will be rest and ending — not for hiding, oh my brother. In days that will be sun and warmth again....

From the darkness, brother, from the darkness coming. But not forgetting, not forgetting.

I'VE got my job back, Jeff Miller said to himself for the hundredth time. All morning he had been saying it, over and over, as if trying in that way to give form to the emotion that struggled for release within him. *I've got my job back.* It was a great exultant shout bottled up inside him, yet he couldn't quite get hold of it, to let it wing free.... It held apart, strangely muffled behind the fuzzy accumulations of the past four years — thought, remembrances that kept shuffling across his mind as if he still belonged to them, as if notice had not yet gone out, echoing, along the thousand tiny trails, that it was over, that this morning had put an emphatic period on all that time of trial and emptiness. All he could really get hold of, all he could really *feel* about the business, was that it was March, and having his job back in March meant oyster stew again in the Grand Central Oyster Bar.

Lord, it was funny, he thought. It must be that the human mind — at least his human mind — was not designed for the proper comprehension of either disaster or miracles. He remembered

vividly that day in '33, just after the bank moratorium, when the
ax had finally fallen at Gormely and Co. Like everybody else he'd
been expecting it for weeks — months. He'd lain awake nights,
thinking about it, cold with fear that went beyond just the idea of
losing his job and what that entailed for himself and Martha. It
was something in the air, that seemed to bespeak not merely the
loss of a job but of all jobs, all sanity, hope, everything that mattered in the world. . . . And when the day had come at last, and Mr.
Gormely had assembled the staff to tell them the news, listening
to the man shaping the unnecessary footnote to the disaster plainly
written on his face, all that Jeff had been able to think about — of
all the things that had kept him awake during the long nights
waiting — was that now he wouldn't have to have the radiator in his
car fixed, after all.

Nuts, that's what it was. Like going balmy without the relief of
being able to jump and bang around and make the appropriate
howling noises. And now he had his job back — and it was the
same thing. Mr. Gormely had said, that day back in '33, 'If ever
a bond means something you can push across a counter again in
this country, if ever Gormely and Co. gets back in the running,
there'll be a place for every one of you boys who still wants it.'
He'd meant it, too. He'd been as good as his word. And
now, of all the things Jeff had imagined, during the intervening
years, he might feel and think and want to do if ever the miracle did
happen — the only thing he could think of, that kept swinging back
into his mind again and again like a slightly mad refrain, was eating
oyster stew at the Grand Central Bar until he was blue in the face!

Benner and Harris and the rest of the old-timers who'd come
back seemed to be having something of the same trouble too. All
they could talk about all morning was going over to Maressi's for
lunch, to celebrate. Jeff had half made up his mind to go along with
them; it would be fun eating with the gang at Maressi's again — if
it was still open. He could hardly believe it would be, after all these
years. But then he was always finding, with surprise, that lots of
things had been going on just as if nothing had happened, the way
they had back in '33. . . . When lunch-time came, however, he
decided suddenly that he would rather be alone. He wanted to be
with the fellows, talk to them, find out how they'd made out during
the four years, but he felt a little strained with them, for some

reason — maybe because he was afraid they might ask *him* what he'd been doing all this time. The idea that they might even *suspect* that he'd been on relief for over a year turned him cold. Besides, he wanted to call Martha and tell her the news, and he wanted to eat oyster stew, and he wanted to get some things straightened out in his mind and try and get hold of this wonderful thing that had happened to him, that had been eluding him all morning behind the clutter and muddledness of the past four years.

He made a pretext of errands to do and went out by himself, and in the lobby of the building, downstairs, he caught up with it at last. Leaving the elevator, he was drawn into a little current of people hurrying toward the entrance, and something about the quality of that movement — less a press of bodies pushing him forward than some compulsion of mass movement that seemed to magnetize his own steps — reached down into a remembrance that had lain buried under the worry and dread and emptiness of these last years.

He stood at the entrance for a moment, controlling his impulse to run, to sing out, to grab some one and whirl him around and shout, 'Hey, brother, what do you know, I've got my job back.'... Then suddenly, looking out at the noonday crowds along Fifth Avenue, gray-black formations moving like sluggish shadows against the glare of stone and pavement, the mood subsided, and a gust of panic went through him. It was strange how ominous they could look, moving along that way, *en masse* — those myriad harmless, destructible worlds, just like himself....

As he turned down Fifth Avenue, he was conscious of the bills in his pocket. What a prince Mr. Gormely was! No gestures, no largesse, just 'Good to see you again, Jeff ... seems like old times again, with you and Benner and Harris....' And then, digging into his pocket, casually: 'Here, you'll probably need a few things.'

And that was a capitalist — an enemy of the working classes — to listen to those guys in Union Square tell it.... Jeff shook his head. Yes, there were some things it was going to take a while to get straightened out in his mind. But meanwhile, he remembered — with an adumbration of eagerness that again didn't quite belong to him now — meanwhile, he was going after that oyster stew in the Grand Central Bar. That, at least, was something it wouldn't take very long to get straightened out — no longer than it would take to get that first clump of hot, soft, rubbery, tasteless deliciousness into his mouth.

He stopped at the corner of Forty-sixth Street to wait for the light, and absorbed in his thoughts, he was a little startled by the sound of a low, intimate voice muttering something, close beside him. He looked up and saw, with a curious dart of recognition, a man of about forty-five standing on the curb alongside; he was wearing a blue camel's-hair coat, obviously of an expensive variety but quite frazzled now about the collar and cuffs; his head was hatless and covered with snarled graying hair, and his face was expressionless.

There was something strangely familiar about the man's aspect, and as he stared at him, trying to fathom that little pang of recognition, it seemed to Jeff, suddenly, unrealistically, and yet with a curious panicky conviction, that he had seen this man before, many tlmes before, on many corners, just like this, waiting for lights — the untidy, graying head, the expressionless face, the toneless, muttering voice. . . .

It was a curious, sick sensation — and it passed, like a beam of darkness drawing aside from his mind. He saw that this was just a man in a frayed blue coat whom he'd probably seen before, somewhere on the Avenue. The light changed, and as he started to cross the street, he saw the man's lips begin to move, heard him murmur in that low, gently chiding voice — as if he were remonstrating quietly with some one: 'But dear, you don't seem to understand, we can't manage it any more, we just can't manage ——'

Jeff hurried by, with his heart in his mouth, remembering oddly a phrase that he'd often heard used in the old days, had used himself, 'Hey, will you cut it out? You'll have me talking to myself in a minute. . . .'

He shook his head, as if defiantly. Well, what of it? This was just another poor lug who'd cracked up and was talking to himself. So what? He'd seen plenty such, and plenty worse. And it wasn't *his* depression any more. Lord, if only he could get hold of that idea once and for all and hang onto it. Sure, it was a bad dream while it lasted — lines of guys with arms and legs and faces, just like him, standing in rain and cold . . . and Martha's face when he first talked about going on relief, and her face when the first relief money came in . . . and waking in the morning with sweat on his face as if he'd

been running all night instead of sleeping . . . and lots of things. . . .
Yes, it was a plenty bad dream. But it was over now. It was *over*.
He was going back to where he left off in '33 and start catching up
with all the things he'd been missing out on all these years — baseball games and shows and new clothes and no debts and good rye
whiskey and apple pie *à la mode*. . . . And the first thing he would
catch up on would be about a gallon and a half of oyster stew, right
now.

He crossed over at Forty-third Street and walked toward Vanderbilt Avenue, springily, trying to recapture in the quality of his
movement the physical elation, the surge of almost animal joy that
had risen in him so wonderfully a while back in the lobby. But as he
approached the Grand Central his steps began to lag, and he knew
finally that it was no use. It was spoiled. He didn't really want
oyster stew any more. His stomach was still queasy with that sickish amalgam of pity and panic. He wouldn't be able to eat for
hours now.

Angry at himself, and a little resentful of the world in general,
he turned back on Vanderbilt Avenue. All this time, years now, he'd
been telling himself that, if ever he got a job again, the first thing
he'd do would be to go down to the Grand Central Oyster Bar and
eat oyster stew until he was ready to bust. And now a guy in a
frayed blue coat talking to himself had robbed him of that — just as
if he'd reached over and snatched it out from under his nose. He'd
always been a sucker for that kind of stuff. But — well, it wasn't
so much that the guy was down at the heels and talking to himself
— there were plenty of worse things he'd seen during the past few
years, that kept coming back to haunt him, wake him up at night
with the fear and shame sticking in his throat. But somehow, all at
once, the poor lug had seemed to epitomize everything that had
happened to people and to the world in the last few years. Sure,
lots of people went around talking to themselves. He could remember his own Grandma Pearson sitting in a rocker, mumbling to herself. But this wasn't an old guy — or somebody who was nervous or
preoccupied and had just forgotten himself for a minute. This was
a young man, maybe forty-five — just a few years older than himself — and he was going around talking to himself because — well,
because he was through, washed up, the depression had finished
him. What did it matter to him that people were saying the depres-

sion was practically over? It wasn't over for him. It would never be over; the armistice wouldn't mean a damn thing to him, one way or the other. Something inside him had folded up.

It had been a time of trouble and loss for everybody — money and jobs and homes, and then self-respect and courage, and worst of all your grip on things, the ability to recognize any more what really counted, to feel badly about the things that should make you feel badly and happy about the things you were sure once would make you feel happy.... But, at least, to keep enough of yourself, that last shred, the ability to walk around with your fright and insecurity and loss *hidden*, deep inside yourself, behind your own inviolable wall of privacy. And to lose that! To walk around naked in the world, the whole story of what had happened to you exposed to public view. Talking to yourself out loud, that way: *'But dear, you don't seem to understand, we can't manage it any more, we just can't* ——'

Jeff Miller shivered a little. Yes, whatever had happened, that much at least had been spared him, that shred of privacy. No one had ever looked at him pityingly, gone off shaking his head, thinking, 'Poor Jeff. The depression's got him.' Yes, that, and standing in the lines — the men standing in the lines, rummaging in the garbage pails, stooping for cigarette butts — that much to be thankful for.

He hunched his shoulders and remembered suddenly that he hadn't yet called Martha. He'd been planning to do it after eating, with his throat still hot and steamy with the good peppery taste, from one of those booths upstairs in the Grand Central, where the operator got the number for you and you could sit with your legs crossed — or nearly — and say, 'Well, Martha, I've got a little news for you. I've got my job back.'

At the corner of Forty-sixth and Madison, he stopped, thinking he might still call her from the drugstore. *'I've been wanting to call you all morning, Martha, but I was too busy. Imagine, Martha, too busy....'* He vetoed the idea abruptly, crossed over and kept up Madison toward Fiftieth Street.

Lord, it was funny. Up there at Gormely's this morning, the same thing had happened to him. He'd been in the midst of his talk with Mr. Gormely, trying to find the right words to tell him how glad he was and grateful and everything, what he was going to do,

all the ideas he'd had.... And all at once, in the middle of everything, there'd flashed into his mind, for no reason at all, out of nowhere, the remembrance of that guy in the doorway on Lafayette
Street that freezing day two years ago — or was it three? — the
blue face and lumps in his jaws that showed how hard his teeth were
clenched and the hands stiff in that awful gesture, like prayer....
Out of nowhere it had come down between him and Mr. Gormely
and what he was trying to say, and it seemed to muddle everything
all at once, take all the kick out of it, and the sense and the reality
— so that he could only stand there, not saying anything at all, not
knowing what to say or think any more.

Yes, it was that, he realized — not the fact that he'd really been
too busy, that had kept him all morning from calling Martha. He'd
been afraid. *Afraid.* How often, during the past four years, in
imagination, he'd heard himself saying, 'Martha, I've got my job
back.' And now it was true, and he was afraid. How often he'd
heard himself saying it to her, feeling it open up between them like a
great shining heaven, blotting out the years, the name on the relief
rolls, the shame, the dread, all of it, having her think, all at once, as
he said it, of coming back from Dotty's, to their own place again,
picking up the old furniture maybe, or some new stuff, paying up
old bills, having people in to dinner again, maybe cocktails....

And now he was afraid, afraid that she would hear it in his voice
— the man in the blue coat and the man with the blue face in the
doorway, and all the rest of it — and she would know, too, that
somehow it was too late, that it didn't matter any more that the
depression was over, that somewhere, some place they'd got to in
the past four years, the depression would never, never be over.

Jeff Miller gave himself a shake as he turned into the Rockefeller
Plaza. Lord, what a way to be going on, at a time like this. It was
stupid, it was asinine.... 'Come on, you lug, snap out of it,' he said
angrily to himself. 'What the hell's the matter with you anyway?'

He got into the elevator. 'Forty-eight,' he said, after a momentary tiny struggle within. He realized, with a rueful, sore smile at
himself, that he'd said it much louder than necessary. Funny, he
thought, some day soon he would be saying it quite naturally, pre-
occupiedly, in fact — maybe not even saying it at all, because the
operators would know him by then, would know he belonged on the
forty-eighth floor.

The doors slid closed, the car began its ascent, in a soundless, tearing gale of emptiness. There was only one other passenger. Jeff observed him from the tail of his eye, a young chap, hatless, needing a hair-cut, wearing the collar of his topcoat turned up around his neck. He was carrying a bag in one hand while in the other he held a dead cigarette from which he'd pinched the lighted end a moment before, as he'd entered the car. Abstractedly Jeff watched him fiddling with the butt, rolling it between his fingers, the charred end flaking off infinitesimally to the floor. ...Yes, he thought, lecturing himself with semi-comic severity, there'd been enough of this nonsense. He'd call Martha, right away, from the extension in Phillips' office, no one would be using it now — poor Phillips, he remembered with a little jolt what Harris had told him this morning. He hadn't known about him committing ——

The indicator began to flash. 28 ... 29 ... Jeff watched the chap with the bag move toward the door. ... Yes, that's what he would do. Right away. From the phone in ... one of the offices. He could hear Martha's voice on the other end of the wire, instantly anxious, as if she couldn't imagine any more that he might be calling to tell her something she'd be glad to hear. '*Jeff, what's the matter, is anything* ——?'

32 ... 33 ... 'Thirty-six,' said the fellow with the bag. Jeff saw him bring his other hand, the one holding the piece of cigarette, toward his pocket, evidently intending to drop the butt there, but somehow the gesture miscarried; the butt skidded off the flap of the pocket and fell to the floor. Involuntarily, the chap made a grab to retrieve it, then straightened up as the doors split open. He stepped off and was abruptly foreshortened, swallowed. The car began to rocket up again, motionlessly.

'*No, nothing's the matter, Martha,*' he would say. '*But something has happened....*' He would allow himself that little luxury of suspense, Jeff thought, his eyes on the cigarette, which was rolling lazily toward the side of the car. Just a moment of suspense. He was entitled to that. Then, '*I've got my job back, Martha,*' he would say.

The tightness in his chest began to relax again, and he felt a little warmth of hope, anticipation, go through him. Sure, it was going to take a little while to get these dizzy ideas out of his system. After all, four years was a long time. He mustn't forget that. He couldn't expect to wash it all out in a day — a morning. It would take a

little time. In a week, two, it would all be gone from his mind —
like a bad dream. As, he remembered with a quizzical smile, the
women said about having a baby.

38 ... 39 ... 40 ... '*Jeff*,' she would cry, '*it isn't true. You're
——*' His eyes were starey, with a little fixed smile of anticipation,
as he watched the butt roll into a corner, teeter a moment uncertainly, then lie still. '*Yes, honey, it's true.* ...' Barely a quarter of it
had been smoked, he noted absently, no more than half a dozen
puffs maybe. ... '*Yes, it's true, honey ... you can come home now.*'

43 ... 44 ... Jeff moved to the side of the car. He wondered what
Dotty would say. She'd been so swell about everything. There
weren't many sisters-in-law who would take the kind of attitude
she had all along. 46 ... Jeff bent down. Just as soon as he was
able to, he was going to show his appreciation to Dotty, in some
tangible ——

He felt the car heaving motionlessly to a stop under him and
with a start, as if waking from a dream, he looked down at his
hand, then in sudden panic jerked his head around to look at the
operator. The other was regarding him curiously, with a kind of
smile on his face. Jeff felt suddenly as if the bottom of his stomach
had fallen out.

'Forty-eight,' the operator said. Jeff raised himself slowly, feeling
his face so clammy where a moment before it had been hot and
prickly. He moved toward the door in an agony of humiliation, his
fist clenched so tightly over the butt that he could feel it turning to
mush in his grasp. ... How could he convey to the man that he
didn't *do* this sort of thing, that he didn't *need* it — that he had a
job. ...

The humor of the situation struck him suddenly, and he saw himself, off to one side, doubled up with uncontrollable laughter. But
when he himself tried to follow suit, the laughter stuck in his throat,
turned him curiously ill, as if he'd failed in an obligation toward his
own sanity. The doors opened. Desperately he pushed his mind
across the abyss of emptiness that gaped before it, toward the
realization that this was the forty-eighth floor, *his* floor, *his* office,
where he worked, *where he had his job back.* ...

For the moment it was dead in his mind, without meaning, without association. For the moment, as he stood at the door of the
elevator, the same sickish, sinking sensation assailed him as he had

got a while back on the Avenue; the unrealistic conviction again flashed in his mind that he was through, washed up, that this was some *Germelshausen* of the spirit into which he had stepped, across time, where having a job meant nothing any more, because it was a land of dead men, ghosts in frayed blue coats mumbling to themselves, or the forever lost and hungry and hopeless. That somewhere he had got to in the last four years, where he had learned so many things, to do without oyster stew, without joy, without pride, to accept charity from the government, to wear second-hand clothes, and even to pick up cigarette butts — from that place there was no returning.

He could feel the operator's gaze still on him, with curiosity — with amusement, no doubt. He looked up now to face him, almost defiantly. But looking at the man, he was startled by the quality of expression on his face. He *wasn't* amused. He wasn't, at all. He was.... Curiously, the image of the man in the blue coat moved, almost like a refrain, across Jeff's mind. And with a sudden, strange impulse he held out his hand, palm up.

'Funny, isn't it, the things you do?' He looked at the bit of mashed paper and tobacco crumbs, laughing a little, strangely. 'And I just got my job back. Today. Just today — after four years.'

'Guess you must be feeling pretty good, eh?'

'Pretty good,' Jeff echoed. 'Yes, pretty good.' He kept looking at his open hand, laughing a little, softly. It wasn't ignominy, it wasn't shame and defeat. It wasn't that at all....

The operator held the door with his foot. 'Who with? The new firm? Gormely...?'

Jeff nodded. No, it wasn't that at all. It was... He looked up now into the other's face, again with that strange new sense of recognition to which all this time he had been so curiously blind. This place, where the last four years had brought him — it wasn't a dead land; it was a place where he could never again be quite alone, never walk alone, or work alone ——

He made a fist, punched lightly on the operator's shoulder. 'Be seeing you,' he said.

In the hall outside the office of Gormely and Co. he stood for a moment staring at the fresh lettering on the frosted glass. 'I've got my job back,' he said, wonderingly. It was still not joy. It was beyond joy.

THE SPANIARD[1]

By PRUDENCIO DE PEREDA

(From *Story*)

WHEN he first came back from the war in the beginning he used to walk around with his bandaged hand swinging in a beautiful black, silk handkerchief sling, and when somebody said, 'What a beautiful handkerchief!' and that it must have cost very much money, he said: 'Surely. General Mola preoccupies himself over the care of his men. Look!' and he showed them a tight little roll of twenty-peseta notes with his good hand.

'You ought to talk to him,' my aunt said to me. 'He might lend you the money to go home to New York with.'

'Do you want me to go home to New York?'

'No, *hombre*, I don't. I don't want you to go, but you're always talking about getting away. I want you to stay here with me.'

'Well, I don't talk to *cabrones*,' I said.

'He is not a *cabron*. He's your cousin. And Lito was very nice to you when you first came here.'

'He was a man when I came here. Now, he is a murderer.'

'According to your ideas! And you? What are you?'

'That worries me very much. I wonder about that very much. Sometimes I think that I am nothing.'

And sometimes I remembered that I was a writer and I would try to write about all of this that was happening, but I could not do it. It never came off. Then I would think about going to Burgos to see the American Consul. I was not registered there, but I had my passport. I thought that if he would send me home I would have to go to Barcelona and then I would stay there and get into the militia. I could see myself, first practicing on the long sewer-pipe range and then in the militia and saying to myself, 'Is this me? Is this really me?' and then going out, but I never went to Burgos. I only stayed in the pueblo and worried about Madrid falling, and sometimes in the night I cried.

Then, on the morning after the night when all of the Burgos papers had announced the fall of Toledo, I was walking in Villarcayo and I passed by Lito standing in the square and talking to a bunch of men, and when I went by I heard them laughing at me. I went home right after that, and in the night I waited for him in the yard by the entrance to the pueblo. He was in Villarcayo every day and he would come home only to take his supper with the family. He was a hero, you know.

And after I had been waiting a little while I saw my aunt coming out on to the balcony to call me for my supper and I went out in the road before she could see me, and then down a little way to wait for him. He came right after that. I saw him walking up in the dark. I was waiting over to the side of the road a little because I did not want anybody else who might be walking along the road to notice me, and now I could see somebody moving up, and the light of the moon was playing on the black silk of his sling and swinging a little as he came on. I had wanted to step out to him when he would be opposite to me and I was sure that it was he. I had planned it like that. I was going to challenge him, to tell him that I was ready; I was only waiting for his hand to heal. We were going to have it out then; but when he came opposite to me and I could see clearly into his face with the same satisfied smirking look on it that he always had on it in Villarcayo, I did not do anything. I could not walk up to him. Even when he looked straight toward me and made a little nod with his head, I did not speak to him and say who it was. I only stood and watched him walk by. I watched him until he went into the pueblo, and then I went up and into the house.

I did not feel like eating anything then, and I went to bed as soon as I got up into the house. Then, while they were still eating, my aunt brought me a cup of *manzanilla* to drink. I held the cup under my nose and breathed in the beautiful smell of the camomile. Then I drank it slowly in sips. It is a wonderful drink. My aunt kept looking at me. Soon she began to smile.

'I love you but I don't know why,' she said.

'You love me because you don't love General Mola.'

'*Vaya!*' she said. 'Always with that!'

'Always! Until they cut him in half!'

'All right! Very good, then! Give me the cup. You go to sleep now. Tomorrow we get up with the sun.'

Tomorrow was the day of fiesta in Sobrepena. 'I have to go, no?' I said.

'Surely, Mickey. It's your grandmother's pueblo and they have only one feast day a year. Anyway, you'll be able to forget all of this for two days.'

But I did not want to forget all of this. I did not want to forget Badajoz and Toledo and the way that they were pounding now at Madrid. I wanted to keep thinking of all that. I wanted to remember that Maria was in Madrid and the looks that the faces of the kids in the People's Militia had when they went to the front in Bilbao. But I did go to the fiesta in Sobrepena, anyway.

The war was there always, too. Even though going in the car we went through the Mazorra Valley — the most beautiful part of the Province of Burgos, or of Spain maybe — even though they danced on the green square in the neat little pueblo, and everybody ate and drank, *arroz con pollo*, red wine and white, cognac with cigarettes and cigars after, and we stayed up in the kitchen all night, you could not think of anything for very long and forget the war. It was there.

I ate very much and I drank all the wine that they gave me, but all of it only made me feel heavy and sleepy and tired. Nobody yelled, '*Animo, hombre, animo!* Perk up! Perk up, kid!' I just sat around there in my American clothes and felt them looking at me.

We were there for a day and a night and another full day, and we left after supper in the car on the second day; but it was midnight before we got to our pueblo. Then, before we went to bed, we drank hot milk and I felt a little easy. When I was in bed I put my hands over my ears so that I would not hear the snoring of the pigs downstairs in the stable, and I went right to sleep.

While we had been in Sobrepena at the fiesta, Lito had gone to bed. He had gone there on the second day. The wound in his hand had not responded to its last treatments, and an early infection was gaining ground and rising slowly up his arm. He had fever, too, and the doctors had thought it best that he take a temporary turn in bed; a temporary turn — he would be up again in two days, in three days, four days at the most, at the very most.

But the four days passed and then another day, and then a slow

week, and Lito was still in bed, up in the big wooden bed by the
window in his house that looked down toward the river; and now the
men from Villarcayo who used to come up to see him on every
afternoon in the beginning did not come any more.

His father told my aunt that he was glad. They had only drunk
his wine and talked rottenness. Foolishly, shamefully, they talked,
he said. He had not liked that at all from the beginning. And how
was the American cousin at this time? he asked my aunt suddenly.
You know, that was what he really desired: that the American
cousin go to visit with Lito sometime. That was a thing that he
would like. He told my aunt, quickly, before she could say anything, that he knew about their quarreling. 'They nearly hit each
other! Two cousins, too!' But Lito had changed. He is quiet and
thoughtful now. The two of them can pass a nice afternoon talking.
Many afternoons! They will not talk about the war. They will
talk about Mickey's first visit to Spain, maybe, eh? Would she tell
me that, suggest it to me?

She did. She told it to me as soon as I had come in from taking
the oxen to graze, when I was rested, and quiet and lonely, and I
said, 'Yes,' without even thinking about it. She was very happy.

On the next afternoon at two o'clock I went from my aunt's place
to his house. It was very hot and quiet in the pueblo and almost
everyone was working in the fields. The people who were at home
were sleeping. I pulled the knocker on the door downstairs and then
let it slam back hard, and he yelled down to me, 'Come on up,
Mickey!' without asking who it was, and I went up the stairs and
along the little hall to his bedroom. I knew this house very well.
We had had wonderful times here. It is strange how long you can
treat with a person before you really know what kind he is.

Now Lito was lying flat on the bed with his left arm bandaged
all the way up to his shoulder and held straight along his side over
the sheet. He was very bad. His face looked terrible, and just as I
was coming into the door I had started to say, 'Hello, you!' calmly
and with confidence, just as I thought of saying it, but when I saw
his face I stopped in the middle of it and with my mouth open. He
kept looking at me.

'At last, little cousin!' he said. 'At last you come!'

'Hello, Lito! How does it go?' I said to him. I went up to the
bed and shook his hand. He had been holding it up to me. I felt

like crying. I said to myself, 'I will only talk about the things that you want to talk about, my cousin that I love.'

'It goes terribly. They caught me, Mickey. They've got me by the *cojones*. By the old *cojones*.'

'Come on, man, not yet,' I said. His body looked strong under the sheet and his voice was low but not weak. 'They haven't finished you yet.'

'Yes. Yes. They caught me,' he said. 'They have caught me.' He shook my hand a little and looked up at me. 'You wanted that, didn't you?'

'I wanted it? I? Somebody else wanted it, not I,' I said. 'You were working for him, Lito.'

'Brave Communist! You brave little *tonto*, you. You still say that, eh? Sit down.' He pushed me a little over to the chair by the bed and then he pushed me back into it and let my hand fall. 'How do they let you stay here? Eh?'

'What can they do?'

'They can string you up somewhere, you little bastard.' He laughed and touched my chin with his fist. 'If they ever did anything, if they would ever try to do anything to you, I would crush them in my hands.' He hit my chin again and laughed. I did not say anything.

Lito turned his head away and lay back on the bed flat. 'They told you that you should not talk about the rebellion to me, no?'

'Yes.'

'We should not talk about it?'

'No, we should discuss something else.'

'Don't talk about it,' he said. 'Don't talk about it. Don't think about it. Just lie here quietly and die.' He was looking straight ahead at the ceiling and the wall, and he was back to all of the things that he had forgotten when I came in.

'Die?' I said. 'Who says it?'

He pushed himself up on his elbow and looked at me. The bandaged arm hung straight down from the shoulder. 'They didn't tell you that I was going to die, eh? They didn't tell you it?'

'No, they didn't tell me.'

'Well yes, I'm dying. I am dying, cousin. They want to take my arm off. I figure to myself that I'll be able to hold the ends of the wheat stalks in my teeth while I sickle them with my one hand.'

He laughed and then he gave a little gasp and his face changed. He had been a wonderful harvester. 'But I will die anyway.' His voice had broken suddenly, become very weak.

I wanted to go on just looking at him and letting this pass me and not saying anything. I held my mouth closed, but then something snapped inside and I began to talk fast and I said, 'Don't you deserve it?'

He swung out his hand to grab my arm that was near to him but I moved it away quickly and he caught only my fist. He tightened his hand on it.

'You can say that!' he yelled out. 'You can say that? I knew that was what you would say.'

'I am Spanish.'

'You are Spanish! You little fool! You are Spanish! You will die just being Spanish. Little Spanish virgin!'

'And you? You will have a harem of frightened young girls.'

'A harem, perhaps, but one is sufficient for me. I go out to fight for the thing I believe in and I do the things that fighting men do,' Lito said. 'You stay in the house and wait for the bombs to come down. You do that. You can do that.'

'You have become bitter,' I said.

'Yes, I know that already. We had better not talk any more about it.' He dropped his hand from my fist on to the bed. I watched him.

'Lito!' I said.

He turned his head to look at me. 'What?'

'You said, "one," Lito. One of the girls. You took one of their women?'

'I got one. She took me. She knew that it was the firing squad or me.' He laughed a little. 'That's part of all this, boy.'

'Yes?' I said. His face had a little satisfied look on it.

I bent down my head. There was a small table between the chair and the bed. It had a marble slab as top. All of the medical things that he needed were on the table. I kept looking at them, and then I noticed that there was a neatly closed straight razor near the edge with the little steel automatic spring button showing on its red celluloid cover. I had seen this little button on large American pen knives. I was thinking about how you pushed it up a little and the blade snapped out, when the thing came to my mind and I picked it up quickly and quietly, snapping it open as I was taking it up, and then I looked at him. He was watching me with that same look on his face. I took his arm by the wrist from the bed and held it out to me, holding it straight with the palm up. I put the edge of the blade slowly down on to the veins of his wrist. He did not try to pull his hand away. He had become a little paler, but he seemed to be amused.

I held his hand tight and pressed the blade down a little.

'Now you are going to die truly, Lito,' I said. He smiled.

'This is for that girl. I just press down on the blade and she will be all right again.' In the white face his eyes looked blacker. 'Eh, Lito? Do I kill you? Do I kill you justly or am I still a Spaniard?' He did not move and he did not stop smiling. I lifted up the razor from his wrist and then set it down on the table again and I threw his hand back on to the bed. I got up.

He had let his arm fall where I had thrown it and it was still lying with the palm showing. I looked at it. There was a thin white line where the blade had been. The hand lay out flat, not limp, but held that way. All of this time he must have been watching me. Then I turned around and went out the door, through the hall and down the steps.

He began to yell when I was at the bottom step. 'Come back! Hey! Come back! Mickey, come back! Kill me! Kill me! Mickey, kill me! Kill me!' He was screaming now. I stopped and began to turn around to go back up the steps, but I did not know what I was doing and I stayed there for a moment thinking, and then went down again and out the door into the pueblo. All of the time that I was walking over to my aunt's house he screamed behind me. When I was in the road someone passed me running toward the house. I think that it was his father. I did not look at him.

After that day the doctor did not come very often in his little blue Citroen that he parked in our yard and then he did not come any more. Lito was getting better? No, they said, he was dying.

He was dying for a week. His house was all quiet and his mother and father did not go to work in the fields. They hired a boy from Campo to work for them that week and they stayed in the room with Lito, their Lito.

'He's waiting for them to get into Madrid, eh?' the Mayor said to Lito's father once.

'No,' he said. 'No. He doesn't say anything about that. He does not talk about that, Don Angel. He talks a little about the days before the war, only.'

'Ah!' said Don Angel.

They had been with him like that for two weeks when the bombardment of Madrid began and everyone forgot about the hero in the excitement. On Thursday night I went to my room early in the night and lay back on the bed with the women and children who were dead in Madrid. 'Wait,' I whispered to them in the darkness, 'wait. Wait just a little while.' Then I heard the knocker downstairs clack twice.

My aunt went to the stairs. 'Who?' she called down. 'Who?' No one answered. We had not heard the door open. The knocker clacked quickly twice again. 'They're outside,' my uncle said. 'The door must be locked.' He went down. It was Lito's father. 'It's I, Domingo,' he said. 'He wants Mickey.'

'Wants me?' I thought in the room. I got up from the bed and stood up. Someone knocked at the door. It was my aunt. 'Mickey!' she said. 'I'm coming,' I said, and I went out. Domingo was upstairs now. He was crying. My uncle kept patting his shoulder. He looked at me as soon as I came out into the hall. 'Lito,' he said.

'Dead?'

'No, not dead. He wants you. He wants to talk to you. Please come.'

My aunt put her hand on my arm. 'Yes, he'll go, Domingo,' she said. She squeezed my arm with her hand. 'He'll go.'

'Right away?' I said.

'Yes, many thanks,' he said.

'Go right away,' said my aunt. 'Go right now.'

I went down the stairs without waiting for Domingo. I could hear them talking to him, going down. Then as soon as I was outside I began to run and I ran all the way up to the door. I remembered to go quietly up the stairs but I was still hopping two at a time.

When I went into the hallway I saw someone standing outside of Lito's bedroom door and crying without making a sound. It was his mother. 'Go in,' she said. 'Go in.' She took a deep breath to clear her voice. 'Lito, here he is. Mickey has come. He's here.' She pushed me into the room.

A candle was burning on the little table with the marble top. The light shone only around the head of the bed. Lito had not changed much. He was only very red now. He looked brownish in the light. I went up to the bed. When he saw me walking into the light he put up his left hand and moved it out to me. I took it in my right hand and then when he squeezed it tightly I put my left hand on and pressed his hand with both of mine. He pulled me down over to him so that I would hear him.

'Mickey, that girl ——' All during that time the girl; and how weak his voice was. 'It wasn't that way. She let me. She wanted me. I found her out on the road alone. They had been scouting and she had been separated from the others. I could have shot her, hombre. She would never have seen me, Mickey.' I went to turn my head to look at him, but he lifted his hand a little and held it that way with my ear by his mouth, without stopping in his talking. 'But I went up to her where she could see me and we challenged each other. She wouldn't put her gun down. We began to talk, then. I made a little joke, you know; about how pretty she was. She laughed. "You are still a little bit like a Spaniard, eh?" she said to me.' He laughed a little. ' "I am all a Spaniard," I said. Then I threw my gun down, and I walked right over to her. She put her gun down and stayed there looking at me. She was very beautiful. I kissed her and she put her arms around my neck.' Lito stopped talking. I could hear his breathing, now. Then when he started to talk again he was gasping a little.

'I made love to her. It was wonderful, Mickito. And then afterward, after that, I showed her the way back. She had never been in that country, but I used to go there very many times when I was doing service in Madrid because I liked it, and then I watched her go. She waved to me. It was still a little dark but I could see her doing it. I know she got back because afterward I heard someone yell and then laughing.

'Two of our men came then. I told them all wrongly about the section. Then, when the rest came, we hit at another part and they were all set in that place. I hurt my arm there. That's all. That's the way it is.'

I held my head like that. I did not want to look at him.

After a moment he said: 'I wanted to — I wanted to tell it to you in an angry, hard voice. Yell it! What you said had made me mad. About the little frightened girls, you know. I'm a Spaniard. I'm a Spaniard, too.'

He took his hand away slowly and then put his arm over my head and pulled it down a little and put his lips on my cheek.

He held it like that until he was dead.

A RUSSIAN IDYLL [1]

By FREDERIC PROKOSCH

(From *The Virginia Quarterly Review*)

ALEXEI *sat by the window and looked toward the Russian church. The sunlight was slanting upon the round spire, liquid and golden. It almost blinded him. His eyes grew blurred for a moment. Then he thought that he saw the flickering sunlight through his eyelashes, lingering not upon the cold, hard ice, but on a summer cloud, a field of wheat, a brown arm. He was deeply touched by the unexpected sweetness of a sudden remembrance, descending upon him in such a gentle, caressing way.*

He turned away from the window and leaned his chin on the palm of his hand. Little by little, with a great bewildered effort he tugged at his memory as if it were a huge rock unmoved for years; and there, beneath it, he suddenly glimpsed a twisted network of grasses and roots, flattened, pale, but still alive.

The farm near Dolya! The pool, and the ducks floating upon it, all snowy white except for the one with the iridescent purple head and the clean grey wings, the bright and knowing eyes, his own pet. The scents of summer, and the little tumbledown summer-house smelling of decayed wood, the boards falling apart and allowing a golden blade of light to glide into the odorous darkness, tipping here a spider solitary in his web and there an old hornet's nest tucked among the rafters. And the fragrance of wet wood, of leaves after rain, of the heavy dripping trees, the hot sun on the wet earth, the water dripping from the berries and from the young bodies beside the pond, the birds quarrelling outside, the musical trickle of water over the dam, the rustling twigs, the breathless whispers, the excitements, the delights.

Once, when Alexei was a boy of ten playing beside the haystack, one of the harvesters, a leering young man of twenty or so, passed by and beckoned to him. 'Come along, I'll show you a thing or

[1] Copyright, 1937, by The University of Virginia.

two,' he whispered. Stealthily they approached the woodshed and peered through a knothole in the door, first the one and then the other. The chap kept tittering and winking his grey eyes, but Alexei could not understand why, until at last he discerned two shapes in the darkness, lying upon the sawdust, kissing and clutching at each other's bodies — his cousin Zofja and the handsome young officer Piotrowski from Kharkov, who had been loitering about the village so much lately.

He caught his breath. He did not understand. But one thing he grasped — the hint of a debased yet sweet excitement, so it appeared to him. From that moment on he could not rest for curiosity and a wistful sort of envy. Everything took on a new significance — the women, with their silky hair and their rich, soft flesh, the older men, all brown muscle and hair, with their bellowing voices. 'I'll be as strong as that one day,' he thought. 'A soldier maybe, like Piotrowski, with a moustache and a uniform....' And there were moments, a year or two later, like the one when he sat with the men out under the trees beyond the field and the girls brought out the food in yellow baskets, and Anna sat down beside him, hot and breathless, leaning back and closing her eyes, her blue skirt rumpled, her forehead pearled with sweat, and he could see her smooth young legs as she raised her knee, and her thighs, mysterious and dark.

And another time, not long after, sitting beside Anna in the hay cart as it rumbled along the road toward Yelenovke at dusk, the air full of the farewells of autumn, the chirping of crickets, the humming of insects. The dust hovered over the road behind them, the sun had set, he could see a single star, just one, no more. He felt the itching of his arm as it rested in the warm hay, and then, as Anna turned to one side, the brief caress of her hair upon his cheek. Then suddenly he put his eager brown arms around Anna's slender waist and placed his face upon her neck, closing his eyes, feeling her warm skin upon his lips, hearing her laughter, her teasing voice slowly growing more tender.

One August morning, six or seven years later, he was walking through the copse behind the Semenenko estate when suddenly he stood stock-still. He saw, on the leafy path before him, the most beautiful creature that he had ever seen.

She wore a big pink hat with flowers on it, and a silky white dress, and she was carrying a parasol. Her sleeves reached down to the elbows, and her forearm was paler and softer than those of the village girls. Her hair was blond, her eyes were blue, her cheeks were rosy. She looked very delicate to Alexei, like a flower or a butterfly.

At first she didn't appear to see him. He stood beside a tree, hand pressed against the bark, and waited breathlessly for her to pass. She walked in soft, timid steps with her eyes lowered toward the ground. Her slippers were tiny and shimmering grey, unlike any he had ever seen, so delicate and outlandish looking.

Then she raised her eyes suddenly and looked at him. A gaze as gentle and calm as that of a deer, but inexpressibly lovely to him, full of a certain fire, too. His heart beat wildly. It seemed that a momentary smile crossed her lips as she passed, a friendly yet dignified smile — or was it more than that? He couldn't be sure, he could be sure of nothing at all now, for the world had suddenly grown new, tremulous, and full of magical expectations.

He saw her a second time, and a third, walking through the copse both times, and by discreet inquiries he discovered that she was a distant Austrian cousin to Mme. Semenenko. Her name was Maria, he found, but her family name he never knew. He now felt that he had come closer to her: no longer a silken evanescent creature out of a fairy tale, but human, sweetly tangible. And one day, seeing her hurrying with a bouquet of bluebells through the garden toward the big white house as it was beginning to rain he suddenly felt like crying out to her, joyfully, intimately, 'Maria, Maria, Maria!'

A few days later he found her sitting upon a tree trunk at the side of the village road, her yellow hat on the grass beside her. She looked hot and tired — but, with the beads of moisture on her brow and the wet curls on her temples, lovelier than ever. He stopped near her with an aching heart. What, oh what might he say? What might he whisper in her ear, to tell her how deeply he admired her, how he longed to kneel at her feet, to write a poem to her, to send her a present of roses, to protect her from the cruelty of the world? He approached, eyes lowered, glanced for one moment at her with an intense shy longing, and then passed on down the road. His heart was overflowing, yet he had said not a word.

But he had seen enough. He had seen, for one celestial and unforgettable moment, her blue eyes meeting his own, the sweet glance of friendly recognition beneath the row of blond little curls that fell upon her forehead.

As he approached the farm he began to leap with joy, he wanted to sing, but then remembered that his voice was hoarse and displeasing. However, he stopped beside an old poplar tree, leaned his head against it for a moment, and then planted upon it a quick, happy kiss.

Several days later he was sent to the big white house with a basketful of cherries for Madame Semenenko.

But instead of waiting in the courtyard he was led by the footman along the mirrored and marbled hall into a large brocaded room. 'Wait here,' said the ugly old footman in his conceited Polish accent. Through a half-open door he could see into the next room — a large yellow room with dark green hangings. In the middle of it sat two army officers playing chess, one old and the other young.

There he stood, with his sunburned arms hanging bashfully out of the torn blue blouse, alternately blushing and blanching in expectation of he knew not what austere or enchanting arrival. He waited five minutes, ten minutes. Then, the basketful of ruby-red cherries dangling from his elbow, he looked about the room more curiously: everywhere were little Chinese figurines, bits of ivory, exotic vases, and toys and such. Upon the mantel in front of a large mirror lay a marble boy, with the long curls and ripe breasts of a girl — on the pedestal underneath he read, letter by letter, the mystifying legend: *Sleeping Hermaphrodite*. A great fire screen stood in front of the hearth and on it were painted in the most charming colours a shaggy man with legs like a goat's and a woman lying under a willow-tree, naked and smiling, eyes lustfully fastened upon the other's body. Alexei found this picture deeply exciting. His heart beat more quickly, and the room seemed suddenly full of strange shadows, visitors out of a curious and fabulous unknown. A great cabinet inlaid with ivory roses and cherubs stood in the corner. Pink ladies rested on golden clouds that were painted on the ceiling. Above all, upon every wall hung paintings framed in the most magnificent golden frames. He looked at one — another naked lady —

and under it he read the name 'Guido Reni'; an Italian, he thought, and his imagination went wild with the thought of a sunny Mediterranean land where men had goat's hooves and women were for ever willing and boys were shaped like girls; and where such lovely unclad figures went leaping across a landscape of ruined towers, streams lined with gnarled trees, grazing sheep, and countless flowers.

Presently the door opened and Maria appeared on the threshold. He was overcome by her beauty, so flawless, so far beyond his reach. She looked at him a moment gently and without a word. She appeared much younger than he had thought. She wasn't after all so very much older than he, perhaps. Her skin was smooth as silk, her eyes were clear as a blue April morning. He caught his breath, stricken, and a sweet melancholy instantly filled his heart.

He nodded, gave her the basket, and mumbled an awkward explanation. How kind she was, how gentle and full of understanding! Her smile was free entirely of that robust irony which twinkled for ever in the eyes of the prettiest village girls. 'Thank you,' she said, in a soft accent, somewhat foreign yet charming and amiable. 'And come again soon, do!' Then she blushed.

Oh, those enchanted and light-hearted days! The delight of arising early in the August morning, leaping into the out-of-doors where the sun was already beguiling each leaf and flower; the rambles in the field where the silky bullocks, their hooves wet and shining with dew, stared at him with their big stupid eyes; climbing the fence, leaping over the brook, skipping past the haystacks and through the orchard, full of the morning's joy and other subtler joys still anticipated. Youth, with the spring in the ankle and the fresh young juice in the knee-joints, the limbs still clear and pliable, the chest firm and smooth, the ribs like soft waves in the warm resilient flesh, the hips slim and white as marble, the hair glowing, the gait careless and graceful, the eyes quick, clear, responsive, innocent, the lips firm and pure, the voice soft and expectant, the spirit so self-forgetful, so ardent! The eyes, the ears, the skin, all were overjoyed to be alive, quivering with delighted surprise at everything they perceived, the green dewy grass, the infinite blue sky, the travelling clouds which assumed strange shapes — a sleeping giantess, a wild boar, a crumbled glove, a wig, an enormous lyre, glowing against the blue so brilliantly that for a moment he longed to be there too, in that soft, white world where no mortal harm could ever reach one and where, no doubt, a continuous heavenly music echoed in one's ears.

He would reach the edge of the wood: the dark level wood of Russia, the ageless, tangled wood where trunks of a thousand years ago were still rotting away and a thousand pale mushrooms guarded their black remains. She would be waiting for him at the edge of the path beside the gate, hidden from the fields and the houses. Then they would walk along the orchard, her hair fluttering in the breeze and her straw-hat hanging on her shoulders by a pink band around her neck. He would watch her, scarcely able to believe her beauty — her flower-like cheeks, her satin neck, her exquisite lips across which she would quickly run her tongue now and again. Even on rainy days she would solemnly wait for him under an umbrella, and they would creep into the old summer-house and sit there, telling old tales, whispering reminiscences. Once she fell asleep there, and his eyes wandered across her face, pausing now at her eyelids, now at her temples, now at her lips still smiling ever so faintly, like a traveller in an enchanted landscape who cannot believe that those trees are truly not of gold, those leaves of emerald, those diamonds nought but daisies. Suddenly, with a glow of surprise, he said to himself, 'I am in love! I am in love!' Then he leaned over and placed on her cheek his first kiss, as timidly as if it were a flower out of the meadow that he was placing in her hand.

And then, those late September evenings! Those prolonged kisses, those impatient fingers sent on their familiar journeys, caressing the fragrant muslin, each new treasure so sweetly attained with wildly beating heart! In the perfect black mirror of the pond he could see reflected the hanging leaves, the darkening sullen clouds, even the devout spire in the distance, all with an amazing exactitude. She would point these out to him, as well as the leaves falling slowly into the water and the fragrance of the fallen leaves: he would be full of surprise at things which he had never noticed before — all the details of this dusky landscape that flowed gradually into such a novel existence before his eyes. Never had he noticed all this before. The mere colour of the leaves seemed suddenly miraculous and touching. That, yes, that was love, so unbelievable, filling the world with intimacy, making it all his own, as if the Lord had tried to please him above all other creatures in creating this charming variety.

And she beside him seemed now no longer an individual but, perhaps, a perfect song created out of all the rest of the world; no longer Maria, but one with the trees, the water, the subdued rhythm of the oncoming night. Oh, lovely, lovely, she was! The loveliness of woman seemed mysterious and marvellous indeed, as variable as the glitter of water, as fresh as the scent of ferns, as consoling as the sound of a violin in the village inn on a cold night. The porcelain hands, the silken hair, the glowing cheeks, all assumed the indefinable hues of mother-of-pearl — like that shell from the Caspian Sea which lay on his mother's dressing-table — as she lay back on the grass and smiled. There only, in those opened arms, did all peace and sweetness of the world seem to be united, while the vast clouds moved above their heads and the trees grew darker and darker.

But September passed, and October, too, little by little. Little by little he felt his lightheartedness vanishing, his delight endangered. He no longer understood the things that went on within him: the wild ambitions, the longing for glory, the gnawing uncertainty, the quick moments of panic and hopelessness and longing to hurt which later on he learned to call 'jealousy.'

Once they quarrelled — about nothing at all, about the hour they were to meet on the next day, perhaps. Full of despair he crept around to the big white house that night and stood outside her window. It began to rain softly. He could see the lamplight fading on the curtain which was drawn across the window, and now and then a momentary shadow cast upon it. Then he climbed the chestnut-tree and crept along the wet branch almost up to the window; by reaching out his arm he could almost touch the casement, but not quite, for the branch began to creak ominously and he didn't dare climb farther. Through a small opening in the curtain he could catch a glimpse of the room. She was sitting by a table, her back to the window, turning over the pages of a large photograph album bound in green velvet; at one page a dead flower fell out and fluttered to the floor, and for some obscure reason he felt a twinge of overwhelming grief in his heart — perhaps to see this fragment of a different love out of a different past so very casually fluttering into oblivion, perhaps because his own heart suddenly recognized how little one can ever possess, how frail and brief the ownership must be. He admired the glow of her hair under the lamplight and the lovely curve of her neck as she leaned over; he longed to touch it with his lips and yet, for the first time, there seemed to be something cruel and perverse in that beauty which he had never yet tasted quite to the full, which still was veiled in mystery.

He broke off a twig and tossed it at the window, and then another. She rose and turned around, with a curious expression on her face. He lost sight of her for a minute; his heart beat madly, for it occurred to him that she might leave the room. However, a moment later the curtain was drawn aside and she stood at the window, only three feet away from him. Yes, there was an unmistakable look of mischievousness in her eyes as she gazed at him and her lips melted into a delicate smile.

He called to her gently, 'Maria,' and slowly she opened the window, reached out and touched his hand. Then he crept forward and clutched at the window sill and leapt into the room. 'Look, your clothes are quite wet,' she said; 'you will catch a cold....' She looked incredibly lovely, never before had her beauty seemed so irresistible, so flame-like, so tormenting. 'Here, slip off your wet things,' she whispered, and held out a blue dressing-robe; 'put this over you.' He took off the wet blouse but did not dare put the silky thing over his wet shoulders, so he sat there, half-naked, unable to think of anything to say.

But, seeing that she had forgotten their quarrel, and seemed indeed more gentle than ever, though he understood nothing at all, himself least of all, he knew that he felt terribly happy, relieved almost to the point of tears to see her being so kind to him. He longed desperately to put his arms around her and press her wildly to his heart. All he dared do, though, was suddenly to run his fingers over her hair in a burst of childish delight.

She smiled, and sat down on the edge of the bed. 'You heard the singing in the village tonight?' she asked in a soft low voice.

He nodded ecstatically.

'Wasn't it agreeable?'

'Oh, yes!' he whispered with enthusiasm. Actually it had only increased his sadness of two hours ago, to hear the music coming from the inn; but now in retrospect it seemed to him wholly delightful.

But as she waited for him to say more, glancing now at the floor and now at him, a little smile for ever at her lips like the clown in a play who peers through the curtain between two acts; during these moments which he never forgot, it never occurred to him that a subtle imperfection existed in this joy; all he knew was that there was something he longed desperately to say, but since words were always very difficult things to him and since no words in the world would have been more difficult to utter than the simple ones 'I love you,' he remained silent.

And presently, carrying his wet blouse in his hand, he was again walking through the orchard on his way home. Now and then he felt an apple being crushed under his heel: the rain had stopped, the leafy darkness was full of the smell of rotting apples and wet autumn foliage. Once he heard an apple falling softly into the grass. High overhead he saw the clouds moving, some stars suddenly appearing, even a little sliver of a moon. Never before in his life had he felt both so unbelievably happy and so inexplicably sad.

Two mornings later Maria departed from Dolya. She was wearing a dark hat and a dark coat and long dark gloves. She looked quite old suddenly. Her two trunks were placed in the carriage beside her, and off they drove. She turned and cast a hurried smile at the servants who were standing in a row beside the stairs, and hardly seemed to notice Alexei at all. Piotrowski was sitting beside her. She was going back to Carinthia, they explained, where she was to marry the son of the mayor of Villach.

He turned and ran to the old summer-house, full of its sweet and fragrant afternoon remembrances. He buried his head in the darkness, but even the power to burst into tears had quite forsaken him. He felt very ignorant, very helpless indeed. And he never saw her again. All he had left of her was a little miniature portrait of her which she had given him a week before, in a mosaic frame of roses and forget-me-nots, and tucked behind the picture, a lock of her hair and a bit of fern that she had once pressed to her lips. And even this small object he could scarcely bear to gaze upon, it hurt him so; he took to wearing it on a red string around his neck until one day a friend of his teased him about it as they were undressing to go swimming in the Kalmius River. Moon-faced, girlish, senti-mental, they called him. After this he simply carried it in his pocket, reaching in to feel it there, ten, twenty times a day. But he rarely looked at it, even long after, for he couldn't do so without feeling an overwhelming longing run through his body and an ache of sadness clutch at his heart.

A REAL AMERICAN FELLOW [1]

By GEORGE THORP RAYNER

From *Story*)

H E SAT in his room, on the edge of his bed, in his dressing-gown. He always took a shower after coming home from the bank, and then a brisk rubdown with a heavy turkish towel. Nothing like it for sending the good old red blood pumping through your veins. But tonight his body felt cold and moist, and he drew the robe closer about him and sat looking around at his room as though he had never seen it before.

It had been about four o'clock when the telephone rang at the bank and Tracey the cashier hollered, 'Hey, Ed, your old lady on the phone!'

He'd said, breezily, 'Hello, Mom!' (always did have a good voice over the phone: full of pep and personality) and she'd said, quick and hoarse as though she were out of breath: 'Grant and May have come home. To stay, I mean. They have to because he's lost his job. I thought maybe I'd better tell you.'

Grant was his older brother. Only that morning he'd been having a chat with Clarke the V. P. out in the washroom about business conditions. (Of course, with this administration, Ed, we can't expect a full recovery.) Clarke had said, 'How's your brother Grant making out, down in New York?' (Nobody ever asked about Pop now, since his little haberdashery had folded.) And Ed had answered, all alive with enthusiasm: 'Swell! Yes, sir, Mr. Clarke; getting orders by the carload. Real results, all the time!' Then Clarke had said something about how he remembered Grant on the High football team and how he'd remarked then that that chap was going to get ahead in the world.

Now Grant had come sneaking home with his wife because he was broke and out of a job. For three months he hadn't been doing a thing; just living on the little they'd saved, and putting up a bluff.

When Ed had come in (tip-toeing up the stairs instead of sounding his heels briskly like he always did), his mother had been waiting for him in his room.

Her face had been gray, like a dishcloth wrung dry, and she kept looking down at the floor.

'We got to keep it from people, somehow,' he'd said. 'We got to play fair by him.'

'Yes,' she answered. 'When you come down to dinner don't let on anything.'

'But those peppy letters he wrote!' Ed had whispered hoarsely. (His kid sister Kate was walking past the door, and they waited a bit, until she'd gone.)

'I know,' Mom said. Her gray hair streaking out in limp wisps; first time he'd ever seen it when every end wasn't in place, so. 'I guess it was his pride. That's the Gardner of it, that pride!'

Then, in a nervous, low voice she'd said: 'I think I better tell you, Ed, not — not to look at May too much! I'm afraid that she — that she's in a delicate condition.'

He hadn't said anything; his throat suddenly dry and tight.

'Where we're going to put them I don't know. I'm sure I don't know.'

So now he sat on the edge of his bed thinking about May and he couldn't help feeling as if something dirty was crawling all over him. It was all right to have a kid when things were going good; but for Grant to have to bring her back here in this state, with no money: it was unclean, somehow.

Sometimes when he looked through his window at night (their house was on a nice street, but the one next was all full of wops; that was the way in a small manufacturing town) he could see people making love to each other. Wops always had their rooms chuck full of beds, anyhow. It sure was disgusting. They never bothered to pull down the shades and when you looked at them — through field glasses, of course — it made you almost ashamed of the human race. It was their faces, though, that were worst of all. Especially the wops. That oily look, that way it was written all over their eyes and mouths.

He couldn't imagine his brother Grant looking like that. *Jesus!*

At the 'Y' rally, last Sunday, they'd had a real peppy speaker from Union and he'd said: 'Now, boys, I want to get right down and talk with you like one fellow to another and I want you to try and remember how often during — say the last week — you have taken the name of the Lord in vain. Even if only in your thoughts — Now, fellows, I'm not going to argue with you on moral grounds, but I'm going to put it up to you the way I would if we were all out on the diamond or the gridiron. I'm going to say to you: "Is it sporting? Is it fair play?"'

He was right, too. But, darn it all, he couldn't help popping out once in a while. After all he wasn't thinking of the Lord when it slipped into his mind like that.

The same speaker had wound up his talk by saying: 'And I think, men, that the ideal we should work toward in our daily lives is becoming what, amongst ourselves, we would call a real American fellow. Now I don't want you to get the idea that I'm a prig or a goody-goody. I enjoy life as well as the next one. (And I might say, in passing, that I am myself the father of four husky young American fellows.) But I do say that it is up to you — to you who represent the right-living, right-thinking vigorous flower of our young manhood to smash your way through ——' But Ed hadn't been able to catch the very end of the talk because the fellows who had charge of serving refreshments were rattling plates and coffee cups around so as to serve everybody right away, and the three ex-convicts who were going to give selections on the cornet had started to unpack their instruments.

Grant had used to be assistant secretary down at the 'Y.'

'If he could only have stuck it out in New York!' Ed thought bitterly. 'If he'd only had the guts!'

Once again he looked slowly about at his room. Because at once, as soon as he'd heard about May, he'd made the decision to give it up. But it was going to be kind of hard to get the right words together. At first he'd thought he'd just tell Mom, on the quiet, but the more he thought about it the more he decided that the right thing was to come plunk out with it at the dining-room table that night.

Gee, it had been one swell room! On the wall there was his high school pennant, a little faded now, and right underneath the picture of the president of his bank that he had cut out of the *Investment Journal*. Opposite, on the other wall, were two shinny sticks, crossed; a picture of Ann Hathaway's cottage, and a pair of boxing gloves. There were his bookshelves that he'd made in carpenter shop in the grades and on them his Alger set and the Tom Swift series. On the floor of the closet were his hockey skates and a rusted iron bank (that had been his, with a five dollar gold piece in it, even before he was born).

But the thing he was proudest of of all was his yearbook from High that he kept out, conspicuously, on the top of the desk. He went over to it now and looked down at its nice leather binding (his Pop had had it specially bound for him with his name in gold lettering on the cover). On the title page it said Editor-in-Chief and, directly following, his own name: Edward Frank Gardner. It was a good name, a real American one, and people hearing it could easily enough take it for that of a V. P. if they didn't know.

It was getting late. Time for dinner. He went over to the closet and took out a fresh set of shirt and shorts. (Then, thinking of something, he went back to the yearbook and leafed the pages over to look at Gert's picture. Gert was his girl friend, and had been for years. Underneath her picture she had written: 'To Ed, a regular guy.')

Somehow he didn't like that inscription. It reminded him of the last time he had dated her. They were out in Bud Payson's car and they were parked somewhere, and he'd been trying a little light necking. She'd said — what was it, now? — oh, yes, she'd said, 'You know, what I like about you, Ed, is you're a nice, decent kind of fellow!'

That was a hell of a thing to say. At petting he was all pins and needles, anyhow, and that didn't help any.

At the bank there was a Polack messenger, a fresh sort of kid, and he was always asking Ed: 'Well, bud, how's it going? You getting much these days?'

Ed always acted up real wise, then. Because after all he was twenty-one and there wasn't any reason why you shouldn't let on to people that you've been around. But only once had he had the nerve. And that was when he was out with a bunch of the fellows and they were all lit. (Only twice in his life was he ever really drunk, and both times before he signed the pledge at the 'Y.') They'd gone to some place up the river. It was a gray clapboard house and they walked up a narrow flight of wooden stairs and then there was this room with a brass bed and a dark splotch of wallpaper where a picture had been. But he was a flop, absolutely. It almost made him sick to his stomach. Going home, the fellows let him in for a lot of kidding, but in his mind he made a vow to remain decent after this; although he didn't tell them that.

He stood in front of the mirror running a wet comb through his hair, and slicking it back with a brush. Then he put on his coat, and he was ready.

But he didn't want to go down. There was a kind of sunk feeling in his stomach as though he'd eaten a lot of hamburgers or something. He didn't want to have to go down into that dining-room and have to look his brother in the face.

As he stood, his legs stiff and cold, he heard a familiar noise from outside the house. It was aways off yet but he knew what it was. It was the wops, parading. Every week or so this time of year they had some kind of fiesta with brass bands and people parading. They were supposed to keep to their own streets but when everybody got well oiled they started sprawling all over the neighborhood.

He went to his window, opened the sash to see if they were coming this way. Sure enough. The street was empty, as yet, the houses cold and shut-up looking in the moonlight. It was a clean street, with the homes all in pastel colors and all the same size. (So alike, his Pop always said, that the cat never knew which one to come home to.) Fifty-foot front, five rooms and bath, with a tin garage and a tiny grass plot. It was so quiet, usually, that when you walked along you could hear the canary birds singing from dining-room windows.

He leaned on the sill watching the glitter of brass teetering crazily in the distance, at the banners that were like lapping tongues of flame. For a while he forgot that it was time for him to go down and face his brother; he just lay resting there on the sill, his body tired as though it had been beaten to exhaustion. Soon the street was full of people; they swarmed over the sidewalks, even over the grass plots and looking at their faces and seeing them so close he felt his hatred of them hot in his throat. Damn, stinking wops! They were laughing and singing, and the noise made the walls of his room shiver. They always looked so happy (although of course they couldn't kid him). Happy? *Happy?*

'Why,' he thought fiercely, 'seventy-five per cent of them are on the Relief!'

That made him feel better at once. He got up and slammed down the window.

When he went downstairs the noise of the wops was only a blurred murmur. As he crossed the little hall to the dining-room his shoulders became at once square-set and his chin firm. Inside the room the family was talking, but the hushed sound of their words made it seem as though somebody had died.

They were all there, at the table, drowned in the light from the green and purple chandelier. Pop, with his bald head shining, a confused, frightened smile trembling on his lips, Mom calm and bent over the vegetable dishes, his kid sister Kate, her mouth held tight as though she'd been warned not to talk.

His brother shuffled to his feet. 'Hi-yah, old scout!'

'Hi-yah!' Ed said, his voice warm and quick. His brother's hand was firm in its grasp, but the palm was moist with sweat.

'Well!' May cried shrilly. 'If it isn't Edward!'

He tried not to look at her, but he couldn't help it. 'Hello!' he said breezily; 'how's tricks?' (But somehow she didn't look like he'd expected. She wasn't getting fatter, so you could notice. Only there was something about her face, as though it had come a little loose, with her features heavier. And her hair looked sloppy.)

'Well!' Pop cried, his voice clammy with amiability. 'Here's the missing link in the family chain! Let's eat!'

They all laughed and sat down at the table.

They bent over their plates as though they were very hungry. It was then that Ed looked at his brother. Sitting so, under the light, his blond hair dry and brittle-looking, his face still held that awful, set smile. Like the face of a drunk, seen under a street lamp.

Only Ed was sitting erect. But all along his body, even in the crook of his elbows, there was this numb feeling, as though he was going to be sick.

'Well, Katie,' May said suddenly, 'how's school these days?'

'Okay,' she answered.

'How's things by you, Ed?' Grant asked. (They sounded like voices in a radio play.)

'Oh, so-so. Of course, with this administration we can't expect a full recovery.'

'No,' Pop said. 'No, that's right. You've got to get money into the people's hands.'

They were quiet then, all at once, and Pop choked a little on what he was eating. In the hall the clock ticked insistently and outside the wops' voices sound up again.

'The eye-talians are having a parade,' Kate volunteered. 'They have confetti. Some red and some yellow.'

'What do you mean?' Grant asked quickly. 'They come on this street?'

'When they're intoxicated they do,' Mom said. 'We've made complaints, but then of course this street is mostly Republican, and you know what that means at City Hall.'

'You leave it to me!' Grant said, coming swiftly to action. His knife and fork rattled down to his plate. 'You just let me fix that! I've a mind to get in touch with Bill McHugh down at the precinct. Let me get to the phone!'

'We haven't got any telephone,' Kate said. 'We haven't had any telephone for a long time.'

'Keep your shirt on!' Ed said. 'I'm going to speak to the Captain myself when he comes in the bank.'

Grant laughed. 'Oh, they won't listen to a kid.'

His brother's saying that made something snap inside him. It was funny. He felt, all at once, warmth, almost liquid warmth, flow over his mind, over all of him, easing that taut numbness. His thoughts swam with words. He wanted to leap up and say: 'Well, that kid's going to support you now, you weak-livered bum! And that kid's been supporting this house for the last two years. What you got to say to that?'

His Mom was saying: 'Here's your dessert, Ed.'

'I don't want any.'

He wanted to say: 'You never had any guts. Just a windbag, that's all. Just a windbag.'

Curiously, in the back of his mind, he was remembering now back to the days when Grant was on the football team at High. He used to be the star player. His name used to be smack up front in all the write-ups. And on the nights of those big games Ed used to lay awake waiting for his brother to come home from parties. They slept in the same bed then. And even after his brother had turned in Ed used to lie there, away over on his side of the bed so he wouldn't disturb Grant, and he used to tremble in a kind of ecstasy, just thinking what a great guy his brother was.

In the silence he could hear their chairs scraping. They were all getting up.

'Say!' Grant said. 'Say, Ed, what do you say to a game of rummy? Remember those sessions we used to have?'

'No,' he said, calmly, 'I guess I'm going to have a little work to do tonight.'

'Work?' May cried. 'You mean you have to work at night?'

'Oh, not at the bank. It's only that — say Grant, I almost forgot! I'm letting you and May have my room. That's what I mean. I've got to get a few things out.'

'But where you going to *sleep?*' May asked.

'In the attic. We've got a flop bed I can put up there.'

They were all just sort of standing around in the hall.

Then Grant said, 'That's white of you, old man!'

'Glad to do it.' Then he turned to go up the stairs.

'Now listen, Ed!' Mom said, bustling after him. 'You let me fix it up a bit for you. You let me make it real comfy.'

He turned, briefly. But he wasn't looking at his Mom. He was looking at Grant standing there staring up at him, not saying anything, his shoulders stooped a bit under the light.

He turned in about eleven. The attic was only high enough to stand up in in certain places, and he had to be careful. But somehow he felt like he was drunk, and he didn't care. There was a fierce righteousness burning inside him.

Mom had given the place a good sweeping and pushed a lot of trunks back in the corner. She'd insisted upon his taking the bridge lamp from the living-room and an overstuffed chair. The flop bed was smoothed down, with clean white sheets on it, and the coverlet was turned back, all ready for him.

As he stood, half bent over, getting undressed, he heard the wop band again. It sounded different up here, the notes high and crazier. They must all be pretty well stewed, now; he could tell by all the hollering and laughing.

There wasn't any window here (only a skylight) and he couldn't look out.

'Damn wops!' he thought. He was going to talk to the Captain, too. He'd tell him a few things!

When the light was out and he was in bed the voices droned away gradually into the distance. He'd tried pulling the coverlet over his ears at first, but that didn't help so much. But after a while they went away altogether and he lay there just listening to the quiet. It was sort of chilly up here, lonely in a way, too.

But he'd get used to it.

He was almost asleep, when something brought him to with a start. At first he didn't know what it was — until he realized that his old room was directly underneath and that the sounds he heard must be Grant and May going to bed.

Or maybe they were in bed already.

He raised himself on his elbow, listening intently. The sounds were so soft, like cats moving around somewhere. He heard some-one murmur. That was Grant. Then everything was quiet again.

Then he heard another sound. Like someone crying. Low-like. (The warm flow was over him once again.) Crying. Well, that was something like!

It was May. He strained avidly to listen. But — he choked, un-believing.

She wasn't crying. She was laughing. *Laughing!* Laughing with that little gurgling sound that a child makes when someone is fondling it.

THE HAUNTED PALACE[1]

By ELIZABETH MADOX ROBERTS

(From *Harper's Magazine*)

THE House stood at the head of a valley where the hollow melted away into the rolling uplands. The high trees about the place so confined the songs of the birds that on a spring morning the jargoning seemed to merge from the walls. The birds seemed to be indoors or within the very bricks of the masonry. In winter the winds blew up the hollow from the valley and lashed at the old house that stood square before the storms. The place was called Wickwood. It had been the abode of a family, Wickley, a group that had once clustered about the hearths there or had tramped over the courtyard or ridden through the pastures.

From a road that ran along the top of a ridge two miles to the east, the House could be seen as a succession of rhomboids and squares that flowed together beneath the vague misty reds of the mass. Or from the valley road to the west, looking up the hollow into the melting hills, in winter it could be seen as a distant brick wall set with long windows, beneath a gray sloping roof. Sometimes a traveler, allured by the name of the place or by the aloof splendor of the walls as seen vaguely from one or the other of these highways, would cross the farmlands by the way of the uneven roads. He would trundle over the crooked ways and mount through the broken woodland to come at last to the House. Leaving his conveyance, he would cross the wide courtyard on the smooth flagstones, and he would hear the strange report his footfalls made as they disturbed the air that had, but for the birds and the wind, been quiet for so great a length of time that it had assumed stillness. He would wonder at the beauty of the doorways and deplore the waste that let the House stand unused and untended. He would venture up the stone steps at the west front and peer through the glass of the side lights. The strange quality of the familiar fall of his own shoe on stone would trouble his sense of all that he had discovered, so that he would at last come swiftly away.

The country rolled in changing curves and lines and spread toward the river valleys where it dropped suddenly into a basin. The farms were owned by men and women who had labored to win them. But among these were younger men who worked for hire or as shareowners in the yield.

One of these last, Hubert, lived with Jess, his wife, in a small whitewashed shelter behind a cornfield. Jess spoke more frequently than the man and thus she had more memory. She had been here two years, but before that time she had lived beside a creek, and before that again in another place, while farther back the vista was run together in a fog of forgetting. She had courted Hubert in a cabin close beside a roadway. She remembered another place where there was a plum tree that bore large pink-red fruits, and a place where her father had cut his foot with an axe. Now, as a marker, her own children ran a little way into a cornfield to play. Beyond these peaks in memory, going backward, the life there rested in a formless level out of which only self emerged. She met any demand upon this void with a contempt in which self was sheltered.

Hubert was a share-laborer, but he wanted to be able to rent some land. He wanted to use land as if he were the owner, and yet to be free to go to fresh acres when he had exhausted a tract as he willed. After the first child, Albert, was born, he said to Jess:

'If a person could have ahead, say, four hundred dollars, and against the Dean land might come idle . . .'

His fervor had the power of a threat. He was knotty and bony and his muscles were dry and lean. He had learned at school to write his name and to make a few slow marks that signified numbers or quantities, but later he had used this knowledge so infrequently that most of it was lost to him. He wrote his name painfully, and writing, he drew his fingers together about the pen. His breath would flow hard and fast under the strain, his hand trembling. If there were other men standing about he would, if he were asked to write his name, sometimes say that he could not, preferring to claim complete illiteracy rather than to undergo the ordeal.

'Against the Dean land might come idle . . .' He had a plan over which he brooded, wanting to get a power over some good land that he might drain money out of it. He was careful, moving forward through the soil, taking from it.

When the second child came they lived at the Dean land, behind the cornfield. Jess would fling a great handful of grain toward her hens and they would come with reaching bills and outthrust necks, their wings spread. She would throw ears of corn to the sow and it would chew away the grains while the sucklings would drag milk, the essence of the corn, from the dark udders.

'We ought, it seems, to build the sow a little shed against winter comes,' Jess said to Hubert.

'We might eat the sow. I might fatten up the sow and get me another.'

'She always was a no-account sow. Has only five or six to a litter. It's hardly worth while to pester yourself with a lazy hog.'

'Fannie Burt asked me what was the name of the sow or to name what kind or breed she was. "Name?" I says. As if folks would name the food they eat!'

Hubert laughed at the thought of naming the food. Names for the swine, either mother or species, gave him laughter. To write with one's hand the name of a sow in a book seemed useless labor. Instead of giving her a name he fastened her into a closed pen and gave her all the food he could find. When she was sufficiently fat he stuck her throat with a knife and prepared her body for his own eating.

Jess yielded to the decision Hubert made, being glad to have decisions made for her, and thus she accepted the flesh of the brood sow. Of this she ate heavily. She was large and often of a placid temper, sitting in unbrooding inattention, but often she flamed to sudden anger and thrust about her then with her hands or her fists. She did not sing about the house or the dooryard. Singing came to her from a wooden box that was charged by a small battery. She adjusted the needle of this to a near sending station and let the sound pour over the cabin. Out of the abundant jargon that flowed from the box she did not learn, and before it she did not remember....

Jess had a few friends who came sometimes to see her. They were much like herself in what they knew and in what they liked. She would look curiously at their new clothing.

But one of them, named Fannie Burt, would come shouting to

the children as she drove up the lane in a small cart, and her coming filled the day with remembered sayings and finer arrangements. When Fannie came Jess would call Albert, the oldest child, and send him on his hands and knees under the house to rob the hen's nest if there were not enough eggs in the basket; for the day called for a richer pudding. Fannie had no children as yet and she could be light and outflowing. She went here and there and she knew many of the people.

'Miss Anne mended the cover to the big black sofa in the parlor ...' She would tell of many things — of tapestry on a wall, blue and gold. Words seemed light when she talked, as being easily made to tell of strange and light matters. Jess was not sure that Fannie knew more of these things than she knew herself since the words conveyed but an undefined sense. The lightness of bubbles floated about Fannie, things for which Jess had no meanings. Fannie had lived the year before at a farm where the owner had been as a neighbor to her. She often went back to call there, staying all day as a friend.

'Miss Anne mended the cover to the sofa where it was worn.' Jess laughed with Fannie, and she scarcely knew whether she laughed at the sofa or at the mended place. She herself could not sew, and thus she could not mend any broken fabric of any kind. She laughed, however, Fannie's call being just begun. She was not yet hostile to it. She tried for the moment to stretch her imaginings to see something desired or some such thing as grace or beauty in the person who leaned over the ancient tapestry to mend it. The effort was spent in wonder and finally in anger. Fannie laughed at the sullenness that came to Jess. The sofa had come from Wickwood, she said. It had been given to Miss Anne at her marriage, for she was somehow related to the Wickleys. Laughing, Fannie tossed the least child and settled to tell again. Her tales would be, all together, a myth of houses and families, of people marrying and settling into new abodes. She was gay and sharp, and her face was often pointed with smiles. Or she would be talking now with the children and telling them the one story she had from a book.

'Then a great ogre lived in the place ... a thing that threatens to get you ... a great Thing ... destroys ... eats up Life itself. Drinks the blood out of Life. It came with a club in its hand. ... It was a fine place, but had a Thing inside it. ... That would be when little Blue Wing went to the woods to play. She found this place in the woods...'

'What was that?' Jess asked suddenly. 'What kind was that you named?'

'A giant. Orgy or ogre. A Thing. Comes to eat up a man and to eat Life itself....'

Fannie would be gone and Jess would be glad to have an end of her. As if too much had been asked of her she would sit now in vague delight, and she would forget to run her radio instrument while she saw Fannie's bright pointed face as something slipping past her. The stories that had been told had become a blend of indistinct mental colorings that would drop out of memory at length, as a spent pleasure no longer wanted. She would reject the visit completely and turn to anger, thrusting Fannie out. Then, complete hostility to the visitor having come to her, she would set roughly upon her tasks. If the children spoke of the stories that had been told she would order them to be quiet.

Some of the farms had lost their former owners. A house here and there was shut and still while the acres were farmed by the shifting men who lived in the cabins or in the town. A man came searching for Hubert at the end of the harvest to offer him a part of the Wickley place to farm.

'It's said fine people once lived there,' Hubert said when he told Jess of his offer.

'If they're gone now I wouldn't care.'

'It's not like any place ever you saw in life. It's good land howsoever.'

Other tenants would be scattered over the acres, laborers who would farm by sharing the crops. Hubert would rent the acres about the house and he would live there.

'Is there a good well of water?'

'Two wells there are,' he answered her.

'I never heard of two wells.'

'One has got a little fancy house up over it.'

'What would I do with a little fancy house built up over a well? I can't use such a house.' As if more might be required of her than she could perform, Jess was uneasy in thinking of the new place to which they would go. She did not want to go there. 'It's a place

made for some other,' she said. She could not see the women of the
place going about their labors. She could not discover what they
might carry in their hands and what their voices might call from
the doorways, or how they would sleep or dress themselves or find
themselves food. In her troubled thought, while she came and went
about the cabin room where the least child lay, shapes without
outline, the women of the Wickleys, went into vague distances
where doors that were not defined were opened and closed into an
uncomprehended space.

But the next day Fannie Burt came and there was something
further to know. The Wickley farm was called Wickwood, she said.
Miss Anne's father had gone there in old Wickley's lifetime. Together these two men had made experiments in the growing of fine
animals. Sometimes it would be a horse old Wickley wanted.
'Egad!' he would say, or 'I'm not dead yet!' Another story running
into a comic ending, 'A good colt she is, but a leetle matter of inter-
ference. Look at her hind feet.' Fannie had something that Miss
Anne had in mind. It was told imperfectly, thrown out in a hint and
retained in a gesture, put back upon Miss Anne, who could tell with
fluent words and meaning gestures. She would be sitting over the
last of the dessert in the old, faded dining room. She would be
telling for the pure joy of talking, laughing with the past. 'Pappy
went over to Wickwood.... It was Tuesday.... Came Sunday
then and we all said, "Where's Pappy?" Came to find out and he's
still over to Wickwood with Cousin Bob. All that time to get the
brown mare rightly in foal. And all still on paper.'

Fannie would seem to be talking fast, and one thing would seem
to be entangled with another, although she spoke with Miss Anne's
quiet, slow cadence. In her telling men would be sitting together in
a library. One would be making a drawing of a horse, such a horse
as he would be devising. A horse would be sketched on paper before
it was so much as foaled. This would be old Robert Wickley, a pen
between his thumb and his fingers. 'What we want after all is a
good Kentucky saddle horse, fifteen hands high and two inches
over. Take Danbury II, say, over at Newmarket...'

'You take Danbury and you'll plumb get a jackass.'

'Pappy laughed over a thing once for a week before he told us,'
Miss Anne's speaking through Fannie's speaking. 'Pappy in a big
tellen way one day and he let it be known what he was so amused
about.'

A man had come in at the door at Wickwood, a hurried man with money in cash saved by. He wanted the Wickley land on which to grow something. He wanted to buy, offering cash.

'Do you think you could live in my house and on my land?' old Wickley asked.

Fannie would be telling as Miss Anne had told and, beyond again, the father who had told in a moment of amusement. Men who came on business were let in at a side door. 'Business was a Nobody then,' Miss Anne said. Mollie would be off somewhere in the house singing. Carline had run off to get married. Old Wickley, father to Robert, rolling back his shirtsleeves because the day was hot, and walking barefoot out into the cool grass, or he would be standing under the shower in the bath house while somebody pumped the water that sprayed over him. Miss Sallie made the garden with her own hands and designed the sundial. They made things for themselves with their hands. Bob Wickley sketching for himself the horse he wanted on a large sheet of manilla paper. His grandmother had, as a bride, set the house twelve feet back of the builder's specifications in order to save a fine oak tree that still grew before the front door. A man wanting to plow his pastures . . .

'Two hundred dollars an acre for the creek bottom, cash money.'

Wickley had called him a hog and sent him away. 'Pappy laughed over it for a week. "You think you could live in my house? Come back three generations from now." . . . "And egad, he couldn't," Pappy said.'

'Hogs want to root in my pasture,' Bob Wickley said. He was angry. . . . Miss Anne speaking through Fannie's speaking, reports fluttering about, intermingled, right and wrong, the present and the past. Fannie could scarcely divide one Wickley from another. One had gathered the books. One had held a high public office. One had married a woman who pinned back her hair with a gold comb. Their children had read plentifully from the books. Justus, William, and Robert had been names among them. Miss Anne now owned the portrait of the lady of the golden comb. There had been farewells and greetings, dimly remembered gifts, trinkets, portraits to be made, children to be born. . . .

In this telling as it came from the telling of Miss Anne, there was one, a Robert, who danced along the great parlor floor with one named Mollie. Mollie was the wife of Andrew. She had come from a neighboring farm. When they danced the music from the piano had crashed and tinkled under the hands of Miss Lizette, Robert's mother, or of Tony Barr, a young man who came to visit at Wickwood. Down would fling the chords on the beat and at the same instant up would fling the dancers, stepping upward on the rhythm and treading the air. Mollie's long slim legs would flash from beneath her flying skirts, or one would lie for an instant outstretched while the pulse of the music beat, then off along the shining floor, gliding and swaying with the gliding of Robert, until it seemed as if the two of them were one, and as if they might float out the window together, locked into the rhythms, and thus dance away across the world.

'Where are they now?' Jess asked.

Fannie did not know. Miss Anne had not told her.

'Where would be Andrew, the one that was her husband?' She was angry and she wanted to settle blame somewhere.

He would be beside the wall. He would look at Mollie with delight. His head would move, or his hands, with the rhythm, and his eyes would be bright. Mollie loved him truly.

Sometimes it would be the old fast waltzes that were danced, and then Miss Lizette and old Bob would come into it. Then they would whirl swiftly about the floor and the music would be 'Over the Waves.' The young would try it, dizzy and laughing, or they would change the steps to their own.

'What did they do?' Jess asked. 'I feel staggered to try to know about such a house.'

'They had a wide scope of land,' Fannie answered her. 'They burned the bricks and made the house. They cut the timber for the beams of the house off their own fields.'

The House had become an entity, as including the persons and the legends of it. All the Wickleys were blurred into one, were gathered into one report.

'There was a woman, Mollie Wickley. She was the mother of Andrew, or maybe she was his wife,' Fannie said. 'I don't recall. It's all one. There was a Sallie Wickley. I don't know whe'r she was his daughter or his wife.'

'Iffen he couldn't keep it for his children,' Jess called out, 'why would he build such a place?'

'He lived in the house *himself*.'

Jess and Hubert would be going to the place where these had been. All these were gone now. The land was still good. Hubert would be able to take money out of it. He would hold the plow into the soil and his tongue would hang from the side of his mouth in his fervor to plant more and to have a large yield. The people would be gone. Jess dismissed them with the clicking of her tongue. They seemed, nevertheless, to be coming nearer. In Fannie's presence, while she sat in the chair beside the door, they came nearer to flit as shapes about her fluttering tongue while Jess fixed her gaze upon the mouth that was speaking or shifted to look at the familiar cups and plates on the table. Shapes fluttered then over the cups. Vague forms, having not the shapes of defined bodies, but the ends of meanings appeared and went. Fannie knew little beyond the myths she had made, and Jess knew much less, knew nothing beyond the bright tinkle of Fannie's chatter.

'It was the horse then,' Fannie said, in part explaining. 'Now nobody wants enough horses.... Now it's tobacco.'

Hubert and Jess came to the place, Wickwood, at sundown of an early winter afternoon. Hubert talked of the land, of the fields, growing talkative as their small truck rolled slowly through the ruts of the old driveway. When they had passed through the woodland, which was now in part denuded of its former growth, they came near to the house. It seemed to Jess that there was a strange wideness about the place, as if space were spent outward without bounds. They went under some tall oaks and maples while Hubert muttered of his plans.

A great wall arose in the dusk. The trees stretched their boughs toward the high wall in the twilight. When it seemed that the truck would drive into the hard darkness of the wall that stood before them as if it went into the sky, Hubert turned toward the left and rounded among the trees. Other walls stood before them. Jess had never before seen a place like this. It seemed to her that it might be a town, but there were no people there. The children began to cry and Albert screamed, 'I want to go away.' Jess herself was frightened.

'Hush your fuss,' Hubert said. His words were rough. 'Get out of the truck,' he said to her. She attended to his short angry speech; it jerked her out of her fear and dispersed a part of her dread of the place. It made her know that they, themselves and their goods, their life and their ways of being, would somehow fit into the brick walls, would make over some part of the strangeness for their own use. He had climbed from the vehicle and he walked a little way among the buildings, stalking in the broad courtyard among the flagstones and over the grass. He looked about him. Then he went toward a wing of the largest house and entered a small porch that stood out from one of the walls.

'We'll live here,' he said.

She did not know how he had discovered which part of the circle of buildings, of large houses and small rooms, would shelter them. He began to carry their household goods from the truck. Jess found her lantern among her things and she made a light. When the lantern was set on a shelf she could look about the room where they would live.

There were windows opposite the door through which they had entered. Outside, the rain dripped slowly through the great gnarled trees. The rain did not trouble her. A press built into the wall beside the chimney seemed ample to hold many things. Hubert set the cooking stove before the fireplace and fixed the stovepipe into the small opening above the mantel. The children cried at the strangeness, but when the lamp was lighted and food had been cooked they cried no more. When Jess set the food on the table they had begun to live in the new place.

Hubert went away across the courtyard and his step was hollow, amplified among the walls of the building. He came back later, the sound he made enlarged as he walked nearer over the flagstones.

'It's no such place as ever I saw before,' Jess cried out.

She had begun a longer speech but she was hushed by Hubert's hostile look. They would stay here, he said. It was the Wickley place. She closed the door to shut in the space she had claimed for their living, being afraid of the great empty walls that arose outside. The beds were hastily set up and the children fell asleep clutching the familiar pillows and quilts. Her life with Hubert, together with her children and her things for housekeeping, these she gathered mentally about her to protect herself from being obliged to know and to use the large house outside her walls. She began to comfort herself with thoughts of Hubert and to court him with a fine dish of food she had carefully saved.

The morning was clear after the rain. Hubert had gone to bring the fowls from their former abode. Albert had found a sunny nook in which to play and with the second child he was busy there.

'What manner of place is this?' Jess asked herself again and again. Outside the windows toward the south were the great gnarled trees. Outside to the north was the courtyard round which were arranged the buildings, all of them built of red, weathered brick. Toward the west, joined to the small wing in which Hubert had set up their home, arose the great house. There were four rows of windows here, one row above the other.

The buildings about the court were empty. A large bell hung in the middle of the court on the top of a high pole. There was a deep well at the back of the court where the water was drawn by a bucket lifted by a winch. Jess had a great delight in the well, for it seemed to hold water sufficient to last through any drought. Not far from the well stood a large corncrib, holding only a little corn now, but ready for Hubert's filling. She went cautiously about in the strange air.

She had no names for all the buildings that lay about her. She was frightened of the things for which she had no use, as if she might be called upon to know and to use beyond her understanding. She walked toward the west beneath the great wall of the tallest house.

There were birds in the high trees and echoes among the high walls. The singing winter wren was somewhere about, and the cry of the bird was spread widely and repeated in a shadowy call again and again. Jess rounded the wall and looked cautiously at the west side. There were closed shutters at some of the windows, but some of the shutters were opened. In the middle of the great western wall there were steps of stone. They were cut evenly and laid smoothly, one above another, reaching toward a great doorway about which was spread bright glass in straight patterns at the sides, in a high fanshape above.

Jess went cautiously up the steps, watching for Hubert to come with the fowls, delaying, looking out over the woodland and the fields. Hubert had said again and again that this would be the Wickley place, Wickwood, that they would live there, tilling the soil, renting the land. Jess saw before her, on the great lefthand door, a knocker. She lifted it and tapped heavily, listening to the sound she made, waiting.

There was no sound to answer her rap but a light echo that seemed to come from the trees. Her own hate of the place forbade her and she dared not tap again. Standing half fearfully, she waited, laying her hands on the smooth door frame, on the fluted pillars and the leading of the glass. A cord hung near her hand and, obeying the suggestion it offered, she closed her fingers about it and pulled it stiffly down. A sound cut the still air where no sound had been for so long a time that every vibration had been stilled. The tone broke the air. The first tone came in unearthly purity, but later the notes joined and overflowed one another.

She waited, not daring to touch the cord again. The stillness that followed after the peal of the bell seemed to float out from the house itself and to hush the birds. She could not think what kind of place this might be or see any use that one might make of the great doorway, of the cord, of the bell. A strange thing stood before her. Strangeness gathered to her own being until it seemed strange that she should be here, on the top of a stair of stone before a great door, waiting for Hubert to come with her hens. It was as if he might never come. As if hens might be gone from the earth.

She saw then that the doors were not locked together, that one throbbed lightly on the other when she touched it with her hand. She pushed the knob and the door spread open wide.

Inside, a great hall reached to a height that was three or four times her own stature. Tall white doors were opened into other great rooms and far back before her a stairway began. She could not comprehend the stair. It lifted, depending from the rail that spread upward like a great ribbon in the air. Her eyes followed it, her breath coming quick and hard. It rose as a light ribbon spreading toward a great window through which came the morning sun. But leaving the window in the air, it arose again and wound back, forward and up, lost from view for a space, to appear again, higher up, at a mythical distance before another great window where the sun spread a broad yellow glow. It went at last into nothingness, and the ceiling and the walls melted together in shadows.

When she had thus, in mind, ascended, her eyes closed and a faint sickness went over her, delight mingled with fear and hate. She was afraid of being called upon to know this strange ribbon of ascent that began as a stair with rail and tread and went up into unbelievable heights, step after step. She opened her eyes to look again, ready to reject the wonder as being past all belief and, therefore, having no reality.

'What place is this?' she asked, speaking in anger. Her voice rang through the empty hall, angry words, her own, crying, 'What place is this?'

At one side of the floor there were grains of wheat in streaks, as if someone might have stored sacks of wheat there. Jess thought of her hens, seeing the scattered grain, and she knew that they would pick up the remaining part of it. They would hop from stone to stone, coming cautiously up the steps, and they would stretch their long necks cautiously in at the doorway, seeing the corn. They would not see the great stairway.

A light dust lay on the window ledges. A few old cobwebs hung in fragments from the ceiling. The dust, the webs, and the wheat were a link between things known and unknown, and, seeing them, she walked a little way from the hall, listening, going farther, looking into the rooms, right and left. She was angry and afraid. What she could not bring to her use she wanted to destroy. In the room to her right a large fireplace stood far at the end of a patterned floor. There were shelves set into the white wall beside the large chimney. She left this room quickly and turned toward the room at the left. Here two large rooms melted together and tall doors opened wide. There were white shapes carved beneath the windows and oblong shapes carved again on the wood of the doors, on the pillars that held the mantel. Before her a long mirror was set into a wall. In it were reflected the boughs of the trees outside against a crisscross of the window opposite.

She was confused after she had looked into the mirror, and she looked about hastily to find the door through which she had come. It was a curious, beautiful, fearful place. She wanted to destroy it. Her feet slipped too lightly on the smooth wood of the floor. There was no piece of furniture anywhere, but the spaces seemed full, as filled with their wide dimensions and the carvings on the wood. In the hall she looked again toward the stair and she stood near the doorway looking back. Then suddenly without plan, scarcely knowing that her own lips spoke, she flung out an angry cry, half screaming, 'Mollie Wickley! Mollie! Where's she at?' The harsh echoes pattered and knocked among the upper walls after her own voice was done. Turning her back on the place, she went quickly out of the doorway.

In the open air she looked back toward the steps she had ascended, seeing dimly into the vista of the hall and the upward lifting ribbon of the stair. A sadness lay heavily upon her because she could not know what people might live in the house, what shapes of women and men might fit into the doorway. She hated her sadness and she turned it to anger. She went from the west front and entered the courtyard. Hubert came soon after with the fowls and there was work to do in housing them and getting them corn.

On a cold day in January when his ewes were about to lamb, Hubert brought them into the large house, driving them up the stone steps at the west front, and he prepared to stable them in the rooms there. The sheep cried and their bleating ran up the long ribbon of the stair. They were about thirty in number, and thus the wailing was incessant. Hubert and Jess went among them with lanterns. The ewes turned and drifted about among the large rooms; but as they began to bear their lambs Hubert bedded them here and there, one beneath the stairway and three others in the room to the right where the empty bookshelves spread wide beside the tall fireplace. The night came, dark and cold.

'They are a slow set,' Jess said. She wanted to be done and she was out of patience with delaying sheep.

'Whoop! here! Shut fast the door!' Hubert called.

Jess was wrapped in a heavy coat and hooded in a shawl. She went among the sheep and she held a lantern high to search out each beast. If a ewe gave birth to three lambs she took one up quickly and dropped it beside a stout young beast that was giving life to but one and she thus induced it to take the second as her own. She flung out sharp commands and she brought the animals here and there. The halls were filled with the crying of the sheep. Threats came back upon her from her own voice so that she was displeased with what she did and her displeasure made her voice more high-pitched and angry. Anger spoke again and again through the room. She wanted the lambing to be easily done, but the days had been very cold and the sheep delayed.

'It was a good place to come to lamb the sheep,' she called to Hubert. 'I say, a good place.' She had a delight in seeing that the necessities of lambing polluted the wide halls. 'A good place to lamb. . . .'

'Whoop! Bring here the old nannie as soon as you pick up the dead lamb,' Hubert was shouting above the incessant crying of the sheep.

The ewes in labor excited her anew so that she wanted to be using her strength and to be moving swiftly forward, but she had no plan beyond Hubert's. 'Whoop, rouse up the young nannie! Don't let the bitches sleep! Whoop, there!'

He was everywhere with his commands. When the task was more than half done he called to Jess that he must go to the barn for more straw for bedding. 'Whoop! Shut the door tight after me. Keep the old ewe there up on her legs.' He went away, carrying his lantern.

Jess fastened the outer door and she turned back into the parlors. Then she saw a dim light at the other end of the long dark space that lay before her. She saw another shape, a shrouded figure, moving far down the long way. The apparition, the Thing, seemed to be drifting forward out of the gloom, and it seemed to be coming toward her where she stood among the sheep. Jess drove the laboring mothers here and there, arranging their places and assisting their travail with her club. She would not believe that she saw anything among the sheep at the farther end of the rooms, but as she worked she glanced now and then toward the way in which she had glimpsed it. It was there or it was gone entirely. The sheep and the lambs made a great noise with their crying. Jess went to and fro, and she forgot that she had seen anything beyond the sheep far down the room in the moving dusk of white and gray which flowed in the moving light of her lantern.

All at once, looking up suddenly as she walked forward, she saw that an apparition was certainly moving there and that it was coming toward her. It carried something in its upraised hand. There was a dark covering over the head and shoulders that were sunk into the upper darkening gloom. The whole body came forward as a dark thing illuminated by a light the creature carried low at the left side. The creature or the Thing moved among the sheep. It came forward slowly and became a threatening figure, a being holding a club and a light in its hands. Jess screamed at it, a great oath flung high above the crying of the sheep. Fright had seized her and with it came a great strength to curse with her voice and to hurl forward her body.

'God curse you,' she yelled in a scream that went low in scale and cracked in her throat. 'God's curse on you!' She lunged forward and lifted her lantern high to see her way among the sheep. 'God's damn on you!'

The curse gave strength to her hands and to her limbs. As she hurled forward with uplifted stick the other came forward toward her, lunging and threatening. She herself moved faster. The creature's mouth was open to cry words but no sound came from it.

She dropped the lantern and flung herself upon the approaching figure, and she beat at the creature with her club while it beat at her with identical blows. Herself and the creature then were one. Anger continued, shared, and hurled against a crash of falling glass and plaster. She and the creature had beaten at the mirror from opposite sides.

The din arose above the noise of the sheep, and for an instant the beasts were quiet while the glass continued to fall. Jess stood back from the wreckage to try to understand it. Then slowly she knew that she had broken the great mirror that hung on the rear wall of the room. She took the lamp again into her hand and peered at the breakage on the floor and at the fragments that hung, cracked and crazed, at the sides of the frame.

'God's own curse on you!' She breathed her oath heavily, backing away from the dust that floated in the air.

Hubert was entering with a load of straw on his back. He had not heard the crash of glass nor had he noticed the momentary quiet of the sheep. These were soon at their bleating again, and Jess returned from the farther room where the dust of the plaster still lay on the air. Hubert poured water into deep pans he had placed here and there through the rooms. He directed Jess to make beds of the straw in each room. Their feet slipped in the wet that ran over the polished boards of the floor.

It was near midnight. Jess felt accustomed to the place now and more at ease there, she and Hubert being in possession of it. They walked about through the monstrous defilement. Hubert was muttering the count of the sheep with delight. There were two lambs beside each of the ewes but five, and there were but two lambs dead and flung to the cold fireplace where they were out of the way. There were thirty-two ewes, they said, and their fingers pointed to assist and the mouths held to the sums, repeating numbers and counting profits.

Lamb by lamb, they were counted. There were two to each mother but the three in the farther room and the two under the staircase. These had but one each. 'Twice thirty-two makes sixty-four,' they said to assist themselves, and from this they subtracted one for each of the deficient ewes, but they became confused in this and counted all one by one. Counting with lantern and club, Jess went again through the halls, but she made thus but forty lambs, for she lost the sums and became addled among the words Hubert muttered. At last by taking one from sixty-four and then another, four times more, in the reckoning they counted themselves thirty-two ewes and fifty-nine lambs. The sheep were becoming quiet. Each lamb had nursed milk before they left it. At length they fastened the great front door with a rope tied to a nail in the door-frame, and they left the sheep stabled there, being pleased with the number they had counted.

BOY IN THE SUMMER SUN [1]

By MARK SCHORER

(From *Story*)

UNALLOYED, summer had lingered miraculously into late
September without a suggestion that autumn was at hand.
Leaves and grass were green still, smoke had not yet come into the
air, and the lake was calm, almost sapphire blue. Mid-mornings
were hot, like mornings in July. So they walked where the woods
were thickest, where the air was always slightly damp and the cool
of night never quite gone. They did not speak much but went
silently along the path, almost shoulder to shoulder, their hands
touching, or their arms, as they moved. Now and then the girl
spoke, quietly, briefly pointed out a bird, a flower, once a green
snake gliding through the grass, and the boy answered with a nod
or a monosyllable, his face touched with abstraction and a slight
worry. After they came to a place in the wood where they stretched
out now with their arms about each other lightly as if the place and
this gesture were habitual, they did not speak at all until at last the
girl, Rachel, asked suddenly: 'Why are you so quiet? Is it Max?
Are you angry because he's coming, Will?'

The boy started and looked into her face. 'Angry? No, I'm not
angry . . . I was just thinking about that lousy job. When I'm out
here it's hard to believe that a job like that can be waiting for me
when I get back. It's foul.'

The girl looked away into the depth of the wood. 'Is it, Will?'
she asked. 'Or is it just that four years of school pretty well spoiled
us for anything else? That we never learn there that for most
people life finally comes down to work?'

'Maybe that's it.'

'Or is it foul, Will? Is it worse than most jobs in the city, in
summer?'

'Maybe not. But it's still foul.'

They were quiet again, and it seemed a long time later, to him,
when Rachel said, 'Anyway, I'm glad it isn't Max.'

His arms tightened around her shoulder. Then he sat up, his eyes
narrowed in the shade, and he asked, 'Why should it be?'

[1] Copyright, 1937, by Story Magazine, Inc.

She said, 'It shouldn't.'

He lay down beside her again. He stared up into the lacework of green leaves arched above them, and at the rare patches of blue sky that the leaves did not cover. Why should it be Max? Or why should she think it might be?

He had been awakened that morning by the ringing telephone, and lay sleepily in bed listening to Rachel's voice talking to someone in a way that did disturb him vaguely then, although now it seemed only mildly irritating that this week end should be intruded upon. 'But darling!' her voice had cried over the telephone. 'What are you doing here? Come over at once! Mind? Of course not! We'll love it! In two hours? Good!'

When he came to breakfast, she smiled brightly and cried, 'Guess who's coming, Will! Max Garey! He got bored and started out early this morning, and just now called from the village. Isn't it grand? Mother's so fond of him — she'll take care of him.'

'Does your mother know him? I didn't know she did.'

'Oh yes, that last week at school, when she came to help me pack, you know ...'

'No, I didn't,' he said. And now he wondered why she had not told him.

Then Mrs. Harley came out on the porch. 'Good morning, Will,' she said brightly as she patted her white hair. 'Isn't it *nice* that Mr. Garey can come! I'm so fond of Mr. Garey!'

'Yes, isn't it?' Will said into his coffee, and looked across the table into Rachel's eyes, which were shining with pleasure and were quite heedless of the question in his.

'Did you have any work with Mr. Garey, Will? Rachel thought him such a splendid teacher.'

'No, I didn't,' Will said. 'His classes were always filled with girls.'

Rachel looked at him quickly. 'Now you're being unfair, Will. He's not one of those. Everybody thinks he's a good teacher.'

'I'm sorry,' he said, and felt suddenly sad, lonely in the bright morning with Rachel only across the table from him.

He felt that loneliness again now. 'Maybe it is more than the job,' he said. 'Everything's different since June. I don't know why.'

'What do you mean, Will?'

'Just that feeling that everything's breaking up, smashing.'

They were quiet then until Rachel said, 'I know. I'm different, too. Something's changed in me. There's something sad, some ache. . . .'

Will knew that something had changed in her. She was older than she had been in June. There was something about her now that bewildered him, the feeling that she lived without him, an aloofness, a self-sufficiency which was new. She was like a woman, sometimes, putting up with a boy. He had felt it almost every week end, and this and the more general sadness of the summer had darkened otherwise golden hours. And yet there was that in her kisses still, in her sweet arms around him, in her yielding body that made him doubt his feeling. With him, there still came from her throat a little moan of pain and passion which he knew no one else had ever heard. And yet, now in the deep cool wood as she lay in his arms, he felt that she had forgotten him beside her.

She spoke at last as with an effort, as if recalling herself from a dream. 'You know, Will, after you left school, in that week I stayed on, I saw Max rather often. Then mother met him. She invited him to come up. He was here earlier in the summer. Didn't I tell you?'

'No,' he said, his throat contracting. 'You must have forgotten.'

His sadness knotted in his throat suddenly, intensely, and he remembered then very clearly, almost as if she were saying it again now, something she had said before he left her in June. 'Sometimes I wonder if this can last, Will, if it mustn't end. It's been almost too lovely, too complete. We've *realized* each other. We know each other as I think people almost never do. Now it begins to seem a little unreal, perhaps because it's been too lovely, part of this unreal life we're leaving. I wonder if that sometimes happens, Will.'

Then he had laughed; but now, as he remembered, his arms tightened around her suddenly, as if from fright, and he leaned down and kissed her. Her lips were quiet, without response. He opened his eyes then to look at her and saw that her eyes were fixed on some remote object in the arch of trees or beyond, some dream, something far from him. He stood up and moved away. 'Let's go back,' he said, and without waiting for her started quickly up the path, toward the house.

All the afternoon they lay on the raft, Rachel between them. Max talked, his voice reflective and lazy, mixing with the sun of that afternoon and the endless laziness in the sounds that insects made in the woods and in the long grass along the shore, his voice spinning itself out, pausing now and then to listen to itself, and going on again, with Rachel lying quiet between them, her eyes closed and the oil gleaming on her brown skin. Will's head was turned toward her, his eyes wandering back and forth from her parted lips and her gleaming lashes to the swell of her breasts under her white swimming suit, to her long browned legs and her crossed feet at the end of the raft.

All the time Max's voice went on, the lazy, professor's voice. Will could tell as he heard it that it was a voice that always talked and that always had listeners, and yet, now, it did not irritate him. He was almost content to lie in the sun with the sensation of burning on his skin, and soft warm glow of skin absorbing bright sun enough in the afternoon to allay for the moment the morning's inarticulate fears, even though it was Max who was lying stretched out beyond Rachel, who was talking, pausing, talking, sometimes falling silent and no word coming from Rachel or himself, and then starting up again, the voice spinning itself out softly in the afternoon sun, with all the laziness of the afternoon in his slow words.

'...and so in Donne the central factor is death...death, of course...he, more than any of the poets, built what he wrote upon what may be called a metaphysic of death...death as the great leveller on the one hand, the great destroyer of everything, beauty, love...and death as the figure at the gate of Heaven... these two, this one...the central factor, always present...'

His voice was slow, modulated, a little affected, quite soft, and in it, Will knew as he looked at Rachel's face, there was some magic, a magic of wisdom and experience that enthralled her.

Rachel's voice began, slow and soft as if infected by Max's voice, as warm as the sun, and speaking lines that Max doubtless first spoke to her, perhaps — only perhaps — in the classroom:

> *'When I dyed last, and, Deare, I dye*
> *As often as from thee I goe,*
> *Though it be but an houre agoe,*
> *And Lovers houres be full eternity,*
> *I can remember yet, that I*
> *Something did say, and something did bestow...'*

Max laughed. 'But darling,' he said, 'that's still another kind of death, not so serious.'

Rachel said nothing. And the sun wove around them its bright and golden web, and the whole world then as they lay there had slipped away and left the three of them stranded together in an unreality of sunlight on burning skin and closed eyelids, and nothing more. And Will, too, felt out of the world of fact, was empty of feeling, as if pure sensation had replaced it. And only slowly did a faint jangling come into his mind, the jangle of Max's word *darling*, like something shaken in a metal box, some harsh sound, or a feeling perhaps, shaking him abruptly from the web. He stirred. He turned. And in turning the web was broken, and he was free of it again, his hand plunged in the cold blue water of the lake and left to dangle there, his eyes turned from Rachel and Max for the moment, but seeing nothing in the indeterminable depths of the blue water that gently lapped his hand.

'Not nearly so serious,' Max said. 'Only a metaphor, a way of speaking...'

Will turned toward them again, and now he saw in Rachel's face how serious it was, for she looked suddenly ill for all the glow of her skin, her face turned away from him and her lips fallen apart, and every line in her face and body taut suddenly, yearning, aching suddenly with sharp longing, sharp pain, she quite sick for love. Will's hands closed at his sides and opened again, turned empty to the sun.

'Poetry is full of such conventions, formalized short cuts to express familiar sentiments,' Max was saying. 'In Donne, of course, there's enough fire, usually, to vitalize them, but in others... mere metaphors...'

Something in Will's mind snapped, then seemed to shout, *Who cares? For God's sake, who cares?* He was enraged beyond endurance by the man's pompous classroom manner, his easy presence, his way of excluding Will, as if he were alone with Rachel and no one else existed. He hated him, and the very presence of Rachel there made his throat ache with something like the pressure of tears coming. The sun had lost its spell. The buzz of insects on the shore seemed for a moment unbearably loud, and the sun no longer warm, but hot, searing, parching his throat and mouth, blinding him. For now he hated Max, and he knew as he remembered Rachel's voice speaking those lines, that she was lost to him, that he had nothing more for her, that Max had all. And there Max lay, as if he belonged there, had every right to be there, talking and priding himself in his talk, delighting to hear his own words, lecturing there as though he were in the classroom and Rachel in the front row looking up at him with wide eyes, lecturing as though Rachel and he were alone in the room, and he, Will, did not exist.

Will's eyes clouded in anger as he stared down into the water disturbed by his hand. He tried not to hear what their low voices said, and only when they were silent did he turn suddenly on the raft again to see how their bodies had moved together, so that their legs touched, and Max's hand lay quite near Rachel's hair. He stood up abruptly, stirring the raft in the water, and then dived deep, swam quickly out and away from them, his arms beating the water in his anger, in a frantic effort to forget the hurt which came from Rachel's willing reception of the man's intolerable arrogance.

He struck out into the lake. The water was cold on his skin, and as he swam, his anger cooled. But when his anger was gone, he felt sad and futile again, swam more slowly, felt helpless and wounded, felt almost weak in the water, so that he grew angry with himself instead and wished that he could hold that other anger. When he turned back and swam slowly toward the shore, only the hurt remained, and he did not go to the raft. There Max's words would still be spinning themselves out in the sunlight, catching Rachel's mind in their spell, catching her heart firmly and her whole mind and life, and holding them there, as if the words were really magic.

He walked up the beach and stretched out on the sand. He lay on his back and looked up into the blue sky, and as he lay there he felt suddenly that this was the last time in his life that he would be doing quite this. All summer he had been coming from the sweltering, grimy city, and in seeing Rachel in the country, in living in her mother's friendly house, in swimming and dancing and drinking and finding cool spots in the woods where the moss was thick and only the trees and birds made sound — in all of this it had seemed that nothing had changed or was ending. And this in spite of the fact that when they parted in June, when they walked for the last time along familiar walks between familiar buildings, they had vaguely felt that an end had come to a period, that a new life was waiting for both of them, and that (Rachel felt) somehow they were therefore ending for one another. But then Max was nothing to him, only a professor whom she liked; so for him nothing really ended.

Now the golden day was unbearable. He turned over on his stomach and put his face in his arms. Almost at once he could feel the sun burning his neck, his back. But it alleviated nothing. There was the dull ache in his chest and throat, the constant feeling that at any moment he would cry out like a child in sobs. It was a pressure in his body that he could not put into thoughts, only the feeling that something was ending, inevitably ending. He thought of his past and it was all gold, all brightness and gold, all magic landscape, all love, all an idyl, all a bright day, and all ending.

He thought he must cry. All his youth was gathered into a knot of pain that choked him, a youth that had been like gold but that pressed against his heart now, dull and heavy. He thought of going back to the city, to the hot office, to the dull and stupid work, sweating over accounts, of the years he had ahead of him in which to slave there. And he knew as he lay in the sand, really *knew*, for the first time, that all of that was no mere interlude, that golden days must end, gold vanish.

He felt a touch on his shoulder, turned, and looked up. It was Rachel, brown in the sun saying, 'Darling, don't be rude.'

He sat up. 'Am I being rude?'

'Does he bore you?'

'Yes. I don't like him much.'

'Well, I'm sorry he came, Will, but I couldn't help it. Come back and try to bear him. He's not bad, you know.'

'No?' Will asked as he got up.

She looked at him swiftly, then smiled. 'Don't be silly, darling.'

'No, *darling*.'

'Good.'

Then they went up the shore, back to the raft where Max still lay in the lessening glare of the sun.

Then finally he could put up with him no longer. The whole thing, suddenly, was impossible, too foul, too much for him. He sat at the table for a minute more and fought against the impulse to leave. But Mrs. Harley, cooing in a voice that almost made him ill ('But how *interesting*, Mr. Garey. *Do* go on! Do you *really* believe that?') and Max, toying with his fork and smiling with what Will supposed was great 'charm' before continuing his monologue,

For over a year . . .' He paused. Then, 'Nothing will ever be the same again — love, or anything.'

'Please, Will. Nothing's happened.'

'Everything's happened. Now it's over.'

She looked at him closely. Then she said, 'I've never heard you talk like that. You're different. Your voice — it's . . .'

'What?'

'You're different. Your voice frightens me. It's so quiet and cold and far away, so different ——' She spoke jerkily. 'So dead!'

He sat up, leaned back on his elbows. The moon was gone, sunk under the water. The sky was darker, and the stars seemed brighter still, separate, and farther away. Then he lay down again and she beside him. They were both very quiet. Finally she said, 'Do you hate me?'

He turned to her. 'No,' he answered. He watched her face. He saw her eyes sparkling with tears. He said, 'What are you crying for?'

'I can't tell you why, I can't say, I don't know. I'm afraid. I do love you, Will. Only now I'm afraid, because I do love someone else — more. I don't want to. But I do. It frightens me!'

Now she was no longer older than he. She was a girl again, her woman's poise, given her briefly by this new love, taken from her again by that same love because, in the face of it, she was afraid. She was afraid of its swiftness, of what it might hold, of her own heart, turning. Now he felt older than she, felt that he could tell her something. He said: 'I know what it is. It isn't just that we've been in love. We've had such a swell time. I don't know if I can say this, but it's something like this anyway — you weren't just yourself for me, and I wasn't just myself for you. We were both in love with much more than each other. You were all of that life for me, and maybe I was that for you, too. We were that whole life for each other, and we didn't want to lose it, but we couldn't help ourselves, couldn't keep it any longer.

She was crying. She put her face on his shoulder and he felt her tears on his neck. Then he put his arms around her and held her close. But he felt no less alone. And he thought then that this aloneness would never entirely leave him again, but that when he got back to the city next day, after he had been there awhile, working in the office, after a week or two or perhaps a whole year, finally anyway, it would have left him somewhat less empty, less deadly calm. Then this day and this summer and all the golden days would have become the dream; and the other life would be real.

'How did your poem go, Rachel? When I last died, and, dear, I die whenever you go from me ...?'

'Please — don't,' she said.

He began to stroke her hair. She was quiet now, no longer crying, held close in his arms. He said, 'Maybe it's always like this. Maybe the end of every love is a kind of little death, when you have to put behind more than just the love itself, but all the life, too, in which the love was wrapped. Maybe that's what living is — a lot of little dyings. I don't know — I can't say it very well. Maybe I don't even know.'

For a moment more they sat together and then she said, 'We have to go back. They'll wonder ...'

'All right,' he said.

Then, clinging together, helping each other up the slope, they went up to the house, where the lights were, and the sounds of voices, clinging together like children still, under the stars.

PRO ARTE[1]

By ALLAN SEAGER

(From *Scribner's Magazine*)

MY LAST porch mate had been a great nuisance — fellow named Porter who cried a little every day because he was sure he was going to die and thought he was too young for it. It made me nervous to watch him, and I was relieved when he did die and was shipped away in a pine box on the nine-fifty train, escorted by a file of weeping kinfolk. Since Porter's translation, I had been quite bored. Under its load of snow, the mountain across the way looked like a bad etching, and at twelve below zero, you cannot try to read, or your hands will freeze holding the book. I was ready to talk, and I don't suppose anyone had ever been so glad to see Henry Comstock as I was.

He followed the head nurse out onto the porch and she introduced him. 'How do you do?' he said politely and gave me a cigarette. He was over six feet tall, with broad, sloping shoulders and blond hair. He wore hardsoled slippers, blue pajamas, and a dark-blue flannel dressing-gown with a monogram on the pocket, the kind given by aunts for Christmas. He carried a copy of Somerset Maugham's *Of Human Bondage*. Evidently he had begun his cure in some hospital, because he was already fat, and when he put his head down, a well-shaved roll of flesh protruded beneath his chin, but even fat he was handsome, and, thinner, he would have been the handsomest man I ever saw. He got into bed and began to read with such concentration that I was sure someone had sent him the book as a gift.

As I looked him over, I thought that Comstock would do nicely. A bit young, perhaps, to be entertaining — he was about thirty — but I did not think he would cry himself to death as Porter had. Also he was well-mannered, and, from his face, he seemed to have a pleasant, youthful candor. But I did not, in spite of my anticipation, rush headlong into conversation.

I knew he was not ready to talk yet. When you first come to a sanitarium from the outside, you do not believe you are quite like the other lungers. They get to be pretty silly from worry and confinement. You will be courteous certainly, but aloof. Then in a couple of days you are telling the nearest person the things that trouble you when you are awake at night.

Comstock read until his hands got cold. He put them under the covers and stared out at the mountain gloomily. I decided to wait until the next day before beginning to talk to him, but the next day I was balked by his visitors.

II

I saw them coming up the icy path through the trees, the girl giving little screams, and laughing when she slipped. The man carried a package under one arm and he made gestures with the other. The girl's coat was sable. They were probably rich.

They entered the cottage. I heard them laughing on the stairs, and then they came out onto our porch. Comstock was asleep, and the man woke him, touching him on the shoulder.

Comstock opened his eyes at once. 'Hello, Arthur. Hello, Mary. God, I'm glad to see you. How are you?' He raised up in bed. 'Oh, congratulations. I saw the papers. I knew it would be like that.'

'Weren't the papers grand? You should have heard me,' the man said, 'I've never played better. Never in my life. I was just an instrument for the real Beethoven, and the papers could see it for once. You know, Iturbi didn't get any better reviews than mine.'

'I liked the *American* best. They called him a "Titan of the Keyboard." Can't you see him playing in a leopard skin and open-work shoes, like Lionel Strongfort?' the girl asked. She was very blonde with brown eyes, and obviously proud of her husband. 'We sat up all night, waiting for the papers and drinking coffee. Arthur couldn't sleep all the next day because of the papers.'

'It was because of the coffee,' he said. 'I bought Mary the fur coat — pose for the gentleman, Mary — and I made her quit her job, and now we are on our way to Montreal, and next year we're going to take a house in Connecticut, with a Steinway for the noise and a Bechstein for the pearly tone.'

'Concert in Montreal?' asked Comstock. 'What are you playing?'
'Bridge. This trip is for fun,' the pianist said.

The girl had stopped looking at her husband. She said, 'Hush, dear, we're being rude. Here is poor darling Henry practically phosphorescent with decay, and you talk about your damned pianos. What do the doctors say, Henry? You look well. I mean, you're not thin at all.'

'Oh, it's nothing. Just a few little holes. I'll be out of here in a couple of months,' he said confidently.

'But what do you do? Just lie here?'

'Lie here and look at the mountains and think. You can do a lot of thinking here.'

'I'll bet you can,' said the man. 'Thinking about your sins. I'd pray if I were you. I've told you about it, haven't I, Mary? Pure Henry's very first affair — his first sane act after a lifetime of celibacy? How Henry trundled his profile round and round the lobby of the hotel in Switzerland? And there was this charming little *Suisse* who spoke only French? She used to come every morning to hear Milstein and Piaty and me play trios. She was trying to learn something about music, she said. But would the wolf Henry let her improve herself? No, by God. He had to be the pupil. He had to learn French.'

I looked at Comstock. He was smiling and fidgeting. Obviously, they all knew the story very well, and this was only a joke which Comstock was enjoying.

'And it wasn't long before it became necessary to hold the lessons in Henry's bedroom. *Voici le lit. Vois-tu le lit?*' Talk some French, Henry; you spent enough time on it. And then, to remove the Swiss flaws from their accent, he must take her to Paris so they could learn together the pure tongue of Île de France, and there they lived, how culturally, talking French like mad, night and day, particularly in the daytime, until Henry began to cough and he couldn't talk any more and he had to come home and lie still. The trick lungs are manifestly your wages from an angry Providence. I hope you see that, Henry. I hope you see it as clearly as I do.'

It had all been very funny up to this point. The pianist was happy and talkative because of his success, and Comstock was pleased because this fooling reflected his prowess as a male, but now his face changed.

'I got it from her, you know. The TB, I mean. She had it then. She told me when we got to Paris.'

'Oh, I'm terribly sorry, Henry. But you never told us,' the man said.

The girl leaned over and kissed Comstock on the forehead and said in a low voice, 'Arthur's such a fool when he's played well. Forgive him, darling. He didn't mean anything.'

'It's all right. I know you didn't mean anything. It isn't as if I were dying,' Comstock said.

'But you are getting along all right, aren't you? I mean, there's no danger of serious complications?'

'No. I'm fine. I'll be back at work in a couple of months.' He seemed anxious to cheer things up again. 'How are the bookings for next season, now that you're the musical white hope of America?'

'Twenty-two already. One date with the Chicago, and I may get a concerto date with Stokowski — the Liszt E-flat, maybe. If you need any money, let me know. Seriously, I mean it.'

'Darling, we've forgotten Henry's champagne. We left it on the bureau in your room there,' said the girl.

'We brought you a couple of bottles because you couldn't celebrate with us. It's Mumm's.'

'That's swell,' Comstock said. 'Let's all have a drink now.'

'We can't, Henry. Our train leaves in a few minutes.'

'Well, it was grand of you to come and see me, and I can't tell you, Arthur, how much your success means to me. You've worked like hell and you deserve all the honors you get and you'll get plenty. I know you will.' Comstock seemed to be making this moment an occasion, as if he wanted the pianist to remember it. 'You'll be the greatest pianist in the world.'

Comstock had a fine forehead. His eyes were very blue and, as far down as his cheek bones, his face was lean, virile, and his expression made it almost heroically earnest. It was like a scene in the movies. I almost expected to see Myrna Loy and Clark Gable turn from his bed and sadly leave the porch.

III

After you have visitors, you are depressed, and when you are depressed, you talk. Comstock watched his guests go down the path. Then he turned, probably frightened that he could envy them so much, and began to talk at once.

Had I noticed his two visitors? They were Arthur Corey, the pianist, and his wife. He had just made his début in New York, and already he was considered one of the finest young American pianists.

He himself was a great friend of Corey's. They had been in college together, where Corey had lived over a garage almost without money, practicing ten hours a day on a rented upright. It was a funny thing, he would strike an octave chord and trill the second and third fingers, and then the third and fourth fingers until he could do it perfectly, sometimes as long as an hour. He had worked incessantly and he deserved all the success he could get, didn't I think? Because a man should have a reward commensurate to his effort.

Opposite me, I reflected, I have one of America's finest young men — tall, callow, and sincere. The reward, so Henry Comstock believed, was equal to the effort. Santa Claus came if you were a good boy, and when you worked nights at the office, the gods made you president of the company. Maybe the gods had sent him as a messenger to tell me that I was cynical and profane and had better watch out. Yet I wondered, according to his system, how Hermes would explain his own disease — he must have done something pretty bad to be punished with TB.

Had I ever heard Vladimir Horowitz play, he asked. His technique was marvelous. Once in Munich, Horowitz had listened to Corey in a small recital, and, being impressed, he had offered to teach Corey something about technique if he would come to Switzerland in the summer. Horowitz had a chalet on the mountainside near Cranssur-Sierre. Last summer Corey had gone to Crans and he had visited Corey there.

(I remember Horowitz playing the *Suggestions Diaboliques* of Prokofieff, leaning over the keyboard, his eyebrows lifted as if in surprise at the swiftness of his fingers with the applause already mounting nervously around him. I remember Prokofieff, too. He was bald and looked like a dentist. You can remember practically everything lying here.)

I was a little impatient. I wanted to hear about the girl, 'pure Henry's very first affair.'

'And the girl? The girl who came to listen to the trios. The one you took to Paris,' I said. 'You forget the porch is only twelve feet square. I couldn't help overhearing.' I cite my behavior as an example of the callousness you acquire in this place.

Comstock accepted my rudeness without offense. 'The girl came every morning. Arthur used to play the trios with Piatigorsky, the 'cellist, and Milstein, the violinist, in the writing-room of the hotel. She sat on a chair just inside the door. Every morning. She was in love with Arthur then.'

'Maybe she just liked the piano,' I offered.

'No. She loved him all right. Or she wanted to be his mistress anyhow.'

'Was she pretty?'

'Beautiful. She was only nineteen, just out of a convent school in Lausanne. I couldn't understand why she was on the make. But don't you have to make a fool of yourself just because they are pretty and want to make love.'

'Depends,' I said. 'After three years here, they would not even have to be pretty now.'

'Well, Arthur made a fool of himself. Evenings he bought her drinks in the bar, and afternoons, when he was supposed to be working with Horowitz, he would be out on the side of some alp, talking to her. The summer before his début, with one of the greatest pianists in the world helping him gratis, and his wife working in New York to help out with expenses, and he gets sidetracked by a girl. It was wrong. It was wrong because of his career and it was wrong because of Mary.'

'Impolitic and wicked,' I said.

'I talked to him. I've always tried to keep him straight, but artists are flighty, you know, and he'd done this kind of thing before. But he just laughed. He said somebody had to make love to her. He said that's what she was living for. I said love was just a nervous habit with him. He laughed some more, so I made love to her myself. You see, I thought he would get to work again if I could draw her away. I couldn't sit by and watch fifteen years of work go to pot, could I?'

'Not as his friend,' I answered.

'Arthur Corey is my best friend. That's why I did it.'

'For art's sake,' I said. 'Sorry.'

He did not get the pun. 'I had never been involved with a woman before, and I didn't know how to start, so I asked her to teach me French. I've always been kind of dumb about languages.'

She probably thought he was crazy, as handsome as he must have been then.

'She had only given me a couple of lessons before I saw I was in for it. She looked at me all the time.'

'If they looked at you like a shot rabbit, it's always love,' I said. 'But what kind of a girl was she? First she falls for Corey; then she falls for you. Her affections were remarkably flexible.'

'She was a good girl, I guess,' he said.

'Was she also a nice girl?'

'Very nice. She used to buy flowers every day while I went for the mail, and I would find them in the room when I came back.'

'She was a wonderful girl.' Then I had an idea. 'When did she tell you she had TB?'

'It was one night when we got to Paris,' he said.

The whole thing was plain now. If she knew that her lungs were bad; if she knew that in six months she would weigh perhaps sixty pounds; and on the table beside her bed, there would lie one of those kidney-shaped hospital bowls filling slowly, but still too fast, with blood and bits of her lung; and then one day she would see the white screen put up around the bed and only barely hear the chuckle of the oxygen tanks, why shouldn't she make love? That really was all she was living for. It was not flexibility. It was desperation. I have seen it here many times. It is a condition quite accepted by the authorities.

'When did you decide to take her to Paris?' I asked.

'About the time I saw that I was going to have to do more than just learn French, if I wanted to keep her away from Arthur,' he said.

When they reached Paris, he was afraid that he might see American friends if they stayed at a good hotel on the Right Bank, so he took her over to a quaint little rat-hole on the *Quai des Grands Augustins* which advertised a *Grand Vue de la Seine*. And the *Vue* was really grand all right, he said. You could see Notre Dame every time you went out the front door.

'I should think it would have been delightful — lovely girl, quaint old-world atmosphere, wine cheap and plentiful, and the cathedral to look at when you got tired. Wasn't it delightful?'

'No. Not to me.' He paused as if he sought the reasons why it wasn't, but the echoes of his mother and his father and his Sunday-school teacher and his headmaster and all the other voices of his upbringing were too faint for him to catch. 'I don't know how you feel about women —— ' he began.

'No, but you will, my dear Comstock,' I said. 'You will if you stay here long enough. You will know how I feel about women, men, small children, the New Deal, interplanetary travel, oysters, everything. It will take me a month to tell you how I feel about everything, and after I have told you, why, we are a month to the good.'

Comstock sat up in bed suddenly. 'Let's have some of the champagne.' We went into his room.

There were two bottles of Mumm's on his bureau. He sat down on the tin wastebasket with the bottle between his knees, undoing the wire and the foil, and I sat in the only chair. We drank from our toothbrush glasses. The wine was cold, dry, and very good.

With the glass in his hand, Comstock began again. 'I'd never had anything to do with women seriously before. I never thought why until I was sick. But I know now. When I was about sixteen, my father was made president of the bank in our home town. He gave me a Model-T Ford. I thought he was a great man and I believed everything he said. One time he told me about things. He said, "Son, keep away from women until you marry." He was embarrassed and so was I, but I promised him. I thought he must be right, because of the Ford, I guess. And then I rowed in college and I never had time to play around with them.'

'You are very handsome. It must have been hard to elude them,' I said politely.

'No. I knew only the sisters of my friends.' He poured out more champagne, and sat looking down into his glass while he made the wine go round in it. 'But they have caught up with me now all right.'

'*Avec ça?*' I said.

'That's French for "So what?," isn't it? If I hadn't learned French, I wouldn't be in this mess.'

'You mean you are worried about the girl?' Then I said heartily, 'Oh, she'll be all right. Very likely your little trip did her good —

travel, change of scene.' I did not believe the trip did her good.
Unless she was a light case, the strain would probably kill her. But
I wanted to be comforting.

'I wasn't thinking of the girl. I was thinking of myself.'

'Oh,' I said, 'what's the matter with you?'

'Well, you may laugh, but I've done wrong,' he said, still looking
into his glass.

'Sinned, you mean?'

'Something like that. I feel as though I'd let myself down and
I'll never be able to look my wife in the face.'

'Have you got a wife?' I asked.

'Not yet. But when I have.'

'She'll never find it out unless you tell her. It's not branded on
your forehead, you know,' I said. I had heard of men like Comstock, but I had never seen one before. I tried changing the subject. 'Did you ever eat at Rouzier's, or La Perouse? They were
both in your neighborhood.'

'We had a baked truffle at Rouzier's. I had never eaten truffle
before and I didn't like it.'

I could see that I was not much help. We finished the champagne, and Comstock did not say any more. He seemed to be depressed, and we went out on the porch and went to bed. It was
snowing hard, and the wind made a lot of noise in the trees. I
would like to have gone dancing some place because of the champagne.

For the next three weeks, Comstock and I had no conversation.
From the little he said, I gathered that he regarded his shame as a
problem which he could solve if he persisted. He lay with his head
propped up, looking out at the mountain, smoking his pipe with
great intensity. Perhaps it could even be totted up and balanced,
red against black, and then he would feel all right. As I watched
him, I could tell that he was trying to save what he could not call
his soul, and he lost just nine pounds doing it, which you may say
is quite cheap for a rescue of that magnitude.

I lay six feet away from him, jealous of the scenes it hurt him to
recall. I did not try to help him, because I was without sympathy.
He had had an affair with a beautiful girl in Paris, and if he wanted
to absolve himself, he could think of the dark inhabited tissues
of his lungs, where in waxen waistcoats (this information is brought

to you through the courtesy of the Rockefeller Institute) untold millions of little creatures, fifty thousand of which could pass, could you persuade them to, through the eye of a needle without touching the steel or one another, were gorging themselves on his flesh, unhindered except perhaps by antibodies, although science cannot tell us much about antibodies yet. He could console himself with that. He had 'betrayed' the girl, and she had given him TB. He was paid if he felt that way.

One day, he asked me to come into his room. 'I think I've got it straightened out,' he said. 'You see, I went into it to help Arthur. It was wrong, but I did it to help him. The girl was willing enough — it isn't as if I'd seduced her. She was willing, and this TB is a punishment. It evens up, doesn't it?'

'Seems to,' I said, wanting to laugh. 'Your good intentions even leave you one up.'

'I did wrong to help a friend and now I am paying for it,' he said. He looked relieved and cheerful, but I couldn't see just why it took him three weeks to find the solution.

'*Nunc dimittis*,' I said.

It is not often that you get a chance to watch a man tinker with his conscience. It is very interesting. It would have been more interesting if Comstock had given even one minute's thought to the girl. He had told me that once in Paris, about dawn, he woke up and he saw against the window the profile of the girl's body in the early light. She was crying. It was that which had wakened him, and, turning from the window, timid, expecting his anger, she told him she was ill.

But in his successful calculation the girl was not included.

IV

After this, Comstock improved rapidly. He gained weight, his X-rays turned out well, and he took to playing bridge in the cardroom evenings. If you are strong enough, you are allowed to play cards until nine o'clock. The authorities consider it a beneficial relaxation.

One morning I stopped at the post-office for the mail. There was nothing for me, but there was a letter and a little package for M. Henri Comstock. The postmark was Davos, Schweiz.

When I got back to the cottage, Comstock was in bed. I gave

him the letter and the package. He opened the letter and read it. Then he jumped out of bed, went into his room, and began to dress. I could hear him. He left the cottage and walked down the hill at much faster than the approved rate.

I thought the girl had died, but I wanted to be sure. So I had no qualms about going into his room to look around. On his bureau was the letter. I picked it up and read. The Directors of the Such-an-Such Sanitarium at Davos had, it appeared, the unhappy duty to inform M. Comstock of the death of Mlle. Albertine Bergier, a patient in their establishment. Before her death, Mlle. Bergier had requested the writer to send M. Comstock her ring as a remembrance. The Directors joined in sending M. Comstock their sincere condolences.

On the bureau, in a pile of tissue paper, lay a pretty little gold ring set with sapphires.

In a few minutes, Comstock returned, still quite agitated. 'She's dead,' he said.

'Mmm,' I said. 'Send a cable?'

'Yes, that's all I could do.' He began to walk back and forth. 'I'll never forgive myself now. This is going to haunt me forever.'

I must have shouted. I was pretty mad. 'For the love of God, Comstock, don't be a damned fool all your life.' He stopped and looked affronted.

'Try to think of the girl for just a minute. Your soul is immortal — it'll keep. She was a young girl from a convent. She knew she was sick,' I said patiently. 'How long do you think it took her to decide to go to Paris with you, to act like a tart so she could see what love was like just once before she died? Not what love was really — she didn't love you — but just a rehearsal in a twelve-franc hotel bedroom.'

'You can't talk to me like this,' he said characteristically.

'I am talking to you like this, and you'll be expelled if you hit me, so you might as well listen. It might even be for your own good. From my obituary, you may find out something about this girl. You see, she knew what the strain of your little jaunt was going to do to her. If you get drunk once in a beer-joint downtown, it sets you back a month, but for a couple of hours you're free. She knew it was going to kill her, but she would be free to find out why she was a woman. And at night when she was frightened by her bargain, she went and stood by the window so she wouldn't wake you crying.' Now that I had worked this off, I felt better. 'Don't let it worry you, Comstock. She had the choice of maybe two more years alone, or the trip to Paris, and she took the trip and the pine box that went with it. It's not your fault. You had nothing to do with it. You were only the male spider.'

He did not say anything for about twenty minutes. Then he said, 'I'm sorry I was angry. Thanks for helping me out. I see what you mean now.'

After that Comstock never spoke of her again. Instead he talked about the romance in the advertising business and the three years he stroked his college boat at Poughkeepsie. Last week he was allowed to leave the sanitarium. He was very fat, looked enormously healthy, and he was beginning to take on the fat man's readiness to laugh.

On the whole, Comstock was good value. He was much more entertaining and instructive than I deserved, and, since no one has been assigned to his bed, I miss him quite a lot. It is a bore not to have anyone to talk to. I lie here and listen to the trees popping. The bole of the tree shrinks away from the bark suddenly when it is cold enough, and there is a loud crack. Since the sanitarium is in wooded country, the cracks come about every half-minute in this weather. Last winter, my porch mate and I used to bet on the length of the interval between the cracks, and I won eight dollars.

THE CHRYSANTHEMUMS[1]

By JOHN STEINBECK

(From *Harper's Magazine*)

THE high gray-flannel fog of winter closed the Salinas Valley from the sky and from all the rest of the world. On every side it sat like a lid on the mountains and made of the great valley a closed pot. On the broad, level land floor the gang plows bit deep and left the black earth shining like metal where the shares had cut. On the foothill ranches across the Salinas River the yellow stubble fields seemed to be bathed in pale cold sunshine; but there was no sunshine in the valley now in December. The thick willow scrub along the river flamed with sharp and positive yellow leaves.

It was a time of quiet and of waiting. The air was cold and tender. A light wind blew up from the southwest so that the farmers were mildly hopeful of a good rain before long; but fog and rain do not go together.

Across the river, on Henry Allen's foothill ranch there was little work to be done, for the hay was cut and stored and the orchards were plowed up to receive the rain deeply when it should come. The cattle on the higher slopes were becoming shaggy and rough-coated.

Elisa Allen, working in her flower garden, looked down across the yard and saw Henry, her husband, talking to two men in business suits. The three of them stood by the tractor shed, each man with one foot on the side of the Little Fordson. They smoked cigarettes and studied the machine as they talked.

Elisa watched them for a moment and then went back to her work. She was thirty-five. Her face was lean and strong and her eyes were as clear as water. Her figure looked blocked and heavy in her gardening costume, a man's black hat pulled low down over her eyes, clodhopper shoes, a figured print dress almost completely covered by a big corduroy apron with four big pockets to hold the snips, the trowel and scratcher, the seeds and the knife she worked with. She wore heavy leather gloves to protect her hands while she worked.

She was cutting down the old year's chrysanthemum stalks with a pair of short and powerful scissors. She looked down toward the men by the tractor shed now and then. Her face was eager and mature and handsome; even her work with the scissors was over-eager, over-powerful. The chrysanthemum stems seemed too small and easy for her energy.

She brushed a cloud of hair out of her eyes with the back of her glove, and left a smudge of earth on her cheek in doing it. Behind her stood the neat white farmhouse with red geraniums close-banked round it as high as the windows. It was a hard-swept look-ing little house, with hard-polished windows, and a clean mat on the front steps.

Elisa cast another glance toward the tractor shed. The stranger men were getting into their Ford coupé. She took off a glove and put her strong fingers down into the forest of new green chrysan-themum sprouts that were growing round the old roots. She spread the leaves and looked down among the close-growing stems. No aphids were there, no sow bugs nor snails nor cut worms. Her terrier fingers destroyed such pests before they could get started.

Elisa started at the sound of her husband's voice. He had come near quietly and he leaned over the wire fence that protected her flower garden from cattle and dogs and chickens.

'At it again,' he said. 'You've got a strong new crop coming.'

Elisa straightened her back and pulled on the gardening glove again. 'Yes. They'll be strong this coming year.' In her tone and on her face there was a little smugness.

'You've got a gift with things,' Henry observed. 'Some of those yellow chrysanthemums you had last year were ten inches across. I wish you'd work out in the orchard and raise some apples that big.'

Her eyes sharpened. 'Maybe I could do it too. I've a gift with things all right. My mother had it. She could stick anything in the ground and make it grow. She said it was having planters' hands that knew how to do it.'

'Well, it sure works with flowers,' he said.

'Henry, who were those men you were talking to?'

'Why, sure, that's what I came to tell you. They were from the Western Meat Company. I sold those thirty head of three-year-old steers. Got nearly my own price too.'

'Good,' she said. 'Good for you.'

'And I thought,' he continued, 'I thought how it's Saturday afternoon, and we might go into Salinas for dinner at a restaurant and then to a picture show — to celebrate, you see.'

'Good,' she repeated. 'Oh, yes. That will be good.'

Henry put on his joking tone. 'There's fights tonight. How'd you like to go to the fights?'

'Oh, no,' she said breathlessly. 'No, I wouldn't like fights.'

'Just fooling, Elisa. We'll go to a movie. Let's see. It's two now. I'm going to take Scotty and bring down those steers from the hill. It'll take us maybe two hours. We'll go in town about five and have dinner at the Cominos Hotel. Like that?'

'Of course I'll like it. It's good to eat away from home.'

'All right then. I'll go get up a couple of horses.'

She said, 'I'll have plenty of time to transplant some of these sets, I guess.'

She heard her husband calling Scotty down by the barn. And a little later she saw the two men ride up the pale-yellow hillside in search of the steers.

There was a little square sandy bed kept for rooting the chrysanthemums. With her trowel she turned the soil over and over and smoothed it and patted it firm. Then she dug ten parallel trenches to receive the sets. Back at the chrysanthemum bed she pulled out the little crisp shoots, trimmed off the leaves of each one with her scissors, and laid it on a small orderly pile.

A squeak of wheels and plod of hoofs came from the road. Elisa looked up. The country road ran along the dense bank of willows and cottonwoods that bordered the river, and up this road came a curious vehicle, curiously drawn. It was an old spring-wagon, with a round canvas top on it like the cover of a prairie schooner. It was drawn by an old bay horse and a little gray-and-white burro. A big stubble-bearded man sat between the cover flaps and drove the crawling team. Underneath the wagon, between the hind wheels, a lean and rangy mongrel dog walked sedately. Words were painted on the canvas in clumsy, crooked letters. 'Pots, pans, knives, scissors, lawn mowers, Fixed.' Two rows of articles, and the triumphantly definitive 'Fixed' below. The black paint had run down in little sharp points beneath each letter.

Elisa, squatting on the ground, watched to see the crazy loose-jointed wagon pass by. But it didn't pass. It turned into the farm road in front of her house, crooked old wheels skirling and squeaking. The rangy dog darted from beneath the wheels and ran ahead. Instantly the two ranch shepherds flew out at him. Then all three stopped, and with stiff and quivering tails, with taut straight legs, with ambassadorial dignity, they slowly circled, sniffing daintily. The caravan pulled up to Elisa's wire fence and stopped. Now the newcomer dog, feeling outnumbered, lowered his tail and retired under the wagon with raised hackles and bared teeth.

The man on the wagon seat called out, 'That's a bad dog in a fight when he gets started.'

Elisa laughed. 'I see he is. How soon does he generally get started?'

The man caught up her laughter and echoed it heartily. 'Sometimes not for weeks and weeks,' he said. He climbed stiffly down over the wheel. The horse and the donkey dropped like unwatered flowers.

Elisa saw that he was a very big man. Although his hair and beard were graying, he did not look old. His worn black suit was wrinkled and spotted with grease. The laughter had disappeared from his face and eyes the moment his laughing voice ceased. His eyes were dark and they were full of the brooding that gets in the eyes of teamsters and of sailors. The calloused hands he rested on the fence were cracked, and every crack was a black line. He took off his battered hat.

'I'm off my general road, ma'am,' he said. 'Does this dirt road cut over across the river to the Los Angeles highway?'

Elisa stood up and shoved the thick scissors in her apron pocket. 'Well, yes, it does, but it winds around and then fords the river. I don't think your team could pull through the sand.'

He replied with some asperity, 'It might surprise you what them beasts can pull through.'

'When they get started?' she asked.

He smiled for a second. 'Yes. When they get started.'

'Well,' said Elisa, 'I think you'll save time if you go back to the Salinas road and pick up the highway there.'

He drew a big finger down the chicken wire and made it sing. 'I ain't in any hurry, ma'am. I go from Seattle to San Diego and back every year. Takes all my time. About six months each way. I aim to follow nice weather.'

Elisa took off her gloves and stuffed them in the apron pocket with the scissors. She touched the under edge of her man's hat, searching for fugitive hairs. 'That sounds like a nice kind of a way to live,' she said.

He leaned confidentially over the fence. 'Maybe you noticed the writing on my wagon. I mend pots and sharpen knives and scissors. You got any of them things to do?'

'Oh, no,' she said quickly. 'Nothing like that.' Her eyes hardened with resistance.

'Scissors is the worst thing,' he explained. 'Most people just ruin scissors trying to sharpen 'em, but I know how. I got a special tool. It's a little bobbit kind of thing and patented. But it sure does the trick.'

'No. My scissors are all sharp.'

'All right then. Take a pot,' he continued earnestly, 'a bent pot or a pot with a hole. I can make it like new so you don't have to buy no new ones. That's a saving for you.'

'No,' she said shortly. 'I tell you I have nothing like that for you to do.'

His face fell to an exaggerated sadness. His voice took on a whining undertone. 'I ain't had a thing to do today. Maybe I won't have no supper tonight. You see I'm off my regular road. I know folks on the highway clear from Seattle to San Diego. They save their things for me to sharpen up because they know I do it so good and save them money.'

'I'm sorry,' Elisa said irritably. 'I haven't anything for you to do.'

His eyes left her face and fell to searching the ground. They roamed about until they came to the chrysanthemum bed where she had been working. 'What's them plants, ma'am?'

The irritation and resistance melted from Elisa's face. 'Oh, those are chrysanthemums, giant whites and yellows. I raise them every year, bigger than anybody around here.'

'Kind of a long-stemmed flower? Looks like a quick puff of colored smoke?' he asked.

'That's it. What a nice way to describe them.'

'They smell kind of nasty till you get used to them,' he said.

'It's a good bitter smell,' she retorted, 'not nasty at all.'

He changed his tone quickly. 'I like the smell myself.'

'I had ten-inch blooms this year,' she said.

The man leaned farther over the fence. 'Look. I know a lady down the road a piece has got the nicest garden you ever seen. Got nearly every kind of flower but no chrysanthemums. Last time I was mending a copper-bottom wash tub for her (that's a hard job but I do it good), she said to me, "If you ever run acrost some nice chrysantheums I wish you'd try to get me a few seeds." That's what she told me.'

Elisa's eyes grew alert and eager. 'She couldn't have known much about chrysanthemums. You *can* raise them from seed, but it's much easier to root the little sprouts you see there.'

'Oh,' he said. 'I s'pose I can't take none to her then.'

'Why yes, you can,' Elisa cried. 'I can put some in damp sand, and you can carry them right along with you. They'll take root in the pot if you keep them damp. And then she can transplant them.'

'She'd sure like to have some, ma'am. You say they're nice ones?'

'Beautiful,' she said. 'Oh, beautiful.' Her eyes shone. She tore off the battered hat and shook out her dark pretty hair. 'I'll put them in a flower pot, and you can take them right with you. Come into the yard.'

While the man came through the picket gate Elisa ran excitedly along the geranium-bordered path to the back of the house. And she returned carrying a big red flower pot. The gloves were forgotten now. She kneeled on the ground by the starting bed and dug up the sandy soil with her fingers and scooped it into the bright new flower pot. Then she picked up the little pile of shoots she had prepared. With her strong fingers she pressed them into the sand and tamped round them with her knuckles. The man stood over her. 'I'll tell you what to do,' she said. 'You remember so you can tell the lady.'

'Yes, I'll try to remember.'

'Well, look. These will take root in about a month. Then she must set them out, about a foot apart in good rich earth like this, see?' She lifted a handful of dark soil for him to look at. 'They'll grow fast and tall. Now remember this. In July tell her to cut them down, about eight inches from the ground.'

'Before they bloom?' he asked.

'Yes, before they bloom.' Her face was tight with eagerness. 'They'll grow right up again. About the last of September the buds will start.'

She stopped and seemed perplexed. 'It's the budding that takes the most care,' she said hesitantly. 'I don't know how to tell you.' She looked deep into his eyes searchingly. Her mouth opened a little, and she seemed to be listening. 'I'll try to tell you,' she said. 'Did you ever hear of planting hands?'

'Can't say I have, ma'am.'

'Well, I can only tell you what it feels like. It's when you're picking off the buds you don't want. Everything goes right down into your fingertips. You watch your fingers work. They do it themselves. You can feel how it is. They pick and pick the buds. They never make a mistake. They're with the plant. Do you see? Your fingers and the plant. You can feel that, right up your arm. They know. They never make a mistake. You can feel it. When you're like that you can't do anything wrong. Do you see that? Can you understand that?'

She was kneeling on the ground looking up at him. Her breast swelled passionately.

The man's eyes narrowed. He looked away self-consciously. 'Maybe I know,' he said. 'Sometimes in the night in the wagon there ——'

Elisa's voice grew husky. She broke in on him: 'I've never lived as you do, but I know what you mean. When the night is dark — the stars are sharp-pointed, and there's quiet. Why, you rise up and up!'

Kneeling there, her hand went out toward his legs in the greasy black trousers. Her hesitant fingers almost touched the cloth. Then her hand dropped to the ground.

He said: 'It's nice, just like you say. Only when you don't have no dinner it ain't.'

She stood up then, very straight, and her face was ashamed. She held the flower pot out to him and placed it gently in his arms. 'Here. Put it in your wagon, on the seat, where you can watch it. Maybe I can find something for you to do.'

At the back of the house she dug in the can pile and found two old and battered aluminum sauce pans. She carried them back and gave them to him. 'Here, maybe you can fix these.'

His manner changed. He became professional. 'Good as new I can fix them.' At the back of his wagon he set a little anvil, and out of an oily tool box dug a small machine hammer. Elisa came through the gate to watch him while he pounded out the dents in the kettles. His mouth grew sure and knowing. At a difficult part of the work he sucked his underlip.

'You sleep right in the wagon?' Elisa asked.

'Right in the wagon, ma'am. Rain or shine, I'm dry as a cow in there.'

'It must be nice,' she said. 'It must be very nice. I wish women could do such things.'

'It ain't the right kind of a life for a woman.'

Her upper lip raised a little, showing her teeth. 'How do you know? How can you tell?' she said.

'I don't know, ma'am,' he protested. 'Of course I don't know. Now here's your kettles, done. You don't have to buy no new ones.'

'How much?'

'Oh, fifty cents'll do. I keep my prices down and my work good. That's why I have all them satisfied customers up and down the highway.'

Elisa brought him a fifty-cent piece from the house and dropped it in his hand. 'You might be surprised to have a rival sometime. I can sharpen scissors too. And I can beat the dents out of little pots. I could show you what a woman might do.'

He put his hammer back in the oily box and shoved the little anvil out of sight. 'It would be a lonely life for a woman, ma'am, and a scary life, too, with animals creeping under the wagon all night.' He climbed over the singletree, steadying himself with a hand on the burro's white rump. He settled himself in the seat, picked up the lines. 'Thank you kindly, ma'am,' he said. 'I'll do like you told me; I'll go back and catch the Salinas road.'

'Mind,' she called, 'if you're long in getting there, keep the sand damp.'

'Sand, ma'am! — Sand? Oh, sure. You mean around the chrysantheums. Sure I will.' He clucked his tongue. The beasts leaned luxuriously into their collars. The mongrel dog took his place between the back wheels. The wagon turned and crawled out the entrance road and back the way it had come, along the river.

Elisa stood in front of her wire fence watching the slow progress of the caravan. Her shoulders were straight, her head thrown back, her eyes half-closed, so that the scene came vaguely into them. Her lips moved silently, forming the words 'Good-bye — good-bye.' Then she whispered: 'That's a bright direction. There's a glowing there.' The sound of her whisper startled her. She shook herself free and looked about to see whether anyone had been listening. Only the dogs had heard. They lifted their heads toward her from their sleeping in the dust, and then stretched out their chins and settled asleep again. Elisa turned and ran hurriedly into the house.

In the kitchen she reached behind the stove and felt the water tank. It was full of hot water from the noonday cooking. In the bathroom she tore off her soiled clothes and flung them into the corner. And then she scrubbed herself with a little block of pumice, legs and thighs, loins and chest and arms, until her skin was scratched and red. When she had dried herself she stood in front of a mirror in her bedroom and looked at her body. She tightened her stomach and threw out her chest. She turned and looked over her shoulder at her back.

After a while she began to dress slowly. She put on her newest underclothing and her nicest stockings and the dress which was the symbol of her prettiness. She worked carefully on her hair, pencilled her eyebrows, and rouged her lips.

Before she was finished she heard the little thunder of hoofs and the shouts of Henry and his helper as they drove the red steers into the corral. She heard the gate bang shut and set herself for Henry's arrival.

His step sounded on the porch. He entered the house calling, 'Elisa, where are you?'

'In my room, dressing. I'm not ready. There's hot water for your bath. Hurry up. It's getting late.'

When she heard him splashing in the tub, Elisa laid his dark suit on the bed, and shirt and socks and tie beside it. She stood his polished shoes on the floor beside the bed. Then she went to the porch and sat primly and stiffly down. She looked toward the river road where the willow-line was still yellow with frosted leaves so that under the high gray fog they seemed a thin band of sunshine. This was the only color in the gray afternoon. She sat unmoving for a long time.

Henry came banging out of the door, shoving his tie inside his vest as he came. Elisa stiffened and her face grew tight. Henry stopped short and looked at her. 'Why — why, Elisa. You look so nice!'

'Nice? You think I look nice? What do you mean by "nice"?'

Henry blundered on. 'I don't know. I mean you look different, strong and happy.'

'I am strong? Yes, strong. What do you mean "strong"?'

He looked bewildered. 'You're playing some kind of a game,' he said helplessly. 'It's a kind of a play. You look strong enough to break a calf over your knee, happy enough to eat it like a water-melon.'

For a second she lost her rigidity. 'Henry! Don't talk like that. You didn't know what you said.' She grew complete again. 'I am strong,' she boasted. 'I never knew before how strong.'

Henry looked down toward the tractor shed, and when he brought his eyes back to her, they were his own again. 'I'll get out the car. You can put on your coat while I'm starting.'

Elisa went into the house. She heard him drive to the gate and idle down his motor, and then she took a long time to put on her hat. She pulled it here and pressed it there. When Henry turned the motor off she slipped into her coat and went out.

The little roadster bounced along on the dirt road by the river, raising the birds and driving the rabbits into the brush. Two cranes flapped heavily over the willow-line and dropped into the river-bed.

Far ahead on the road Elisa saw a dark speck in the dust. She suddenly felt empty. She did not hear Henry's talk. She tried not to look; she did not want to see the little heap of sand and green shoots, but she could not help herself. The chrysanthemums lay in the road close to the wagon tracks. But not the pot; he had kept that. As the car passed them she remembered the good bitter smell, and a little shudder went through her. She felt ashamed of her strong planter's hands, that were no use, lying palms up in her lap.

The roadster turned a bend and she saw the caravan ahead. She swung full round toward her husband so that she could not see the little covered wagon and the mismatched team as the car passed.

In a moment they had left behind them the man who had not known or needed to know what she said, the bargainer. She did not look back.

To Henry she said loudly, to be heard above the motor, 'It will be good, tonight, a good dinner.'

'Now you're changed again,' Henry complained. He took one hand from the wheel and patted her knee. 'I ought to take you in to dinner oftener. It would be good for both of us. We get so heavy out on the ranch.'

'Henry,' she asked, 'could we have wine at dinner?'

'Sure. Say! That will be fine.'

She was silent for a while; then she said, 'Henry, at those prize fights do the men hurt each other very much?'

'Sometimes a little, not often. Why?'

'Well, I've read how they break noses, and blood runs down their chests. I've read how the fighting gloves get heavy and soggy with blood.'

He looked round at her. 'What's the matter, Elisa? I didn't know you read things like that.' He brought the car to a stop, then turned to the right over the Salinas River bridge.

'Do any women ever go to the fights?' she asked.

'Oh, sure, some. What's the matter, Elisa? Do you want to go? I don't think you'd like it, but I'll take you if you really want to go.'

She relaxed limply in the seat. 'Oh, no. No. I don't want to go. I'm sure I don't.' Her face was turned away from him. 'It will be enough if we can have wine. It will be plenty.' She turned up her coat collar so he could not see that she was crying weakly — like an old woman.

HUEY, THE ENGINEER [1]

By JESSE STUART

(From *Esquire*)

CAN'T you hear that whistle still — can't you hear it! Can't you hear the tee rails popping and the flat cars lumbering around the curves and the big-bear engine — fat as a bear — huffing and puffing like a tired horse up a hill with an overloaded express — that humpy-dumpy old E-K engine with her pistons screaking and the long line of black smoke laid back from the stack — following the way the wind was blowing — can't you see it all and the long train of seven cars — two for the passengers — two for coal and two for logs and cattle — maybe I don't remember the two rusted streaks of tee rails running south through the Plum Grove hills — two streaks of rust fastened to the decayed and cinder-buried crossties — rotted at the necks where the tee rails kissed the crossties. Maybe my Pa and my Pa's Pa didn't help make the crossties and my Pa's Pa helped lay the big tee rails in them days — rails that three men could lift — yes, they helped to put the thirty-six miles of track over these Kentucky hills back to the coal, crossties, chickens, and the ore — maybe I haven't heard about it all my life — maybe I don't remember the first time I saw that train and ran away through the sassafras sprouts like a scared rabbit.

My Pa will tell you. He was taking me to school. I was a big shaver for the years on my head — for the seven springs and six autumns we'd had — for we start to school in Kentucky in July to save a coal bill in the country school — coal all around us too — coal in the high hills and the low hills under the shaggy tough-butted white oak roots — fire clay there too, and that's why the E-K run wild over the hills for thirty-six miles — that's why we saw the big engine pulling seven coaches over the road just a-snorting and a-huffing and a-puffing, and sometimes on this seven-coach train the engineer would reach his hand out and try to shake hands with the conductor who rode in the back coach. Oh, you couldn't quite do it,

you know, but he just tried and the people would laugh. Once
John Isom saw 'em do that. And John said he did and he said he
hollered at 'em among all that noise, 'Watch you don't break the
train's ribs pulling stuff like that!' He said he didn't think they
heard him. That was all. Wind a-blowing in the corn along the
train — an autumn wind and apples falling from the apple trees.
A body could see just loads of them in the Sandy bottoms. God,
but falltime along the E-K — don't you remember — train huffing
and puffing like a bull coming right out of a hole in the hill — eight
of them big holes on thirty-six and one-half miles of track.

After I saw the E-K Pa used to say to me: 'Son, what do you want
to do when you get to be a man — teach school, run a big store, run
a big farm — Son, just what do you want to do?' And I says to Pa:
'I want to be a man like Huey — sit up in that engine and pull the
throttle and let 'er fly. Pa, that's what I want to do. Want to have
white hair like Huey too and let it fly to the wind when the engine
rocks, and I want my hair to be long and follow the wind like Huey's
hair does when he's pulling that engine. I want to be an engineer.'

Pa would look at me as if to say: 'Engineer — huh — w'y the
train is a ghost against the wind now — the big train — the C & O
has come to the big valley and people don't come out to see the E-K
pass like they used to come in for miles and watch it before there
was another railroad around. The old E-K is a dead duck trying to
swim. The old E-K is a goner — w'y I've worked on the section and
don't you think I know a sick track? The E-K track is not only a
sick track but it is a dead track.' That is what Pa kept trying to
say. But Huey stayed right on that track. Huey kept pulling the
throttle and don't you know people rode that train. A lot of them
said it was dangerous to ride it. But Huey said it was not. People
believed Huey. People liked Huey for thirty-six miles — they all
knew him, and when they heard his whistle moan they would pull
out their watches and get the time. One would say: 'Here comes
Huey. Set your watches. Never over thirty minutes off unless a
tunnel fell in, or the cut caved in, or a tree fell across the track — a
trestle fell in or a bridge washed out ——' No, never, never — Huey
at the throttle and that engine always rode the rails — over the two
rusty streaks that run to the north to the Ohio River and to the
south — Ah — let me see over the hills — no, under the hills —
eight of them, people! And the bridges and trestles — ah, let me see

fifteen miles of them? No, that is not right when there are eight miles under the ground or something near that. That would leave only thirteen miles of easy sailing track. The way you count it you add the holes in the ground plus the bridges and the trestles and subtract that from thirty-six and one-half miles of the old E-K. The Lord knows I can count for I have been to school. When I used to go to school — I used to see Huey every morning. Just one place on the patch to school we saw Huey. We waited for him. Hid in the willows by the track and jumped out and waved our dinner buckets at Huey to surprise him. But he always had his eye on the spot where the willows were so he could wave at us and rare back at the throttle and laugh — don't think I don't remember how we used to quarrel over who was going to be like Huey. Walter Felch used to say he's going to be like Huey when he got to be a man — sit up in a train and ride and have everybody watching him pull at the throttle — never the brake — And I said I was going to be like Huey too and then he said only one of us could be like Huey. And I told him that Pa told me that Huey learnt a lot of the men that was out on the main line to pull a engine right on the old E-K. They tried to get Huey to go out and pull an engine there and he just laughed. He wouldn't leave where he'd been for years for no strange track. He wouldn't leave the people and the curves, the tunnels and the stores along the tracks. God no, he wouldn't leave all this and the bridges. Huey was in many a wreck but he never got a bone broke. He knew where to take it easy and where to take it fast. He'd been over the bumps and the bridges and in and out the holes under the hills enough until he ought to have known what was what along that track.

He knew the patches of sprouts along the track and the barns and the apple orchards. W'y Huey knew who owned the bulls along the road and who had in this patch of tobacco and that patch of cane. He knew all about the boys along the track. And you can just see honest Abe Johnson over there now in his corn knee-high to a grasshopper — without a shirt on his back plowing in the hot sun. That's the way Abe went most of the time. And he'd stop his mule and rest between the plow handles till Huey went by. He'd wave at Huey and holler and Huey would wave. And the wind would blow down the corn if it was a windy day along the Sandy bottoms. Smoke from the engine would blow back across the fields like a ribbon in the wind when sister Mary is running against the wind. Huey would just wave at everybody. W'y old Winston Leppor said he believed Huey could be elected President of the United States because he knowed so many people. Thirty-six miles long and God knows how many miles wide for the people used to come in to see the train — all the people knowed Huey.

'Good old days they used to be,' said Grandpa, 'good old days.' Not back in the Rebellion. It was a bad time then to ride the train. But later on through the days of Grant, Garfield, and Hayes — w'y they's more butter and eggs and crates of chickens come in on that train then than you could shake a stick at if you stood and shook a stick all day. Train stopped at every station and loaded on chickens. Everybody raised chickens along the E-K. It was a chicken country. People had to have salt and soda and coffee for their tables I guess. Couldn't very well raise them here in Kentucky. Let the hens pay for them. And calico and percale for dresses and silks and satins. Had to have some of them to go along for the well-dressed people and the girls getting married. Wasn't married at all unless she was married in a silk dress. Let the hens pay for that too. Well — you'd be surprised what a flock of hens can do in the spring and by grabs they don't do it — up and sell the hens and get you some that will do it. That's what Mom always done. Pa was always for giving the hens the second chance if they didn't do any good one spring. But Mom just give 'em one chance. She said that was enough when there were other hens just waiting for the chance. And she'd up and crate the old hens that perhaps didn't find any gravels for their craws Pa said — well gravels or no gravels — Mom just up and crated them and we hauled them to the station and waited for Huey. That's what we done with a bunch of lazy hens. And Lord how mercy — you ought to have just seen the turkeys that come down that E-K in the fall. Lord how mercy — it was one more sight — it was a plum sight. John Anderson would pass and he'd say: 'If Huey don't quit hauling so many turkeys w'y people going to call him "Turkey Huey."' Great loads of turkeys — a whole carload a day all through November and a bunch of wagons and them old fizzling automobiles at the other end of the track to get the loads — them old automobiles that scared the wits out 'n the people and made the horses break the tongues out of the wagons. Well, a lot of women had to quit driving the

mules and horses after them things come into use. That's just
exactly what happened. Who was going to run the risk getting a
leg, arm, maybe a neck broke over them infernal automobiles! Big
things waiting for the turkeys. Yes — and they'd haul them to the
Produce House in Greenupsburg too — a town that never did grow
much — has had about a thousand people since 1816. No place to
build and when it did build baby by baby — w'y they always told
me when a baby was born in Greenupsburg two men left the town.
That's what I always heard. Pa told me and his Pa told him. But
that's where the turkeys went. And a lot of people would just ride
the train in to get to see a Darkie. Never had any back in the hills.
They all live in town you know. And they'd drive them automobiles
that hauled the turkeys. They all had the prettiest teeth — white
as a hen egg laid by a white leghorn and just dropped in the nest.
They'd sweat and lift the big crates of turkeys and the white men
would just show 'em how to do it. They done the work. Honest to
God they did. Smokey-Bill, Abe and Honest Jim and old Uncle
Dick, and all that bunch of Darkies. And you ought to hear them
sing too. They just sung away and the turkeys would stick their
necks out the crates and go 'plop — plop — kirt — kirt — kplop —
kplop — kirt — kirt' and old Abe would laugh and show his big
white set of teeth and say: 'You's goin' to kplop when that ax am on
your neck. That's what you am — turkey!' And he would laugh.
Turkeys wanting back to green fields on the Sandy River — back
among the hills where it had the big fields to run over — not just
crowded in a little crate a sweating and sweating — a huffing
and puffing like the engine that pulled them there. But let me tell
you when the engine is going toward the north — it don't have to do
much pulling the last fifteen miles of the way. It goes downhill —
just nearly has to lock the wheels and it blows like a blowing viper
snake all the time like 'sssssssssssssss' and there's just a little stream
of smoke that goes up from the stack. And in the winter that train
always brought two carloads of coal from the mines in the low hills
and they said on the other end of the track it hauled six or seven
carloads from the Hammertight mines down to Grayson. Yessir —
I've heard it but I never got to 'tother end of the E-K, more than
twice or three times in my life. Just went there then to ride the
train the first time and the next two times to see about some cattle.
I know they hauled a lot of ties. Grandpa said when he was a young

man it was a sight what they hauled down to Greenupsburg and
there they took it on the Greyhound. That big boat that used to
run on the river — and he said there's a lot of other boats that
hauled from the E-K too. Huey could tell you. If Huey was here he
could tell you a lot that happened in the half a hundred years he was
a hold of that throttle. He could tell you about the cattle too they
hauled in the fall and in the spring — two carloads of cattle a week
— sometimes four and five and they always had four or five crates
with bawling calves in them — veal calves shipping them from
their mothers and they'd cry for them all the way. Huey said he
just made himself get used to it. It bothered him a little at first.
That was back in the days when the road was good and Huey could
pull the train in on time. And in the spring it was a sight at the
cans of cream and milk that come in on the E-K — and the lumber
and the people going to Greenupsburg with baskets on their arms.
Going to town with baskets of eggs, baskets of butter done up
pretty with a buttermould and a swan on the top of the yellow
pounds and some with a horseshoe. All depended on the kind of
buttermoulds the women wanted. Horseshoe was better luck.
Could sell the butter easier in Greenupsburg maybe — good fresh
yellow country butter — and they'd have baskets of ducks and
duck eggs, turkeys and turkey eggs, geese and goose eggs and guin-
eas and guinea eggs — I tell you the women back in the days of
Grant, Garfield and Hayes — w'y they went loaded on that train to
Greenupsburg. After the Rebellion you know. Them was good days
and Huey pulled long trains. W'y yes — there was another train on
that road in them days — Jonas Black, I believe, let me see wasn't
he from Grayson and didn't he run that train? Now, I may have it
wrong but I believe he did. He come from the other end of the
line — started eight o'clock in the morning and passed Huey at
Midway — and Huey started from our end of the road at eight in
the morning and passed him at Midway. I believe he beat Huey
there because Huey had to go uphill going out and kindly downhill
coming back. Well when they done that we got mail twice a day
at the Riverton post office. You see Jonas brought it from the
other end of the line and Huey brought it from the other end of
the line. Huey took it out from our end of the line and Jonas took
it out. That was when we got mail twice a day in them good old
days. Believe me it was a lot better to ride on a train the old people

will tell you than it was to ride a mule to death. Just like one end of
you had growed in the saddle when you started to get off — just
have to heave and pull to get yourself limbered up and to pull your
bones in shape and get the stuck end out of the saddle. Old people if
they were a-living — people in the days of Grant, Garfield and
Hayes will tell you too that it was a lot better than listening to the
gravel fly against the dashboard of the surrey all day long and see
the wheels roll around the flanks of the oak covered hills. Better
than to hear the wheezing of the axles and the horses getting their
wind and seeing the foam fall from their flanks. Better to listen to
the chug-chugging of the train any time and to see the white and
black clouds of smoke roll out over the green hills — better to see
it roll with the wind over the winter barren hills — honest it was —
And boy them excursions back in the old days. Ask the men about
them. Ask me too boy — I remember them and I'm of the new generation — I'm of the third. I remember them. I'll let the old tell
you first about what they saw and I'll tell you what I saw. 'W'y in
the days of Grant, Garfield and Hayes — they'd have some of the
awfulest baseball games down at Greenupsburg and people would
come with the team. The other end of the line would play our end
of the line. Grayson would play Greenupsburg and the train would
pull seven coaches — all the coaches they had and they'd put on
box-cars sometimes to hold the people. They'd be on top the engine
and Huey'd go out and say: "Boys, don't care where you get so
you get down low when we pass through them tunnels. If you get
your heads knocked off it is your own risk. Get me, boys?" "Yes,
Huey, we got you. We'll watch our heads for they are our own."
And they would laugh. And they'd follow the boys to the game. Of
all the people. Some said there's where the E-K used to make their
wheelbarrow loads of money was on them excursion ball games.
W'y everybody saved for a week to get to come to the ball game on
Sunday. Girls all trigged up and the boys too and they'd come and
hold hands — drink that red pop from the stands and lots of times
the boys would be drinking something else for red pop can't make
them stagger — and they'd holler and whoop. I wish I could just
tell you about it the way it was. I wish you could have just seen
one of the games. They'd holler "batter Up!" And they dust the
plate with a broom and they'd start the thing. The people would
get on their own sides and start hollering. When the score got

close men would go to meeting one another between the sides and they'd start fighting. More men would go out to get them out of the fight and they'd get into it. And the fight would start. And the baseball bats would start. People would go to hauling guns and the Sheriff would go out with his deputies and he'd deputize more men to help him break up the fight. If they was on our end of the line we just fined their men. If we was on their end of the line they just fined our men. So we just about broke even on fines. Huey would be there. He'd just sit there and look on. Huey was a young man in them days. They'd try to get Huey to root for this side and that side. Of course I'll always believe Huey felt for our side for he was from this end of the line. We'll never know. But Huey would say: "Boys, I can't be for neither side. I haul all of you. I live among all of you. I'll just watch the game." And Huey didn't even get on neither side. He sat back off on the old E-K railroad bed where the fielders always got — right about where the center fielder stood. He said he could see it better from there. And Huey couldn't a taken sides for if he had the people wouldn't have ridden on the train. It would have hurt the company if Huey had got on one side or the tother side. So Huey just set there between the two sides out where the pizen vine was on that old diamond at Greenupsburg.

'And after the game the boys would get on the train — sweaty and tired and a lot of them with their lips busted and noses smashed — and they'd get their bats and balls and water jugs and go home. They'd holler smart things at us and lick out their tongues and we'd holler smart things at them and lick out our tongues. I guess we had the right to lick out our tongues at them if they had the right to lick out their tongues at us. We'd nearly all the time win the game when they come and played us and we'd nearly always lose when we played them. You know you can play better ball and fight harder on your own territory. Look at Gettysburg back yander in the Rebellion won't you. Fit on Yank territory and they winned that battle. First big one for them to win. They ought to a fit on their own territory and they'd a fit harder. That's the way it is in a ball game. I know it used to be that way with us here.

'Well, I remember the last hanging we had here and the scaffold out in the open for people to see. Had to put on a lot of box cars that day and then couldn't haul 'em all. It was a sight at the people that went out on that train — went to the hanging. W'y after you got there you couldn't get to see anything for so many people. You couldn't get near the scaffold to see him hang and you couldn't get near enough to hear his confession. Too much hollering and going on. People having a good time and there with smiles on their faces — glad to see the man hang for what he had done to a woman. It was a awful day and the people all got worked up there that day and bloodthirsty and started a lot of fights. Two trains on the track that day. They run two excursions — one from our end of the track and one from the other end of the track. Hanging took place in an old orchard not far from Midway. Dinners on the ground that day to feed the people. They was warned to bring their own grub and they brought it and spread it on the ground. People had a good time that day all but the few fights on the ground and they can always be expected when a crowd of strange people get together at a hanging.'

And in the spring the E-K always hauled the people to the big Baptis Association — that was always held on the upper end of the line. That's where all the Baptis live — back up yander! And they had their big Association and big revils and preachings that lasted a week where every Baptis preacher had a chance to preach. Some went four hours long. That's the one that got most of the yaller pullets to eat I always tell my wife. She's a Baptis and I kindly tease her a little bit. And they'd preach of a night and wash feet of a day. Lord what times they used to have back there in them groves by Little Sandy. That old river could sure tell some tales and that train can, too. Come right off the train a-preaching and a-singing — that old E-K Huey could tell you about it. It was back in the days of Grant, Garfield and Hayes — and God Almighty it comes right on up from that. That's when it started — w'y just a short time ago they had enough for a train load — they had to have an excursion. People just wanted to go along the track and they demanded it. Just told Huey they wanted an excursion and they got it. Tramped the weeds down under them groves till it looked like where General Morgan's men used to camp back yander in that Rebellion when them old Abolitionists use to swarm through here.

I tell you the train didn't haul so much in the early nineties. It just hauled big loads of money — carloads of money for the hills. You talk about awful times. We had them back then. God I remember taking bushels of money home and putting it under the bed when Grover Cleveland was President of the United States. We paid off in corn — in seed corn and lassies. A bushel of seed corn for a day's work — seed corn or bread corn — either one you wanted to call it. I remember Pap bringing corn home and putting it under the bed. Wouldn't let us kids have any to parch in grease on the griddle. Huey was pulling them train loads of corn back then — train loads of money. Couldn't sell a turkey, couldn't sell a chicken without you got paid in lassies or corn. Two gallons of lassies for a day's work under Cleveland. Talk about hard times. And people saying we's going to have another Rebellion — going to have a big war. And people got scared, afraid the World was coming to an end. But we pulled out of that without a war. The War come later though. Just to think the people among the hills couldn't take lassies and corn for their chickens, ducks, turkeys, butter, cream, milk — they already had lassies and corn. They had all the money and it's just as bad to have all the money on your hands than it is not to have any. So — they couldn't trade it in at the stores. Banks wouldn't hold corn and lassies. And the girls couldn't be married in silks and satins. Lots of people couldn't ride the train. They couldn't give Huey a peck of corn to ride over the two streaks of rust that run to the north and to the south. God no they couldn't do it when they didn't have a place to put it, Huey's Conductor Bill couldn't put it in his pocket. No sir, he couldn't.

Well, the War did come. It come with Spain. Huey took many a man down to Greenupsburg to enlist for the Stars and Stripes. Band was a-playing and the boys coming up to march away. They rode from the hills over the two streaks of rust — and Huey's hair was getting gray then. He was behind the throttle pulling them someplace. He pulled them down past where they use to break bottles and bats at the ball games but they didn't stop there to fight. They went on to fight with Teddy. They can tell you about it.

Yes — I remember when they took one train off, said they couldn't get the money they used to get. Coal leaving the hills around Hammertight and not as much ore as the people thought. Ore playing out. Train wasn't near as big as it used to be — dwindling down. People thought first Little Sandy would be a rival to the E-K and get a lot of the trade. Well, the Little Sandy couldn't float big barges of pig iron from the old furnaces. They tried it and one couldn't get over the Riffles. It went to the bottom. People say that load of ore is right over from the old Scott place in the Little Sandy River now. They say it's buried in the sand at the bottom of the river. Little Sandy couldn't haul pig iron and ore like the E-K and Huey at the throttle. His gray hair in the wind and the men on the section stepping aside — four men to twelve miles of track — stepping aside and the bossman that worked with them made five. 'Hello, Huey,' they would say, 'look at old Huey pulling her won't you — a load this time — watch them cars weave in and out.'

Seems like I remember — as the ghosts of leaves in autumn remember and as the smoke from the stack remembers — the days that used to be — days when there were two trains on the E-K when we got mail twice a day and now with one train Huey brings us mail once a day when the tunnel don't fall in and a bridge ain't washed out — a cut's not slipped in — and a tree's not across the tracks — yes — yes — I remember as the ghosts of leaves remembers — that was long ago — you remember Grant, Garfield, and Hayes — you remember the two streaks of rust over the sand-filled yellow blooming between the rotted crossties — you remember the corn by the tracks and the apple trees loaded with apples — you remember the corn and the wheat — And you remember the four men on the twelve-mile section — section one, two, three, or four — do you remember how the bosses worked, four bosses worked with their men to get the Thanksgiving turkey — Do you remember — seems like I hear the songs they used to sing: 'I'd Knocked the Devil or I'd a Got My Joe,' 'Corena, Corena, Where Did You Stay Last Night — Come in this morning and your clothes don't fit you right —' Yes, it seems like I remember seeing one look at the sun and then at his watch. I remember hearing him say: 'It's about time for Huey to be getting in here.' And the way the wind blew — the dead leaves — yes as the smoke goes to the thin air — yes, I remember — and the click of the shovel and the pick — the hammer against the tee rail and the shovels against the cinders — I remember — as the ghosts of dead leaves flying in the wind remember —

One train a day — and we would run to see Huey. We would come from the Hollow. We would run to the willows. We had heard the dreams of yesterday — only one train now. It was Huey: 'Kept Huey on the old E-K to pull that train — the old Eastern

Kentucky — yes sir. Will be missed if she ever leaves these hills.'
And we saw the crowds around the depots a-holding their horses and
mules. 1909, 1910, 1911, 1912 — and the years go by. The tee rails
gather more rust and the crossties get more rotten around the necks.
Sections been cut down. Three men and the boss and they work
for the turkey — sections one, two, three, and four. And Huey's
hair is getting white — white to the wind — a white morning streak
in the wind as the train goes out over the red streaks through the
weeds. And we go to the tracks and pick wild strawberries by
place in the track. Walter Felch says it's a cattle guard. I don't
know but it cuts our feet and we can walk on the cinders with our
feet. I don't guess the cattle could get over it. And there's a little
place hollowed out under the ties and a fence comes down to the
place, a fence all painted white — it's right in front of the first tunnel — maybe it's to keep cows out of the tunnel. And we argue
whether a cow can wreck the train or not. We put little cinders on
the track and that big engine Huey pulls crushes the cinders. We
hide in the weeds to see. We don't let Huey see us. We can see
Huey from the weed patch. And one would say: 'God how I would
love to be Huey and set up there in that engine and ride — never
have to look at a book all day or go home get in the wood, get up
the water and slop the hogs.'

1913, 1914, 1915, 1916, '17 — and believe you — another war —
believe it or not — no more good big ball games when old left-
handed John give them the slow drop and fanned them fast as they
stepped up — only the Darkies could hit 'Mighty John.' They
stepped up on the slow ball before it started that slow drop. They
hit 'Mighty John.' Knocked him clean over the haystacks. That's
what they done. But no more good ball games. Boys left the hills
again for to cross the waters. 'I've seen it happen,' said Huey,
'before. I've pulled the men from the hills right down this line.'
And Huey smoked his pipe. His white hair flying to the wind and
the white smoke, the gray smoke, the black clouds of smoke going
out over the fields into the thin air. Lord them dark days. I was
there when they loaded the boys on the train. So many of them so
drunk they didn't know where they's a-going. I was there when they
put Kim on the train. He never sobered up until he was wearing
Uncle Sam's uniform — and that boy of Amos Allbright's — just a
strip of a boy fifteen or sixteen — was there to see the boys off.

Some crying and some laughing — some singing and some preaching
and some cussing — I remember it — and when the train started
Owl Allbright swung on the car and says I'm going too — and he
went right along. No keeping him back. He went to France. Got
in some way. You know Uncle Sam was wanting men in them days
— begging them to work and making some of them fight. Didn't
have to make the E-K boys fight — of course we missed them at
the ball games and we missed them at the church — two years was
awful long and the girls around just a-going with little strips of boys.
Courting right up a limb. I'll tell you single men were scarce as
hen's teeth here among the hills. And people would be at the post
offices along the track back in them days. They'd come and say:
'Hello, Huey, what's the news today?' And Huey would say:
'Heard we got a lot more Germans today — all the papers filled
with it.' And they'd jump up and down and laugh. Don't think I
don't remember it all and how they run to the post office and ask
for a letter from Kim, Gaylord, Owl, Frank, John, Henry, Joe,
Martin, Dan, Silas — yes — I remember how Huey would talk
from the engine to the boys along the station and tell them the
news he'd heard in Greenupsburg and how the people would say:
'Wouldn't be so afraid if that fighting was on our own land. A dog
can't fight near so good when it is away from home among strange
people. You know that.'

Two years away from home's a long time. You know that. And
them building roads back into the hills. Cars going out now and
hauling chickens, lassies — barrels of them and the turkeys and
eggs. Times changing. Amos Allbright said: 'Them automobiles
will never last. Make too much noise. Smell too bad. Scare too
many horses on the road. People won't stand for it. Ought to elect
a Representative and send to Frankfort agin 'em.' But Amos
was wrong. They did last. And they started to beating Huey.
W'y people anymore even rode to town in them holding baskets of
eggs, butter, and chickens on their laps — the good women even
done it — their dresses flying up over their heads when they stood
up behind in the truck and rode — right out in public — women
that brazen. Lord have mercy — no wonder the younger children's
so hard to do anything with — old people acting like that — and
the old E-K — is it just a rattletrap against the wind —

God a uniform in 1917 — W'y it was the hunkey-dora thing —

now look at it. No one didn't care for the boys in their pretty uniforms like they did when they come back to the hills on furloughs and told about what they's going to do to the Germans. And Huey would listen and laugh: 'Going to do the same things to the Germans old Teddy's boys done to the Spaniards are you? Going right after 'em. Need old Teddy over there. I'd feel better satisfied.' 'Yes — we're going to pour the hot lead right in 'em. I hope they got good guns. One a body can shoot good with — heavy and easy to hold. One of these like them old rifle with six sides ——'
But now: 'That damn war. What the hell did we ever get mixed up in that thing for. German people good people. I liked the Germans. Englishmen think they're something on a stick, Huey.' 'Is that right, boys? And we're about all English ——' 'Can't help that. That's right.' 'Well get on the old boy and I'll haul you back where you belong,' Huey would say. And the soldier going home would say: 'How's Pa and Ma, Huey?' And Huey would say: 'Saw them at the post office yesterday. Come up at Hopewell when I stopped there. And I talked to them a good little bit. Your Pa's got a bad cough. Nothing don't ail your Ma. She's well and hearty for her years. Yes — starting to farm a lot out there. Got in all that horse-shoe bottom this year. Going right after it.'

1920, 1921, 1922. And did you hear about it? Well they plan to take the old E-K away. Yes — that is right. I'm wondering what old Huey will do now. Getting so they can't make it pay. W'y it's not safe to ride on anymore they tell me. They tell me the crowd has been condemned. You see they've cut the sections down to two men and the boss. Yes, that is what has happened you see.

Is that the E-K just coming in? Look at my watch. Nine o'clock at night. Huey's due in here at the three o'clock in the afternoon. Guess a tunnel's fell in. Have been having a time here lately. Three wrecks in one week. Three too many. Used to be a fellar had to go to the station to catch the train. But I can stand out there with my basket anymore and flag the train and go from anyplace along the track. Say, did you hear what old Huey had a fellar to pull on him the other day? He was some fellar standing by the track and a right smart dressed fellar you know. He flagged Huey and Huey stopped. He got on the train and rode over to the station. And when Conductor Bill started to get his fare — W'y he just got off and said: 'Gentlemen, I just wanted to be neighborly and ride with you. I didn't know you had to pay.' And the fellar said he didn't have no money. Huey just let it go. Well there wasn't anything he could do about it but let it go. We've been a-laughing about Huey's neighbor ever since. And since that time Huey don't pick up no more strangers unless they look good. Huey's liable to lose his job you know.

When the boys went out to the pond to frog, w'y Huey stopped the train and put them off at the right place. You know up there at that Reeves pond. A bunch of good fellars and Huey he knows 'em all you know. I tell you Huey's been on that road a long time, boys. Ever since I can remember. W'y he knows everybody in the country. They just come and ride the train to say they've been on Huey's train. W'y they say they're really afraid to ride the train but they can stand one trip of what Huey has stood a lifetime of. Just the other night when the train pulled in late — w'y the tunnel fell in when the train was going through it. Murt Hensley said she heard a lumbering in the coach and when they come out on the other side to where the daylight was there was a rock big enough for twenty yoke of cattle to pull laying right in the coach beside her and the whole top of the coach caved in where it had come through from the top of the tunnel. W'y Huey puts that train over nothing but two streaks of rust and the wind. And Huey is right there pulling that train every day. Don't pull much anymore. Just two and three people sometimes. But the old E-K keeps going on two streaks of rust — red streaks through the ragweed tops and the dewberry briars and the sankfield.

The other day when Huey was taking a crowd of big Hunters out to Anglin — w'y they had the dogs tied in the coaches and when they come to Hilltop — w'y one of the boys saw a covey of birds and Huey stopped. They unfastened the dogs and got out and got ever last one of the birds and got back on the train and went on to Anglin. I tell you a lot of Engineers wouldn't let you do that. But it's just as Huey says. If he says we can bird-hunt I guess we can bird-hunt and he don't have so awful much to haul anyway. Hauls out an awful bunch of baseball players and froggers to the ponds and hunters to the hills. But they say the old road is just ready to play out.

1923, 1924, 1925, 1926, 1927, 1928 — The old E-K goes on. Huey is at the throttle. His hair is white as clean sheep wool and he has a big head of hair. The years pass. Men come and go from the track. Some go to better jobs on the C & O. 'I'll stay with my throttle, boys,' says Huey, 'been here a long time. And I know everybody. Know this country like a book. Schoolboys all come to the track out through the hills and watch me — holler at me. Want to be like me. I want them to be like me. The things they don't know. I've lived so I can die — I've pulled my train as near on time as my track would let me. And I've loved it. Never had trouble with my men in my life. They've never had trouble with me. Say what they will — I've been an engineer that's kept my eye on my rails. Never had an accident in my half-a-hundred years. I'm still pulling my train.'

Can it be the truth? Is the old E-K a ghost that has come to stay — no one rides the train. And people come to look at it. It goes on. People come to the post offices along the track and get the mail and wave at Huey. His white hair in the wind. Maybe it is the ghosts of yesterday — one man and the section foreman to a section now and no more Thanksgiving turkeys. Maybe it is the ghosts of the days of Grant, Garfield and Hayes — who knows and who remembers — maybe Huey remembers the boys by the tracks and the paw-paws on the hills — the gold and light gold leaves in autumn and the haw trees with their iron colored leaves and their red and dark red berries — maybe Huey remembers the old cornfields, the apple orchards, the old houses, the bridges and the trestles and the cattle guards. The cattle guards are gone now and the sankfield and dewberry briars have covered up the crossties. The crows fly overhead and caw-caw at two men straining at the tee rails. But two men by doing a little spiking handle them all right. Maybe as the thin smoke to the wind and Huey's white hair to the wind — maybe they are the ghosts that remember — what about the dead leaves in the wind and August heat from the streaks of rust. All right — they bear the train twice a day. Huey pulls that train and it is 1930. Huey's hair is white as cotton. His eyes are a little dimmed. But he can see a man or a cow on the track. Guess he can when he sees a cow on the track w'y he gets out of the engine and shoos the cow off. And if Martha Higgins is close w'y Huey will say: 'Better keep that cow off the track here, Martha, or you'll get her killed. Your Grandpa used to have a roughish cow that come nigh as a pea getting bumped off here a couple of times.' And Huey will get back in his engine and start pulling the throttle.

Well it was in the fall all right. Falltime — yes — I remember the corn in the shock and the briars with brown leaves on them — just the color of the rusted rails — and I remember the boys going along and just pulling out a few spikes and lifting the rails up. Took Huey's Old Faithful to the other end of the line. Left Huey on this end of the line where he lives. I remember we'd heard so many times they's going to tear up the tracks and they didn't do it — w'y we just didn't believe them. But this time the train didn't whistle for Three Mile and we went to see. Sure enough they were taking up the rails. Had a bunch of boys working and they were eating apples and throwing the cores at one another. Had one old sour-faced fellar on there and I says to myself: 'Hit that bird with a apple core and you'll have him to fight.' And there was the devilish boy of Mort Anderson's on there. Call him Possum and I just ups and says to myself: 'They'll be a fight on this work car before the day is over.'

When I passed by Riverton I saw Hester Anderson. He had a pistol and he said: 'I'm looking for that sour-faced dough-bellied fellar that hit my brother Possum over hitting him with an apple core. He mashed my brother Possum's face — Possum just sixteen years old and one hundred and fifty pounds — that fellow two hundred and forty pounds and thirty years old. But I got the difference and I want to see him.' And there were no trains that day.

That was the day the engineer fell asleep. He fell asleep not to wake up for a long time — perhaps in another morning — not just to get off at eight o'clock and to pull the throttle over the rusted rails. But no more trains and Huey — he passed on. We heard about it. 'Huey is dead.' W'y the schoolboys all cried. They wanted to be like Huey. Pulling a train over two rusted streaks of steel — through the spring, summer, autumn, winter — unafraid of track and weather — he pulled his train. It was his train — he knew every bolt and every piece of steel. It had been faithful to him and to us. We knew them too.

There wasn't any train to pull us to his funeral. It would have been a big excursion. And if we had just had Huey to have pulled us there. Of course he got a little tottery toward the last but a lot of people said it was the track that Huey was going over that made him scoot all over his cab — If he had just been here to have pulled us to his own funeral. There were enough there for a big excursion — the biggest funeral that has ever been in these parts. It would have taken both trains to have pulled them all to Huey's funeral.

We saw Huey there. He was quiet. He was dressed up a little bit now — Didn't have the glasses up on his forehead and the red bandanna around his neck like we used to see him wear. But his eyes were the same and his lips were the same. He had his eyes set on the rails — half a hundred years and not an accident. And in his face were the dreams that we remembered and soon would not be remembered — the great crowds at the ball games and the train loads of boys and girls — the boys that rode for Teddy and the boys that crossed the waters. Some were not hauled back alive — and the noise at the ball games — the section men a-singing and the click of the shovel, spade, mattock, hammer, hoe. The click of steel battering steel and the wind a-whining through the dewberry briars — and Huey with his hand on the throttle and the scream of the whistle — and us down behind the willows waiting to wave at Huey — all wanted to be like him. But now — the silent hands — the steady quiet eye and we stand and shed our tears unashamed of tears for our engineer that once pulled the train where no track now is — nothing but the wind and dents in the earth and cinders ground down and old bridges — but we remember — we'll always remember — and Huey — our engineer — we wonder on what silent train and to what silent land our engineer has gone.

THE AMATEURS[1]

By HARVEY B. SWADOS

(From *Contemporary*)

IT WAS cold as hell that night. When Joe and I opened the door
marked 'Taj Mahal Theater — Stage Entrance' the heat sort of
rushed over us and our breaths disappeared again. An old guy was
sitting on a chair with the front rung missing, reading the 'International Musical.' There was a bulb hanging on a wire from the
ceiling and it made a big white shiny patch on his bald head. He
had a light grey unbuttoned vest over his potbelly — it fitted him
smooth and snug, something like the way an egg looks when you've
peeled off the shell. His thighs were flattened out wide on the chair,
wrapped tight in old dark grey pants.

When we came in the old guy looked up and said, 'Amadjoor
tryouts?' kind of half asking and half telling us. Joe said, 'Yeah,
yeah,' quick; I guess he was nervous. Then the old guy walked over
to the little old elevator and stood there waiting for us. I carried
the flute and stand and Joe carried the music. We figured it looked
more dignified that way, Joe being the accompanist.

Between the second and the third floor I said, 'Boy, she sure is a
freezer tonight,' and the old guy didn't say a word. Just stood there.
The hell with him, I said to myself. At the seventh he opened the
elevator and we got out and walked down a hall and into a little
room jammed with people.

The announcer was standing by the door with a bunch of cards
in his hand. He was a baldish good-looking young fellow, with
glasses and a hundred-dollar suit on. I filled out a card and put
down my age two years older than I am, like everybody told me to.

We dumped our coats on top of a big pile over in the corner and
by that time the first ones were trying out — I think it was three
saxes. Anyway, they were pretty good and one of them sure could
ride. When they got done everybody clapped just so much, trying

to show they were good sports. A middle-aged Italian was next. He was about five feet tall and pretty fat. He sang some Italian love song with gestures and everybody snickered. But it must have meant a lot to him, because he was practically crying with his big wobbly voice.

Then a girl gets up and takes off a bathrobe she's got on, and I see she's wearing just tights and a brassière. Her garters left red itchy marks on her legs. A guy starts pounding the piano, and the first thing you know she's tying herself up in knots. It was an old costume she had on and the floor was dirty as hell. The kid must have been about fifteen or sixteen and she didn't have any breasts or any hips or anything. God, I felt sick. It reminded me of way back when we were young kids we used to sneak in a backyard and watch a girl about eleven get undressed.

Finally this kid finishes and she gets a big hand. My turn was next, so I got out my flute and put it together. It was colder than a damn iceberg, and besides the pads were wet and the keys were sticking. People kept walking in front of me. And when Joe hits A, I see the piano's a half-tone flat.

I didn't take out my stand because I figured that would look like I was trying to lay it on, so I stuck the music on the piano and I had to bend half-way over to see it. The piece was one of those French semi-classical, not Victor Herbert stuff, but the kind of chamber music Canadian stations broadcast afternoons. I did my best with it, but I could tell right away that it wasn't flashy enough.

When I finished, I turned to the announcer and said, 'O.K.?' and right away I could have kicked myself for saying it. He sort of jumped and said: 'Yes. You play very well,' or some bull like that. Joe and me put on our coats and beat it.

The elevator wasn't there and there was no push-button so we had to walk down seven flights. I guess we were both thinking about the same things all the long way down. Joe had always figured some day he'd make his living as an accompanist. When we reached the ground floor we saw the old guy standing there, moping around.

Neither of us was in any hurry to go out into the cold, so we sort of nosed around, fiddling with our mufflers. We walked into a cubbyhole (I guess it was the old guy's office) and I picked up the *International Musician* and Joe dropped the music on the table and stretched himself out in the chair. Pretty soon the old guy wandered in, looking to see if we were swiping anything. When he saw the music he brightened up a little and picked it up. 'Now what?' I thought. He talked with a thick German accent. 'There is in this number too much repetition. The theme is three times repeated. This page you should cut out.'

'Yeah?' I said.

He looked at me funny. 'You think I am ignorant of music, hah?' Then he reached in his back pants pocket and dragged out a little red booklet. It said American Assn. of Professional Musicians or something like that. The old guy didn't have to turn any pages — it opened right where he wanted it. 'Look,' he said. E flat Clarinets. He was pointing out a name to me and I noticed for the first time that he had nice long thin fingers, the kind you read about, clean as hell. You know how rough the ends of your fingers are after you've had a long bath? Well, that's how his were from opening and closing the keys. 'Emil Durkheim. But now I am retired.' And he turned around and walked out of the room.

In about half a minute he came back, his face all twisted up from thinking about his years of misery. Suddenly I felt mad, and licked, and ashamed, all at the same time. He just stood there like that.

Then the outer door opens up and a flashy-dressed bird comes in with a tenor sax and a clarinet and says, 'Top floor, Grampa.' The old guy walks slow over to the elevator. 'Well, g'nite,' I said.

Joe and me both looked up to watch the brass pointer that showed where the elevator was. It turned around pretty fast till it got to the middle, then it got slower and slower and finally stopped at seven with a little bump. I thought back to how I'd grinned at the old guy when I first came in, and even after the tryout, when he tried to explain to me about my music. Then, God damn it, the feeling came over me that I was just a fat, middle-aged busted bum, with the flute in my hand nothing more than an old grey lumpy piece of lead pipe.

CHRISTMAS GIFT [1]

By ROBERT PENN WARREN

(From *The Virginia Quarterly Review*)

THE big white flakes sank down from the sagging sky. A wet grey light hung over everything; and the flakes looked grey against it, then turned white as they sank toward the dark earth. The roofs of the few houses along the road looked sogged and black. The man who sat in the wagon that moved slowly up the road wore an old quilt wrapped around his shoulders and a corduroy cap pulled down over his eyes. His ears stuck out from under the cap, thin as paper and lined with purplish veins. Before him, vanishing, the flakes touched the backs of the mules, which steamed and were black like wet iron.

When the man spoke to the boy on the seat beside him, the ends of his mustache twitched the amber drops that clung to it. 'You kin git off at the store,' he said.

The boy nodded his head, which looked tight and small under the rusty-felt man's hat he wore.

The hoofs of the mules cracked the skim ice in the ruts, and pale yellow mud oozed up around the fetlocks. The wagon wheels turned laboriously, crackling the ice with a sound like paper.

The man pulled on the reins, and the mules stopped, their heads hanging under the sparse downward drift of flakes. 'Whoa,' he said, after the mules had already stopped. He pointed his thumb toward the frame building set beside the road. 'You kin git off here, son,' he said. 'Most like they kin tell you here.'

The boy climbed over the side of the wagon, set his foot on the hub, and jumped. His feet sank in the half-frozen, viscous mud. Turning, he took a step toward the building, then stopped. 'Much obliged,' he said, and started on. For a moment the man peered after him from small red-rimmed eyes. He jerked the reins. 'Giddap,' he said; and the mules lay against the traces, their hoofs crackling the skim ice.

The boy mounted the steps to the sloping boards of the porch, and put his sharp grey claw-like fingers on the latch-bar. Very quietly, he pushed the door inward a little space, slipped his body through the opening, and closed the door, letting the latch back down without a sound. He looked down the shadowy corridor of the store between the shelves of cans and boxes and the clothing hung on racks against the other wall. At the end of the corridor some men sat, their bodies in huddled outline against the red glow of a stove.

With hesitant steps, the boy approached them, stopping just behind the circle. A big man, whose belly popped the broad leather belt he wore, let his chair come forward to rest on the floor, and surveyed him. 'What kin I do for you today, buddy?' he said.

The tight skin of the boy's face puckered greyly toward the lips, and his Adam's apple twitched up his throat. The big man kept on looking at the boy, who stood dumbly beyond the circle, the over-size mackinaw hanging to his knees, and shook his head at the big man.

'You wanter git warmed up?' the big man said.

The boy shook his head again.

'Naw, sir,' he managed.

'You look cold,' the big man said. 'You come round here.' He motioned to the open space in front of the stove.

Eyes fixed in question on the big man's face, the boy obeyed the gesture. He came round, carefully stepping over a man's out-thrust leg. He stood inside the circle, about six feet from the stove, and spread his hands out to it.

'Git up closter,' the big man said. 'Git yore bottom up to hit.'

The boy moved forward, and turned his back to the stove, his hands behind him working weakly toward the warmth. The men kept looking at him. Steam from the mackinaw rose up against the stove, with the sick smell of hot, wet wool.

'Now ain't that better?' the big man demanded.

The boy nodded at him.

'Who are you, pardner?' one of the men said.

The boy turned toward him. He was a short stocky man, bald and swarthy, and he sat with his booted legs bunched under him like an animal ready to spring.

'I know who he is. I've seen him,' another man said. 'He's one of Milt Lancaster's kids.'

Another man beyond the stove leaned forward, bucking his chair nearer to the boy. 'Now ain't that nice,' he said. 'Pleased ter meet you. So you're one of Milt's little bastards.'

The bald, swarthy man glared at him. 'Shut up!' he ordered abruptly.

The other man leaned elaborately back and studied the ceiling, softly whistling between his teeth.

'In doing yore Satiday trading?' the bald swarthy one said.

The boy shook his head. Then he looked at the big man. 'I wanter git the docter.'

'That's what he's for,' the big man admitted, and blinked at the stove.

'Yore folks sick?' the bald, swarthy man said.

'My sister,' the boy said, 'she's gonna have a baby.'

The man who was whistling stopped. 'Yore little sister, buddy?' He addressed the ceiling in mock solicitude, and shook his head. 'Them Lancasters allus did calf young.'

'Hit's my big sister,' the boy said to the bald man. 'She come up here last summer. She ain't nuthing but my sister on my ma's side.'

'Well, well,' said the man who was looking at the ceiling. He let his chair thump down on the front legs and spoke to no one in particular. 'So they's gonna be another little bastard out to Milt's place.'

The bald swarthy man stared glumly across at the speaker. 'Bill Stover,' he commented with no feeling, 'you gonna make me stomp hell outer you fore sun.'

The boy glanced quickly from one to the other. The bald swarthy man stared across the space, his legs bunched under him. The other man grinned, and winked sidewise.

'I oughter do hit now,' the bald swarthy one said as if to himself.

The other stopped grinning.

'If you want the doc,' the big man said, 'you go up the road four houses on the right-hand side. It ain't no piece. That's where Doc Small lives. They's a office in his front yard right smack on the road, but you go up to the house, that's where he is.'

'Hit's a chicken office,' one of the men said. 'That's where the doc keeps his chickens now going on twenty years.'

'You ain't gonna miss hit,' the big man said.

The boy came out of the circle and stopped before the big man. He looked up with a quick, furtive motion of the head. 'Much obliged,' he said. He pulled his mackinaw about him, taking up the slack in the garment, and moved down the corridor toward the door.

'Wait a minute,' the big man called after him. He got up ponderously to his feet, hitched his belt up on his belly, and went forward to the single glass showcase. The men watched him, craning their necks, all except the bald swarthy one, who crouched and stared at the red bulge of the stove.

The big man reached into the glass showcase and took out a half dozen sticks of red-striped candy. He thrust them at the boy, who, looking suspiciously at the objects, shook his head.

'Take 'em,' the man ordered.

The boy kept his hands in the pockets of the mackinaw. 'I ain't got nuthin' ter pay fer it with,' he said.

'Here, take 'em, buddy,' the man said.

The boy reached out his hand uneasily, all the while studying the man's face, which was without expression. The fingers, scaled grey by cold like a bird's claw, closed on the candy, jerked back, clutching the sticks. The hand holding the candy slipped into the loose mackinaw pocket.

'Beat it,' the big man said, 'afore they beat hell outer you at home.'

The boy slipped out the door, quick and quiet as a cat.

The big man came back to the stove and sank morosely into his chair. He tilted it back and put his arms behind his head, on which the thin brown hair was slickly parted.

'You sick, Al?' one of the men said to him.

He did not answer.

'You must be sick, giving something away just off-hand like that.'

Bill Stover again leaned forward, wet his lips, and winked at the man who spoke. He himself seemed about to speak. Then he saw the face of the bald swarthy man, whose dark eyes burned with a kind of indolent savagery.

'You go straight to hell,' the big man was wearily saying.

The snow had almost stopped. It was getting colder now. The flakes were smaller now, drawing downward breathlessly like bits of white lint. They clung to the soaked grass by the road and lay on the frozen mud. The boy's feet cracked the skim ice on the mud, then, in withdrawal, made a sucking sound.

Two hundred yards up the road he came to the place. Jutting on the road, the one-room frame building stood beside a big cedar. A tin sign, obscured by rust and weather, was nailed to the door, carrying the words: *Doctor A. P. Small, Office.* The boy turned up the path by the cedar, whose black boughs swooped down toward the bare ground. The house was set far back from the road, half hidden by trellises to which leafless horny vine clutched and curled. The windows of the house gave blankly, without reflection, on the yard where grass stuck stiffly up from dirty ice-curdled pools at the roots. The door had a glass pane in it; behind the glass a lace curtain hung like a great coarse cobweb.

He tapped the paintless wood of the door.

It was a woman who, at last, opened the door.

'What do you want, boy?' she said.

'I wanter git the docter,' he said.

She said, 'Clean your feet and come in,' and abruptly turned down the low hall. He scraped his shoes, stooped to wipe them with his fingers, and then, wringing the mud from his hands, wiped them on the mackinaw. He followed her, with quick secret glances from one side to the other. She was standing before a door, her thin arm pointing inward. 'You come in here,' she ordered. He stood back from the hearth while the woman thrust her hands nervously at the blaze. She was a little woman, and while she warmed her hands, she kept looking over her shoulder at him with a wry bird-like asperity. 'What's the matter?' she said.

'My sister's gonna have a baby,' he said.

'Who are you, boy?'

'Sill Lancaster's my name, mam,' he said, looking at her little hands that approached and jerked from the bright blaze.

'Oh,' she said. She turned fully at him, inspected him sharply from head to foot. 'You ought to take off your hat when you come in the house, boy,' she said.

He took the big hat off his head, and standing before her, held it tight in both hands.

She nodded at him; said, 'Wait a minute'; and was gone out the door.

With a dubious, inquiring step, as on suspected ice, he went across the straw matting toward the hearth, and put his back to the fire. He looked at all the objects in the room, covertly spying on them as though they had a life of their own: the gilt iron bed covered by a lace counterpane, the unpainted rocking chairs with colored pillows on the seats that were pulled up to the hearth, the table on which stood a basket full of socks rolled up in neat balls. The fire spat and sputtered in mild sibilance, eating at the chunks of sawn wood on the hearth. And the clock, its face supported by plump cupids of painted china, ticked with a small busy sound. The boy laid his hat on the yellow cushion of one of the chairs and put his hands to the fire. Against the plump little cushion, its color so bright, the hat was big and dirty. With hands still stretched out, the boy regarded it. It was soggy black with wet flecks of mud clinging to it; at the creases it was worn through. The boy took it quickly off the chair.

With that neat industrious sound the clock kept on ticking.

'Hello, son,' the man in the door said.

The man was buttoning up a brown overcoat that dropped to his ankles. Beneath the coat his small booted feet stuck out. The woman slipped in past him and came to the fire, put her hands toward the blaze again, jerked them back, all the while looking at the boy. The man pulled a black fur cap on his head and turned down the ear-flaps. 'Les go,' he said.

The woman went up to him, touching his breast with a quick indecisive motion as when she spread her hands to the fire.

'Don't wait up for me,' he said.

He put his face down, a sharp expressionless face that seemed inconsequential under the big fur cap; and the woman kissed his cheek. Her kiss made a neat, dry sound, like a click.

'Les go,' he said.

He went into the hall, the boy following to the door of the room, where the woman stood aside to let him pass. He paused an instant at the threshold. 'Much obliged,' he said to her, and slipped down the hall after the man like a shadow.

A horse and buggy, the curtains up, stood beyond the cedar at the corner of the office. The powdery flakes of snow drifted cautiously downward, were lost in the dark branches of the tree, on the road where the horse stood, head down in patience.

'You get in,' the man said, and went around to the driver's side. The boy climbed into the buggy, slipping under the curtain. The man got in and bent to fasten the curtain flap on his side. 'You fix 'em over there,' he said, and picked up the reins. The boy fumbled with the metal catch, the man, reins in hand, watching him. 'Don't you know nothing, son?' he said.

'I ain't never fixed one afore,' the boy said.

The man thrust the reins into the boy's hands, leaned across his knees to latch the curtain, straightened up, and took the reins as though lifting them from a peg. 'You pull that rug off the seat back of you,' he said, 'and give it here.'

The boy obeyed, unfolding the rug. The man took an end, jabbed it under his thigh and wrapped it around the outside leg. 'Now fix yourself up over there,' he ordered. He shook out the reins through the slit in the curtain.

The horse swung into the road, the front wheel groaning and scraping with the short turn, the buggy jerking sidewise over the ruts. The buggy straightened out, and drew more easily. The hoofs crunched and sloshed, the wheels turning.

'That's right, ain't it,' the doctor said, 'we go outer the settlement this a-way?'

'Yes, sir,' the boy said.

'I thought I recollected it so.'

They drew past the store. A man went down the steps and started to walk up the road, walking with a plunging, unsteady stride, plowing the mud. His high shoulders hunched and swayed forward.

'John Graber.' The doctor jerked his mittened thumb toward the man. 'He better be gitting on home, his woman sick like she is.' He shook his head, the sharp features without expression. 'A mighty sick woman. Kidneys,' he said.

'Yes, sir,' the boy said.

'Graber'll be cooking his own supper fore long.'

They passed the last house, a small grey house set in the open field. Yellow gullies ran across the field, bald plateaus of snow-smeared sod between gully and gully. A mule stood close to the barbed-wire fence which separated the field from the road, and the fine flakes sank in the field and the gullies. From the chimney of the house a line of smoke stood up very still amidst the descending flakes.

'Graber's house,' the doctor said.

The boy sat up straight and peered through the isinglass panels at the house and the smoke and the gutted field.

'Do I turn off up the creek?' the doctor asked.

'Yes, sir.'

They crossed the wood bridge, where the timbers creaked and rattled loosely with the turning wheels. Beneath it the swollen water plunged between limestone rocks, sucking the yellow foam. The flakes touched the spewing foam, the water plunging with a hollow constant sound.

'What's your pappy doing now?' the doctor said.

'My pappy's croppin' on a place fer Mr. Porsum, but hit ain't no good.'

'Uh-huh,' the man grunted. He looked through the isinglass in front. They had turned off the main road up the road by the creek. On one side, the limestone stuck out from the bluff side, thin grey icicles hanging from the grey stone among the shriveled fern fronds. The creek, below the dead growth of the gorge on the other side, made its hollow sound.

'Hit ain't worth nuthin'. Cain't even grow sassafras on hit.'

'Uh-huh,' the man said.

'We be leaving this year. We ain't gonna have no truck no more with Mr. Porsum that ole son-of-a-bitch. He ain't done nuthin' like he said. He ain't ...'

'That's what your pappy says,' the man said.

'My pappy says he's a goddam sheep-snitching son-a-bitch.'

The man stared through the isinglass pane, his sharp nose and chin sticking out in front, his head wobbling with the motion of the buggy. Then he opened his mouth: 'I reckon Jim Porsum's got something to say on his side.'

The boy took a stolen glance at the man's face, then relapsed to the motion of the buggy. Out of the red mess of the road, limestone poked, grey and slick like wet bone, streaked with red mud. The wheels surmounted the stone, jolting down beyond on the brittle mud. On the bluff side the cedars hung. Their thick roots thrust from the rotten crevices of stone, the roots black with moss, garnished with ice; their tops cut off the light.

The man reached the reins over to the boy. 'Hold 'em,' he said.

The boy drew his hands from under the rug and held the reins. He grasped them very tight with both hands, the knuckles chapped and tight, and peered through the isinglass panel at the horse; the head of the horse, under the cedars, bobbed up and down.

Clamping his mittens between his knees, the man rolled a cigarette. His breath, as he licked the paper, came frostily out from his mouth in a thin parody of smoke. He lighted the cigarette; then, as he reached for the reins, he found the boy observing him, observing the twisted paper that hung from his lips. He did not put the tobacco sack in his pocket, but, after a moment of hesitation, held it toward the boy. 'All right,' he said, 'go on and take it.'

The boy shook his head, watching the sack.

'Aw hell,' the man said, and dropped the sack on the boy's lap.

The boy took the sack without assurance, adjusted the paper, poured tobacco into it. Biting the string with his teeth, big square teeth irregularly set in the tight mouth, he pulled the sack together, and dropped it. Then he lifted the paper to his lips; the tip of his tongue darted out between his lips, strangely quick from the stolid, pinched face, and licked the edge of the paper. With that delicacy of motion, with the sharp grey fingers bunched like claws together to hold the bit of paper to his mouth, the boy, crouching there in the dim interior, looked at that instant like a small coon intently feeding.

He took a deep drag of the smoke, the end of the cigarette shriveling with the sucking coal, and his thin chest expanded under the cloth of the mackinaw.

Balancing the sack in his mittened hand, the doctor regarded the process. The smoke drifted colorless from the boy's nostrils, which were red and flattened. 'You ought not to do it,' the doctor said, 'and you just a kid like you are.'

'I'm ten,' the boy said.

'It's gonna stunt your growth all right.'

'Hit never stunted my pappy's growth none, and he's been a-smokin' ever since he was eight. He's big. Ain't you never seen him?'

The doctor looked at the lips which puckered greyly to the twist of paper, the pale eyes set close together under the man-size hat. The two cigarettes, the man's and the boy's, glowed indecisively in the shadow. 'I've seen him all right,' the man said at length.

'He's a plenty strong son-a-bitch,' the boy said.

The man pushed his cigarette through a crack in the curtain, and sank back. His torso, swathed in the heavy overcoat, rolled and jerked to the impact of rut or stone like some lifeless object in uneasy water. Down the gorge, like the sound of wind driving through woods, the creek maintained its hollow constant plunging. 'I didn't know Milt Lancaster had any girl big enough to be having babies yet,' the man said.

'He ain't. Not I knows anything about.'

'You said your sister, didn't you?'

'She's my sister on my maw's side. That's what she says and that's what my maw says.'

The live cigarette, burned almost to the very end, hung at the corner of the boy's lips, glowing fitfully and faintly with his speech. It hung there, untouched by his hands, which were thrust under the rug. He no longer drew the smoke in; it seemed to seep in without conscious effort on his part, drifting from his nostrils thinly with his breath.

'She just come up here last summer,' the boy said. 'I never knowed nuthin' 'bout her afore that. Maw was glad ter see her, I reckin. At first, I reckin.

'Uh-huh,' the man said absently, his sharp features fixed forward apparently without attention.

'But pappy warn't, he just raised holy hell fer sartin. She just worked round the house and never said nuthin' ter nobody. 'Cept ter me and the kids. Then pappy got so he didn't pay her no mind ter speak of.'

The cigarette burned close to the lip, the paper untwisting so that bits of red ash slipped from it and fell toward the rug. The boy withdrew one hand from beneath the rug, and with thumb and forefinger pinched together, removed the cigarette. The paper had stuck to the flesh of the lip; he jerked it free, licking the place with that strange darting motion of the tongue tip. The tongue was pink and damp against the dry grey flesh of the lips. 'Then she up and got sick and she's gonna have a baby,' he said.

'So that's why she's up here,' the man said.

The boy shook his head. 'I dunno,' he said. 'She just come.'

In the gloom of the buggy, their bodies, one long and lax against the back of the seat, the other short and upright, jerked and swayed.

The road climbed a little. The bluff wall lost its steepness, falling to heaps of detritus among boulders. No cedars showed here, only stalks of weeds and the wiry strands of vine showing on the broken surface. Then the road went down again, swinging away from the creek. There was no further sound of the water.

At the foot of the slight grade the bottom spread out: bare corn fields with stubble and shocks that disintegrated to the ground, rail fences lapped by the leafless undergrowth. Away to the left a log house stood black under bare black trees. From it the somnolent smoke ascended, twined white and grey against the grey sky. The snow had stopped.

Beyond the bottoms, the knobs looked cold and smoky. From them, and from the defiles, fingers of mist, white to their blackness, crooked downward toward the bare land. The horizon rim, fading, sustained a smoky wreath that faded upward to the space without sun.

They drew to the lane that led to the log house.

'You go on past here,' the boy said. 'Hit's up them knobs.'

The boy, almost surreptitiously, took a stick of candy from his pocket, broke off half, and stuck it between his lips. He looked at the man's sharp, expressionless profile. Then he held out the piece to him. Without a word the man took it and stuck it between his lips, sucking it.

They moved forward between the empty fields.

— Lily's not going to get married, that's just an idea she's got in her head.'

'More power to you, ladies,' said Ed Newton, spanking himself with a tablet.

They saw Estelle Mabers sitting on the rail of the bridge over the railroad track, slowly drinking a Ne-Hi orange drink. 'Have you seen Lily?' they asked her.

'I'm supposed to be out here watching for her now,' said the Mabers girl, as though she weren't there yet. 'For Jewel. Jewel says Lily come in the store while ago and took a two-ninety-eight hat and wore it off. Jewel wants to swap her something else for it.'

'Oh, Estelle, Lily says she's going to get married!' cried Aimee Slocum.

'Well, I declare,' said Estelle; she never understood anything.

Loralee Adkins came riding by in her Willys-Knight, blowing the horn to find out what they were talking about.

Aimee ran waving out into the street and yelled: 'Loralee, you got to ride us up to Lily Daw's. She's up yonder fixing to git married!'

'Well, that just shows you right now,' said Mrs. Watts, groaning as she was helped into the back seat. 'What we've got to do is persuade Lily it will be nicer to go to Ellisville.'

'Just to think.' While they rode around the corner Mrs. Carson was going on in her sad voice, like soft noises in the henhouse at twilight. 'We buried Lily's poor defenseless mother. We gave Lily all her food and kindling and every stitch she had on. Sent her to Sunday school to learn the Lord's teachings, had her baptized a Baptist. And when her old father commenced beating her and tried to cut her head off with the butcher-knife, why, we took her away from him and gave her a place to stay.'

The paintless frame house was three stories high in places and had red and green stained-glass windows in front and gingerbread around the porch. It leaned steeply to one side and the front steps were gone. The car drew up under the cedar tree.

'Now Lily's almost grown up,' Mrs. Carson continued; 'in fact, she's grown,' she concluded, getting out.

'Talking about getting married,' said Mrs. Watts disgustedly. 'Thanks, Loralee, you run on home.'

They climbed over the dusty zinnias onto the porch and walked through the open door without knocking.

Lily was there, in the empty dark center hall, kneeling on the floor beside a small open trunk. ('There certainly is always a funny smell in this house. I say it every time I come,' said Aimee Slocum.)

When Lily saw them she put a zinnia in her mouth.

'Hello, Lily,' said Mrs. Carson reproachfully.

'Hello,' said Lily, and gave a suck on the zinnia stem that sounded exactly like a jay-bird. She was wearing a petticoat for a dress, one of the things Mrs. Carson kept after her about. Her milky-yellow hair streamed freely down from under a new hat. You could see the wavy scar on her throat if you knew it was there.

Mrs. Carson and Mrs. Watts, the two fattest, sat in the double rocker. Aimee Slocum sat on the wire chair donated from the drugstore that burned.

'Well, what are you doing, Lily?' asked Mrs. Watts.

Lily smiled.

The trunk was old and lined with yellow and brown paper with an asterisk pattern showing in darker circles and rings. The ladies indicated mutely that they did not know where in the world it had come from. It was empty except for two bars of soap and a green washcloth, which Lily was trying to arrange in the bottom.

'Go on and tell us what you're doing, Lily,' said Aimee Slocum.

'Packing, silly,' said Lily.

'Where are you going?'

'Going to get married, and I bet you wish you was me now,' said Lily. But shyness overcame her suddenly and she popped the zinnia back in her mouth.

'Talk to me, dear,' said Mrs. Carson. 'Tell old Mrs. Carson why you want to get married.'

'No,' said Lily, after a moment's hesitation.

'Well, we've thought of something that will be so much nicer,' said Mrs. Carson. 'You can go to Ellisville.'

'Won't that be lovely?' said Mrs. Watts. 'Why, yes.'

'It's a lovely place,' said Aimee Slocum uncertainly.

'You've got bumps on your face,' said Lily.

'Aimee, dear, you stay out of this if you don't mind,' said Mrs. Carson anxiously. 'I don't know what it is comes over Lily when you come around her.'

Lily stared at Aimee Slocum meditatively.

'There — wouldn't you like to go to Ellisville now?' asked Mrs. Carson.

'No'm,' said Lily.

'Why not?' All the ladies looked down at her in impressive astonishment.

''Cause I'm goin' to git married,' said Lily.

'Well, and who are you going to marry, dear?' said Mrs. Watts. She knew how to pin people down and make them deny what they'd already said.

Lily bit her lip and began to smile. She reached into the trunk and held up both cakes of soap and wagged them.

'Tell us,' said Mrs. Watts, 'who you're going to marry, now?'

'A man last night.'

There was a gasp from each lady. The possible reality of a lover descended suddenly like a summer hail over their heads. Mrs. Watts stood up.

'One of those show fellows! A musician!' she cried.

Lily looked up in admiration.

'Did he — did he do anything to you?' It was still only Mrs. Watts who could take charge.

'Oh, yes'm,' said Lily. She patted the cakes of soap fastidiously with the tips of her small fingers and tucked them in with the washcloth.

'What?' demanded Aimee Slocum, tottering before her scream.

'Don't ask her what,' said Mrs. Carson. 'Tell me, Lily, are you the same as you were?'

'He had a red coat, too,' said Lily graciously. 'He took little sticks and went ping-pong! ding-dong!'

'Oh, I think I'm going to faint,' said Aimee Slocum.

'The xylophone!' cried Mrs. Watts. 'The xylophone player they talked about! Why, the coward, he ought to be run out of town on a rail.'

'Oh, he is out of town by now,' cried Aimee. 'Don't you know — the sign in the café — Victory on the ninth and Como on the tenth? He's in Como! Como!'

'Then we'll bring him back!' cried Mrs. Watts. 'He can't get away from me!'

'Hush,' said Mrs. Carson. 'I don't think it's any use following

that line of reasoning at all. It's better in the long run for him to
be gone out of our lives for good and all. That kind of a man. He
wanted Lily's body alone. He wouldn't make the poor little thing
happy, even if we was to force him to marry her like he ought, at
the point of a gun.'

'Still,' began Aimee.

'Shut up,' said Mrs. Watts. 'Mrs. Carson, you're right, I
suppose.'

'This is my hope chest, see?' said Lily. 'You haven't looked at
it. I've already got soap and a washrag. And I have my hat — on.
What are you-all going to give me?'

'Lily,' said Mrs. Watts, starting over, 'we'll give you lots of
gorgeous things if you'll only go to Ellisville instead of getting
married.'

'What will you give me?' asked Lily.

'I'll give you a pair of hem-stitched pillowcases,' said Mrs. Carson.

'I'll give you a big caramel cake,' said Mrs. Watts.

'I'll give you a souvenir from Jackson, a little toy bank,' said
Aimee Slocum. 'Now will you go?'

'No'm,' said Lily.

'I'll give you a pretty little Bible with your name on it in real
gold,' said Mrs. Carson.

'What if I was to give you a pink crepe-de-chine brassière with
adjustable shoulder straps?' asked Mrs. Watts grimly.

'Oh, Hermine.'

'Well, she needs it,' said Mrs. Watts. 'Unless she'll wear dresses
in Ellisville.'

'I wish *I* could go to Ellisville!' said Aimee Slocum luringly.

'What will they have for me down there?' asked Lily softly.

'Oh! Lots of things. You'll weave baskets, I expect...' Mrs.
Carson looked vaguely at the others.

'Oh, yes, they'll let you make all sorts of baskets,' said Mrs.
Watts; then her voice too trailed off.

'No'm, I'd rather git married,' said Lily.

'Lily Daw! Now that's just plain stubbornness!' cried Mrs.
Watts. 'You almost said you'd go and then took it back.'

'We've all asked God, Lily,' said Mrs. Carson finally, 'and God
seemed to tell us — Mr. Carson too — that the place where you
ought to be, so as to be happy, was Ellisville.'

'We've really just got to get her there — now!' screamed Aimee Slocum suddenly. 'Suppose — ! She can't stay here! *You* know — *you* know!'

'Oh, no, no, no,' said Mrs. Carson hurriedly. 'We mustn't think that.'

'Could I take my hope chest — for Ellisville?' asked Lily shyly, looking at them sidewise.

'Why, yes,' said Mrs. Carson blankly.

'If I could just take my hope chest!'

'All the time it was just her hope chest!' cried Aimee Slocum.

'It's settled!' Mrs. Watts struck her palms together.

'Praise the fathers,' murmured Mrs. Carson.

'O.K. — Toots!' said Lily, her eyes gleaming with the triumph of a quotation.

The ladies were backing away to the door. 'I think I'd better stay,' said Mrs. Carson, stopping in her tracks. 'Where — where could she have learned that terrible expression?'

'Pack her things,' said Mrs. Watts. 'Make the 12.35.'

In the station the train was puffing. Nearly everyone in Victory was hanging around waiting for it to leave. The Victory Civic Band was scattered through the crowd. Ed Newton gave false signals to start on his bass horn. Everybody wanted to see Lily all dressed up, but Mrs. Carson and Mrs. Watts had sneaked her into the train from the other side of the tracks. The two ladies were going to travel as far as Jackson to help Lily change trains.

Lily sat between them with her hair combed and pinned up into a figure-eight knot under a small blue hat without flowers. She wore a thin made-over black dress from Mrs. Watts's last summer's mourning. Pink straps glowed through. She had a purse and a Bible and a cake in a tin box, all in her lap.

Aimee Slocum had been getting the outgoing mail stamped and bundled. She stood in the aisle of the coach now, tears shaking from her eyes. 'Good-bye, Lily,' she said. She was the one who felt things.

'Good-bye, silly,' said Lily.

'Oh, dear, I hope they get our telegram to meet her in Ellisville!' Aimee cried suddenly, as she thought how far away it was. 'And it was so hard to get it all in ten words, too.'

'Get off, Aimee,' said Mrs. Watts, all settled and waving her dressy fan from the funeral parlor. 'I declare I'm so hot, as soon as we get a few miles out of town I'm going to slip my corset down.'

'Oh, Lily, be good down there, weave baskets and do anything else they tell you — it's all because they love you.' Aimee drew her mouth down and backed down the aisle.

Lily laughed. She pointed across Mrs. Carson out the window toward a man who had stepped off the train and stood there in the dust. He was a stranger and wore a cap. 'Look,' she said, laughing softly through her fingers.

'Don't look,' said Mrs. Carson, very distinctly, as if to impress these two solemn words out of all she had ever spoken upon Lily's soft little rain. 'Just don't look at anything till you get to Ellisville.'

Outside, Aimee Slocum was crying and almost ran into the stranger. He wore a cap and was short and seemed to have on perfume.

'Could you tell me, lady,' he said, 'where a little lady lives in this burg name of Miss Lily Daw?' He lifted his cap; he had red hair.

'What do you want to know for?' asked Aimee.

'Talk louder,' said the stranger. He almost whispered, himself.

'She's gone away — she's gone to Ellisville!'

'Gone?'

'Gone to Ellisville!'

'Well, I like that!' breathed the man.

'What business did you have with the lady?' cried Aimee suddenly.

'We was only going to get married, that's all,' said the man. He laid the cap back on his hair and gave an agitated pat to the plaid-covered button.

Aimee Slocum started to scream in front of all those people. She almost pointed to the long black box she saw lying on the ground at the man's feet. Then she jumped back in fright. 'The xylophone! The xylophone!' she cried, looking back and forth from the man to the hissing train. The bell began to ring hollowly and the man was talking.

'Did you say Ellisville — that in the state of Mississippi?' He

was writing in a red notebook entitled *Permanent Facts & Data*.
'I don't hear well.'

Aimee nodded her head up and down.

Under 'Ellis-Ville Miss' he was drawing a line; now he was flicking it with two little marks. 'Maybe she didn't say she would. Maybe she said she wouldn't.' He suddenly laughed very loudly, after the way he had whispered. Aimee cringed. 'Women! — Well, if we play anywheres near Ellisville, Miss., in the future, I may look her up, and I may not,' he said.

The bass horn sounded the true signal for the band to begin.

'Wait!' Aimee Slocum did scream. 'Wait, Mister! I can get her for you!'

Then there she was back on the train screaming in Mrs. Carson's and Mrs. Watts's faces. 'The xylophone player! He meant it! He wants to marry her! There he is!'

'Nonsense,' murmured Mrs. Watts, peering over the others to look where Aimee pointed. 'If he's there I don't see him. Where is he? You're looking at One-Eye Beasley.'

'That little man with the cap — no, with the red hair! Hurry — the train ——'

'Is that really him?' Mrs. Carson asked Mrs. Watts in wonder. 'Mercy! He's small, isn't he?'

'Never saw him before in my life,' cried Mrs. Watts.

'Come on!' cried Aimee Slocum. Her nerves were all unstrung.

'All right. Hold your horses, girl,' said Mrs. Watts. 'Come on,' she cried thickly to Mrs. Carson.

'Where are we going now?' asked Lily as they struggled down the aisle.

'We're taking you to get married,' said Mrs. Watts. 'Mrs. Carson, you'd better call up your husband from the station.'

'But I don't want to git married,' said Lily, beginning to whimper. 'I'm going to Ellisville.'

'Hush, and we'll all have some ice cream cones later,' whispered Mrs. Carson.

Just as they appeared on the steps of the train the band went into the 'Independence March.'

The xylophone player was still there. He came up and said, 'Hello, Toots. What's up — tricks?' and kissed Lily with a smack, after which she hung her head.

'So you're the young man we've heard so much about,' said Mrs. Watts. Her smile was brilliant. 'Here's your little Lily.'

'What say?' asked the xylophone player.

'My husband happens to be the Baptist preacher of Victory,' said Mrs. Carson, in a louder voice. 'Isn't that lucky? I can get him here in five minutes.'

They were in a circle around the xylophone player, all going into the white waiting-room.

'Oh, I feel just like crying, at a time like this,' said Aimee Slocum. She looked back and saw the train moving slowly away, going under the bridge at Main Street. Then it disappeared around the curve.

'And whom have we the pleasure of addressing?' Mrs. Watts was shouting.

The band went on playing. Some of the people thought Lily was on the train, and some swore she wasn't. Everybody cheered, though, and a straw hat was thrown into the telephone wires.

OFF THE HIGHWAY [1]

By IRA WOLFERT

(From *Esquire*)

WHAT he heard first was the tap of the bullet against the rock. Then the crack of the rifle came to him, something bright, sharp, a noise that leaped into the air. Then the soft, endless silence of a drowsy morning in June. And as he lay pressed flat with fear, he could hear the suck and gurgle of his own blood and hear his heart beat like a fist through his chest against the earth.

He had been looking exactly where the bullet struck — a little scuffed-up pile of dust and gravel, yellow, gray, brown, all white now in the bright sun and the pile suddenly had been snatched from under his eyes, vanishing abruptly with a scuttling sound. The dust had risen into the air in a bodiless mound, as if stretching; had hung motionless for a moment in the windless air and then had muttered down, looking like a cloud stooping under a puff of wind.

'My God,' he thought. 'Oh my holy Jesus God,' and lowered his face into the dust of the earth.

The sput of dust had bellied due north, and he knew the man who was shooting at him was firing from the south. He couldn't see him. He lay in a scoop of earth behind a huge, flat slab of rock whose tip, protruding from the earth, formed a natural parapet, and he was afraid to look over it, afraid he would draw more of this crazy, remorseless fire. How he had gotten there he did not know, except hastily, in bounding, scrambling terror. He had been there ten minutes.

A half-hour before his car had run out of gasoline on a dirt road crossing scrub country — dead trees standing naked in stone-littered fields, no houses, the horizon scraggly with stunted woods, weeds growing seedily among the stones, thistles, burrs, the rusted carcass of a car, its front wheels off, its motor squatting on the earth. He had waited a long time, peering down and up the road, listening for the sound of an oncoming car or wagon or person, hear-

ing nothing except the rustle of the world living out of sight. He
spread paper before sitting on the running board, hiking up his pants
carefully, careful of the crease. He was a salesman and had to look
neat for his customers.

Then he tired of reading the small items in the newspaper and
started to worry about finishing up his route, about Harry Barton
up in Titusville closing up his store for lunch before he could take
his order and about having to wait around in Titusville for Harry
to come back and fill in his stock of canned goods and packaged
cakes and bacon and the wait making him late for the rest of the
route so that he would have to come back over it again the next day
and waste half a day just getting to three or four stores. So he put
away his paper, folding it neatly and stowing it on the shelf in the
back of his two-seated business coupé to save the comics for his
children. My holy cats, he thought, if it was up to them kids they'd
run up a newspaper bill that would keep me broke just to get the
funnies. Was it three or four or five miles back that he had seen
the gasoline pump standing out in front of a general store at a
crossroads? He couldn't remember. He came over this way so
seldom. He thought maybe he would pass a house before then and
borrow a quart or a gallon of gasoline and pay for — pay extra for it,
too. Time is money, he told himself.

So he started walking down the road, a thin, youngish man with
pouched eyes, his brown eyes soft and tired over the sagging pouches
and his chin drooping under his mouth, his nose soft and pudgy
down his small, weak, pale face. A thin, youngish man with a faintly
fussy manner, something old-maidish about the prim, firm way he
held his arms, not tall enough to be tall, not short enough to be
short, walking down a rutted country road through rocky, scrub
country, twelve and four-tenths miles from the town of Emmitsville,
Pa., population 8001, the one being the owner of the mill when he
came down from the New York office, on a day in June of 1936
when the Spanish war was still a plot and Mrs. Simpson a rumor
behind the backs of certain manicured hands. A thin, youngish man
dressed in square-cut, sober, unobtrusive, cheap store clothes, no
stain on the vest, no wrinkle in the collar, picking his feet up high
and setting them down gently to avoid raising dust. Once he
started, he walked rapidly with the quick, short steps of the man
accustomed to the crowds on city sidewalks.

Then he heard a shot and he stopped at once, curious, eyes alert, neck stiff, a human animal cocked to hear. And then he heard another shot, the bullet smacking flat against a dead tree trunk not five feet from him. 'Hey!' he yelled, feeling foolish because he couldn't see at whom he was yelling. His voice came mangled through his throat. There was another shot, stinging low over his head, splashing loose a flutter of twigs. He wasn't ashamed to yell after that. 'Hey!' he yelled. 'What the hell do you think you're doing?' Then there came two shots in quick succession. One of them sputtered along the dirt before his feet and the second bullet brushed him with a cone of air.

He started running then down the road and the bullets kept coming after him, two, three, four of them, and he cut off the road and went bounding blindly over swollen, hard tufts of earth and rock, gravel dusting up from his heels, and flung himself behind the ridge of stone into the scoop of earth.

There he lay, his breath whistling, his thoughts panicked. What was happening? God Almighty, what in The Hell was happening? Who was shooting at him? Why should anybody shoot at him? What kind of a lousy Goddamn fool kind of a Goddamn joke was this anyway? 'Hey!' he yelled. 'Hey, you Goddamn fool,' and stopped and heard his voice sink into silence. He waited a minute in the drowsy, warm, white sunlight and yelled, 'Hey,' again and then raised his head over the parapet. For a moment he could see nothing. Then far off he saw a man in blue overalls and trench helmet wriggling along the ground toward him, inching along a rifle as he wriggled.

Warily the salesman stood up and said, 'Hey, mister! Hey, mister!' and waited and added querulously, 'What the hell you think you're shooting at?' The man stopped wriggling and lifted his head. He poised that way a moment. Then he brought the rifle to his shoulder and the salesman flung himself back into his scoop of earth.

That way he lay for a short while, fear curdling him. Then, desperately, he called again, 'What do you want, for Christ sake, tell me what you want?' and waited a moment, but no answer came from anywhere. 'I'll give you what you want,' he cried again, his voice trembling. 'For Christ sake, tell me what you want. I've got a family,' and waited again. His neck quivered with the effort of supporting his head and he dropped his heavy, teeming head, letting his starched collar cut into his chin. His eyes had grown large with pain and when he lifted his head again, his chin shook and his mouth sagged open. The skin of his face, too, seemed to be shaking, so wildly did the blood run through it, almost as if it were tumbling.

But no sound came in reply. He heard only the sounds of the world as they had melted together in the air, and the sound of himself living, breath bursting from between his hanging lips, the booming of his heart in his chest and the knocking of the blood against his temples. And he began suddenly to fill with rage, literally to fill to bursting, his ears ringing and hot, his blood draining from his fingertips and bounding up his body to his head, his throat swelling into a red, corded pillar.

Holding me here like I was an animal, he thought. Something crazy, he thought, like I was in a war. All right, you fight a war for democracy or something like that, but you don't get fooled into walking into it. When you walk into a war, you know why, you know the Germans are going to run over the country and cut off babies' arms, but this here had no sense to it. If he was killed here now, what would be the point?

'This isn't my fight,' he thought. 'I've got my work to do. I've got my responsibilities and my life to live. I'm a family man. I've got kids and a woman looking to me for food.'

And here it was, something outside his life, something that had not the remotest connection with him, except that it was happening, to him. A mad, horrible thing, created by a force of which he had no knowledge and over which he had no control, had taken complete charge of the structure of his existence, had brought the entire routine of his life to a halt and had commanded him, on penalty of death, to lie quaking against the earth like an animal, his blood pounding hot, his skin drenched with sweat, his stomach knotted in a cramp and on the edge of retching, the nape of his neck prickling with fear.

'A guy walks down a country road,' he thought, 'and it's like walking into somewhere in Goddamn France.'

'What do you want of me?' he whimpered suddenly, his rage gone. 'I'll give you anything. I'm a family man.' He stopped and waited for an answer and when none came shrieked with all the force within him, 'I'm a family man!'

Abruptly his assailant replied, the voice sounding shockingly close: 'You're in the army now.'

And the salesman thought he had never heard such a strange, dead voice, barren, mechanical.

'You're not behind a plow,' the voice went on methodically, the words evenly toned and spaced as on a printed page.

'You son of a bitch,' it said emotionlessly.

'You'll never get rich.'

'You're in the army now.' And there it stopped, like a squad ordered to halt. There had been no form to the words, as if the throat that uttered them were full of gears grinding and now the gears had stopped grinding.

The salesman listened stunned. A nut, the man was a nut. Oh Jesus God, a looney trying to kill him. He must get away. He must escape. But the country was so thin. There were twenty feet of humpy ground to cover between the ridge behind which he lay and the first cluster of stringy trees and yards more of openness between that and the next cluster and then a roll of ground to the horizon. No good, no more good than running down the road.

But he must do something. He thought of shouting for help. Surely in this country, in this complex and civilized state, where every rock and twig and blade of grass was owned by someone, where every bug must be a trespasser crawling over titled, deeded, warranted property, there would be someone to hear him.

Sounds carried far through the warm quiet, he thought, and when he stopped and concentrated he could disassociate from the air around him a blurred roar that could only be motor traffic, cars, busses, trucks bowling along swiftly, serenely, sure in the wonderfully blessed routine of their progress.

'How many hundreds of people,' he thought, 'must have heard the nut shooting at me. Why don't they come? Does a guy get shot at every day in this dump of a hole in the ground?' But he knew, as he argued with himself, why they didn't come. He himself, stretched in a hammock in the country, had heard shooting many times and had never stirred because it was always some farmer hunting crows or buzzards. And he knew, as he argued with himself, why he didn't yell for help, why he couldn't. The cry would only force the maniac's hand and the help couldn't possibly come in time. If he only had some weapon, some ruse, some something to stave off attack if only for a few moments until help could come, but he had nothing and no way and he must lie and hope and wait.

'Look,' he called suddenly, his voice heavy with pleading, 'I just want to go away, that's all. I just want to go away. Honest to God, believe me, believe me.' He trembled in his earnestness and he found his voice getting erratic and he stopped and tried to pull himself together. After a moment, he began again. 'I won't do nothing,' he said. 'I just want to go away. I won't say a word. I won't tell anyone. Why should I tell? I promise. I promise on the grave of my mother.'

He stopped and listened and waited, cocking his head, screwing up his face unconsciously in an agonized effort to hear some response, but there was none and he began to talk again. 'I just need some gasoline,' he said. 'I'll come right back. It won't take me five minutes and I'll be back. You can walk along with me to make sure. Honest to God, I swear it, I swear it, I swear it, I'll be right back.'

He stopped again and listened again, with the same helpless cock of his head, wrinkling his gray sweated forehead, pinching up his eyelids. He waited a long time and then the mechanical voice answered, 'You're in the army now.'

The salesman's face unfolded slowly, his mouth sagging down, his eyes drooping wide, only the wrinkles remaining fixed in his brow, looking like gashes in the fat, flat layer of sweat. He lay a long time staring straight ahead of him, thinking nothing, feeling only the hopelessness that engulfed him. Then, in a sudden spurt of fear, he began once more, his voice so thin and desperate it sounded strange in his ears.

'Have you got a cigarette?' he said. He tried to get some chattiness into his voice and couldn't and kept trying. 'I'm dying for a smoke. Let me come over for a cigarette and then I'll come right back here and we can start again, start playing again just where we left off,' thinking that if he could only get close he might have a chance to jump him or at least if he could see this lunatic, if he could talk eye to eye with him, he might change him back into the docile fuzzy-wit he must be ordinarily to be let loose like this.

'Against regulations to fraternize with enemy troops,' said the barren, mechanical voice and methodically sent over the shot that had scuffed the gravel and had set dust to nestling up the salesman's nose.

So the waiting took over again, the salesman flat in his scoop of earth, smelling the earth as he had smelt it before only on picnics or one day in August so many years before on his honeymoon when he had lain with his wife in the grass, feeling herself close beside him, fleshless and haunting, as if she were music, and thinking over and over again, 'By God, I'm married. By God, I'm married now. I'm a married man. I'm married,' the words having meaning as they had never had before and had had only rarely since.

He thought of that now and thought, without emotion, if he were killed, would she too be destroyed, as once she would have been, something going dead forever inside of her, or would she be glad secretly of the chance to take up a new life?

But how, he wondered, could he think like this, tranquilly, when all his heart revolted at the thought of smashing his family, setting them adrift in the stream of living — a widow who had never worked, two children not old enough to work, $2800 insurance, $750 down payment on a house for which there was no market, $329 in the bank, $175 owed on a car.

He must do something. God Almighty, he must do something. He crawled to a depression in the stone ridge before him and over it he saw the madman, or the tip of him protruding from the side of a huge boulder across the road, gun at the ready, eyes squinting keenly down its barrel as he waited for more target to show. The salesman shuddered back hastily out of sight. What in the name of all the hell on earth was the man waiting for? Why didn't he just walk ten feet down the road and shoot him dead from the side? He must know his opponent wasn't armed.

The minutes dragged on, each one silent as a tick that has ended, until finally, from across twelve and four-tenths miles of country air came winding faintly the noon hoot of Emmitsville's factory whistle. The voice of civilization speaking in his ear and the salesman realized with new anxiety that the end of this lunatic catastrophe was nearing. People were starting home for lunch, field-hands, hunters, fishermen, school-children, shopkeepers, and who-ever passed would pass not ten feet from where he lay.

What should he do? Should he call out? He couldn't, but he must. It was impossible to stay where he was. I can't stand any

more. I just can't stand any more, he thought, and sooner or later
the madman would lose interest in whatever game he was playing
and come over and finish it. He'd yell and run. That was the answer. Yell and run like hell, dodging and weaving and hoping that
the maniac would lose lifegiving seconds making up his mind at
whom to shoot. Let the one who came along take care of himself.
Say, a man can stand only so much. If it were a car that came, all
the better. He'd try to get it to stop and keep it between him and
the gun.

But it wasn't a car. Footsteps, far off, a light, easy patter of
them, crunching the ruts softly around a distant curve. Then he
saw two boys, brothers they seemed, slouching along both sides
of the road, their mouths sucking their tongues, their long red faces
bored, the dust kicking up from their swiftly moving, careless feet.
He thought, sickly, they would pass so close he could smell them.

If it had been anybody, anything else! But how could he drag
them into this? Schoolboys hearing his cry to LOOKOUTDUCK!
standing openmouthed, dumbfounded, rooted with surprise. Both
would be killed and he'd be to blame. How possibly could he do
it? And the thought struck through his brain that they might see
him lying there, might become terrified, might run of their own
volition and then he would not be to blame. Then he too could
run, dodging and weaving, to the first cover.

He could see them easily now. But they could not see him unless
they looked directly at him and they weren't looking at anything,
just down the road at the world with the shining, blind eyes of
children in a hurry. The salesman held himself tense, every muscle
bunched to quivering, his breath strangling into snorts, as they
came scuffling along patiently, saying no words, their little boy feet
chunky in black ribbed stockings, the flesh plumping above their
high shoes. They looked to be eight and ten years old, maybe
eleven, and the eight-year-old had a face like a man, only smooth.
Long and shrewd-looking, the nose sharp, the lips thin, the chin
square. His brother's face was rounder and duller. Under thin
blond hair it had a look of kind emptiness.

He was shot first. He was shot in the heart and died instantly,
his face stretched into prodigious astonishment by a wide-open
mouth. Dead, he stood stock still for a moment, trapped by death
as by a camera, and then melted slowly down to earth. The

younger boy was shot in the neck, the bullet riding up to blunt against his collarbone and mushroom through his throat. It was as if he had been kicked. He bounded up and backward, his little feet flinging wildly up to the level of his chin, and he landed with a scraping jar and sat upright and startled in the road, his mouth working like that of a fish out of water. Half his neck had been shot away by the spreading bullet, but by some miracle of cruelty no nerves had been severed. And he sat there, almost motionless, shocked into paralysis, bleeding to death, his fuzzy ball of a head wobbling slowly on half a neck. Once he tried to speak, and he squeaked, 'Ma,' and then he couldn't hold himself up any more and began to sway back and forth sluggishly and finally he went all the way over backwards and hit his head with a thump against the road and was still.

The salesman's face had become like a mask, so stricken it was, so frozen, so unreal, as if his flesh were cardboard and his features lumps and creases in it. He was sick. Inside he had dissolved and a stink rose up from him, filling his mouth, drenching his nostrils. 'Oh,' he said, pushing the word up through his constricted throat. 'Oh, oh, oh, oh, oh!' and he was not conscious at all of the sudden roar of silence that came pouring over the ridge to him and did not hear the madman say abruptly:

'I call on you to negotiate under a flag of truce for full surrender.'

He didn't answer. No words could come to him through the clattering in his ears. I'm so tired, he thought, I'm a sick man, and he lay flat, his wet face resting on the warm, dry stone and let his body bang and shake and flop as if he himself were not there.

'Why should you waste any more of your men?' came the voice from across the road. And suddenly the voice boomed large as the world, filling it with its flat, mechanical tone. 'Two minutes to surrender,' it said, 'then I shall order an advance.'

The salesman heard. He tried to say 'yes.' For a moment he could not utter a sound. Then he said in hardly more than a whimper, 'Yes, yes, yes, yes.'

'I give up,' he roared suddenly at the top of his voice. 'I surrender, I surrender,' the words teetering crazily on the edge of each other as they shrilled from his mouth.

'Stand up,' replied the madman. 'Throw away your guns.

Every one of you. Throw them in front of you. Hold your hands up. Come out hands first.'

The salesman's body felt light and empty, but it was hard to stand up. His muscles lay nerveless, flat against his bones and his bones hurt as if they had been trampled. All the life was out of him and he had to drag himself erect ponderously and he stood lurching and lunging on trembling knees. He clung to the ridge of stone to stay himself from falling. 'Hold your hands up high,' said the madman, and the salesman slowly raised his gray hands high above his head. He looked grotesque, dust and burrs and wisps and bits of gravel thick up the front of him clear past his chin, a man smashed into dead-eyed emptiness.

The madman lifted himself cautiously from behind the boulder, gun at the ready, and walked warily, step by slow step to the middle of the road and halted. A small, dumpy, middle-aged man, his blue eyes dancing wildly in his slack, quiet, red face. A pathetic creature caught up in a frenzy of alertness. Once he had been a farmer and now he was a lunatic, and the tin khaki helmet bulging over his bald skull made him look sad and frightened. 'Jenkins, Williams, Johnson, and you, you Hall there, fall out, take these prisoners to the depot and bring the receipt back to me right away,' he called loudly, his darting eyes never leaving the salesman. Then suddenly he turned around and whispered loudly: 'They put up a good fight. Remember these no-good killing bastards put up a good fight and held up our advance.'

His back was turned and the salesman thought, now was the time to jump him. But he couldn't do it. He wanted to lie down and let his body go banging and shaking and flopping on by itself, just let everything go.

'They're heroes in their own army,' the lunatic was whispering hoarsely, 'and I don't want them killed. You hear you, you there, Hall, they're not to be killed. If that receipt doesn't read for all prisoners, you'll answer to me. I'll have you court-martialed for murder. They're heroes all right.'

He turned back. 'All right, let's go,' he said and stepped warily around the salesman, not looking at him, looking straight ahead, his eyes racing in his head, his gun cocked, looking funny, looking crazy in his faded blue overalls and stained, scuffed workshoes and sweat-blackened galluses and tin helmet, the smell of the barn thick and sweet on him and the acrid smell of the chicken coop stinging out from him.

He clambered warily over the ridge and, crouching almost double, worked his way across the field and crawled under a barbed-wire fence and out of sight down a roll of ground.

THE YEARBOOK OF THE AMERICAN SHORT STORY

STORY

JANUARY 1 TO DECEMBER 31, 1937

ABBREVIATIONS

I. Periodicals

A.L.	American Literature.
A.Merc.	American Mercury.
A.Y.B.	American Yellow Book.
Af.	Afro-American.
Am.	American Magazine.
Am.P.	American Prefaces.
Asia	Asia.
Atl.	Atlantic Monthly.
Bea.	Beacon.
Books	Books (New York Herald-Tribune).
Bull.N.Y.P.L.	Bulletin of the New York Public Library.
C.For.	Canadian Forum.
C.S.M.	Christian Science Monitor.
Cat.	Catamount.
Cath.W.	Catholic World.
Chal.	Challenge.
Chame.	Chameleon.
Champ.	Champion of Youth.
Coa.	Coast.
Col.	Collier's Weekly.
Colo.	Colophon.
Colum.	Columbia.
Com.	Commonweal.
Con.	Contemporary.
Cor.	Coronet.
Corn.	Cornhill Magazine.
Cos.	Cosmopolitan.
Esq.	Esquire.
Fan.	Fantasy.
Fight	Fight.
For.	Forum.
Frontier	Frontier and Midland.
Fur.B.	Furman Bulletin.
G.H.(N.Y.)	Good Housekeeping (New York).
Glo	Globe.
Hai.	Hairenik.
Hard.	Hardboiled.
Harp.B.	Harper's Bazaar (New York).
Harp.M.	Harper's Magazine.
Hin.	Hinterland.
Hor.	Horizon.
House	Household Magazine.
Husk	Husk.
I.L.	International Literature.
I.R.	Intermountain Review.
J.o'L.	John o'London's Weekly.
L.H.J.	Ladies' Home Journal.
L.L.	Life and Letters To-day.
L.Merc.	London Mercury.
Lam.	Lamplighter.

II. Books

Benét...............Benét. Devil and Daniel Webster.
Benét B.............Benét. Thirteen o'Clock.
Benson E............Benson. Portrait of an English Nobleman.
Benson F............Benson. Janet.
Benson G............Benson. Friend of the Rich.
Benson H............Benson. The Unwanted.
Bensusan B..........Bensusan. Marshland Echoes. (English edition.)
Blair...............Blair, *editor.* Native American Humor (1800-1900).
Brewster B..........Brewster, *editor.* A Book of Contemporary Short Stories.
Brownlee...........Brownlee. Corporal Wanzi. (English edition.)
Calder-Marshall.....Calder-Marshall. A Date with a Duchess. (English edition.)
Canfield E..........Canfield. Fables for Parents.
Chekhov T...........Chekhov. Plays and Stories.
Chesterton K........Chesterton. The Paradoxes of Mr. Pond. (English edition.)
Clarke D............Clarke, *editor.* Cats and Cats.
Coppard Q...........Coppard. Ninepenny Flute. (English edition.)
Corcoran...........Corcoran. This Man Joe Murray.
Deland.............Deland. Old Chester Days.
Dobie B.............Dobie. San Francisco Adventures.
Duranty B...........Duranty. Babies without Tails.
Edmondson..........Edmondson. Old Amos. (English edition.)
Faber..............Bowen, *editor.* The Faber Book of Modern Stories. (English edition.)
Farrell B...........Farrell. Can All This Grandeur Perish?
Field..............Field. The Cock's Funeral.
Fitzpatrick........Fitzpatrick. They Lived in County Down. (English edition.)
Gibbons............Gibbons. Roaring Tower. (English edition.)
Goodwin............Goodwin. The White Farm. (English edition.)
Goudge.............Goudge. A Pedlar's Pack. (English edition.)
Greenwood..........Greenwood. The Cleft Stick. (English edition.)
Gregory C...........Gregory, *editor.* New Letters in America, I.
Hanley F............Hanley. Half an Eye. (English edition.)
Hansen E............Hansen, *editor.* O. Henry Memorial Award Prize Stories of 1937.
Hill...............Hill. Loving Memory.
Holme..............Holme. The Wisdom of the Simple.
Holtby B............Holtby. Pavements at Anderby. (English edition.)
Hurst H.............Hurst. We Are Ten.
Isherwood..........Isherwood. Sally Bowles. (English edition.)
Jarrett............Jarrett. I Asked No Other Thing.
Johnston B..........Johnston. Laleen. (English edition.)
Jones B.............Jones. The Blue Bed. (English edition.)
Joseph B............Joseph, *editor.* 'The Editor Regrets...' (English edition.)
Kafka B.............Kafka. The Metamorphosis. (English edition.)
Kantor C............Kantor. The Romance of Rosy Ridge.
Lagerlöf D..........Lagerlöf. Christ Legends. (English edition.)
Laing..............Laing, *editor.* The Haunted Omnibus.
Lehmann C..........Lehmann, *editor.* New Writing. III. (English edition.)
Lehmann D..........Lehmann, *editor.* New Writing. IV. (English edition.)
Lobell.............Lobell. The Fire Door.
Low................Low. No Green Pastures. (English edition.)
Lucas..............Lucas. The Woman Clothed with the Sun. (English edition.)
Lyons F.............Lyons. Tom, Dick and Harriet. (English edition.)
Maginn B...........Maginn. Ten Tales. (English edition.)
Mansfield J.........Mansfield. Short Stories.
Maugham H.........Maugham. My South Sea Island.
Meynell............Meynell. Kissing the Rod. (English edition.)
Miller D............Miller. Ana the Runner. (English edition.)
Nature.............Century of Nature Stories. (English edition.)
Nogales............Nogales. Heroes and Beasts of Spain.
O'Brien SS..........O'Brien, *editor.* Elizabethan Tales.
O'Brien TT..........O'Brien, **editor.** The Best Short Stories: **1937.**

ADDRESSES OF MAGAZINES PUBLISHING SHORT STORIES

I. AMERICAN AND CANADIAN MAGAZINES

American Magazine, 250 Park Avenue, New York City.
American Mercury, 570 Lexington Avenue, New York City.
American Prefaces, University Hall, Iowa City, Iowa.
American-Scandinavian Review, 116 East 64th Street, New York City.
Asia, 40 East 49th Street, New York City.
Atlantic Monthly, 8 Arlington Street, Boston, Mass.
Canadian Forum, 28 Wellington Street West, Toronto, Ont., Canada.
Canadian Home Journal, Richmond and Sheppard Streets, Toronto 2, Ont., Canada.
Canadian Magazine, 345 Adelaide Street West, Toronto, Ont., Canada
Catamount, P.O. Box 183, Montpelier, Vt.
Catholic World, 401 West 59th Street, New York City.
Chatelaine, 143 University Avenue, Toronto, Ont., Canada.
Chicago Tribune (Syndicate Service), 220 East 42nd Street, New York City.
Coast, 130 Bush Street, San Francisco, California.
Collier's Weekly, 250 Park Avenue, New York City.
Columbia, New Haven, Conn.
Commonweal, 386 Fourth Avenue, New York City.
Coronet, 919 North Michigan Avenue, Chicago, Ill.
Cosmopolitan, 57th Street and Eighth Avenue, New York City.
Country Gentleman, Independence Square, Philadelphia, Pa.
Elks Magazine, 50 East 42nd Street, New York City.
Esquire, 919 North Michigan Avenue, Chicago, Ill.
Fantasy, 950 Heberton Avenue, Pittsburgh, Pa.
Fight, Room 701, 268 Fourth Avenue, New York City.
Forum, 441 Lexington Avenue, New York City.
Frontier and Midland, University of Montana, Missoula, Mont.
Globe, 157½ West 5th Street, St. Paul, Minn.
Good Housekeeping, 57th Street and Eighth Avenue, New York City.
Hairenik, 13 Shawmut Street, Boston, Mass.
Harper's Bazaar, 572 Madison Avenue, New York City.
Harper's Magazine, 49 East 33rd Street, New York City.
Hinterland, 624 Third Avenue, S.E., Des Moines, Iowa.
Holland's Magazine, Dallas, Texas.
Household Magazine, Topeka, Kansas.
Husk, Cornell College, Mount Vernon, Iowa.
Intermountain Review, Box 907, Cedar City, Utah.
Kansas Magazine, Kansas State College, Kansas.
Ladies' Home Journal, Independence Square, Philadelphia, Pa.
Liberty, 1926 Broadway, New York City.
McCall's Magazine, 230 Park Avenue, New York City.
Maclean's Magazine, 481 University Avenue, Toronto, Ont., Canada.
Mademoiselle, 79–89 Seventh Avenue, New York City.
Menorah Journal, 63 Fifth Avenue, New York City.
National Home Monthly, Bannatyne and Dagmar, Winnipeg, Manitoba, Canada.
New Challenge, 43 West 66th Street, New York City.
New Masses, 31 East 27th Street, New York City.
New Mexico Quarterly, University of New Mexico, Albuquerque, N.M.
New Republic, 40 East 49th Street, New York City.
New Yorker, 25 West 43rd Street, New York City.

North American Review, 587 Fifth Avenue, New York City.
Opportunity, 1133 Broadway, New York City.
Partisan Review, 22 East 17th Street, New York City.
Pictorial Review, 57th Street and Eighth Avenue, New York City.
Prairie Schooner, Box 1232, Station 'A,' Lincoln, Nebraska.
Queen's Quarterly, Queen's University, Kingston, Ont., Canada.
Redbook Magazine, 230 Park Avenue, New York City.
Saturday Evening Post, Independence Square, Philadelphia, Pa.
Scribner's Magazine, 597 Fifth Avenue, New York City.
Short Stories, Doubleday, Doran & Co., Garden City, L.I., N.Y.
Signatures, c/o John H. Thompson, 58 West Adams Avenue, Detroit, Mich.
Southern Review, Louisiana State University, Baton Rouge, La.
Southwest Review, Dallas, Texas.
Story, 432 Fourth Avenue, New York City.
Tanager, P.O. Box 66, Grinnell, Iowa.
This Week, 420 Lexington Avenue, New York City.
Toronto Star Weekly, Toronto, Ont., Canada.
University Review, University of Kansas City, Kansas City, Mo.
Virginia Quarterly Review, 8 West Lawn, University, Va.
Westways, 2601 South Figueroa Street, Los Angeles, Cal.
Woman's Home Companion, 250 Park Avenue, New York City.
Woman's World, 461 Eighth Avenue, New York City.
Yale Review, 125 High Street, New Haven, Conn.
Yankee, Dublin, N.H.

II. British, Irish, and Colonial Magazines

Adelphi, The Adelphi Centre, Langham, near Colchester.
Argosy, Tallis House, Tallis Street, London, E.C. 4.
Blackwood's Magazine, 45 George Street, Edinburgh, Scotland.
Blue Peter, 12 St. Mary Axe, London, E.C. 3.
Britannia and Eve, 346 Strand, London, W.C. 2.
Bulletin, 214 George Street North, Sydney, N.S.W., Australia.
Bystander, 346 Strand, London, W.C. 2.
Chamber's Journal, 11 Thistle Street, Edinburgh, Scotland.
Cornhill Magazine, 50 Albemarle Street, London, W. 1.
Criterion, 24 Russell Square, London, W.C. 1.
Daily Express, Fleet Street, London, E.C. 4.
Daily Herald, 12 Wilson Street, Long Acre, London, W.C. 2.
Daily Mail, Northcliffe House, London, E.C. 4.
Dublin Magazine, 2 Crow Street, Dublin, Irish Free State.
Evening Standard, 46 Shoe Lane, London, E.C. 4.
Fortnightly Review, 8 More's Passage, 51 Carey Street, London, W.C. 2.
G.K.'s Weekly, 2 Little Essex Street, Strand, London, W.C. 2.
Good Housekeeping, 28–30 Grosvenor Gardens, London, S.W. 1.
Grand Magazine, 8–11 Southampton Street, Strand, London, W.C. 2.
Happy Magazine, 8–11 Southampton Street, Strand, London, W.C. 2.
Harper's Bazaar, 9 Stratton Street, Piccadilly, London, W. 1.
Illustrated London News, 346 Strand, London, W.C. 2.
John o'London's Weekly, 8–11 Southampton Street, Strand, London, W.C. 2.
Lady, 39 Bedford Street, Strand, London, W.C. 2.
Left Review, 2 Parton Street, Red Lion Square, London, W.C. 1.
Life and Letters To-day, 26 Maiden Lane London, W.C. 2.
Lilliput, Lincoln's Inn Chambers, 40–43 Chancery Lane, London, W.C. 2.
Listener, Broadcasting House, Portland Place, London, W. 1.
London Mercury, 10 Great Turnstile, London, W.C. 1.
Manchester Guardian, 3 Cross Street, Manchester.
New English Weekly, 7 and 8 Rolls Passage, Chancery Lane, London, E.C. 4.
New Statesman and Nation, 10 Great Turnstile, London, W.C. 1.
News-Chronicle, 19–22 Bouverie Street, London, E.C. 4.

Novel Magazine, 18 Henrietta Street, Covent Garden, London, W.C. **2**.
Outspan, P.O. Box 245, Bloemfontein, Orange Free State, S. Africa.
Pearson's Magazine, 18 Henrietta Street, Covent Garden, London, W.C. **2**.
Queen, Hatfield House, Stanford Street, London, S.E. 1.
Quiver, Fleetway House, Farringdon Street, London, E.C. 4.
Red Magazine, Tallis House, Tallis Street, London, E.C. 4.
Sketch, 346 Strand, London, W.C. 2.
Spectator, 99 Gower Street, London, W.C. 1.
Sphere, 346 Strand, London, W.C. 2.
Story-Teller, Tallis House, Tallis Street, London, E.C. 4.
Strand Magazine, 8–11 Southampton Street, Strand, London, W.C. 2.
Sydney Mail, 38 Hunter Street, Sydney, N.S.W., Australia.
Tatler, 346 Strand, London, W.C. 2.
Time and Tide, 32 Bloomsbury Street, London, W.C. 1.
Truth, 10 Carteret Street, Queen Anne's Gate, London, S.W. 1.
20-Story Magazine, 93 Long Acre, London, W.C. 2.
Violet Magazine, Fleetway House, Farringdon Street, London, E.C. 4.
Windsor Magazine, Warwick House, Salisbury Square, London, E.C. 4.
Woman's Journal, Fleetway House, Farringdon Street, London, E.C. 4.
Woman's Magazine, 4 Bouverie Street, London, E.C. 4.

ROLL OF HONOR
1937

NOTE: This list excludes reprints

I. AMERICAN AND CANADIAN AUTHORS

ABBE, GEORGE.
    Two Deaths.
ANDERSON, SHERWOOD.
    Moonlight Walk.
ARMSTRONG, MATT.
    Iscariot.
ASCH, NATHAN.
    Heart's Desire.
AYRE, ROBERT.
    Mr. Sycamore.
BAUM, R. F.
    Pond.
BENEDICT, LIBBY.
    Blind Man's Buff.
    Day of Triumph.
BENÉT, STEPHEN VINCENT.
    Tooth for Paul Revere.
BERKENFELD, EMANUEL.
    Leave One Tree Standing.
BISHOP, ELIZABETH.
    Baptism.
BJORKMAN, EDWIN.
    Nemesis Medusa.
BOND, NELSON S.
    Mr. Mergenthwirker's Lobblies.
BOYLE, KAY.
    Herring Piece.
    King of the Philistines.
CALLAGHAN, MORLEY.
    Boy Grows Older.
    Cheat's Remorse.
    Evening in Madison Square.
    Homing Pigeon.
    Little Beaded Bag.
    Pair of Long Pants.
    Rendezvous with Self.
    This Man, My Father.
    Very Merry Christmas.
CHEEVER, JOHN.
    Brothers.
CHERKASSKI, VLADIMIR.
    What Hurts Is that I Was in a Hurry.
CONIGLIO, ANINA.
    Wedding.
COOK, WHITFIELD.
    Dear Mr. Flessheime.
    Portable Mrs. Tillson.

CREYKE, RICHARD PAULETT.
    Niggers Are Such Liars.
DONATO, PIETRO DI.
    Christ in Concrete.
DURANTY, WALTER.
    Explosion in Russia.
FAST, HOWARD MELVIN.
    Children.
FAULKNER, WILLIAM.
    Monk.
FESSIER, MICHAEL.
    Black Wind and Lightning.
FITZGERALD, F. SCOTT.
    Alcoholic Case.
FLANDRAU, GRACE.
    At the Farm.
GELLHORN, MARTHA.
    Exile.
GEROULD, CHRISTOPHER.
    Night Before.
GODCHAUX, ELMA.
    Horn that Called Bambine.
GORDON, CAROLINE.
    Brilliant Leaves.
    Women on the Battlefield.
HANNUM, ALBERTA PIERSON.
    Turkey Hunt.
HETH, EDWARD HARRIS.
    Something to Tell the Boys.
HOKE, TRAVIS.
    Nice Quiet Apartment.
KAPSTEIN, I. J.
    Song the Summer Evening Sings.
KOMROFF, MANUEL.
    Whole World Is Outside.
LARSEN, ERLING.
    Birds and Present Rain.
LE SUEUR, MERIDEL.
    Girl.
LUDLOW, DON.
    She Always Wanted Shoes.
LUMPKIN, GRACE.
    Dory.
MCCLEARY, DOROTHY.
    Little Bride.
MALTZ, ALBERT.
    Hotel Raleigh, The Bowery.

MARCH, WILLIAM.
  Last Meeting.
  Listening Post.
MATHESON, JAMES.
  But That Was in Another Country.
MOLL, ELICK.
  To Those Who Wait.
NEAGOE, PETER.
  Little Marie, the Goosegirl.
PEREDA, PRUDENCIO DE.
  Bullfighter.
  Spaniard.
PORTER, KATHERINE ANNE.
  Noon Wine.
  Old Mortality.
PROKOSCH, FREDERIC.
  Russian Idyll.
RAYNER, GEORGE THORP.
  Real American Fellow.
RICHMOND, ROALDUS.
  Big Brother.
ROBERTS, ELIZABETH MADOX.
  Haunted Palace.
ROSS, LEONARD Q.
  K*A*P*L*A*N and Pythias.
  Mr. K*A*P*L*A*N and Shakespeare.
  Mr. K*A*P*L*A*N Cuts a Gordian
    Knot.
  Mr. K*A*P*L*A*N's Dark Logic.
  Mr. K*A*P*L*A*N's So-and-So.
  Mr. K*A*P*L*A*N's White Banner.
  O K*A*P*L*A*N! My K*A*P*-
    L*A*N!
RYAN, STELLA.
  Manhole.
SALTZMAN, ELEANOR.
  Pastoral.
SAROYAN, WILLIAM.
  Locomotive 38.
  Trains.
  Vision.
SCHACK, WILLIAM.
  Old Man's Choice.
SCHORER, MARK.
  Boy in the Summer Sun.
  Not Devoid of Feeling.
  To Make Life Seem Full.
SEAGER, ALLAN.
  Pro Arte.

SMITTER, WESSEL HYATT.
  Hand.
STEGNER, WALLACE.
  Remembering Laughter.
STEINBECK, JOHN.
  Chrysanthemums.
STILL, JAMES.
  Brother to Methuselum.
STUART, JESSE.
  Blue Tick Pig.
  Fast-Train Ike.
  Goin' to th' Buttin'.
  Huey, the Engineer.
  Land Beyond the River.
  Little Giant.
  One of God's Oddlings.
  Pa.
  Sunday Afternoon Hanging.
  Uncle Fonse and the Starlings.
  War and Cousin Lum.
  Whip-Poor-Willie.
  Zeke Hammertight.
SULLIVAN, RICHARD.
  Paper Costume.
SWADOS, HARVEY B.
  Amateurs.
THIELEN, BENEDICT.
  Haunted House.
  This is My Own, My Native Land.
  Warrior's Return.
TREMAINE, PAUL.
  Tramp Love.
WARREN, ROBERT PENN.
  Christmas Gift.
WEIDMAN, JEROME.
  Everybody Wants to Be a Lady.
WELTY, EUDORA.
  Lily Daw and the Three Ladies.
WICKENDEN, DAN.
  Journey through Sunlight.
WILCOX, WENDELL.
  Nostalgia.
WOLFE, THOMAS.
  Lost Boy.
WOLFERT, IRA.
  Off the Highway.
WOOLRICH, CORNELL.
  Goodbye, New York.
ZUGSMITH, LEANE.
  Lie.

II. British and Irish Authors

Austin, F. Britten.
  Persian Idyll.
Bates, H. E.
  Cloudburst.
  Finger Wet, Finger Dry.
  Something Short and Sweet.
Bates, Ralph.
  Death of a Virgin.
Burke, John T.
  Linden Leaf.
Coppard, A. E.
  Were Deceivers Ever.
Davies, Rhys.
  Mourning for Ianto.

Hanley, James.
  World Laughs.
Knight, Eric.
  Bit of a Do.
  Flying Yorkshireman.
  Mary Ann and the Duke.
O'Connor, Frank.
  Story-teller.
O'Faoláin, Seán.
  Kitty the Wren.
  Old Master.
Strong, L. A. G.
  Mr. Dallas Has a Quiet Evening.
  Soldier's Song.

III. Translations

Chamson, André. (*French.*)
  Enemies.
  White Animal.
Frank, Bruno. (*German.*)
  Moon Watch.
Gergely, Sandor. (*Hungarian.*)
  Heroes.
Gorky, Maxim. (*Russian.*)
  Bawdy Face.

  Life in a Prison Cell.
  Song of the Blind.
Neumann, Robert. (*German.*)
  Blind of Kagoll.
Nexö, Martin Anderson. (*Danish.*)
  Overhead Has Swallowed Everything.
Zweig, Arnold. (*Austrian.*)
  Man Against Man.

BIOGRAPHICAL NOTICES

NOTE. These notices refer only to American authors whose work appears in the Roll of Honor in this series for the first time. Biographical notices of other authors included in this year's Roll of Honor may be found, with one or two exceptions, in earlier volumes of the series.

ABBE, GEORGE. Born in Somers, Connecticut, 1911. Educated at the University of New Hampshire and Union Theological Seminary. Married. Lives in Guilford, Connecticut.

ARMSTRONG, MATT. Born in Scotland, 1903. Came to Canada in 1910. During the past fifteen years has worked as a telephone trouble shooter, hydro-electric lineman, woollen spinner, and brush salesman in thirty-three Canadian towns. Has now settled down to write short stories and sell life insurance. Married. Lives in Dunnville, Ontario.

AYRE, ROBERT. Born of Irish parents in Manitoba, 1900. Lived in Winnipeg till he was twenty-seven except for a year in San Francisco and Hawaii. Became a railway man. Has moved about Canada for ten years. Associated with the Canadian National Railways. Lives in Montreal.

BAUM, RICHARD FITZGERALD. Born in Chicago, 1913. Educated at Harvard University. Lives in Lake Forest, Illinois.

BISHOP, ELIZABETH. Miss Bishop is a young American poet who lives in New York City.

BJORKMAN, EDWIN. Born in Stockholm, Sweden, 1866. Came to the United States in 1891. On New York newspapers for about fifteen years. Has published seven books including two novels. Now North Carolina State Director of the Federal Writers' Project. Lives near Asheville, North Carolina.

BOND, NELSON S. Is twenty-nine years old and married. Has been a civil engineer, an electrical engineer, a newspaper reporter, and a publicity man. Lives in Augusta, Georgia.

CONIGLIO, ANINA (MRS. HENRY BRANSON). Born in western New York, 1904. Educated at a small college in Michigan and at the University of Michigan. Married. Lives in Ann Arbor, Michigan.

COOK, WHITFIELD. Born in Bloomfield, New Jersey, 1909. Grew up in a whole series of towns in Wisconsin, Minnesota and Illinois. Educated at Yale University. For the past few years he has been stage managing and doing technical work for various New York theatrical producers. Lives in Hadlyme, Connecticut.

CREYKE, RICHARD PAULETT. Born in Farmville, Virginia, 1915. Has spent most of his life in Washington, D.C. Educated at George Washington University. Is business manager of the Roadside Theatre near Washington. Also broadcasts. Lives in Washington, D.C.

DONATO, PIETRO DI. Born in West Hoboken, New Jersey, 1911. Left grammar school at thirteen to support widowed mother and seven brothers and sisters. When his father was killed on the job, he picked up his tools and went to work on the scaffold as a bricklayer. Has been tied to the job ever since. Lives at Northport, Long Island, New York.

FAST, HOWARD M. Born in New York City, 1914. High School education. Wandered through the South for a while, worked in the Everglades, rode freights, studied art, worked at lumbering, shipping, clerking, plumbing, and carpentry. His first novel is forthcoming. Lives in New York City.

FENSTAD, TRONDBY. Born in Chicago, 1910. Raised on a farm in the Catskill Mountains with a year on the plains of Colorado, and educated at Crane College and Northwestern University. Published the *Midwestern Observer*. Lives in Chicago.

GELLHORN, MARTHA. Born in St. Louis, 1908. Author of 'What Mad Pursuit' and 'The Trouble I've Seen.' Has been in Spain. Lives in New York City.

GEROULD, CHRISTOPHER. Born in Princeton, New Jersey, 1911. Educated at Princeton University and in Switzerland. Has been a newspaper reporter and now writes advertising. Married. Lives in Berwyn, Pennsylvania.

HANNUM, ALBERTA PIERSON. Born near Condit, Ohio, 1906. Educated at Ohio State University and Columbia University. Author of 'Thursday April' and 'The Hills Step Lightly.' Married. Lives in Moundsville, West Virginia.

HARDMAN, F. A. He is twenty-seven and married, and has been a reporter, sailor, real estate salesman, taxidermist, and writer. Lives in San Antonio, Texas.

HOKE, TRAVIS. Has been a newspaper man, associated with book publishing, and editor of Popular Science Monthly. Has published several books, was for several years a columnist for the New Yorker, and in 1936–37 was State Director in New York City for the Federal Writers' Project. Lives in New York City.

KAPSTEIN, I. J. Born in 1904. Educated at Brown University. Married. Now Assistant Professor of English Literature at Brown University. Lives in Providence, Rhode Island.

LUMPKIN, GRACE. Born in Milledgeville, Georgia. Has spent most of her life in South Carolina. Studied writing at Columbia University. Has published two novels and had a play produced on Broadway. Lives in New York City.

MAXWELL, WILLIAM. Born in Lincoln, Illinois, 1908. Educated at the University of Illinois and at Harvard. Author of 'Bright Center of Heaven' and 'They Came Like Swallows.' Is on the editorial staff of the New Yorker. Lives in New York City.

MOLL, ELICK. Born in New York City, 1903. Grew up in Chicago. Educated at the University of Chicago. Married. Lives in New York City.

PEREDA, PRUDENCIO DE. Born in Brooklyn, New York, 1912. Educated at the College of the City of New York. Has been in Spain. Lives in New York City.

'ROSS, LEONARD Q.' (LEO C. ROSTEN.) Is twenty-nine years old. Educated at the University of Chicago and abroad. Has been a night school teacher, a reporter, a professional lecturer, and a member of the research staff of President Roosevelt's Committee on Administrative Management. Author of 'The Education of H*Y*M*A*N K*A*P*L*A*N' and 'The Washington Correspondents.' Lives in Beverly Hills, California.

SCHACK, WILLIAM. Born in New York City, 1898. Educated at Cornell University. Has studied chemistry, done research work in teaching, edited trade and technical journals, and is a dramatic and art critic. Has spent a year in the Near East and written extensively on Palestine affairs. Lives in New York City.

STEGNER, WALLACE. Born in Lake Mills, Iowa, 1909. Has lived in North Dakota, Washington, Saskatchewan, Montana, Utah, California and Wisconsin. Educated at the University of Utah, the State University of Iowa, and the University of California.

Has taught at several universities and colleges and is now in the English Department at the University of Wisconsin. Married. Author of 'Remembering Laughter.' Lives in Madison, Wisconsin.

STILL, JAMES. 'Born on Double Creek in the hills of Alabama. One of ten children. My father is a "horse doctor." As a child I spent many nights in moggy barn lots and frosty pastures. Attended a mountain college near Cumberland Gap, Tennessee. Paid my expenses by working two years in a rock quarry, and two in the school library. Later attended Vanderbilt University. Am librarian of Hindman Settlement School at the forks of Troublesome Creek in the Kentucky hills. Along with my work in the Settlement, I conduct a library-on-foot, carrying books in a pasteboard box on my shoulder to nineteen one-room schools. Collections are changed every two weeks. I'm called the "book boy" in the coves and hollows. I can play a few ballads on the dulcimer.' Author of 'Hounds on the Mountain.' Lives at Hindman, Kentucky.

SWADOS, HARVEY B. Born in Buffalo, New York, 1920. Is a student at the University of Michigan. Lives in Buffalo, New York.

TREMAINE, PAUL. Has led a wandering life full of incident and adventure. Married. Lives in Topinabee, Michigan.

WARREN, ROBERT PENN. Born in Todd County, Kentucky, 1905. Educated at Vanderbilt University, University of California, Yale University and Oxford. Has published a volume of poems and a life of John Brown. Received a Houghton Mifflin Literary Fellowship in 1936. Is one of the founders and is managing editor of The Southern Review. Teaches at Louisiana State University. Lives in Baton Rouge, Louisiana.

WICKENDEN, DAN. Born in Tyrone, Pennsylvania, 1913. Educated at Amherst College. Connected since 1936 with the Columbia Broadcasting System in New York City. Author of 'The Running of the Deer.' Lives in Manhasset, New York.

WILCOX, WENDELL. Born in Albion, Michigan, 1906. Brought up in Chicago. Educated at the University of Chicago. Lives in Chicago.

WOLFERT, IRA. Born in New York City, 1908. Worked his way through high school and college. Is a newspaper man and married. Lives in New York City.

WOOLRICH, CORNELL. Born in New York City, 1903. Spent his early boyhood in Mexico. Educated at Columbia University. Unmarried. Lives in New York City.

THE BEST BOOKS OF SHORT STORIES
1937

I. American Authors

1. BAHR. All Good Americans. Scribner.
2. BENÉT. Thirteen O'Clock. Farrar and Rinehart.
3. CANFIELD. Fables for Parents. Harcourt, Brace.
4. DOBIE. San Francisco Tales. Appleton-Century.
5. FIELD. Cock's Funeral. International Publishers.
6. GREGORY, *editor*. New Letters in America, I. Norton.
7. ROSS. Education of H*Y*M*A*N K*A*P*L*A*N. Harcourt, Brace.
8. SAROYAN. Little Children. Harcourt, Brace.
9. STEGNER. Remembering Laughter. Little, Brown.
10. WHARTON. Ghosts. Appleton-Century.
11. ZUGSMITH. Home Is Where You Hang Your Childhood. Random House.

II. British and Irish Authors

12. BEACHCROFT. You Must Break Out Sometimes. Harper.
13. HOLME. Wisdom of the Simple. Oxford University Press.
14. MANSFIELD. Short Stories. Knopf.

III. Translations

15. CHAVES NOGALES. Heroes and Beasts of Spain. Doubleday, Doran.
16. SNOW, *editor*. Living China. Reynal and Hitchcock.
17. WERFEL. Twilight of a World. Viking Press.

VOLUMES OF SHORT STORIES

PUBLISHED IN THE UNITED STATES AND CANADA

1937

NOTE. An asterisk before a title indicates distinction.

I. AMERICAN AND CANADIAN AUTHORS

*American Stuff. Viking Press.

BAHR, JEROME. *All Good Americans. Scribner.

BALDWIN, FAITH. Manhattan Nights. Farrar and Rinehart.

BARTLETT, STANLEY FOSS. Beyond the Sowdyhunk. Portland, Maine: Falmouth Book House.

BEACH, ROY. White Quartz and Gold. Placerville, Cal.: Davis Press.

BECK, SHI. Wimmen an' Men. Dallas, Tex.: Tardy.

BENÉT, STEPHEN VINCENT. *Devil and Daniel Webster. Farrar and Rinehart. *Thirteen O'Clock. Farrar and Rinehart.

BLAIR, WALTER, editor. *Native American Humor. American Book Co.

BREWSTER, DOROTHY, editor. *Book of Contemporary Short Stories. Macmillan.

BROWN, BRUCE. Arkansas Tales. New Vernon, N.J.: Cassowary Press.

BURGESS, GELETT. Murder at the Dôme. San Francisco: Book Club of California.

CANFIELD, DOROTHY. *Fables for Parents. Harcourt, Brace.

CARMER, CARL. *Hurricane's Children. Farrar and Rinehart.

CHAMBERS, ROBERT E. S. John Tom Alligator and Others. Dutton.

CLARKE, FRANCES E., editor. Cats and Cats. Macmillan.

CORCORAN, WILLIAM. *This Man, Joe Murray. Little Brown.

DELAND, MARGARET. *Old Chester Days. Harper.

DOBIE, CHARLES CALDWELL. Crystal Ball. San Francisco: Book Club of California. *San Francisco Tales. Appleton-Century.

DOUGLAS, LLOYD C. Home for Christmas. Houghton Mifflin.

DUMVILL, WILLIAM SOLOMON JOSEPH. Conversion of Mr. Banks. Christopher.

DURANTY, WALTER. Babies without Tails. Modern Age Books.

EVERETT, LILY ABBOTT. Dance or Die. Atlanta, Ga.: Brown.

FARRELL, JAMES T. *Can All This Grandeur Perish? Vanguard. *Short Stories. Vanguard.

FIELD, BEN. *Cock's Funeral. International Publishers.

FOOTE, JOHN TAINTOR. Sporting Days. Appleton-Century.

FOOTNER, HULBERT. Casual Murderer. Lippincott.

GILPATRIC, GUY. Glencannon Omnibus. Dodd, Mead.

GREGORY, HORACE, editor. *New Letters in America, I. Norton.

HANSEN, HARRY, editor. *O. Henry Memorial Award Prize Stories of 1937. Doubleday, Doran.

HAWKES, CLARENCE. Igloo Stories. Christopher.

HILL, JAMES. *Loving Memory. Little, Brown.

HOWELL, H. D. Strange Negro Stories of the Old Deep South. Los Angeles: Wetzel.

HURST, FANNIE. We Are Ten. Harper.

JARRETT, CORA. I Asked No Other Thing. Farrar and Rinehart.

KANTOR, MACKINLAY. *Romance of Rosy Ridge. Coward-McCann.

KIRBY, LOUIS PAUL. First Ophelia. Boston: Meador.

LAING, ALEXANDER KINNAN, editor. Haunted Omnibus. Farrar and Rinehart.

LELAND, EFFIE WILLIAMS. Crossin' Over. Columbia, S. C.: State Co.

LOBELL, WILLIAM. *Fire Door. Reader Press.

LUNDEBERG, OLAV K. Enchanted Valley. Augsburg Publishing House.
McDONALD, LEONARD. Music Box. Washingtonville, N.Y.: Clough-Bush Press.
McGAVIN, ELMER CECIL. Christmas Bells. Meador.
MASON, TALLY. Consider Your Verdict. Stackpole.
MILLER, MADELEINE SWEENY. Journey of the Christ Child. Revell.
MULLALY, CHARLES J. Bravest of the Virginia Cavalry, Apostleship of Prayer.
O'BRIEN, EDWARD J., editor. Best Short Stories: 1937. Houghton Mifflin.
PARKER, JAMES REID. *Academic Procession. Harcourt.
PENDLETON, LEWIS. Down East. Harcourt.
PERKINS, CHARLES ELLIOTT. Pinto Horse. Santa Barbara, Cal.: Fisher and Skofield.
PHILLIPS, MARIE TELLO. There's a Divinity. Pittsburgh, Pa.: Observer Press.
PORTER, KATHERINE ANNE. *Noon Wine. Detroit: Schuman's.
Post Stories of 1936. Little, Brown.
RANDOLPH, RICHARD W. Sweet Medicine. Caldwell, Idaho: Caxton Printers.
RIDGWAY, WILLIAM HANCE. Christian Gentleman. Wilde.
RIDING, LAURA. *Progress of Stories. Random House.
RINEHART, MARY ROBERTS. Married People. Farrar and Rinehart. Tish Marches On.
    Farrar and Rinehart.
ROBINSON, ROWLAND E. *Out of Bondage. Rutland, Vt.: Tuttle.
ROSS, LEONARD Q. *Education of H*Y*M*A*N K*A*P*L*A*N. Harcourt, Brace.
ROTOR, A. B. Wound and the Scar. Manila: Philippine Book Guild.
SANGSTER, MARGARET E. Flower Wagon. Round Table Press.
SAROYAN, WILLIAM. *Little Children. Harcourt, Brace.
SCHRAMM, WILBUR L., editor. *American Medley. Muscatine, Iowa: Prairie Press.
SHEEAN, VINCENT. Pieces of a Fan. Doubleday, Doran.
SINCLAIR, UPTON. No Pasaran! Pasadena: The Author.
SMITH, EDMUND WARE. Tomato Can Chronicle. Derrydale Press.
STEGNER, WALLACE. *Remembering Laughter. Little, Brown.
STEINBECK, JOHN. *Nothing So Monstrous. Pynson Printers. *Of Mice and Men.
    Covici-Friede. *Red Pony. Covici-Friede. *Saint Katy the Virgin. Covici-
    Friede.
STONE, ELINORE COWAN. Binks, His Dog and His Heart. Appleton-Century.
STRAUSS, THEODORE. *Night at Hogwallow. Little, Brown.
TRAIN, ARTHUR. Mr. Tutt's Case Book. Scribner.
VAN ETTEN, WINIFRED MAYNE. Four Stories. English Club of Cornell College: Mount
    Vernon, Iowa.
WARREN, ROBERT PENN, editor. *Southern Harvest. Houghton Mifflin.
WHARTON, EDITH. *Ghosts. Appleton-Century.
WRYNN, ANTHONY. Someone Who Will Not Believe It. Philadelphia: Ritten House.
WU, W. Y. Old Story in Tsin. Boston: Christopher.
ZUGSMITH, LEANE. *Home Is Where You Hang Your Childhood. Random House.

II. BRITISH AND IRISH AUTHORS

ALLINGHAM, MARGERY. Mr. Campion, Criminologist. Crime Club.
ARLEN, MICHAEL. *Crooked Coronet. Doubleday, Doran.
AYRES, RUBY M. Our Avenue. Godwin.
BAPTIST, R. HERNEKIN. *Cargo of Pirates. Little, Brown.
BEACHCROFT, T. O. *You Must Break Out Sometimes. Harper.
BENSON, E. F. *Old London. 4 vols. Appleton-Century.
CHARTERIS, LESLIE. Ace of Knaves. Doubleday, Doran.
CHESTERTON, G. K. *Paradoxes of Mr. Pond. Dodd, Mead.
CHRISTIE, AGATHA. Dead Man's Mirror. Dodd, Mead.
DINNIS, ENID. Curtain Rises. Herder.
FRANKAU, GILBERT. Experiments in Crime. Dutton.
GIBBONS, STELLA. *Roaring Tower. Longmans.
GIBBS, ARTHUR HAMILTON. Young Prince. Lippincott.
GOUDGE, ELIZABETH. *Pedlar's Pack. Coward-McCann.
HOLME, CONSTANCE. *Wisdom of the Simple. Oxford University Press.
JOHNSTON, MYRTLE. *Laleen. Appleton-Century.

McFee, William. Sailor's Bane, Philadelphia: Ritten House.
Mansfield, Katherine. *Short Stories. Knopf.
Mather, Edward. Chaste Polygamy. Harper.
Maugham, W. Somerset. My South Sea Island. Chicago: Argus Book Shop.
O'Brien, Edward J., *editor*. Best British Short Stories: 1937. Houghton Mifflin.
  Elizabethan Tales. Houghton Mifflin.
Oppenheim, E. Phillips. Ask Miss Mott. Little, Brown.
Stoker, Bram. Dracula's Guest. Hillman-Curl.
Wells, H. G. *Croquet Player. Viking.
Williams, Valentine. Curiosity of Mr. Treadgold. Houghton Mifflin.
Wodehouse, P. G. *Crime Wave at Blandings. Doubleday, Doran.

III. Translations

Chavos Nogales, Manuel. (*Spanish.*) *Heroes and Beasts of Spain. Doubleday,
  Doran.
Le Braz, Anatole. (*French.*) Forest Fire of Good Friday. Washington: St. Albans
  Press.
Maurois, André. (*French.*) *Ricochets. Harper.
Snow, Edgar, *editor*. (*Chinese.*) *Living China. Reynal and Hitchcock.
Werfel, Franz. (*Austrian.*) *Twilight of a World. Viking Press.
Zaitsev, Boris. (*Russian.*) *Anna. Holt.
Zweig, Stefan. (*Austrian.*) *Buried Candelabrum. Viking Press. *Old-Book Peddler.
  Evanston, Ill.: Northwestern University.

ARTICLES ON THE SHORT STORY IN
AMERICAN PERIODICALS

1937

A

American Short Story.
  By Eugene Armfield. Sat. R. (N.Y.) Sept. 4. (10.) Dec. 18. (10.)
  By Ben Belitt. Nat. Jan. 30. (144:131.)
  By Stephen Vincent Benét. Books. Sept. 5. (11.)
  By Alvah C. Bessie. Fight. Mar. (19.)
  By Estelle H. Blumenthal. Books. Mar. 14. (21.) Jun. 6. (12.)
  By James Broughton. Books. Nov. 21. (10.)
  By Mary M. Colum. For. Feb. (97:96.)
  By Jack Conroy. N. Mass. Sept. 14. (24.)
  By Bernard De Voto. Sat. R. (N.Y.) Sept. 25. (3.) Oct. 9. (3.)
  By Horace Gregory. Nat. Sept. 11. (145:272.)
  By L. C. H. Sat. R. (N.Y.) Dec. 18. (21.)
  By Granville Hicks. N. Mass. Sept. 28. (22.)
  By Aldous Huxley. Sat. R. (N.Y.) Jul. 17. (10.)
  By Peter Monro Jack. N.Y. Times. Jan. 17. (2.) Oct. 3. (2.)
  By Alfred Kazin. Books. Sept. 26. (13.)
  By Weldon Kees. Pr. S. Spring. (11:87.) Winter. (11:319.)
  By H. T. M. N. Rep. Jan. 13. (89:338.)
  By Arthur Mizener. Part. R. Dec. (72.)
  By Henry Lee Moon. N. Chal. Fall. (2:88.)
  By Fletcher Pratt. Sat. R. (N.Y.) Jul. 3. (3.)
  By Vance Randolph. U. R. Winter. (4:101.)
  By George S. Schuyler. Opp. Dec. (15:377.)
  By Philip Stevenson. N. Mass. Jan. 26. (30.)
  By R. V. N. Rep. Jul. 7. (91:259.)
  By E. H. W. N.Y. Times. Mar. 28. (20.)
  By M. W. N.Y. Times. Nov. 21. (28.)
  By Eda Lou Walton. N.Y. Times. Aug. 29. (2.)
  By Edith H. Walton. N.Y. Times. Jun. 6. (7.) Nov. 21. (7.)
  By T. K. Whipple. N. Rep. Oct. 20. (92:318.)
  By Katherine Woods. N.Y. Times. Jul. 25. (5.)
  By Frances Woodward. Sat. R. (N.Y.) May 15. (15.) Jun. 12. (8.)
Andersen, Hans Christian.
  By Julian Clausen. Scan. Spring. (25:58.)
Andreyev, Leonid.
  By Maxim Gorky. I. L. No. 8. (47.)
Arlen, Michael.
  Anonymous. C. For. Nov. (17:290.)
  By Rose Feld. Books. Nov. 21. (14.)
  By Peter Monro Jack. N.Y. Times. Nov. 21. (24.)
  By F. W. Sat. R. (N.Y.) Dec. 4. (54.)
Austin, Mary.
  By T. M. Pearce. S. W. Winter. (22:140.)
  By Dudley Wynn. Va. Spring. (13:243.)
Ayres, Ruby M.
  By E. C. B. N.Y. Times. Jan. 10. (17.)

B

Bahr, Jerome.
    By Milton Meltzer. N. Mass. May 18. (29.)
    By George Milburn. Books. Apr. 4. (29.)
    By Harry Thornton Moore. Bea. Aug. (19.)
    By Edith H. Walton. N.Y. Times. Mar. 28. (6.)
Baldwin, Faith.
    By Lisle Bell. Books. Dec. 12. (10.)
    By Drake De Kay. N. Y. Times. Dec. 5. (4.)
    By K. S. Sat. R. (N.Y.) Dec. 18. (21.)
Balzac, Honoré de.
    By Obed Brooks. N. Mass. Jun. 22. (23.)
    By Ralph Fox. N. Mass. May 11. (15.)
Bandello, Matteo.
    By Olin H. Moore. M. L. N. Jan. (52:38.)
Baptist, R. Hernekin.
    By Howard Mumford Jones. Sat. R. (N.Y.) Oct. 9. (13.)
    By Fred T. Marsh. N.Y. Times. Oct. 10. (21.)
    By William Soskin. Books. Oct. 17. (10.)
Beachcroft, T. O.
    By Fred T. Marsh. Books. Mar. 7. (16.)
    By Eda Lou Walton. N.Y. Times. Mar. 7. (6.)
    By T. C. Wilson. N. Mass. Apr. 6. (24.)
Bell, Henry Glassford.
    By Walter G. Neale, Jr. A. L. May. (9:237.)
Benét, Stephen Vincent.
    By Robert P. Tristram Coffin. Books. Oct. 17. (7.)
    By William Maxwell. Sat. R. (N.Y.) Oct. 23. (11.)
    By M. W. N. Rep. Nov. 17. (93:55.)
    By Edith H. Walton. N.Y. Times. Oct. 24. (7.)
Benson, E. F.
    By May Lamberton Becker. Books. Oct. 3. (14.)
    By Louise Maunsell Field. N.Y. Times. Oct. 17. (24.)
Benson, Stella.
    By E. C. Kyte. Q. Q. Spring. (44:123.)
Bierce, Ambrose.
    By Wilson Follett. Atl. Jul. (160:32.)
Boccaccio, Giovanni.
    By Thomas Caldecot Chubb. N.Y. Times. Oct. 10. (4.)
    By Ernest Boyd. Sat. R. (N.Y.) Sept. 25. (25.)
    By Joseph Wood Krutch. Nat. Oct. 2. (145:350.)
    By Arthur Livingston. Nooks. Oct. 31. (7.)
    By Frances Valensi. N. Rep. Dec. 22. (93:207.)
British Short Story.
    By Ruth Bower. Books. Nov. 21. (16.)
    By Eleanor Clark. N. Rep. Jan. 27. (89:390.)
    By Peter Monro Jack. N.Y. Times. Oct. 3. (2.)
    By Alfred Kazin. Books. Sept. 26. (13.)
    By E. H. W. N.Y. Times. Nov. 7. (24.)
    By T. K. Whipple. N. Rep. Oct. 20. (92:318.)
Brown, Bruce.
    By L. L. D. Hin. No. 2. (2:56.)

C

Caldwell, Erskine.
    By William Troy. Nat. Jan. 16. (144:76.)
Callaghan, Morley.
    By Weldon Kees. Pr. S. Spring. (11:87.)

Canadian Short Story.
    By Regina Shoolman. Sto. Mar. (2.)
Canfield, Dorothy.
    By Margaret Culkin Banning. Books. Sept. 12. (2.)
    By Edith H. Walton. N.Y. Times. Sept. 5. (7.)
    By Isabel Wilder. Sat. R. (N.Y.) Sept. 18. (12.)
Carmer, Carl.
    Anonymous. Sat. R. (N.Y.) Dec. 11. (6.)
    By Ellen Lewis Buell. N.Y. Times. Dec. 19. (9.)
    By Zora Neale Hurston. Books. Dec. 26. (4.)
Cather, Willa.
    By Lionel Trilling. N. Rep. Feb. 10. (90:10.)
Chambers, Robert E. S.
    By George Conrad. Books. May 23. (14.)
    By E. H. W. N.Y. Times. May 23. (23.)
Chekhov, Anton.
    By John Cournos. Va. Summer. (13:440.)
    By Alexandre DeRore. N. Mass. Feb. 2. (24.)
    By Dorothy Dudley. N. Rep. Mar. 3. (90:116.)
    By Walter Prichard Eaton. Books. Jan. 17. (3.)
    By Henry James Forman. N.Y. Times. Jan. 24. (3.)
    By M. G. Sat. R. (N.Y.) Feb. 6. (22.)
    By Nina A. Toumanova. Sto. Feb. (2.)
Chesterton, G. K.
    By Will Cuppy. Books. Apr. 4. (30.)
    By Peter Monro Jack. Yale. Winter. (26:426.)
    By Joseph J. Reilly. Cath. W. Jan. (144:496.)
Chinese Short Story.
    By Florence Ayscough. Books. Apr. 4. (2.)
    By H. Chen. N. Mass. May 18. (28.)
    By Ch'ao-ting Chi. N. Rep. Sept. 1. (92:110.)
    By Dorothy Graham. Cath. W. Jun. (145:378.)
    By Alice Tisdale Hobart. Sat. R. (N.Y.) Jun. 26. (11.)
Chopin, Kate.
    By Joseph J. Reilly. Com. Mar. 26. (25:606.)
Corcoran, William.
    By Howard Mumford Jones. Sat. R. (N.Y.) Oct. 9. (13.)
    By Fred T. Marsh. N.Y. Times. Oct. 10. (19.)
    By William Soskin. Books. Oct. 17. (10.)
Cunninghame Graham, R.B.
    By Isidor Schneider. N. Rep. Jan. 6. (89:308.)

D

Deland, Margaret.
    By P. H. N.Y. Times. Aug. 29. (7.)
Deloney, Thomas.
    By G. W. Kuehn. M.L.N. Feb. (52:103.)
    By Edward Wagenknecht. Cor. Oct. (42.)
Dobie, Charles Caldwell.
    By James Broughton. Books. Oct. 3. (19.)
    By Anita Moffet. N.Y. Times. Oct. 17. (24.)
Douglas, Lloyd C.
    By Margaret Wallace. N.Y. Times. Nov. 21. (6.)
Doyle, Sir Arthur Conan.
    By Logan Clendening. U.R. Winter. (4:81.)
Dreiser, Theodore.
    By Ford Madox Ford. A. Merc. Apr. (40:488.)
    By John F. Huth, Jr. A.L. May. (9:208.)
Duranty, Walter.
    By N. L. Rothman. Sat. R. (N.Y.) Sept. 25. (24.)

E

Edmonds, Walter D.
    By David McCord. Sat. R. (N.Y.) Dec. 11. (10.)
Elizabethan Short Story.
    Anonymous. Sat. R. (N.Y.) Sept. 18. (16.)
    By Percy Hutchinson. N.Y. Times. Sept. 19. (2.)

F

Farrell, James T.
    By Bernard De Voto. Sat. R. (N.Y.) May 22. (20.)
    By F. W. Dupee. N. Mass. May 25. (21.)
    By Otis C. Ferguson. N. Rep. Nov. 10. (93:22.)
    By Alfred Kazin. Books. May 16. (6.)
    By Weldon Kees. Pr. S. Summer. (11:188.)
    By Fred T. Marsh. N.Y. Times. May 16. (7.)
    By S. L. S. Mod. M. Aug. (16.)
Field, Ben.
    By N. A. N. Rep. Jun. 23. (91:202.)
    By Alvah C. Bessie. Fight. Sept. (19.)
    By Robert M. Coates. N. Mass. May 4. (30.)
    By Alfred Kazin. N.Y. Times. Jul. 11. (7.)
    By C. E. MacG. Sat. R. (N.Y.) Jul. 3. (21.)
    By Harry Sylvester. Books. Apr. 25. (10.)
Filipino Short Story.
    By A. B. Rotor. Phil. Jan. (34:19.)
Fitzgerald, F. Scott.
    By John Peale Bishop. Va. Winter. (13:106.)
    By James Gray. Sat. R. (N.Y.) Jun. 12. (3.)
Flandrau, Charles Macomb.
    By James Gray. Sat. R. (N.Y.) Jun. 12. (3.)
Flandrau, Grace.
    By James Gray. Sat. R. (N.Y.) Jun. 12. (3.)
Flaubert, Gustave.
    By Ralph Fox. N. Mass. May 11. (15.)
France, Anatole.
    By Haakon M. Chevalier. N. Rep. Jul. 21. (91:313.)
    By Bertrand L. Conway. Cath. W. Sept. (145:755.)
    By Alfred Kazin. Books. Oct. 17. (18.)
    By Harry Levin. Nat. Jul. 10. (145:51.)
    By M. L. Radoff. Sat. R. (N.Y.) Jul. 3. (6.)
    By Harold Strauss. N.Y. Times. Jun. 27. (6.)

G

Galsworthy, John.
    By Percy Hutchinson. N.Y. Times. Mar. 14. (9.)
    By Edith Mirrielees. Sat. R. (N.Y.) Jul. 17. (19.)
Gibbons, Stella.
    By E. C. Kyte. Q.Q. Summer. (44:256.)
    By Louise Townsend Nicholl. Books. Apr. 25. (3.)
    By E. H. W. N.Y. Times. Apr. 25. (21.)
Gorky, Maxim.
    By Isaac Babel. I.L. No. 6. (87.)
    By Ivan Bunin. Yale. Spring. (26:533.)
    By Georgl Storm. I.L. No. 6. (81.)
Goudge, Elizabeth.
    By Louise Townsend Nicholl. Books. Nov. 21. (5.)
    By Edith H. Walton. N.Y. Times. Nov. 21. (6.)

H

Haardt, Sara.
  By Maud Ethel Ely. S.W. Winter. (22:210.)
Harte, Bret.
  By Jacob Blanck. Pub. W. Nov. 28, '36. (130:2102.)
Hawthorne, Nathaniel.
  By Oscar Cargill. P.M.L.A. Sept. (52:848.)
  By Donald C. Gallup. N.E.Q. Dec., '36. (9:690.)
  By Manning Hawthorne. Colo. Winter. (2:262.)
  By Randall Stewart. Sew. R. Oct.–Dec., '36. (44:434.) N.E.Q. Sept., '36. (9:504.)
    S.P. Jan. (34:91.)
  By Arlin Turner. M.L.N. Nov., '36. (51:426.)
Hearn, Lafcadio.
  By Edward Larocque Tinker. A.L. May. (9:261.)
Hemingway, Ernest.
  By John Peale Bishop. Va. Winter. (13:106.)
Henry, O.
  Anonymous. Red Bk. Jan. (7.)
  By George A. Boissard. Sat. R. (N.Y.) Jan. 9. (13.)
  By Percy H. Boynton. N. Rep. Aug. 25. (92:82.)
  By Fred B. Millett. A.L. May. (9:264.)
  By Mrs. S. L. C. Porter. Red Bk. Mar. (8.)
Hill, James.
  By Howard Mumford Jones. Sat. R. (N.Y.) Oct. 9. (13.)
  By Mabel L. Rossbach. N.Y. Times. Oct. 24. (25.)
  By William Soskin. Books. Oct. 17. (10.)
Horgan, Paul.
  By Alfred Carter. N.M.Q. Aug. (7:207.)
  By George Milburn. N. Mass. Jan. 5. (24.)
Hurst, Fannie.
  By M. B. N. Rep. Oct. 20. (92:322.)
  By Lisle Bell. Brooks. Sept. 26. (12.)
  By Zora Neale Hurston. Sat. R. (N.Y.) Oct. 9. (15.)
  By E. H. W. N.Y. Times. Sept. 26. (27.)
  By Isabel Wilder. Sat. R. (N.Y.) Oct. 9. (15.)
Huxley, Aldous.
  By Cecil Day Lewis. N. Mass. Aug. 10. (17.)

I

Irving, Washington.
  By Jacob Blanck. Pub. W. Nov. 28, '36. (130:2101.)
  By Francis Prescott Smith. A.L. May. (9:228.)
  By Mary Zirkle. C.S.M. Mar. 20. (14.)

J

James, Henry.
  By Robert Cantwell. N. Rep. Jun. 23. (91:177.)
Jarrett, Cora.
  By William Soskin. Brooks. Jun. 27. (6.)
  By Edith H. Walton. N.Y. Times. Jun. 20. (7.)
Jewett, Sarah Orne.
  By Olive Beatrice Floyd. Yale. Winter. (26:430.)
  By Katherine R. Merrill. N.Y. Times. Sept. 12. (18.)
Johnston, Myrtle.
  By B. E. Bettinger. Books. Nov. 21. (16.)
  By L. Cabot Hearn. Sat. R. (N.Y.) Nov. 6. (10.)
  By E. H. W. N.Y. Times. Nov. 7. (24.)

K

Kafka, Franz.
  By Stephen Spender. N. Rep. Oct. 27. (92:347.)
Kantor, MacKinlay.
  By Drake De Kay. N.Y. Times. Sept. 12. (7.)
  By R. P. Harriss. Books. Sept. 19. (18.)
  By Amy Loveman. Sat. R. (N.Y.) Sept. 18. (12.)
Kipling, Rudyard.
  Anonymous. N.Y. Times. Feb. 7. (2.)
  By Elliot Balestrier. Sat. R. (N.Y.) Feb. 27. (6.)
  By Stephen Vincent Benét. Books. Feb. 28. (1.)
  By Henry Seidel Canby. Sat. R. (N.Y.) Feb. 27. (5.)
  By Clifton Fadiman. N.Y. Mar. 6. (85.)
  By Maxwell Geismar. Nat. Feb. 27. (144:243.)
  By Granville Hicks. N. Mass. Mar. 30. (25.)
  By Percy Hutchison. N.Y. Times. Feb. 28. (1.)
  By L. A. MacKay. C. For. May. (17:65.)
  By William Lyon Phelps. Yale. Summer. (26:810.)
  By John W. Thomason, Jr. A. Merc. Jun. (41:244.)
  By Frederic F. Van de Water. Harp. M. May. (174:569.)
  By Edmund Wilson. N. Rep. Mar. 24. (90:214.)

L

Lagerkvist, Pär.
  By J. B. C. W. Scan. Spring. (25:87.)
Lawrence, D. H.
  By Ernest Boyd. Sat. R. (N.Y.) Jan. 2. (16.)
  By Kerker Quinn. Yale. Summer. (26:847.)
  By Edward Larocque Tinker. N.Y. Times. May 9. (24.)
Lobell, William.
  By Edith H. Walton. N.Y. Times. Apr. 25. (7.)
Longstreet, Augustus B.
  By Carl J. Weber. Colo. Spring. '36. (1:525.)
Lovecreft, H. P.
  By August Derleth. Riv. Jun. (1:88.)

M

Mann, Thomas.
  By Victor Lange. C. For. Oct. (17:243.)
Mansfield, Katherine.
  By Ben Belitt. Sto. Dec. (4.)
  By Kay Boyle. N. Rep. Oct. 20. (92:309.)
  By Katherine Anne Porter. Nat. Oct. 23. (145:435.)
  By George Stevens. Sat. R. (N.Y.) Oct. 2. (11.)
Mather, Edward.
  By B. E. Bettinger. Books. Apr. 25. (10.)
  By R. V. N. Rep. Jun. 23. (91:203.)
  By E. H. W. N.Y. Times. Apr. 18. (23.)
Maurois, André.
  By Mary Ross. Books. Dec. 12. (5.)
  By Harold Strauss. N.Y. Times. Nov. 21. (7.)
Melville, Herman.
  By Robert F. Almy. Colo. Winter. (2:27.)
  By James D. Hart. A.L. Mar. (9:49.)
  By Luther Stearns Mansfield. A.L. Mar. (9:26.)
  By Willard Thorp. U.R. Summer. (3:254.)

Moore, George.
    By Conrad Aiken. N. Rep. Feb. 17. (90:52.)

O

O'Hara, John.
    By John Peale Bishop. Va. Winter. (13:106.)
Oppenheim, E. Phillips.
    By E. C. B. N.Y. Times. May 16. (21.)
Ondard, Georges.
    By Charles Cestre. N.Y. Times. Nov. 21. (8.)

P

Parker, James Reid.
    By M. B. N. Rep. Oct. 20. (92:322.)
    By Drake De Kay. N.Y. Times. Oct. 17. (17.)
    By Edward A. Fitzpatrick. Com. Nov. 12. (27:82.)
    By C. H. M. Sat. R. (N.Y.) Oct. 9. (42.)
Pendleton, Lewis.
    By Lincoln Colcord. Books. Feb. 7. (7.)
    By Stanley Young. N.Y. Times. Feb. 14. (7.)
Perkins, Charles Elliott.
    By P. H. N.Y. Times. Sept. 5. (10.)
Pirandello, Luigi.
    By Edward Larocque Tinker. N.Y. Times. Nov. 7. (31.)
Poe, Edgar Allan.
    By Roy P. Basler. A.L. May. (9:232.)
    By Ruth Leigh Hudson. A.L. Jan. (8:402.)
    By Joseph Wood Krutch. Books. Apr. 18. (8.)
    By William McKee. Com. Jul. 30. (26:350.)
    By Walter G. Neale, Jr. A.L. May. (9:237.)
    By J. H. Whitty. R.N.L. Apr. 24.
    By Yvor Winters. A.L. Jan. (8:379.)
    By Frances Winwar. N.Y. Times. Jun. 13. (2.)
Porter, Katherine Anne.
    By Ben Belitt. Nat. May 15. (144:571.)
    By Dorothy Brewster. N. Mass. May 25. (25.)
    By Edith H. Walton. N.Y. Times. Apr. 11. (7.)
Powys, Llewelyn.
    By Petronius Applejoy. Cath. W. Apr. (145:31.)
Pushkin, Alexander.
    Anonymous. I.L. No. 1. (66.) No. 2. (60, 86.)
    By V. G. Belinsky. I.L. No. 1. (69.)
    By Nikolai Bogoslovsky. I.L. No. 2. (43.)
    By John Cournos. Yale. Spring. (26:595.) Va. Summer. (13:440.) N.Y. Times.
        Jun. 20. (2.)
    By Paul Crowley. Com. Mar. 12. (25:561.)
    By F. W. Dupee. N. Mass. Feb. 23. (14.)
    By Manya Gordon. Sat. R. (N.Y.) Feb. 13. (3.)
    By Alexander Kaun. Books. Feb. 14. (1.) Feb. 21. (4.)
    By Guichard Parris. Opp. Feb. (15:48.)
    By William Lyon Phelps. Sat. R. (N.Y.) Feb. 13. (13.)
    By Victor Shklovsky. I.L. No. 1. (7.)
    By Irina Skariatina. N. Rep. Apr. 7. (90:274.)
    By Alexander Tarsaidze. Books. Mar. 14. (28.)
    By Nina Andronikova Toumanova. N.Y. Times. Feb. 7. (1.)
    By V. V. Veresayev. I.L. No. 1. (23.)
    By Avrahm Yarmolinsky. Nat. Feb. 20. (144:218.) May 1. (144:515.)

R

Reed, John.
  By Granville Hicks. N. Mass. Oct. 19. (9.)
Richter, Conrad.
  By Stanley Vestal. S.W. Autumn, '36. (22:107.)
Riding, Laura.
  By Richard Vaughan. N. Rep. Oct. 6. (92:250.)
Rinehart, Mary Roberts.
  By Lisle Bell. Books. Mar. 14. (21.) Nov. 28. (22.)
  By Charlotte Dean. N.Y. Times. Nov. 28. (26.)
  By L. M. F. N.Y. Times. Feb. 28. (6.)
  By Eleanor Godfrey. C. For. May. (68.)

S

Saroyan, William.
  Anonymous. Sat. R. (N.Y.) Aug. 14. (10.)
  By Robert M. Coates. N. Mass. Aug. 31. (23.)
  By Eleanor Godfrey. C. For. Dec. (17:328.)
  By Alfred Kazin. Books. Aug. 15. (4.)
  By T. S. Matthews. N. Rep. Aug. 25. (92:81.)
  By William Phillips. Nat. Aug. 21. (145:203.)
  By Harold Rosenberg. N. Mass. Feb. 9. (24.)
  By Harold Strauss. N.Y. Times. Jan. 3. (14.) Aug. 15. (6.)
  By William Troy. Nat. Jan. 16. (144:76.)
Sedgwick, Anne Douglas.
  By Fred Lewis Pattee. A.L. Jan. (8:480.)
Sheean, Vincent.
  By Clifton Fadiman. N.Y. Nov. 6. (92.)
  By Mary Ross. Brooks. Nov. 21. (3.)
  By K. S. Sat. R. (N.Y.) Nov. 13. (20.)
  By Edith H. Walton. N.Y. Times. Nov. 14. (7.)
Short Story.
  By John Rood. N.M.Q. Aug. (7:197.)
  By T. C. Wilson. N. Mass. Oct. 26. (23.)
Silone, Ignazio.
  By Lionel Abel. Part. R. Dec. (33.)
Sinclair, Upton.
  Anonymous. New Masses. May 18. (30.)
Snelling, William Joseph.
  By G. H. Orians. A.L. May. (9:269.)
Stegner, Wallace.
  By William Soskin. Books. Sept. 26. (6.)
  By Phil Stong. Sat. R. (N.Y.) Sept. 25. (5.)
  By Edith H. Walton. N.Y. Times. Sept. 26. (6.)
Steinbeck, John.
  By Henry Seidel Canby. Sat. R. (N.Y.) Feb. 27. (7.)
  By John Chamberlain. Scr. Mar. (78.)
  By Clifton Fadiman. N.Y. Feb. 27. (79.)
  By Joseph Henry Jackson. Sat. R. (N.Y.) Sept. 25. (11.)
  By Fred T. Marsh. N.Y. Times. Feb. 28. (7.)
  By Harry Thornton Moore. N. Rep. Mar. 3. (90:118.)
  By Christopher Morley. Sat. R. (N.Y.) Sept. 25. (18.)
  By Rosemary Paris. Mod. M. Apr. (14.)
  By Louis Paul. Books. Feb. 28. (5.)
  By Philip Rahv. N. Mass. Mar. 16. (22.)
  By Burton Rascoe. Esq. May. (105.) Aug. (97.)
  By Edward C. Richards. N.A. Rev. Summer. (243:406.)
  By Mark Van Doren. Nat. Mar. 6. (144:275.)
  By Edith H. Walton. N.Y. Times. Oct. 10. (7.)

Stevenson, Robert Louis.
    By Lucile Harrington. Com. Mar. 26. (25:618.)
    By Peter Monro Jack. N.Y. Times. Aug. 22. (1.)
    By Clara Gruening Stillman. Books. Apr. 4. (5.)
    By Isobel Osbourne Strong. Sat. R. (N.Y.) Sept. 25. (9.)
    By Katherine Woods. N.Y. Times. Mar. 28. (4.)
Strauss, Theodore.
    By Howard Mumford Jones. Sat. R. (N.Y.) Oct. 9. (13.)
    By Samuel Sillen. N. Mass. Oct. 26. (23.)
    By William Soskin. Books. Oct. 17. (10.)
    By Robert Van Gelder. N.Y. Times. Oct. 17. (7.)
Strindberg, August.
    By L. A. MacKay. C. For. Jul. (17:144.)
Stuart, Jesse.
    By Burton Rascoe. Esq. Mar. (104.)
    By W. S. Wabnitz. N.M.Q. Aug. (7:161.)

T

Tecchi, Bonaventura.
    By Henry Furst. N.Y. Times. Jan. 10. (8.)
Tolstoy, Count Lyof N.
    By Mary M. Colum. For. Mar. (97:159.)
    By Alexandre De Rore. N. Mass. Feb. 2. (24.)
    By Babette Deutsch. Books. Jan. 24. (6.)
    By Dorothy Dudley. N. Rep. Mar. 3. (90:116.)
    By Manya Gordon. Sat. R. (N.Y.) Jan. 30. (12.) Apr. 10. (9.)
    By Anita Marburg. Nat. Mar. 6. (144:272.)
    By Aylmer Maude. Sat. R. (N.Y.) Mar. 27. (9.)
    By Alexander Nazaroff. N.Y. Times. Jan. 31. (8.) Dec. 5. (8.)
    By Catherine Radziwill. Com. Feb. 12. (25:447.)
Twain, Mark.
    By Jacob Blanck. Pub. W. Oct. 30. (132:1740.)
    By W. J. Burke. Bull. N.Y.P.L. Jun., '36. (40:499.)
    By De Lancey Ferguson. Colo. Winter. (2:189.)
    By John T. Flanagan. Minn. H. Dec., '36. (17:369.)
    By Louis H. Swain. Fur. B. Apr. (19:48.)
    By Hyatt Howe Waggoner. A.L. Jan. (8:357.)

U

Unamuno, Miguel de.
    By F. V. Kelyin. I.L. No. 2. (80.)

W

Wells, H. G.
    By May Lamberton Becker. Books. Feb. 28. (5.)
    By Ben Belitt. Nat. Mar. 20. (144:329.)
    By John Chamberlain. Scr. May. (82.)
    By H. J. Davis. C. For. May. (17:64.)
    By Clifton Fadiman. N.Y. Feb. 27. (79.)
    By Louise Maunsell Field. N.Y. Times. Feb. 28. (6.)
    By Richard Greenleaf. N. Mass. Mar. 2. (25.)
    By Timofei Rokotov. I.L. No. 6. (113.)
    By George Stevens. Sat. R. (N.Y.) Feb. 27. (10.)
    By Harvey Curtis Webster. N. Rep. Apr. 14. (90:300.)
Werfel, Franz.
    By Nathan Asch. N. Rep. Jun. 2. (91:108.)

INDEX OF SHORT STORIES IN BOOKS

1937

I. AMERICAN AND CANADIAN AUTHORS

II. BRITISH AND IRISH AUTHORS

INDEX OF SHORT STORIES

379

Adam and Eve and Pinch Me. Laing. 75.
All the World a Stage. Coppard Q. 209.
Badge. Coppard Q. 257.
Cherry Tree. Laing. 809.
Chronicles of Andrew. Coppard Q. 173.
Clorinda Walks in Heaven. Laing. 717.
Deserter. Coppard Q. 81.
Good Samaritans. Coppard Q. 187.
Gudgeon and the Squirrel. Coppard Q. 33.
Halfyard Ham. Coppard Q. 297.
Hannibal's Bust. Coppard Q. 267.
His Worship Receives. Coppard Q. 63.
Jack the Giant Killer. Coppard Q. 131.
Jove's Nectar. Coppard Q. 19.
King of the World. Laing. 75.
Kiss the Book, Beezer. Joseph B. 279.
Landmark. Coppard Q. 221.
Life is Like That. Coppard Q. 233.
Mordecai and Cocking. Faber. 91.
Ninepenny Flute. Coppard Q. 1.
Philosopher's Daughter. Coppard Q. 49.
Six Sad Men. Coppard Q. 199.
Sofa One, Sofa Two. Coppard Q. 157.
Some Talk of Alexander. Coppard Q. 245.
Speaking Likenesses. Coppard Q. 95.
Were Deceivers Ever. Coppard Q. 279.
COTTRELL, DOROTHY.
'Uncommon Stupid Dog.' Nature. 719.
CRACKANTHORPE, HUBERT.
He Wins Who Loses. Rowland. 203.
CROFT-COOKE, RUPERT.
Banquo's Chair. Walpole D. 1015.
CURREY, R. N.
Black Dog. Standard B. 327.

DAVIES, HYWEL.
Five Eggs. Welsh. 430.
DAVIES, RHYS.
First Patient. Rowland. 65.
Mourning for Ianto. O'Brien UU. 54.
Resurrection. Welsh. 39.
Revelation. Steele F. 237.
DE LA MARE, WALTER.
Physic. Faber. 264.
Trumpet. Walpole D. 357.
DEKKER, THOMAS.
Tinker's Bargain. O'Brien SS. 290.
DELONEY, THOMAS.
Jack of Newbury and the Widow. O'Brien SS. 224.
Old Cole's End. O'Brien SS. 279.
DEVEREUX, BLANCHE.
Bull Giant Head. Welsh. 358.
DEWES, SIMON.
Prize. Rowland. 101.
DU MAURIER, DAPHNE.
Doll. Joseph B. 257.

DUNSANY, LORD.
Drink from a Running Stream. Standard B. 941.
DYMENT, CLIFFORD.
Departure. Lehmann C. 185.

EDMONDSON, ARNOLD.
Billy the Lamb. Edmondson. 272.
Cowslip Lee. Edmondson. 203.
Crime. Edmondson. 257.
Dark Days. Edmondson. 219.
First Aid. Edmondson. 159.
Good by Stealth. Edmondson. 101.
Good Sam. Aritan. Edmondson. 328.
I Will Arise. Edmondson. 371.
In the Know. Edmondson. 140.
Keeping His Lead. Edmundson. 43.
Miss 'Ilda. Edmondson. 83.
Peace and Goodwill. Edmondson. 346.
Presence of Mind. Edmondson. 27.
Salmon Catch. Edmondson. 64.
Tally Ho! Edmondson. 182.
Very High Politics. Edmondson. 122.
Wedding Guest. Edmondson. 11.
William's Uncle Joshua. Edmondson. 292.
Winning a Bride. Edmondson. 240.
EDWARDS, DOROTHY.
Conquered. Welsh. 21.
ELYOT, SIR THOMAS.
Titus and Gisippus. O'Brien SS. 35.
EVANS, CARADOC.
Way of the Earth. Welsh. 177.
EVANS, MARGIAD.
Country Dance. Welsh. 241.
EVANS, SIAN.
Davis. Welsh. 58.
EWART, WILFRID.
Flats. Rowland. 77.
'EX-PRIVATE X.'
Oak Saplings. Walpole D. 459.

FITZPATRICK, KATHLEEN.
Bantam Hen. Fitzpatrick. 104.
Best Finder. Fitzpatrick. 79.
Chief Mourner. Fitzpatrick. 129.
Child Samuel. Fitzpatrick. 67.
Cruel Harm. Fitzpatrick. 184.
Day of Growth. Fitzpatrick. 52.
Dorcas Society. Fitzpatrick. 115.
English Aunt. Fitzpatrick. 208.
English Uncle. Fitzpatrick. 231.
Jane at Miss Courtney's School. Fitzpatrick. 171.
Jane's Conversion. Fitzpatrick. 36.
Jimmie Burke's Wedding. Fitzpatrick. 155.
Rowallan. Fitzpatrick. 13.
Safeguard. Fitzpatrick. 145.
Stocking. Full of Gold. Fitzpatrick. 89.
Why Mrs. McRea Returned to the Faith of her Fathers. Fitzpatrick. 23.

III. TRANSLATIONS

MAGAZINE AVERAGES

JANUARY 1 TO DECEMBER 31, 1937

The following table includes the averages of distinctive stories in fourteen American periodicals. One, two, and three asterisks are employed to indicate relative distinction. 'Three-asterisk stories' are considered worth reprinting in book form. The list excludes reprints. Figures in columns three and six represent stories with one or more asterisks: figures in columns four and seven, stories with two or more asterisks: figures in columns five and eight, stories with three asterisks.

PERIODICALS	Number of Stories Published	Number of Distinctive Stories Published			Percentage of Distinctive Stories Published		
		*	**	***	*	**	***
American Mercury..............	11	8	3	1	73	27	9
American Prefaces................	28	20	9	3	71	32	11
Atlantic Monthly..................	20	19	8	3	95	40	15
Cosmopolitan.....................	105	5	4	0	5	4	0
Esquire..........................	152	84	48	27	55	32	18
Frontier and Midland.............	19	10	5	1	50	25	5
Harper's Bazaar (New York)........	46	23	12	8	50	26	17
Harper's Magazine.................	20	15	10	4	75	50	20
Prairie Schooner..................	23	13	4	1	57	17	4
Red Book Magazine................	95	20	7	3	20	7	3
Saturday Evening Post.............	234	41	11	0	18	5	0
Scribner's Magazine...............	41	29	13	8	71	32	20
Southern Review..................	14	13	8	4	91	57	43
Story............................	81	73	59	32	90	73	40

The following tables indicate the rank, by number and percentage of distinctive short stories published, of eleven periodicals coming within the range of my examination which have published an average of 50 per cent or more of distinctive stories. The list excludes reprints, but not translations.

By Percentage

1. Atlantic Monthly.............. 95%
2. Southern Review.............. 91%
3. Story........................ 90%
4. Harper's Magazine............ 75%
5. American Mercury............. 73%
6. Scribner's Magazine........... 71%
7. American Prefaces............ 71%
8. Prairie Schooner.............. 57%
9. Esquire...................... 55%
10. Harper's Bazaar (New York).. 50%
11. Frontier and Midland........ 50%

By Number

1. Esquire....................... 84
2. Story......................... 73
3. Scribner's Magazine............ 29
4. Harper's Bazaar (New York)..... 23
5. American Prefaces.............. 20
6. Atlantic Monthly............... 19
7. Harper's Magazine............. 15
8. Southern Review............... 13
9. Prairie Schooner.............. 13
10. Frontier and Midland.......... 10
11. American Mercury............. 8

The following periodicals have published during the same period seven or more 'two-asterisk' stories. The list excludes reprints, but not translations.

1. Story.......................... 59	8. American Prefaces............. 9
2. Esquire........................ 48	9. Atlantic Monthly.............. 8
3. New Yorker.................... 20	10. Southern Review.............. 8
4. Scribner's Magazine............ 13	11. Hairenik..................... 8
5. Harper's Bazaar (New York)..... 12	12. Yale Review.................. 7
6. Harper's Magazine............. 10	13. Red Book Magazine........... 7
7. Saturday Evening Post........... 10	

The following periodicals have published during the same period four or more 'three-asterisk' stories. The list excludes reprints, but not translations.

1. Story.......................... 32	5. Harper's Bazaar (New York)..... 8
2. Esquire........................ 27	6. Southern Review................ 8
3. New Yorker.................... 9	7. Yale Review.................... 8
4. Scribner's Magazine............ 8	8. Harper's Magazine............. 8

Ties in the above lists have been decided by taking relative rank in other lists into account.

***Cheat's Remorse. Esq. Oct. (75.)
***Evening in Madison Square. Esq. Jun. (56.)
***Homing Pigeon. Harp. B. (N.Y.) Jun. (76.)
***Little Beaded Bag. Harp. B. (N.Y.) Sept. 1. (69.)
**Night Out. House. Oct. (44.)

***Pair of Long Pants. J. o'L. Jan. 22. (36:685.)
***Rendezvous with Self. Esq. Mar. (46.)
***This Man, My Father. Maclean. Mar. 15. (15.)
***Very Merry Christmas. Harp. B. (N.Y.) Dec. (70.)
CREIGHTON, LUELLA BRUCE.
  *Cornfield. C. For. Jun. (17:97.)

III. BRITISH AND IRISH AUTHORS

AUSTIN, F. BRITTEN.
***Parisian Idyll. Esq. Jan. (92.)
BATES, H. E.
***Cloudburst. Front. Summer. (17: 258.)
***Finger Wet, Finger Dry. Sto. Jan. (9.)
***Something Short and Sweet. Glo. Sept. (24.)
BATES, RALPH.
***Death of a Virgin. Sto. May. (66.)
BOTTOME, PHYLLIS.
  *Pair. Harp. B. (N.Y.) Mar. (96.)
BURKE, JOHN T.
***Linden Leaf. Sto. Apr. (56.)
'CHANDRAPAL.'
  **Bandicoot. Sto. Jun. (9.)
COPPARD, A. E.
***Were Deceivers Ever. Harp. B. (N.Y.) Dec. (100.)
CORKERY, DANIEL.
  *Death of the Runner. Colum. Aug. (7.)
DAVIES, RHYS.
***Mourning for Ianto. Esq. Feb. (92.)
FLEMING, PETER.
  **Story to Tell. Cos. Jan. (54.)
HANLEY, JAMES.
  *Machine Stops. Pop. May. (1.)
***World Laughs. Cor. May. (147.)
HILTON, JAMES.
  *Bat King. Col. Jul. 3. (14.)
  *Mr. Chips Meets a Sinner. T.W. Sept. 12. (11.)
  *Mr. Chips Takes a Risk. T.W. Jan. 17. (4.)
  *My Aunt Lavinia. G.H. (N.Y.) Dec. (39.)
HOUSEHOLD, GEOFFREY.
  **Bribe. S.E.P. Jul. 31. (12.)
  **Unconsidered Factor. Atl. Mar. (159: 297.)
KAYE-SMITH, SHEILA.
  **Intimate Stranger. Harp. B. (N.Y.) Sept. 1. (86.)
KNIGHT, ERIC.
***Bit of a Do. Sto. Oct. (51.)
***Flying Yorkshireman. Sto. Jul. (66.)
***Mary Ann and the Duke. Esq. Dec. (92.)

McLAVERTY, MICHAEL.
  *Stone. Colum. Apr. (5.)
MANHOOD, H. A.
  **Worm in Oak. Pop. Mar. (16.)
MAUGHAM, W. SOMERSET.
  **Lion's Skin. Cos. Nov. (36.)
  **Official Position. Cos. Jul. (32.)
O'CASEY, SEAN.
  **Dream School. Yale. Jun. (26:718.)
O'CONNOR, FRANK.
***Story-Teller. Harp. B. (N.Y.) Nov. (76.)
O'FAOLÁIN, SEÁN.
***Kitty the Wren. Sto. Apr. (81.)
***Old Master. Sto. Aug. (38.)
OUTERSON, WILLIAM.
  *Fire in the Galley Stove. Atl. May. (159:542.)
PREEDY, GEORGE.
  *Cuckoo Spit. Pop. Mar. (74.)
ROBINSON, LENNOX.
  *Bloom on the Plum. Harp. B. (N.Y.) Jan. (50.)
SMITH, A. W.
  *Old Uncle. Atl. Aug. (160:189.)
STRONG, L. A. G.
***Mr. Dallas Has a Quiet Evening. Harp. M. Jan. (174:148.)
***Soldier's Song. Atl. Apr. (159:456.)
  *West Highland Interlude. Com. Dec. 3. (27:153.)
TOWNEND, W.
  *On Greenside Island. Harp. M. Feb. (174:239.)
TRAVERS, P. L.
  *Fine Boy-o. Harp. B. (N.Y.) Aug. (64.)
WALPOLE, HUGH.
  *Revolt. Am. Apr. (56.)
WARNER, SYLVIA TOWNSEND.
  *Drought Breaks. Fight. May. (16.)
WYLIE, I. A. R.
  *Champion Luck. S.E.P. Nov. 6. (8.)
  *Curtain Rising. S.E.P. Jun. 19. (20.)
  **'We Have Come Through ...' Cos. Jun. (34.)
YOUNG, FRANCIS BRETT.
  **Cotswold Honey. Harp. M. Feb. (174: 290.)

IV. TRANSLATIONS

To Catherine

God Bless you

Robert P Byrd